THE SECOND
DEATH OF
SAMUEL AUER

THE SECOND
DEATH OF
SAMUEL AUER

Bernard Packer

HARCOURT BRACE JOVANOVICH
NEW YORK AND LONDON

Requests for permission to make copies of any part of the work should be mailed to:
Permissions, Harcourt Brace Jovanovich, Inc.
757 Third Avenue, New York, N.Y. 10017

Printed in the United States of America

Library of Congress Cataloging in Publication Data

Packer, Bernard.
   The second death of Samuel Auer.

   I. Title.
PZ4.P117Se   [PS3566.A316]   813'.5'4   78-10728
ISBN 0-15-179955-5

First edition
B C D E

THE SECOND
DEATH OF
SAMUEL AUER

PART ONE

Sam Auer never forgot that fight. Hot Saturday nights, there were always brawls at Zacky's. He was waiting in the employment agency, next door to the bar, along with other grocers, bill collectors, and salesmen. Zackman merely tolerated their presence. There was one strict rule. Nobody could dun the pickers returning from the Jersey bogs until they first collected their pay and cleared their accounts with Zacky. It was a sound rule, Auer noted, as he sat on a back bench in the grubby hall. Once Gottlieb, the accountant, was through subtracting Zacky's percentage for all the outstanding debts on the books, there was little left over for all these other hyenas. Zacky had these black berrypickers coming and going. They owed him for the weekly room rent, the food bill from his market at Eighth and Grenoble, loans from his pawnshop and lending agency at Ninth and Cottonwood, and many had a liquor bill at his bar, though it was illegal to serve whiskey on the tab in the state of Pennsylvania.

Auer felt uneasy about being in this filthy office with these scavengers. Bunny put him up to it. His wife exploded when she heard that Howie Williams had run his grocery bill over one hundred dollars and insisted he come round here for a showdown. It was not his style. Sam Auer still had a reputation as a nice guy around this neighborhood, a tough guy, but a man who did not get on people.

A crowd was gathering outside the employment agency. Wives, children, spongers. Since dusk they had been filtering down Seventh Street, waiting for the three yellow school buses to turn the corner of Green Garden. Even after Gottlieb finished his mathematics there would be enough money for a good Saturday night, money to hit Zacky's, Shor's or the Green Room.

In the oppressive heat Auer smoked a Lucky and thanked

God he was not a *shvartzer*, especially not a picker. He had seen these old buses leave before dawn, smelling of pocket flasks, sardine and sweet roll sandwiches, Red Apple chewing tobacco, and unwashed feet. The pickers put in six days a week under the hot Jersey sun and had enough for one Saturday blast after Zacky took his huge bite off them. Winters they went on relief. And now he was sitting in this office to put the arm on Howie Williams after the guy had put in twelve hours of stoop labor.

A cheer from the crowd outside as the first yellow bus was spotted. The salesmen rose from their benches, and Zacky signaled for everybody to remain calm and seated. On the street there was a wild scramble as the women and children pushed and jockeyed to get a good position for their man. Big Zeke came out of the bar with a billy club to shape things up in case the line did not settle down, and the hundred pickers poured out of the three buses before they had even stopped, charging toward the front door with friendly ferocity, scuffling, pushing, anxious to get up front, get that cash payoff, get in some drinking time before the blue laws closed the saloons at midnight. They were mostly laughing, but with all the elbowing and shoving several quick punches were thrown, and two women emerged from the crowd, swinging.

Big Zeke, a bull who once played semipro football, moved in to separate Big Vye and Peggy Moore, but the pickers began to boo and the girls shook off his interference. They circled around in the crouch of veteran boxers, jabbing, weaving in and out, throwing quick combinations. A red car pulled up near the electric factory, and Auer wondered when the cops would step in. They just sat there with front-row tickets to the main event.

Peggy Moore was getting all the best of the first round. She was little and wiry with sharp knuckles, while Vye was a slow, ponderous woman with the bunched muscles of a stevedore. Peggy Moore picked away deftly at Vye's bleeding nose, flicking fast jabs and ducking back. She might have won it on her jab alone, till she danced into a barn-door right.

The crowd whooped as Peggy landed plunk on her ass. It looked like she was knocked silly, but Peggy got to her knees, shook the stars away, and was so furious she scrambled to her feet and shockingly hiked up her tight green skirt to her waist so she could dance more freely. The long lines of pickers roared, the women cackling louder than the men at the sight of her torn pink bloomers, while the Puerto Ricans in line jabbered *"Mira, mira, mira"* in appreciation of her slim thighs.

Sidonia, the iceman, was rolling on the ground, clutching his guts to control his laughter as Peggy Moore charged in with a flurry of hooks and rights before Big Vye caught her by the shoulders, shook her like she was a wet cat, and with one mighty effort slammed her against the concrete wall of the electric factory.

That finished off Peggy Moore. She slumped to the sidewalk. Her current man, Melvin, made the mistake of trying to tug Big Vye back. Vye was so incensed she spun round, grabbed Melvin by the collar and the seat of the pants, and rushed him right against the lamppost banging his skull against the hollow iron.

Vye stood there, legs wide apart, sobbing, tears streaming down her black cheeks and blood dripping from her nostrils. Watching from the window, Auer shuddered and thought about calling the station at Twelfth and Cottonwood and reporting this to Doheny, how two of his men just sat there on their asses while this went on. He might have done so if he had not seen Zacky, of all people, make a move. Zackman the slumlord was not famous for his generous gestures, but it was Mutty who walked across Seventh and raised his arm. A rotund man in a sleeveless undershirt, Mutty gave Vye a pat on the rear, and it was finished. He immediately covered the kindness by snarling, "That's it! Show's over. Get in line if you want to get paid tonight. I don't give a damn."

Auer hovered in the background till Howie Williams got up to the table. Williams threw his slips down enthusiastically, six slips for six days of work. Gottlieb, with his right hand, flipped the ledger to Williams's page and, with his left, totaled up the six slips on his adding machine. He made three notations in the ledger, dipped into the metal money box for several bills, and said, "Yeap. Thirty-five bucks, Howie."

"What the hell you mean?" Williams exploded. "Them six slips come to eighty-eight dollars and sixty-three cents. I counted them twice."

Gottlieb swung the ledger around. "Take a look, Howie. You're over three hundred down. You're lucky I don't keep the whole six slips."

"Shit, man. I should get more than half, man."

"C'mon, Howie. Before I change my mind. There's a hundred people behind you in this line, and they all need a drink, too."

Big black Zeke, seemingly impassive, was sitting against the water cooler, tapping his billy club in his palm. He stirred, as if to rise, and Howie spun round saying, "Shit."

At the exit, three more salesmen were waiting to pounce on Williams. The insurance man, the door-to-door Bible man, and Roth from the furniture outlet blocked his way, plucking at his sleeve, their black books open and fountain pens out, whining in his ear, "C'mon, Howie. You missed last week. Just a buck. C'mon, Howie boy."

Auer slipped out to the heat and sultriness of Seventh Street without bothering to add to the man's woes. Blood from a stone he was not going to get tonight. He walked up Seventh and then down Cottonwood toward his place at Sixth. Leah Dobry was sitting in front of her store with her sons, Maddy and Herbert. He accepted her invitation to a glass of lemonade and sat down on a milk crate. The boys, engrossed in their chess game, mumbled greetings and then ignored him.

"What are you doing down here so late?" Leah asked.

"Oh, I was over at Zacky's to catch one of my people. Howie Williams. He's into me for over a hundred bucks."

"Williams? He's into me for thirty."

They both chuckled and Leah said, "We'll probably never see a dime. One morning they'll skip."

"It was pretty rough at Zacky's tonight. A terrible fight."

"You shouldn't go by that place. It's no place for you."

He described the fight to Leah and saw a tear glint in her eye. She blinked it away and said, "But Peggy and Vye are friends. How could they do that to each other? I've seen them together a thousand times."

Auer shrugged. "The heat. The irritation. It's August. It gets pretty wild over there when they pour out of those buses. Probably tomorrow they'll kiss and make up."

Four black children came racing up and entered Leah's store. Auer saw Herbert get up grudgingly and go in to sell them Cokes and three-for-a-dime comics with the covers ripped off. The three Dobrys took turns waiting on trade. The life of a storekeeper.

Auer accepted another glass of lemonade and found it soothing to be talking to Leah Dobry. With all her gossip, she had a bad word for nobody. Both of them could remember a time, not too long ago, before the neighborhood changed and everybody moved to the suburbs, when there were block parties at Seventh and Grenoble on Saturday night, nuns running bingo tables, charity bazaars for the synagogue, when the police turned a blind eye to an innocent roulette wheel and not to bloody brawls. . . .

Sam Auer was raised at the corner of Sixth and Cottonwood when the area north of Franklin Square and stretching from the Delaware Avenue waterfront to the Reading Railroad tracks was mostly called "Northern Liberties." During the Depression he dropped out of Southern High to help his family and worked for a while as a loader and truck driver for a wholesale produce market on Second Street. In 1940 he married Bunny Stein of Stein's dry-goods shop on Marshall Street, and on December 8, 1941, he enlisted in the Army against his wife's wishes. While serving in Europe, he received word his father had died, and when Auer was mustered out in 1946 he took over the family luncheonette and grocery. Shortly afterward he used his veteran's benefits to purchase a heavily mortgaged home in

Oxford Circle and lived there with his women: one wife, two daughters, and his mother, who had her own room with a private bath on the second floor. Since moving to the Circle, he had to make the same trip every morning: the bus ride down to the Frankford Elevated, the El till his stop at Fairmount Avenue, and then walk from Fairmount Avenue down to Green Garden, up Green Garden to Sixth, and one block down to Cottonwood. This area was laced by many side streets such as New Market and Oriana which appeared on few maps, and the walk was longer than it might seem. It was about a mile from the El stop to his corner. He walked it at dawn, and after a twelve-hour shift in his store.

Nobody called Auer "Sammy," because the diminutive did not fit his rugged build. After thirty-four Auer still had the cocky swagger of the best fullback who never graduated South Philly High. Auer knew he was an attractive man. The secretaries and shopgirls who took the El all the way down to the department stores and offices on Market Street sometimes peeped at him sideways as he left the car at Fairmount. Big Vye had measured him up and down for size, and Vye was not a girl to examine every man.

In winter that walk was much longer. With two feet of snow on the ground and more falling, it became a damn ordeal. Winter had hit early, in November this year, and the wind slashed into his face as he pushed up Green Garden Avenue, gusts whipping powdery snow over his recently shaved cheeks, stinging the nicks. Behind blinded eyes he remembered that battle last summer, the dazzling movement Peggy made, hiking up her skirts, and found it difficult to believe it had ever been so hot, windows open, people on their steps, everybody in shirtsleeves.

Auer huddled his chin deeper inside his woolen scarf, and a treacherous updraft almost lifted his cap from his skull. He reached up frantically to tug it down tighter and then thrust his hands back into the warmth of the jacket pockets, fingered the accumulations of wrappers, threads, and tobacco dust. Only one pedestrian had preceded him up the sidewalk, puncturing prints in the drifts, and with his lashes tearing under the frigid spray Sam wondered whether it might not be easier to walk in the street. The mat of snow over the four lanes of Green Garden Avenue was already plowed and slashed into a mucky brown tundra that reminded him of the battlefields in Belgium after the Panzers and Shermans had torn at each other, crisscrossing and maneuvering with their blunt treads. The partially demolished warehouse at Third and Green Garden, with its naked, rusty girders and exposed brick walls, reinforced that recollection of devastation and desolation. In this blizzard Green Garden Avenue looked like the perimeter of a combat zone, one of those Belgian industrial towns in the coal region.

A mist of frost drifted from his lips and Auer chuckled, tasted the snow on his tongue. This was peace. He preferred the Army. The Army was supposed to be bad times. Except for his starring at fullback for Southern, those were his best times. The rifle range and whores and poker games and drinking. Whenever his dealers and salesmen complained about their military experiences, he thought, "Bullshit, you fruity punk. They took you away from mama and made you play with the big boys for once." The clerk-typists at Fort Dix, they were the ones who griped most. He liked it. Sam Auer was a combat infantryman. He liked to lick that title around on his tongue without saying it out loud: combat infantryman. When he shot that German in the forest, his Sarge from Kentucky said, "Got your first scalp, Jewboy." He never minded the Sarge calling him that, because he knew the Sarge had a high opinion of him. Funny—he never realized how few Jews there were in this country till he enlisted. That first Friday night in basic training the Sarge barked, "All Jews, fall out! Auer, Brodsky, Wasserman, and Zaslofsky, front and center!" The four of them were pulled out of ranks and had to stand there in front of the hundred men in their outfit, face down all those Negroes from Philly, soda jerks from Camden, and hillbillies from West Virginia. They were cut out like strange cattle and released from sharing in the first Friday night barracks party. The other three characters, wise guys from

South Philly, bragged about how they were escaping from the drudgery of scrubbing the walls and floors. But Sam Auer, the good soldier, hurried back after the service to do his share of work. He always got along.

Nothing good happened to him since the Army. Nothing special. Some mornings he wished a car would swerve out of control and splatter him instantly. On a freezing November dawn like this, snowflakes blinding his eyes, he wondered where he got the tenacity to go on. Customers were enjoying the light and warmth in the diner at the corner of Fifth and Green Garden. Over and over, trudging up Green Garden, he dreamed the same dream: stopping for a leisurely cup of steaming coffee at the diner, ordering a taxi, and taking a bus for San Francisco. It would have to be done with no bag, no suitcase, cleanly and sharply. One day he would not be there. The store would remain closed, and his *shvartzers* could bang on the door till they froze. If he mentioned a divorce to Bunny, if they started discussing it—separation, maintenance, the children, dividing property— it would never happen. She would cry and promise to stop nagging and whip up enthusiasm in bed for a night or two, and in three days it would be the same old story all over again.

Then he ran into the same dead end. He thought of his daughters and could not leave them. It was a dead end. For five years he had been eating shit, ever since he was mustered out of the Army. Which meant he had a lot of practice and could put up with the diet for another fifty years. His father had that old saying, "*Es dreck und mehn'tze honig*." Eat shit and call it honey.

His smile drained away as Auer rounded the corner at Sixth and immediately sensed that something was wrong. He blinked into the flurries attacking his lids. At the end of the block, directly in front of the store, the falling snow was acting strangely. It twisted around in a tight maelstrom, swirling like a tornado rooted over one spot, and then flew in his window as if sucked into a vacuum. Without thinking, Auer hurried down the narrow path of packed ice, almost slipping with every step, and from twenty yards away he spotted the slivers of glass planted upright in the drifts. Automatically he glanced over at Leah's store and grimaced in envy. Her front window was intact. Only his had been broken.

Tears from the cold now mixed with tears of rage as he surveyed the wreckage of smashed glass and toppled displays. A rough red brick nestled among his damp school supplies. Nothing had been stolen. It was such a senseless, ignorant act, but nothing was stolen. What did these *shvartzers* want with school supplies? The wind was blowing in and sprayed his sheafs of looseleaf paper, notebooks, and colored dividers, at least thirty dollars worth of merchandise. Another wave of anger washed through him, and he glanced over his shoulder at Leah's. Her store was untended. Little Leah had the knack for handling these people. She took the surly drunken bucks by the arm and rushed them right out of her store, saying "C'mon, c'mon, c'mon, that's enough of your nonsense," and they left, chuckling at her spunkiness. He was too big a man to get away with that approach.

It was wiser to leave the shattered splinters of glass lodged in the frame, Auer decided. If he yanked them out, the snowy gusts would sweep through the whole store and wreck all the goods on the candy counter. If anybody was dumb enough to poke around and cut himself, they could sue. Why else had he helped put a brother through law school?

He had a fairly accurate idea as to which sonofabitch threw this brick. It gave him knots in his gut. Yesterday he slapped little Johnson's hand at lunchtime for stealing a piece of candy. Not even slapped it really, just tapped it. The kids from the school across the street always tried that trick, crowding around the candy counter while he was busy behind his lunch counter at twelve and trying to palm two pieces of candy for one penny. He always caught them. Their eyes gave them away, became vacant and innocent as they thrust a penny at him and spun to rush out.

Auer sniffed at his running nose as he unlocked the front

door. He had merely tapped Johnson's hand, and the savages sent round one of their fourteen brothers to smash his window during the night. A fine way to train a boy. A fine example to set for a child.

Driver after driver in the cars chugging down Sixth peered quickly at the shattered window as Auer made several trips to carry his crates of milk, boxes of Danish, and bundle of morning *Inquirers* inside. Nothing was touched. During the summer bums from Franklin Square crept up this way to snitch doughnuts and pints of milk, but winter held them trapped around Vine Street. Winter brought other problems; the weather froze the cream on top solid and popped the paper tops on his quart bottles. The edges of newspapers were muddied by brown slush because the driver was too lazy to get out of his truck and place the bundle on the sheltered steps. Nobody took care anymore. They went through the motions, bitched, and cashed their paychecks.

After starting his coffee urn, Auer took ten minutes to Scotch-tape sheets of wrapping paper across the front window frame. Leah was already up and preparing her urn of coffee. They could hardly be called competitors. With the Irish and Jews moving out and the Negroes and Puerto Ricans moving in, every month there was slightly less money in the neighborhood. The lunch trade kept them both going, but if Starker closed up his factory at Fifth and relocated out in Jersey as he was threatening to do, then everybody could lock up shop. He saw Leah shaking her head at him, in sympathy for his window. He sold more groceries, but Leah had her dress racks and junk and antiques to stay above water.

His hands trembled and there was a curdling in his intestines as he picked up the damp red brick and dropped it into his garbage can. He was an individual that liked everything to go smoothly, eventlessly, and suddenly he was faced with all these disagreeable duties: He would have to call his insurance agent when the office opened at nine, call the hardware store, eventually call Bunny. And grab Johnson at noon and tell him he wanted to talk to his mother or father. It was calling Bunny he dreaded most. Bunny always assumed that when a disaster occurred he was at least partially to blame. When that moron scratched his fender last summer, Bunny bitched at him all the way to Atlantic City as if he had been the one straying over the lane. If he phoned Bunny it would merely disturb her entire day, and she would call back every hour to hear the latest developments, demand some kind of specific action from him.

The bell tinkled over the door. It was seven by his Pepsi-Cola clock, and the first customer of the morning entered, the postman with his leather sack. Mr. Beaumont eyed the wrapping paper taped over the shattered window and said, "Looks like you got it, Sam."

"A brick through my window last night. They had nothing better to do, so they use my window for target practice."

Auer winced. He had almost added "the goddamn Niggers," but Beaumont was a high yellow with a Ronald Colman moustache, a soft-spoken graduate of Temple University, and married to a schoolteacher. He had almost stuck his foot in it.

"It keeps on getting worse," Beaumont agreed as he accepted his cup of coffee. "I remember when this was an all right place, Sam. No trouble at all. Only trouble I ever had was from that West Virginia trash up by Seventh and Green. Those hillbillies set their dogs on me for the hell of it. And laughed when their animals tore my trouser cuffs. I finally had to tell that white trash that I intended to plant poisoned hamburger round their alleyways if they did not leash their animals properly. . . ."

The mailman droned on with his lament about the ferocious beasts at Seventh and Green. Auer scraped his grills and nodded periodically to indicate he was still attentive. His breakfast trade was only half what it used to be, so he needed only half of the grill's surface. Since they eliminated the southbound trolley on Sixth, the people heading to work in the morning bought their cigarettes and papers, had their coffee and doughnuts, at the stores on Fourth and Eighth while they waited for their trolley. The merchants on Sixth wanted to form an association, set up a jitney service. At the big hearing at City Hall they have all kinds of experts, maps, charts, statistics, and agree to study the proposal. One year later, it's no dice. It did not fit in with the master plan for transportation. Auer scraped furiously at the grease on his grill. Since when did they have master plans in this country? He thought Philadelphia was for the Philadelphians, and not for goddamn drivers from Jersey who wanted a racecourse down to the bridge.

From eight o'clock on, Auer hovered by his front door. He served bacon and eggs to the few customers who still ate hearty breakfasts and wrapped sandwiches for the polishers from the cabinet factory, bachelors who had no woman to fix them a bagged lunch. Everybody had a comment about the window. He was already sick of it. Through the Cottonwood side window he could see the schoolyard, children in leggings and galoshes wrestling in the snow. He hoped to spot Johnson out there but guessed that the little sneak would cut around to Grenoble Street and creep in through the rear gate. It was almost all Negroes in the schoolyard now. Twenty-five years ago, when all the Auers attended the Thurston School, there were possibly fifty *shvartzers*. Now maybe there were fifty white kids over there, from the Irish and Polish families left around York Avenue. From west of Sixth came only blacks.

It had stopped snowing by the time the first bell rang, and the children began to form their lines. Auer found it impossible to make out any faces through his flyspecked, frosted Cottonwood side window. He was reminded of his need to visit an oculist. Mislaid in a bottom drawer somewhere in his home was a pair of standard Army-issue spectacles he had not worn since his discharge. First Bunny made fun of the old-fashioned glasses, and then she wanted him to wear them.

The second bell rang and the lines began entering the building. Mrs. Lewis was directing traffic. She was a fine-looking woman, a redheaded *shvartzeh* with a cute sprinkling of freckles and a figure that showed through her heavy overcoat. One day he was going to speak to her.

After the final bell rang with no Johnson in sight, he measured his window, entered his parlor behind the store, checked through his faded list of important numbers, and dialed Manny's hardware store at Franklin and Green Garden. Manny's helper answered and informed him they could give no service till the following day as the truck had already left.

Auer said, "Look. With you I'm getting nowhere. Put your boss on."

"Up yours, *putz*," Auer thought as the helper made an exasperated noise on the other end of the wire. The receiver banged around against the wall, and he heard it being recovered and Manny's familiar voice.

"What's the problem, Sam? What can I do you for?"

"I'm stuck here. Some *shva'* tossed a brick through my window last night, and the cold winds are blowing in. All my radiators are turned up full blast, but I can't have the place freezing when my workingmen come in for lunch. You know that."

"The truck's already left," Manny said apologetically. "And we're all backed up with orders. I don't know how much I can do for you today."

"Manny," Auer pleaded, "give me a break, will you? My family has been dealing with you for over forty years. Last year you got a hundred-and-fifty-dollar paint order off me. Doesn't that rate me some kind of special attention in an emergency?"

"All right, all right. I'll try to catch my driver at his next stop. But I can't guarantee anything before two, Sam. And that was a big window you got there. I'm not even sure we carry panes that size in stock anymore."

Auer reminded him how big it was exactly, hung up, and frowned as the bell tinkled and Barry, Fat Grace's man, slouched in. From his worn couch Auer motioned to Barry to hold on. The book trade could always wait. Barry was not about to demand deluxe service or storm out. Barry parked on a stool as Auer dialed his insurance agent and encountered the same initial resistance from underlings. Feinberg was extremely busy, and the secretary wished to know if she might help him.

"Mostly you can help by stopping being an obstruction and letting me speak to your employer."

He lit a cigarette before Feinberg picked up the extension, and after an exchange of greetings Auer cheerfully announced, "Well, it looks like I'm finally going to get some mileage out of that policy you nailed me with, Milton. I'll be having a fat, juicy bill for you."

"What's that supposed to mean?"

"It means some *shva'* tossed a brick through my window last night. I found it in the middle of my school supplies."

A protracted pause, a throat cleared, and Feinberg ventured, "Well . . . we'll see whether it's covered, Sam."

"Oh?" Auer strummed his fingertips against his temple and then awarded a mocking salute to his reflection in the parlor mirror, congratulating himself for anticipating the reaction.

"Yes, you could check into that. Unless my premiums only go to finance your Chrysler, or so your company can build skyscrapers. My policy, I believe, mentioned breakage and vandalism. A brick should enter those categories."

"Don't get your balls in an uproar," Feinberg said in his Chestnut Street office. "I'll give your clauses an immediate look-see, and I'm pretty sure you'll be all right."

"Let us both hope we're all right, OK? Red Newman's kid up the street has just gone into the insurance game and has been trying to sign me on, but I've remained loyal to you, Milton. So let us have some reciprocity."

"Send us the bill," Feinberg said wearily. "I'll push it through myself. I don't make a practice of letting my clients down. You remember when your father died? We had the check for your mother in two weeks. That was real service, wasn't it?"

"Was there any doubt he was dead?"

"C'mon, Sam. Give credit where credit is due. Two weeks is fast service."

"I was in Europe at the time. Protecting the Four Freedoms and Sixth and Cottonwood. But thanks, anyway. I'll send the bill by mail. Good-bye, Milton."

Auer returned to the store and Barry immediately began shaking his head and making clucking noises. He picked up a loaf of Bond bread and indicated the window with his chin. "Now ain't that a goddamn shame, Mister Sam? Who the hell would want to do a rotten thing like that? That's an ignorant thing to do."

"I've got a fairly good idea who did it, and so do you. You can tell him for me that the next time I see him I'll break his jaw." Auer hunched his shoulders and was reassured by their massiveness. They were adequate for the task.

Barry added four cans of sardines to the low pyramid of groceries he was constructing between the meat slicer and the scale. He said, "I don't know. These people moving around here now, Mister Sam. They come up here and don't know how to act yet. They don't act right. They sit in Zacky's, and sit in front of Shor's, and I go by and I don't know what's the matter with them."

"I hope you've got the cash to pay for that stuff," Auer cut him off. He wondered where Barry got the gall to criticize his cousins from down South. Barry had two long stretches on Fairmount Avenue on his record, and whenever a corpse was found outside Zacky's, the first place the squad car checked was Fat Grace's to find out where Barry was that evening.

"You mean that?" Barry asked incredulously. His chin dropped to his collarbone as though his feelings were hurt.

"Don't give me that hangdog look, man. You and Grace have thirty-nine dollars on the books right now, buddy. I don't see the bill coming down any."

"C'mon, Mister Sam," Barry said and touched Auer's wrist. "My check is coming in on Friday. Right on Friday. A check for one hundred and sixty-three dollars. I saw my boss last Saturday, and he swore he'd fix me up. Don't you worry. I'll give you something against it. You treated me all right, and I'll do right by you.''

Auer flicked away the black hand touching his sleeve, opened his ledger, and began adding the bill. With regret he marked down exactly two dollars and eighty-seven cents.

Barry helped him pack the groceries into a paper bag and then casually reached for a can of Planter's salted peanuts. Auer placed a hand over his and, after a short tugging battle, removed the can from his grasp. The withered old black grinned at him quickly, appreciatively.

''You sure are a hard man, Sam. I thought my captain in the Army was hard-ass, but you take all the prizes.''

''How can I stay soft dealing with you, you bum? No money for groceries, but last night I caught you staggering back from Shor's with cartons of beer. You see this book, Barry?'' Auer flipped open the green ledger again and with his thumb spun the dog-eared pages of smeared, penciled columns of figures, now indecipherable with age. ''Take a good look, you bum. My old man died with thousands and thousands of dollars of deadbeating in this book. If I had all the dough you deadbeats owed him, and me now, I could be in Florida sunning my ass instead of running it off up here.''

Barry shuffled out into the snow after more promises of dropping by on Friday. A sharp burst of wind crackled the wrapping paper over the window. Auer climbed up and balanced himself amid his school supplies to Scotch-tape on another layer of newspaper sheets. The society pages. He blinked away a tear. For a penny they broke a window. Very constructive. A fine way to raise a boy. He was born around here, too, and his parents taught him better. If he were a *gonif* like all the other grocers, he would have tacked another thirty cents to that total. With total justification. They never paid their last bill. When the bill hit twenty, they paid ten. Next week it was up to thirty-five, and they paid fifteen again. And played the same game till it ran up over a hundred. Dubin, the rental agent, faced the same situation. They paid two weeks' rent, and then missed one. And paid another and missed one. And when they owed every grocer from Kaminsky on Third to Newman on Eighth and Cottonwood and were three or four months behind on the rent, they brought in a car or team of horses in the middle of the night, moved everything out, stripped the room bare, and took the stoves and radiators if they could unbolt them. Then they started the same routine all over again up by Columbia Avenue or down by South Street. Yet he, Sam Auer, was guilty as accused of making money. Sure. Naturally. Working from seven in the morning till eight at night, he was not starving.

He knew why he had butterflies in his belly. At two, when he locked up for his rest hour, instead of napping on his parlor sofa or having a beer and watching television, he would walk over to Seventh Street and warn the Johnsons against repetition of this conduct. The prospect was making him nervous. Everyone knew Sam Auer had a foul temper. He could talk to people for a while, reason with them, "discuss" matters rationally, but if they did not respond to reason, something snapped inside him. Which was why he took so much crap off Bunny at home. If it ever came to raising his hand to her, it wouldn't be a slap; he might kill her.

"Looks like you've had some action," the Tastykake driver said as he came in with the daily order. The driver began arranging his boxes more favorably on the pastry counter, and Auer told him the entire story of the penny pinwheels and the light tap on the wrist. He told him about the Johnson family, the worst pack on Seventh Street, fourteen brothers and sisters, all foul balls, and of his intention to call on the Johnsons this afternoon and warn them against further repetitions of this incident.

The Tastykake driver agreed and told him that almost every store along his route had been robbed or vandalized over the last two years. Auer found himself repeating the same story to his Freihofer breadman, his *Daily News* driver, and Larry Hermans, who came in for the monthly grocery order. They all reacted in the same fashion; they clucked in sympathy and then minimized his misery by topping him with stories of bloody muggings and burglaries. Hermans recalled how old Phil Basarov had been pistol-whipped to death closing up his saloon on Callowhill Street last year, skull cracked, all for a stinking thirty-seven dollars. The assailant had just been released from Moyamensing on parole, a twenty-year-old *shvartzer*, out on the street because of some technicality, free to bash in another skull.

Hermans drove off in his Plymouth, and Auer wished that he had not opened his mouth so wide. Talking about it had not quieted the trickling looseness in his gut. Actually, he had boxed himself in. By telling them that he had a suspect, that he intended to confront the Johnsons in their lair, he had made a commitment. Tomorrow everybody would want a report.

At ten-fifteen Auer was surprised to hear the first recess bell ring. Through his Cottonwood window he watched the children pour out of the fire exits and start sliding around on the schoolyard ice. In such lousy weather Thurston usually held its recess indoors, but he guessed that the teachers probably felt more cooped up than the kids. He peered through his pyramids of fruit juice and cleanser cans, searching for Johnson among the three hundred or so children slipping around and banging each other against the long board fence that separated the yard from the adjacent empty lot. From this angle the line of the school building sliced off his view, and he could command only half the yard. Without doubt, little Johnson would be skulking down the other end, staying carefully out of sight.

A caressingly warm sensation curled through his chest as he saw that it was Mrs. Lewis on recess duty. The poor girl had all the duties today. She was bundled up in her practical brown tweed coat, green woolen scarf, boots, and a fur cap that came down over her ears and made her look like a pixie. He smiled as she quickly jumped in to separate two boys wrestling in the snow banks. The woman gave him strange pleasurable tingles when he watched her. So innocent. There was no creeping in the balls or stiffening toward an erection, just an unidentifiable sense of well-being at observing her exist. He had never even noticed her till last fall when he paused to watch her play dodge ball with the kids and suddenly noticed how athletic she was. More lithe and agile than any of the boys as she ducked and twisted. Then, shockingly, she jumped high to escape a ball and her skirts flew up, revealing splendid thighs and a pretty contrast between her cinammon skin and the white panties. She quickly tucked her skirts down and looked around in embarrassment. Heinie Schmidt was in the store at the time and said, "You ever try any of that black stuff, Sam?" He had responded, "Yeah, sure," but that was a lie. He had never dabbled with them. Before he was married, he had screwed a lot of *shiksas,* Irish girls from Oriana Street and Italian girls from South Philly, but he had never messed around with any *shvas*.

No customer was approaching, and Auer could control himself no longer. He hurried to the parlor and dialed his home number. Bunny and he were not speaking when he left the house this morning, but this was more important than their habitual dawn squabbles.

A loud squawk from a radio blasted him as the phone was picked up in Oxford Circle. A hoarse, watery "Hello!" was blurted in his ear, and he remembered that his five-year-old had a sore throat.

"Stephanie, it's Daddy. Let me talk to Mommy."

Shouts of "Mommy, Mommy, Mommy," and the receiver dropping and banging around. Skating sounds. She was skating on his hardwood floors.

The extension was picked up in the kitchen, and he was attacked by total silence. Bunny had to remind him that they were not speaking when he left this morning. She had to punish him and force him to make the first move. Seconds dragged by before Bunny said, "What's the matter? I was down in the basement monkeying with the oil burner. It's got that funny knock again."

He braced himself, drawing on his reserves of strength and patience.

"My front window was smashed this morning."

"Wha'?"

"The front window was broken."

"How?" she asked angrily.

"With a brick. Probably from the empty lot. It was sitting there in the school supplies."

"Have you done anything about it yet?"

"What's to do? I've called Manny's hardware store, and they're sending the truck around. I've called the insurance, and we're covered. So now it's a matter of holding on tight till Manny's truck arrives."

"How come the window was broken?" Bunny demanded in exactly the tone he had anticipated, one that implied that he was in cahoots with the perpetrators.

"If I knew I'd tell you. I think it's the Johnsons. Yesterday I slapped one of their brats on the hand for stealing. They're the worst troublemakers in the neighborhood. Leah won't even let them in her place."

"You should have the police get them. Have the police go round there and throw a scare into the sonsofbitches."

"What can I tell the police?" he asked wearily. "I only surmise it's the Johnsons. I have no substantial proof. Instead of taking my nap, I'll talk to them myself. Johnson's not so bad. It's his wife who's the real bitch-on-wheels."

"What?"

"I'll just warn them that I don't want any repetitions of this incident."

"I don't like it, Sam. Be careful. Call the police and go round there with the red car. If you go there by yourself, all that miserable slop might jump you."

"*Ach,*" he scoffed, "I can take care of myself. I was born around here, too, y'know. When I was a kid, I must have punched it out with every *shva'* in the schoolyard."

"Just be careful," she admonished him. "I don't like this. A husband in bed I don't need."

Auer scowled at his reflection in the parlor mirror. She meant that in more ways than one.

"Are you feeling any better?"

"I wasn't feeling ill this morning, Sam. I was just sick and tired of it. You don't need a home to live in, you need a pigsty. If I didn't have enough trailing around after the kids all day, I have to follow you with a bucket and mop. I can't live like that, Sam. I'm at my wits' end."

"You passed that point a long time ago."

"Don't start," Bunny warned him.

"What else can I do but start? I call up to discuss a serious problem, and all you can do is put on the same tired record and give me a load of crap."

"If you don't want to hear the same tired record, try to show a little more consideration around the house. I'm tired of nagging you but I'm really at my wits' end."

"Good-bye. The store is filling up. I have to run."

"Don't forget the list I gave you. The car's all snowed in in the driveway, and with Stephanie sick I won't be able to get away from the house to do any shopping."

He hung up without bothering to reply. They were not speaking this morning, but her isolation was not so complete she could not hand him a grocery list as he went out the door. Twice a week she forced him to trudge home with a bag of groceries as if the two bucks saved on a ten-dollar order were worth his pain and humiliation in having to carry the heavy bag all the way to the El Station at Fairmount, sit on the El with a bundle of groceries like a goddamn greenhorn, bump into all the passengers when he took the crowded bus to Oxford Circle, and carry it the whole long block to their corner over a pavement slippery with ice. Two dollars she saved by subjecting him to this ordeal, and then she dropped twenty on some junky doodad for her fucking mantlepiece. Bunny did it on purpose. She knew that on nights he lugged a box of groceries he couldn't stop off at the diner for a coffee with Zig and Gall. With a box of groceries on his lap, no woman peeked at him on the El. They examined the groceries with amusement or contempt. Women were all screwed up mentally. First they scrambled to get married and then felt contempt for any individual who looked too married.

The messenger from Starker's was crossing Sixth to pick up the office order at Leah's. Just seeing the boy always triggered in his mind visions of Sophie Bitko, Starker's executive secretary, gleaming back there in the office cubicles. He could almost smell her creams and powders, sense her strong legs under the desk, the nylon stretched tight by her garter belt, her breasts high in that red blouse she flaunted last summer.

Sophie was one of his daily bright spots. He managed to always be outside at five-thirty when the factory let out, washing the windows or sweeping the pavement, so he could enjoy her striding by. Sophie, of course, was aware of it. Hurrying past the dumpy, frowsy women from the components department, she seemed like a superior creature from a greater planet—a tall, arrogant blond widow of thirty-five, the boss's mistress, and they could all kiss her ass. Yet they still played that game. Sophie went to Leah's, had a cup of tea, and then Starker picked her up at six. Everybody knew she had been running around with Starker since his wife's heart attack made her an invalid; and yet year after year Sophie pretended to wait for the trolley at Eighth and Green Garden, and Starker picked her up as if it were a chance meeting.

Nobody messed with Sophie, none of the production workers, not even the Puerto Ricans who whistled at all the girls, since Al Dominic was fired. There had been a two-by-four card on the company bulletin board:

"Mister Starker has lost his rubbers. Anybody finding a box of Sheiks, please return to Sophie in the office. Thank you."

Starker blew up. He charged right over to Al Dominic, the plant wise guy, ran his finger across the television cabinet Dominic was polishing, and said, "Dominic, you do a crummy job. Punch your card and get the hell out of here."

Dominic was back in five minutes with the shop steward, and there was a threat of a strike. Starker told them go ahead. He snorted, because most of his better employees were old German cabinetmakers with homes in Jersey. They minded their own business and were not about to go against the boss in a dirty matter like this. . . .

Auer dropped another clove of garlic into his stew. He did not envy Leah her connection with the factory management. It stemmed from the fact that Sophie used Leah as her confidante. He managed to split the lunch trade with Leah quite nicely. She catered to the fancier business, the Negro teachers from Thurston, the few stenographers from local firms, Starker executives, and he fell heir to the rough types, Starker's polishers, truck drivers, laborers from the lumberyard at Sixth and Grenoble. Leah could keep her Negro schoolteachers. A lot he needed them. They ordered a twenty-five-cent grilled cheese sandwich and a cup of tea and wanted to occupy a booth for the whole lunch hour, oh-so-refined, linger elegantly over their tea like they were parked on their own veranda till the first bell rang for the afternoon session.

The colored volunteer women in their navy blue uniforms and white crossed belts were chatting in front of Grace's steps, waiting to direct traffic when the children came out at twelve, detain the cars chugging down Sixth. His stomach was twisting. He would have to go out there and grab Johnson. He felt as though he were in a dangerous countdown, like ready to bail out with the Airborne.

The bell ripped through the silence, and the timing could not have been worse. Manny's truck pulled up on Cottonwood just as the buzzers ceased snarling. In less than a minute his counter was crowded with impatient workingmen, paint-stained, smelling of dye, varnish, sawdust. They were snatching pints of milk from his wall refrigerator, Cokes from the soda case, all of them demanding service and barking their orders simultaneously. The kids were crowding around the candy counter up front, grabbing pinwheels and Fig Newtons and chocolate buds and tossing their pennies into the cigar box.

He signaled to the two Negroes Manny had sent to proceed directly to their task; he had no time to talk to them. They tore the sheets of paper away, and a freezing blast and light entered the store. To the normal confusion they added a nerve-racking pounding and chipping, as the wind fluttered the newspapers in his stand. His daily rush was always fifteen minutes of pandemonium. Every day he had to put out, apply, prove himself, ladle out his stew or daily special with a slice of pickle and buttered roll, wrap up the prepared hoagies, keep everybody happy. A worker around here liked fast service so he could gobble his food down and use the rest of his lunch hour to smoke and rest.

"Watch it over there," Auer snarled at the children swarming around the candy counter. He could see nobody stealing, and the warning was general in nature. He never lost much, because they would all gladly squeal on each other and moaned loudly when a buddy tried to cheat.

All the while he kept one eye on the glass pane in his front door, hoping to catch Johnson skipping across Sixth. He was responding mechanically to the greetings and orders and questions, nodding, "Yeah, Joe. Rotten weather. Car broke down, Benny? Yeah. A brick through my window. Found it there this morning when I opened up. Another slice of pickle, Al?"

"Hey," Heinie Schmidt shouted, "wouldn't it be cheaper to wash that window, Sam? I knew it was dirty, but you didn't have to toss a rock through it."

Heinie Schmidt was an unsuccessful joker, but that never stopped him. Auer winced at all the racket Manny's helpers were making with the glass removed, banging away with their hammers and chisels at the decayed putty in the old frame. That huge open space gave him a queasy sensation. The cars were too close as they raced and bumped down Sixth. With the glass gone, it seemed as though he had raw flesh exposed to the wind and cold, as though part of his own skin had been ripped away.

At least the cold had helped to invigorate him. He had really been fast today. It was not that he was too stingy or tightfisted to hire a helper. The real scurrying and hassle only lasted ten, fifteen minutes, and if he moved his butt he could handle it all himself. Helpers hardly helped. They all started out like balls of fire, and within three weeks they were eating and pocketing more than they took in. Nobody was as fast as he was on his feet. If he ever finally ran away to California, he could make one-fifty a week as a short-order cook.

Auer was satisfied to note that all his boys were chewing avidly at their hoagie sandwiches and wolfing down his stew. They were loyal to him. They did not complain about the cold and banging. The volunteers with their orange caps and crossed belts were detaining traffic again, and he spotted Louis Johnson slipping across Sixth Street, flanked by two bigger boys that he was obviously trying to use as shields. Rushing out from behind the counter, Auer pushed his way through the children gathered around the soda box, blanched as the cold air swept over him on the front step, and put his hands to his mouth to bellow, "Johnson! Get over here!"

With that roar everybody at the intersection turned around to look at Auer. The children, the teachers on Leah's steps, Fat Grace with her ponderous breasts resting on the window ledge, they were all staring at him expectantly. Johnson pretended not to have heard anything. He rolled his rear in a little hucklebuck step as he passed Grace's window, and Auer again shouted, "Johnson! C'mere!"

Louis Johnson stopped. He froze theatrically with one foot poised in midair as if he had been paralyzed in flight. He spun around and pointed to his chest with his thumb. An impish grin was on his face.

"That's right, Johnson," Auer called to him. "You!"

Manny's repairmen continued chipping away methodically at the crumbling putty in the stripped frame. They had dumped all the glass slivers into a cardboard container and were scraping and banging energetically, anxious to escape this cold. Johnson ambled through the brown slush with an impudent hitch in his stride for the benefit of all his buddies. He crossed diagonally from Fat Grace's building, slowly and deliberately, like he was a gunslinger sidling down the main road of Dodge City. He took so much time that the cars stopped by the volunteers, and backed all the way up to Green Garden, began honking their horns, and the heavyset women in the crossbelts finally shooed him along.

Traffic rolled again, and for a second, as the boy posed in front of him, legs wide apart, hatless, corduroy jacket unzipped, Levis ripped at the knee, and only a thin polo shirt protecting his chest from the cold, Auer felt ashamed to be menacing a seventy-pound child. His determination was restored by the nasty sound of the repairmen tearing away splintered wood stripping from the window ledge. The glass was not enough; now he was going to be stuck with a doozy of a carpentry bill.

"You wanted me, mister?" Johnson asked.

"No, Johnson. I don't want you. I want you to run home and tell your father or mother I want to see them. Right now."

"What for?" His features twisted with the grief of injured innocence. Like all his large family, he had green eyes and a reddish tint to sparse kinky hair, a sprinkling of freckles around his nose. They seemed faintly Teutonic.

"Never mind, Johnson. You just tell them I want to see them. You get me, boy?"

"I never stole no pinwheel, Mister Auer. I had that pinwheel in my pocket from the time before I came into the store."

Auer made a rasping noise. "Sure. I'm not worried about any pinwheel. It's my front window I want to see them about. Tell them that if they're not around here to see me by two o'clock I'll be paying them a little visit. With the red car."

The boy's stance melted from hands-on-hips defiance to a Sunday-go-to-church reverence as he politely said, "All right, Mister Auer, I'll be sure and tell 'm. They gotta come right around here and see you."

Without even glancing over his shoulder, Johnson abruptly flung himself into the street, dodged through one lane of traffic, paused stiffly between the trolley tracks to let one car go by, and then raced for Leah's pavement as an oncoming upholstery truck braked with an agonizing screech and barely missed clipping him. The upholstery driver slapped his forehead and then shook his fist at Johnson. He started up again as Auer watched the boy hop down the ice on Leah's long Cottonwood sidewalk, dancing with disjointed elbows and rolling his skinny buttocks, happy to be released.

"What was that all about?" Heinie Schmidt asked as Auer returned to the relative warmth of the store.

"Oh, the little bastard. I grabbed him stealing yesterday and his brothers are my prime suspects. A rotten family like you've never seen."

Auer gathered up the crumpled napkins and soiled paper dishes as all the men at the counter shared the moment of high drama. Nobody had complained about the cold, and they all appeared interested in the project. Perhaps all laboring men were interested in labor, Auer thought, in observing how another worker plied his trade. The fresh white putty was daubed in, and now they all shared in the suspense as Manny's men slid the cumbersome pane of fresh glass from the truck, wobbling as they carried it across the slippery, treacherous ice, almost dropping it when the skinny helper banged his foot against the wrought-iron heelscraper next to the step, and then they all winced together as the glass rose, and there was a loud crunch as the pane fitted into the frame. It was in fast. The men at the counter broke into cheers and applause, and the two helpers gave loud sighs of relief.

Strangely, with the brilliant new glass in, everything looked worse. Leah's window, a jumbled mass of groceries, ceramics, and antiques, loomed much closer, a mere jump away over a cobbled black marsh. Grace's hideous building, a four-story rectangular structure, seemed even ghastlier today, like a second-grader's drawing, covered with a smeared puckering

gray concrete, a rusting fire escape hanging over the Cottonwood pavement, and Fat Grace herself filling her window next
to the green double doors and broken side steps. The spar-
klingly clean glass let in more of the dismal November overcast, and under this new lens the rest of his fixtures aged and
withered. His place was shabby. The icebox windows were
painfully spotted, and there were dents in his cans of Franco-
American spaghetti. Everything seemed magnified or di-
minished.

Across the street Mrs. Lewis was coming out of Leah's,
laughing at some comment Mr. Silverman, the principal,
whispered in her ear. The laughter produced a twinge of resentment. Since when had Silverman stooped to having his lunch at
Leah's? Usually Silverman walked up to the fancy Oyster
House at Glendolph and Green, had lunch with the bank executives from Sixth and Green Garden, liked to pass himself off as
a member of the elite.

The second bell rang, and the lines in the schoolyard filed
into the fire exits in orderly fashion, kindergarteners, first- and
sixth-graders bringing up the rear, with the boys swaggering
rebelliously and punching each other when the teachers were
not looking. Auer saw the more responsible boys from the
safety patrol dawdling as they strolled down Cottonwood, picking at each other to delay the return to classes. They were about
to start a snowball fight when the volunteer woman blew her
whistle and ordered them to hurry inside.

Poor kids, Auer thought. Whistles, bells, buzzers, clocks.
He himself lived like Pavlov's dog, tied to the school and factory
schedule of whistles, bells, buzzers, and clocks. A caveman
visiting the twentieth century would think that everybody was
nuts, jumping up and down to whistles, bells, buzzers, and
clocks.

It was quiet now, without the children yelling in the yard,
just the not unpleasant chipping at the window of Manny's
helpers putting on the finishing touches and the music of the
chains and snow tires on the rough cobbles. He always looked

forward to this stretch of tranquillity after lunch. He could wash his dishes with a cigarette burning in the ashtray, straighten up the place, sweep the floor, put away his grocery orders. Just a few customers came in for groceries now. They knew better than to bother him during his busy lunch hour.

Often, as he put cans on shelves and puttered around, he wondered how he could be so content working and so miserable at home. Work was supposed to be the lousy part of life, home the goal and refuge of joy. With him it was all ass-backwards: his best moments came here in the store, while in his mind the home was some kind of horrid castle in the dim northern region of the city, presided over by a wicked witch whose clutches he was obliged to return to every night.

The green doors next to Grace's window opened, and he saw Barry stagger out. Perhaps those *shvas* had the right idea. When a woman became too much for them, they cut out and tried another town. Barry was supposed to have a family in Tennessee and another pack of kids over in Cincinnati. Who was better off? Barry was free to bum around out there, and he was trapped in his store, trapped behind this sink.

Auer dumped more Duz into his hot dish water and snapped on his radio. The radio was stolen goods. Peggy Moore's ex-boyfriend Winston brought it in and wanted fifteen dollars for it. Hoo-hah. Fifteen bucks for a burglarized Philco not even Zacky's hock shop would touch. Winston accepted five and was glad to get it.

Slipping off his Omega wristwatch, Auer recalled that this was also a swiped item. Some *schlech* from Shor's taproom brought it in. A grand espionage network they operated here. With all the cleaning women working up in West Oak Lane and Wynnfield, the local burglars always knew who was away on vacation, which addresses had mail sticking out of the boxes or newspapers piling up in the storm door.

Auer flipped the dial till he found a foreign language station where he could not understand the advertisements and jingles. He wanted romantic mandolins and guitars, and not "Won't

you try Wheaties? They're whole wheat with all of the bran."
Even on the foreign stations they attacked. He would hear
"Jabber Jabber Jabber Household Finance Company Jabber
Jabber Jabber."

Washing his dishes was relaxing. Bunny bitched about washing dishes, and he washed a huge load every day and found it
relaxing. It gave him time to daydream. He knew exactly how
silly his favorite daydream was, and every day he concocted
increasingly elaborate versions: He graduated Southern with a
scholarship to the University of Pennsylvania. Three varsity
seasons with the Red and Blue, All-American, and he got in one
season with the Eagles after graduation. Then came Pearl Har-
bor, and he was commissioned an officer. Captain Auer returned as a bemedaled war hero and starred for the Eagles five
years at fullback. This season he was retiring as the grizzled old
pro, and they were giving him a testimonial dinner at the Warwick Hotel. His farewell address was broadcast over both
WCAU and WFIL. The main fun came in drawing up the list of
distinguished guests at the head table: Steve van Buren, repre-
senting the team; Joe Fulks from the Warriors; Del Ennis and
Bob Carpenter for the Phillies; Connie Mack for the A's; Uncle
Wip, Eddie Fisher, Albert E. Greenfield, and John B. Kelly,
the construction magnate. Mayor Samuels and the Governor
telegrammed their regrets.

This was all seen so clearly. With his savings Sam Auer
opened a classy lounge at Broad and Spruce, a block up from
Lew Tendler's spot. The walls were knotty pine and decorated
with football trophies and autographed photos of chorus girls,
strippers, boxers, comics, and actresses from the Walnut and
Shubert theaters. Celebrities, gamblers, and sporting figures
dropped by to ask who he liked on the Friday night card at the
Arena and. . . .

Totally silly. It was absurd for a man to dream about being
himself and yet a success. It was ridiculous for a man to wish to
be himself while recalling an entirely different background, a
string of victories, triumphs, and awards. To be exactly the

same yet totally different. And twenty times a day he furnished that lounge at Broad and Spruce and composed spectacular guest lists of notables for his testimonial dinner at the Warwick Hotel.

It was two-fifteen, and his scalp was tingling. Nerves. No matter what he told himself that was a sure sign he was nervous. For those bastards he would lose a few more hairs. His stomach was turning, but he still had to go around there and advise them that he would brook no further repetitions of this behavior.

Between customers, he sat at the counter and munched on a salami, tomato, and onion sandwich with hot mustard on a seeded roll. He sipped at a bottle of 7-Up, to help him belch afterward, and browsed through the newspapers. Korea and McArthur he did not need. Nor more crap about Joe McCarthy. He flipped to the funny pages. It was the only section of the newspaper where the good guys consistently won. He turned to the sports pages but found them unsatisfying in winter. In spite of playing football for Southern, he was essentially a baseball fan and impatient for next season to start. During the regular season he often read the same box scores over three times: first in the *Inquirer,* then in the *Daily News,* and a few hours later in the *Bulletin.* He would feel elated when Del Ennis, a hometown boy, went two for four, and depressed if it were all goose eggs for one of his favorites like Andy Semenick. He rooted for the guys who extended themselves beyond their natural talents.

The hands on the Pepsi-Cola clock said three P.M. and still no sign of the Johnsons. There was no escape. Auer kneaded his scalp to stop the tingling and then drew the bolt on his front door. He flipped the Closed/Open sign and adjusted the dials to three-thirty. Back in the parlor he slipped into his black leather jacket and checked the effect in the mirror. It would do. In this leather jacket he still looked like a tough truck driver, and not a porky grocer.

Fat Grace grinned at him as he crossed Sixth, and Auer winked back. She was an ugly black sow and a nice person, all four hundred pounds of her, with the fist marks and battle scars crisscrossing her enormous face. Day after day she sat in that window, grinning at the passing scene, the kids heading for school, the cars racing toward the bridge, the fights and squabbles. He had never seen her outside. Rumor had it that she had not left her apartment for the last four years because she had grown too wide to squeeze through the vestibule door. Another rumor had it that she was only thirty-five, though she looked sixty with half her teeth gone and crow's-feet under her sleepy eyes. He wondered what she did with her money. Grace had money from the moonshine she sold after hours, and when the relief checks came there were poker games in her rooms with hundreds of dollars in the pot.

Leah had strung barbed wire down her long yard fence. The storefront church facing Marshall had also strung barbed wire along their Cottonwood fence. *Shvartzers* protecting themselves from their fellow *shvartzers*. Newman up by Eighth Street had the right idea. His brick wall in back was topped with chips of broken bottles planted in concrete. Anybody trying to climb over that would cut himself up good. A man staying in business around here lived in a state of siege. Slip up for two seconds, and they would steal everything except the *mezuzahs* off the door.

Down snowy Marshall Street the steps were empty, and the shades drawn on all the three-story rooming houses. The freight cars on the tracks south of Grenoble blocked off any view of Franklin Square farther down. It was sad. Ten, fifteen years ago those big houses were for one family, with maybe a few boarders upstairs. He had screwed Dora from #417 and Dirty Gertie from #412. Esther from #426 Marshall had worn his varsity sweater with the big "S," though he had never made it with Esther. Now they had all moved out. To Oak Lane and Logan and Merion and Cheltenham. Once they occupied solid blocks, and now Jews only lived on the corners down here. Since they moved out, the bricks were never pointed or stenciled anymore. All the fronts were a muddy brownish red that looked terrible with the dirty yellow window shades and green doors.

The scene at the corner of Seventh and Cottonwood was strange. It seemed unreal, like from a movie, even though he knew everybody there. Like some kind of pagan ritual.

On the empty lot by the icehouse the Negroes were gathered around a bonfire, and Sidonia was tossing a broken sofa onto the flames. They were warming their hands, burning a rickety pushcart, scrap wood, and the old sofa, with the sparks crackling in the straw, sputtering and snapping and spitting smoke. They tossed empty beer bottles into the flames, and it seemed weird, like a Druid funeral pyre surrounded by rubbish and blackened snow, with the smoke rising into the grim sky above the telephone wires.

Auer could not explain why, but the five Negroes in their motley outfits, civilian clothes mixed with Army jackets and fatigue trousers, seemed alien and lonely today, lonelier than he was. Sidonia, the iceman, led a good life, no? It was said that Sidonia had the longest and most active *shvuntz* in the neighborhood, eleven inches dangling, and all kinds of bastards from York Avenue to Franklin Street. If that mattered. Auer shrugged under his leather jacket. The Italian guys on his football team always used to rib him about it and say, "Hey, Sam, we thought you Jews were supposed to have short dicks, but you need a goddamn harness for that cannon you got down there." If that mattered. Bunny said he carried a big *shmuck* and was a big *shmuck*, and that was all the credit she gave him.

"Pretty nasty day, Mister Sam," Sidonia called to him as he passed the icehouse. Rhythm and blues music was coming out of Shor's taproom.

"Rotten," Auer agreed with a cloud of frost flowing from his lips. He blinked away tears from the acrid smoke wafting his way from the bonfire. Sidonia was all right. Sidonia just minded his own business, delivered his ice, and fucked a lot.

He walked down Seventh, and from the middle of the block he could hear Zacky's jukebox: "That's the story of, That's the glory of . . . love." Already pouring it down in there in the middle of the afternoon. Terrible. Endless. Seventh Street was a replica of Marshall, except the rooming houses on the west side were only two stories high. They all had the same dull red unpointed bricks, grimy tan window shades, and green doors. One decoration on the block, a sign that read "Rooms for Rent—Inquire at Zacky's Employment Agency." Auer snorted. That *genzil,* Mutty Zackman, had moved up in the world; from cheap chiseler to big-time operator. Only in America.

Suprisingly, the bell at #424 was working. He gave it five sharp bursts and then waited. The Johnsons occupied the second floor back, and their eldest daughter had the whole third floor with all the kids up there. A minute crawled by and he heard steps on the staircase inside, a door creaking, slamming shut.

Nobody was volunteering to open the front door. He felt the eyes on his back. The roomers were peeking at him from behind their curtains and shades. A scabby mutt was picking through an overturned garbage can at the corner. He jiggled the door handle and leaned on the bell again. Everybody knew him around here, but a white man on this block was generally a bill collector. He held his thumb on the buzzer and pounded on the door with a heavy, thumping beat till he heard a screeching in the first-floor hallway.

The green door was unlatched and Auer scowled down at little Brenda Williams, Howie Williams's youngest. He wondered what she was doing out of school. Before he could say anything, Brenda dashed back down the unlit hall. As he pushed the door open wider, his nose turned at the stench of cooking turnips, unwashed floors, and sluggish plumbing that attacked his nostrils before dissolving into the cold air of the street.

He sensed, rather than saw, a presence on the staircase, by the second-floor landing, a weight leaning against the banister without coming down far enough to be seen.

"Anybody home?" he called out.

"Who the fuck making all that racket down there?" a woman's voice answered.

"It's Sam Auer. I want to talk to Mister Johnson."

"He ain't here!" the voice rasped. "He went to the hospital. Now get the hell off that bell."

"Tell him," Auer shouted, "that if he doesn't come down, I'll be back with a red car and talk to him then."

"I told you the fuck he ain't here. What you want?"

At Cottonwood the smoke was billowing as the damp straw of the couch burst into full flame. The gang from the icehouse had gathered to discuss the situation and watch the fun. He did not want to go inside and meet the Johnsons on their own grounds. Once inside those hallways anything could happen, with no witnesses. Over his shoulder, to his right, he saw loafers had come out of Zacky's to enjoy this spectacle.

"Then you come down here, and I'll talk to you," Auer roared.

"You'll shit talk to me. I ain't got nothing I need to talk to you about."

"C'mon down, or I'll be back with the red car."

A whine of loose, creaking steps, muttered curses, and he saw the squat, lumpy shape of Linda Johnson, breeder of the fourteen troublemakers, approaching him in the dark hallway. He backed down off the steps, just in case she took it into her mind to push him down. Auer folded his arms across his chest, and Linda Johnson stopped in the vestibule, with her fists planted on broad hips. She tossed her head in anger and snapped, "Now what the fuck you want?"

A beauty she was not, Auer decided. Her yellowish tinted hair was tortured high in pink curlers and the fat hung over her arms to form puffy mounds of cinnamon dough at the elbows. He wondered how Johnson could have brought himself to do the dirty deed with this slob fourteen times.

"I want to talk to your husband about the brick in my window."

"We don't know nothing about no brick through nobody's window, so you can just get out of here."

"Well, I think you do, and I'm putting my foot down. Tell

your husband, or your man, or whatever he is, that if there are any more repetitions of this incident I will deal with him personally."

"We don't know nothing about no brick," Linda Johnson spluttered. "We was at a party last night. Ask Shor. We was in Shor's taproom till two oh-clock."

"I think you were involved, and I think you're lying. It didn't have to be your husband. Any of your brats could have done it."

"Yeah? You got any proof?" she asked triumphantly.

"I don't need any proof."

"Then what the fuck you mean coming around here accusing us of this shit? You got no proof, you get your fucking ass out of here, stop bothering me, or I'll call my son downstairs on you."

"I'm very worried," Auer said smugly. "You tell your man that if I have any more trouble with him, I'll break his head and then throw his ass in jail so fast he won't know what hit him."

People were coming out on their steps and opening their windows to tune in on the cursing match. Linda Johnson shook a fist at him and shouted, "Yeah? And you listen to me. The next time you touch my boy Louis, my men'll go around your Jew store and drag you out and kick your Jew ass all over the schoolyard."

"Don't worry," Auer assured her. "The next time I catch Louis stealing, I won't slap his hand; I'll break his fucking arm."

"Fuck you, you Jew motherfucker," Linda Johnson screamed and slammed the door.

Auer stood there with the sharp click of the metal latch and the reverberation of the damp wood still humming in the air, while all the spectators laughed and shook their heads. He shrugged as he went back up Seventh. His cheeks felt scorched. Arguing with that woman was like poking a sleeping bear or getting your face too close to the oven. Yet it had done him some good. He felt oddly relieved. A soft punk did not stand a chance around here. It was all are you game or are you lame, put up or shut up, and go down to play at the other end of the schoolyard with the little kids.

The bums in front of the icehouse were nodding to him. They respected him. Sidonia drawled, "Peace on earth, Sam. Peace on earth."

"That's all I want, Sidonia. Take it easy."

"Guts was all," Auer reminded himself as he sloshed through the pulverized ice on Cottonwood Street. Guts was all. Sidonia had guts. Sidonia needed that icepick for more than chipping ice when he made his deliveries. Guts was all. When Southern played West Catholic for the city championship, everybody was yakking about how Red Scoletti would cream Sam Auer. All over South Philly and West Philly they were predicting that Scoletti would take him out on the very first play.

On all the corners and in all the candy stores around Snyder Avenue they were making bets about that showdown. And in front of fourteen thousand fans in St. Joe's stadium it was Sam Auer who got his helmet down lower, charged right into Scoletti on that opening kickoff, and sent him to the hospital. Sure it cost. It cost him a broken collarbone. But so what?

Auer suddenly stopped. The story had an unhappy ending. Two years later Scoletti was starring at halfback for Alabama, and Sam Auer had to read about his exploits after a day of pushing a wheelbarrow at Second and Callowhill, read about the college hero while smelling like a sack of dusty Idaho potatoes.

He had missed his three-thirty rush, the flurry of messengers coming in to get doughnuts and coffee and the penny trade of the kids leaving school. He changed from his wet shoes and for the remainder of the afternoon read "Amazing Stories" between grocery customers. The new window still disconcerted him. It looked like a gleaming new plate in a mouth full of rotten teeth. For forty years the old window had sat in that frame. This one was like another nail in his father's casket. His father was deader, and his mother was older.

At five-thirty he was irritated to be trapped behind his fountain, preparing two fried egg sandwiches to travel for Heinie Schmidt, who was bitching about working overtime. He hurried so as not to miss Sophie Bitko going by, but when he reached the steps he saw that Sophie was skipping her chat with Leah today and was already up at Sixth and Green Garden, turning the corner at the bank. For one second he had Sophie, a quick flash of golden hair in the dusk, a smart fur jacket, black boots. Then nothing. He was staring at the leather factory across Green Garden from the bank.

Turning, and as if in compensation for his loss, he glanced down Cottonwood, and Pauline Kozak was coming around from Glendolph Street. He lit a cigarette so as to have an excuse to be out there when she passed. A few years back, three-thirty was the crucial hour for him to be outside, when Pauline returned from school. She was fourteen, dumpy, gawky, still played softball with the boys, swinging the bat with all her might and letting her skirts fly up as she ran the bases. In one year that baby fat melted away, her complexion cleared, and her blouse swelled. All so fast. Now she had dropped out of William Penn, went to a modeling-and-poise academy, and worked illegally as a hostess in a nightclub. In her pea jacket and with a pert sailor's cap, she looked like a rose growing out of this shitpile.

"Hi, Sam," Pauline said unenthusiastically.

"Hi, kid," he answered in a warm, paternal tone. He stepped inside so as not to be too obvious. Through the door glass he watched her mince through the banked snow, hurry across Sixth as quickly as her tight skirt permitted. Pauline was a woman already, well aware of her charms. She went to Leah's. She also used Leah as an adviser. And Maddy got the chance to look at her. Some kids had all the luck. Goddamn Maddy had all the luck in the world and did not know it yet.

Closing time approached, Auer took out his grocery list and began filling a cardboard carton with items that Bunny could have bought almost as cheaply at the supermarket on Cottman.

He fought to resist the sluggish backwash and sense of useless-ness that often seeped through him around nightfall. There were no agonizing problems at the moment: the Johnsons were warned, the window was fixed, the insurance was coming through, and yet he would not object if he fell in front of the El tonight when it came roaring down the tracks. He was heading home for a fight. About what, he did not know. He only knew that before bedtime he and his wife would quarrel. About some-thing he did. Or something he failed to do. About something he always did. Or something he never did. If nothing else was handy, she got him for smoking. She would provoke him till he was on the verge of strangling her, and then accuse him of blowing matters out of all proportion and having a terrible temper. Then she would roll over in bed, give a nasty tug to the blanket, point her fat *tochis* at him, and fall asleep. . . . Tonight, he sensed it would really be hot and heavy. Because of the window.

Locking his side door, he stared at the old kerosene drum next to the steps and reminded himself for the ten-thousandth time that it was no longer used and he should get rid of it. Across the street, through the ceramics and comic books in Leah's window, he saw Maddy and little Herbert playing chess in the cluttered store. Maddy he had never been able to figure out. An unusual kid. Maddy started out just like little Herbie, a fat-assed little brain reading *War and Peace* at the age of ten, the quiz kid with all the answers, and then he suddenly slimmed down and became a pool shooter and roughneck.

The chess match was a curious scene for this neighbor-hood. The life of the mind. With the lights burning, Leah's store seemed like some kind of outpost of warmth and education and culture in this harshness. People always did a double take when they went in there and found that jumble of groceries and dress racks, antique lamps and ceramic ovens.

He could not compete with Leah for the night trade. With her apartment in the rear, she merely threw the bar over her door, drew the bolt, and was home, while he now had an hour trip to Oxford Circle coming up. It had been better with Bunny when they lived in an apartment over the store. But what kind of rotten father would raise his daughters around here?

Glazed snow gleamed luminously under a frigid sky on Green Garden Avenue. The meat trucks and tractor trailers from the terminals had slashed the snow into a brown syrup that was churned and kneaded by chains and tires into a fine brackish powder at dusk. After the evening rush hour the powder again froze into flaky sheets of obsidian that contained and reflected the shivering moon above. In winter the earth seemed to tilt on its axis and cover Green Garden Avenue with skies that belonged to the endless marshes north of Hudson Bay.

The lights were blazing in the diner at Fifth Street. Auer adjusted the carton of groceries in his arms to a less uncomfortable position. His knife was right on top, right where he could grab it in case anybody jumped him on the solitary trip down to the river. At this hour there was not one light, one business open, one stray soul out, past the diner down to the Delaware. Under the El rails he could see the deck lights of a freighter sailing out to sea. The few dim street lamps made the broad avenue look like a Siberian tundra lined by sinister warehouses and menacing truck terminals. He realized there was nothing threatening about depots and parked vans. It was people who were dangerous, muggers lurking in the alleys. The odds were against him. One night they could get him for the cash in his pockets.

With the bundle in his arms he could not drop in the diner for his regular cup of coffee. He saw Zig and Gall in the rear, holed up in their usual booth, and could not bring himself to cross the avenue and tolerate the ribbing they would give him for the grocery carton. Bunny did this on purpose. She gave him this chore to deny him the half hour he always looked forward to, a half hour when he could talk dirty with Della the waitress and kid around with the old gang, tell jokes and argue boxing and baseball and broads and movies. For a while he could feel like he was single again, free, loose, ready to hop into the car and drive down to Wildwood for a few suds. But with the groceries, the ribbing became too cruel. Especially from Zig. Zig had a vicious streak, that dirty trick of coming on with a real sincere expression on his face, sucking you in, and then really slipping that blade in. . . . That was a funny hangout, that diner. Half the scrounges in there were the gang from the schoolyard from twenty years ago. Many had married and divorced, to return and hang out at the diner. That was their real life—the diner.

Auer thought about that all the way to his station at Fairmount. Knocking up Bunny had saved him from a life as a diner scrounge. He stood on the El platform and gazed out at the ships docked for miles up and down the waterfront, the powerful sweep of the bridge crossing over to Camden, the immense warehouses and piers, the freight cars on the Delaware Avenue tracks. Next to these plants and smokestacks stretching from Frankford down to the Navy Yard, nothing else counted. This was raw power, production, money, and he counted for nothing. He was a mere blob of shivering flesh, hardly there.

To alleviate the freezing pain in his toes, he did a brisk tap dance while the river breezes burned his cheeks. They were loading steel at the Poplar Street wharf, lowering steel beams into the lit hatches with four cranes in tandem. The steel gang was collecting a special bonus for the dangerous duty. They worked like a team when they loaded these beams and ingots, cursing up at the winchmen, shouting orders in the hatches. Every year one of the team was splattered against a bulkhead.

The dingy waiting room beckoned to him as a refuge from the winds, but he could not go in there. The waterfront looked too magnificent after being cooped up all day. The docked freighters had their mast lights on, lights from their portholes shining on the gloomy wharves. It hurt adding up how much he had missed. Gall once shipped out. Zig had his papers. In the old days everybody from the neighborhood took a few trips to Europe or the Caribbean. You were not a man until you had fucked a Cuban whore. Maybe if he talked to Gall, Gall could take him down to the union hall on Market Street and plug him on. Without some kind of "in" the union was a closed shop. He could sign on as a cook or messman. He was a crackerjack cook. But he could just hear Bunny's reaction: "What, are you crazy, Sam? You're a married man with two daughters. . . ."

A distant rumbling on the tracks snapped his head up, and he leaned forward to see the lightbeam on the El rushing at him. When he was a kid, the waterfront had not seemed so raw and inhuman. The docks seemed lively and kind when he was a kid. They all piled down here to watch the horses pull the garbage and trash wagons up the ramp, and when the derrick turned the wagon over and dumped the trash on the fires below, the smoke shot up and they all moaned with pleasure. Then they headed to the next wharf, where the fishermen were chopping up huge critters, hundred pounders, split wide-open, scaled right there with the blood oozing out of them. The fishermen sometimes gave them chunks from the marlin they were roasting over the stones, and that was great eating with lots of salt and Tabasco sauce.

Auer yelped as the door snapped shut immediately, banging against his arms and box, almost tripping him. He looked around for a conductor to curse, but none was in sight. First they show up late on a freezing night, and then they don't even give a man with a box in his arms three seconds to get through the doors.

As he flopped down on the dirty yellow rattan seat, he wondered when they were planning to install new cars on this line, like they had on Broad Street. Perhaps Broad Street was supposed to have a higher type of clientele? It was a crime to charge for transporting people in these filthy cattle cars. He stared at the red-cheeked Irishwoman sitting across from him and wondered what she thought about the situation. From the glazed look in her eyes, she probably thought nothing about the situation.

With the car swerving and swaying, he had to hold one hand over his carton so it would not topple off the bench at an abrupt stop. Now that his toes were beginning to thaw and tingle he could use a smoke. Nerves. Already on his third pack today. Though he hardly smoked them. While he bustled around the store there was always a cigarette burning in the ashtray, but he drew only maybe five puffs per smoke, so he could actually claim he was under a pack per day. A smoke would really fill the bill right now.

The "No Smoking" sign under the subway map of Philadelphia glinted back at him. "Smoking Prohibited. The carrying of a lighted cigarette, cigar, or blah is prohibited by blah and subject to blah-blah of not more than twenty-five blahs or thirty days' imprisonment blah-blah-blah."

Two more old women got on at Girard. Leather shopping bags. Babushkas. Thick ankles. Probably Ukrainians from Third Street.

He slowly brought his pack of Luckies out of his jacket pocket. The eyes of the Irishwoman widened as if he had un-zipped his fly. The whole trio was squinting at him. Why, was it their business? Goddamn busybodies. This was precisely the trouble with the world: everybody minding everybody else's goddamn business. Except when a man was in trouble and needed help. Then nobody wanted to know from nothing.

Sitting erect, he lit his Lucky and defiantly flipped his match down the aisle. The women glared at him, and he sneered back till they were forced to turn away. A moral victory. He wondered what the hell was the matter with the newsy old bitches. If the car were crowded and there was a chance he might burn somebody, he could understand their objections. But with the car so empty, there was absolutely no reason why a workingman should not relax with a well-earned smoke. Point two: they were too far away for the smoke to irritate them, so there was no call for those sour pusses. Point three: there was no worry about litter, because the floor was already filthy. So it was just to be mean, the old bags. The papers talked about un-employment. What unemployment? To reduce the unem-ployment, they could let well-behaved passengers smoke and hire some of the parasites off the relief rolls to sweep out the cars when the subway pulled into the Sixty-ninth Street station. Unemployment here and unemployment there, and there were thousands of useful tasks to be performed.

The Ukrainians and Irish left at Allegheny, but he had already crushed out his cigarette, unable to enjoy it with their grim jaws and narrow eyes spoiling the flavor. Just as the doors were about to bang shut, four teenage girls came rushing on board and flung themselves down on the seats. They were giggling and carrying ice skates. Quite an improvement. He slouched lower in his seat to get a better view of the slim redhead. She tugged her hem down over pleasing knees, and he wondered how anybody had the audacity to call women the weaker sex. He had been freezing his balls off on that El platform, and here were these little *shiksas* gadding about in short pleated skirts, with the cold wind swirling around their panties.

Nice legs. Pretty, muscular legs from roller skating and ice skating. Jewish girls never skated. The Jewish girls had the *bupkas*, and the *shiksas* had the legs. Strange customs. He had never been able to figure out the *goyim*. The *goyim* were truly mysterious creatures. They drank at their clubs, and they all wanted to be Lions and Elks and Eagles and Mooses and Knights of Columbus and march around with red fezzes playing clarinets. They ran the show. They fished at Cape May and probably thought Heaven was some kind of golf course. A Jew never had to belong to an organization. Some did, but it was superfluous. Just coming into the world as a Jew was like entering a club with your papers filled out and your dues paid up. . . .

From his El stop Auer had to dash for his bus, which was already pulling out of the depot. He bustled over the choppy ice with the bulky box in his arms, and the driver was kind enough to hold it up for him. Uptown there were these courtesies. He moved to the rear, frowning at the prospect of another long ride and then wheezed with relief as he took a seat. A quick survey of all the faces on the bus. A pleasure, all these normal-looking white faces. After a day down at Sixth and Cottonwood he felt like Doctor Livingstone on the Zambezi. All Oxford Circle faces here, except for three boys with thin Nazi noses and ducktails who had to be from Mayfair. That was the reassuring thing about this town; everybody knew who everybody was and where they came from. To come from Strawberry Mansion, or Fishtown, or Ninth and Snyder meant something. Everybody stuck in his place and nobody minded. Except the *shvartzers*. They wanted to spread out and change everything. But nothing would change. The rich *goyim* would still pull all the levers. The rich *goyim* merely took the suburban train out to the Main Line and were never heard from again. They ran everything and went down to their bank vaults at Fifteenth and Chestnut to clip a few coupons or sell a few stocks and escape to Paris. . . .

Fresh air filled his nostrils as he stepped off at his stop. Clean, pure, sweet air. That was the first thing he always noticed. The snow was cleaner on the front lawns, the air was purer, wide paths were cleared on the sidewalk, the stars were available in the sky.

He was at the end of his trek. On certain nights, trudging up this long block, he felt like one of those British heroes in the Rommel Desert Fox movies, valiantly lugging a buddy on his back to the next oasis. Only that was no oasis at the end of the block. There were thirty houses on this side facing thirty twins. Last night they all looked the same, and tonight more so, like couples growing old together. Thirty identical twins set back on lawns, yellow sandstone false fronts, bay windows on the first floor, two windows with shutters on the second floor, shingled roofs, and ornate gas lamps over the doorbells.

That was quite an equation: downtown—shitty; uptown— boring. Last winter, straggling home drunk along this block, the first solid drunk he tied on since the service, a weird notion hit him. He felt like a monster, one thousand feet tall, crushing glaciers in Greenland as he crunched through the ice. For fun he could march into any of these thirty houses, or the thirty houses directly across, barge in, kick off his shoes, and slip into the slippers. Around here they called him the *zhlub*, the ignoramus, because he never finished high school. They said he was crude and primitive, even though he read more books than any of them. Most of the husbands along this street had more education than he did, graduated Central or Olney, and a lot had college—Temple, West Chester, Philadelphia College of Pharmacy; but in their beach chairs on their front lawns, in their undershirts, they all looked, smelled, talked, and sounded alike, the meatman and the math teacher. Not one had any imagination. He could walk into any of these parlors, snap on the television, separate the brats and tell them to settle down and pick up their toys, *plotz* down at the supper table, scarf up whatever specialty was being dished out, take up whatever argument was in progress, and the lady of the house might not note the difference.

After supper they would squabble over what to watch on television, have a snack at eleven, walk the dog, put the garbage out, and later, in bed, nothing would happen unless it was Saturday night. Maybe in the morning the lady might yelp, "Hey! You're not Seymour!" and maybe she wouldn't. It all depended and hardly mattered.

His sidewalk was cleared, which meant that the kids with the shovels had been around. Fifty cents they charged nowadays, and Bunny gave them a dime tip. The rock salt crackled under his heels as he went up his cement path. Still a fairly thick sheet of ice. Those kids had done a very slipshod job, not put much muscle into it for sixty cents.

With difficulty he got the storm door open and balanced his heavy carton as he rang the doorbell with his shoulder. Through the small window cut in the door he could see the television blaring away in the parlor and the usual daily eruption of plastic dishes, teddy bears, dolls, crayons, and torn magazines spewn over the rug and sofa. He pressed again with his shoulder, and this time the buzzer sounded, producing cacophonous shrieks of "Daddy, Daddy, Daddy!" as his Sheila and Stephanie rushed in unison toward the vestibule, fighting and pulling at each other for the privilege of opening the door while he shivered outside with the box hurting his forearms and the storm door pressing into his side.

"C'mon, c'mon, c'mon," he barked. "Cut out the nonsense and let me in."

Sheila finally broke loose and undid the latch. He was instantaneously assailed by the aroma of the Tuesday night spaghetti sauce. As usual, the green peppers were underdone. The girls continued jumping all over him and pulling him down for kisses as he set the box down and began pulling off his rubbers. All he had to do was track up the parlor rug, and more than the spaghetti would hit the fan tonight. Prim Sheila received her kiss on the cheek, and he bent low to give Stephanie a more affectionate hug and kiss, tousled her blond curls and cooed, "Hi, honey. Hi, darling."

This was the moment when Bunny invariably asked him if it did not make him feel grand and needed and loved to come home to such a wonderful reception. "Sometimes" was the proper answer.

Tonight his wife was not bothering to come to the door. He picked his way through the clutter on the living room floor with the rankness of the raw green peppers growing pervasively more repulsive. At least she had set a place in the dining room for him. A green mat, a glass of wine, dish of pickles, and the salad bowl. She was not going to consign him to the kitchen this evening.

His daughters abandoned him as he entered the dining room. They resumed their tussling amid the torn sheets of the evening *Bulletin* on the sofa. In the kitchen Bunny was stirring the overly red ripe casserole of bubbling sauce. Without glancing back at him she said, "I thought you were going to call this afternoon."

"What about?"

He dumped his box on the white metal table and refrained from patting his wife, his attractive brunette, on the bottom. It was hoisted nicely into position by a girdle and attractively displayed in a yellow skirt. At thirty his wife had the ample figure of a movie star. Men still peeked at Bunny on the Boardwalk.

"You had me worried this morning when you told me you were going to see the *shvartzers*. I was sure you'd call back."

"Telephones work both ways, don't they? If you were that concerned, you could have called me."

He began putting the groceries away, cans on the pantry shelf, boxes of soap powder in the cupboard, twelve eggs into the egg slots in the refrigerator shelf. His nostrils dilated at the red sauce. Pimento-colored. Almost as if it had been dumped from the can and the onions, hamburger, and peppers added five minutes before he arrived.

"You shout at me when I call too much, and tell me I take you out of the store with the customers in there, and they steal. What about the *shvartzers*? Did you settle anything with them about the police and the window?"

"The king of the house was not at home. I had an interview with his queen."

"What did she have to say for herself?"

"Nothing too much. She said 'Fuck me,' and I said 'Fuck her,' and not too much was accomplished."

"Shhh," Bunny murmured, and wrinkled her nose toward the living room. "The girls." She positioned her lips for a brief kiss and responded to his embrace, but when his hand slipped down to her behind she flicked it away.

Auer returned to putting away the groceries. He discovered that they were low on tuna fish and asked, "How come Sheila was at home, too? Was school called off for the snow?"

"Steppie had the sniffles and a slight fever, so I thought it was best to keep them both home. I want you to look at Steppie's doo-doo when she goes to the toity. Her poo is much looser than I like it to be. You can give me an opinion as to whether I should call the doctor."

"Yeah."

Bunny prepared herself a cup of tea and sat at the dining room table with him as he ate the spaghetti. Her eyes narrowed as he sprinkled on an abundant amount of ground oregano and then a whole handful of the grated cheese. He savored the sauce, added more salt and another pinch of pepper. After one more bite he added more pepper, and Bunny said, "If you had a decent job and came home at a decent hour, I could prepare you a decent supper."

"That's not too logical," Auer said after sipping at the wine. "Logically, I should think that the fact that I get home late, at nine-thirty, would give you ample time to prepare a decent meal. You've already got the kids fed and bathed, and you've got nothing else to do."

"Sure, Sam. And I have to eat alone with the kids like an animal at six and worry about cooking for you again in the middle of the night. Other men get home at a decent hour and spend some time with their children and wives, while you go on and on in that goddamn store and show up in the middle of the night expecting a catered feast."

He pinched on more grated cheese. Not for the flavor now, just specifically to irritate her. This argument was over four years old and fought out an average of three times a week. Other arguments were enjoying longer runs. He almost admired her endurance, her tenacity, her ability to repeat herself night after night, month after month, year after year without visible signs of exhaustion.

"I would not gripe about that store so much," he said slowly, with the lettuce crunching in his teeth. "It provides you with a damn good living. You were the one all set on moving up here. If we'd kept the apartment over the store, we could be together all day long. . . ." He stared up at the ceiling and controlled an urge to grin at the ghastliness of that prospect. "But you wanted to be ritzy in Oxford Circle, so we're stuck with this arrangement. In any arrangement, you take the good with the bad."

"So much bad for so little good? Other men provide decent livings for their families without arriving for dinner in the middle of the night like Dracula. You're practically a stranger to your own children. On the one day you're home—Sunday—you park behind the newspapers, and I don't see your face till one o'clock. Then, as the big concession, you take me and your mother and the children out for a drive. I really bought myself a bargain, didn't I?"

Auer meticulously buttered his slice of garlic toast. He tapped a bit more hot pepper on the remaining spaghetti. Except for the girls, absorbed by a shoot-'em-up on the television, there could well be a brutal homicide on Burtonrose Lane tonight. The Apaches were skulking behind the rocks, and the sturdy pioneers were entering the pass.

"Bargain?" he asked Bunny with false brightness. "When you shop in bargain basements, you rarely come up with pearls. What were you, Bunny, that you should come up with a prize? Were you a nurse, that you should meet a doctor? Were you a legal secretary, so you could show your knees to a young lawyer? No. You waited on store in a dry goods shop on Marshall Street, and you rubbed your belly against all the boys at the 'Y' dances, till I was the lucky fellow who knocked you up with Sheila. And, if I recall, you were very glad to get me, Bunny. Suddenly I was Flash Gordon and Prince Valiant all rolled up into one."

"*Uch*," she groaned and, glancing quickly at her oldest daughter, brought her finger to her lips.

"Very glad to get me," he repeated in a hard, metallic tone. "My buddies told me I was nuts. Zig and Gall advised me to take off, cut out of town. And I, the sap, went through the whole cruddy production—the reception at the Ambassador, with a band and all your dumpy girl friends and sloppy relatives in a circle and applauding as we waltzed to. . . ." He began to sing, "Oh, how we danced on the night we were wed. If you think we danced, you got rocks in your head."

"Will you shut up already?" Bunny pleaded. "Just shut up!" She pinched his wrist, and he refused to yank his arm away, let her dig her nails in till she was tired of the sport.

He licked away a tiny drop of blood off the wrist and said, "I'd be delighted to shut up. After twelve years of holy matrimony, all I ask for is a bit of peace and quiet. When I was in the Army, when I was in Europe, don't you think I could have had other women? Sure. But I was concerned about you. And V.D. I wanted to come home clean. I should have brought you back a case of leprosy."

"You make me sick sometimes," Bunny said, rising from the table.

"Sometimes? You make me sick all the time, but do I say anything?"

The girls were too fascinated by the massacre on television to pay attention to their parents. Auer watched bemused as Bunny stormed into the living room and began clearing up in a whirlwind of energy. She did not even scream for the children to help as she dumped the toys and dolls and stuffed bears and plastic dishes into their toy chest and slammed the lid down. He looked at his wristwatch. One minute flat. Then she furiously snatched up the shreds of the *Bulletin* and plopped down on the easy chair in front of the TV set. After a few smacks at the paper, she had it in some kind of shape.

Auer made a face at the back of her head. Lately, he was bringing in his big guns and heavy artillery too early in the battle. He should not commit his reserves that early. It was ceasing to produce the desired effect. Bunny was becoming inured to being reminded of her delicate condition when she waltzed in that white gown at the Ambassador. It no longer completely squelched her and drove her out of the room. Quiet without peace had been achieved. He chuckled sourly. What a great life he led: the Johnsons by day and this battle-ax by night.

As he finished his plate, Stephanie came in and cuddled in his lap, wanted a sip of wine. The sauce, he decided, was not that bad when doused with lots of oregano and cheese and pepper. He was delighted by the way his four-year-old refused to relinquish the wine glass, held on to the last drop. If anything, Steppie was his consolation. He was crazy about his girls. When Steppie lost that ugly gray and purple nubbin on her belly, from the umbilical cord, blood oozed out, and both he and Bunny became frantic. Bunny leafed through the Spock and sent him to the druggist because Doc Kluger's answering service could not locate him. He ran like a madman to Doc Fine's pharmacy at Seventh and Green Garden, but Fine's was closed for the summer vaction, and he dashed all the way to the pharmacy at Eleventh Street, only to find Hanson's closed, too. He banged on Hanson's door till the old man came down in his bathrobe, and he spluttered, "Please, sir. I've got a baby-button with a belly coming off." That was the standing joke in the family: "I've got a baby-button with a belly coming off."

A long while back. He rose to clear off the dinner dishes, and as he placed them in the kitchen sink he contemplated washing them as a mollifying gesture. With a splatting noise, he rejected the idea. Too much like cowardly appeasement. Every marriage had about five hundred Munichs. These conciliatory gestures sometimes helped, but it was too easy to convert them into habits. Bunny was just devious enough to provoke fights in order to get him to perform tasks and make up with gestures.

Instead, he cut himself a thick slice of fruitcake, poured another cup of coffee, and carried his tray to the living room. His daughters, rooting for the Seventh Cavalry, pretended he did not exist. Bunny was making sounds upstairs, and they were ignoring her also as they concentrated on the spurs and mayhem, the sabers cutting down the savages.

"Young ladies, isn't it past your bedtime?"

That produced no results, but the clatter of Bunny's high heels approaching the steps galvanized them into scurrying up as she shouted, "Sheila! Stephanie! I've told you to get up here and brush your teeth. Now get up here before I come down there and give you one. I'm tired of repeating myself."

"Then why does she do it so well?" Auer wondered.

Stephanie scrambled over the couch to peck him on the cheek. Sheila, his firstborn, was now a staid and sedate eleven-year-old. She primly said "Good night, father" from the two-step landing and waited gravely for Steppie to waddle by her, then assumed all the airs of a protector, letting Steppie climb up first, step by step, following her with a straight back and highly conscious of her duties.

He chewed at his fruitcake and was proud of the blond, talcumed princesses climbing the stairs. That much he could allow Bunny. She did a first-rate job of keeping them spruced up. On other matters he could fault her. Like forgetting how privileged she was. Bunny should have been out on the steps today to get a whiff of that hallway when Brenda Williams opened the door. Up here, in this gleaming living room with its modernistic furniture, she forgot how hard this world could be, and her need to take care of the man who provided all this soap and talcum powder.

More banging and stalking around upstairs, doors slamming, water sloshing in sinks, teeth being brushed, Stephanie shoving Sheila against the laundry basket, and Bunny's groan of "I can't take it anymore! Get in bed, or I'm really going to give it to both of you."

A minute later Bunny came clacking down the hollow stairs. She swept by him and parked herself on the sofa. He let silent seconds slip by before glancing up from his book to examine the set of her jaw. Bunny obviously did not approve of his bringing his desert and coffee into the living room. Nor of the smear on the table where his ashes missed the ashtray. Nor of his stockinged feet resting on the coffee table. She might well have expressed objection to all three items if she were talking to him. Tough. Now she was learning the drawbacks of the freeze treatment.

Auer deliberately popped a chocolate-covered cherry into his mouth. Bunny opened her copy of *Life* magazine, folded the cover back with an unnecessarily loud crackle. To inform him that she intended to read and was incommunicado. That was all

right with him. Lately, the most he could hope for was silence.
He preferred his book to her complaints about the cleaning girls
or her gossipy neighbors. First she gave him two ulcers and a tin
ear to move up here, and then it was constant complaints against
her gossipy neighbors. Perhaps she would prefer Big Vye, Fat
Grace, and Linda Johnson.

He read. He was always reading. Science fiction. The Tarzan books. War novels. Books on Chinese Gordon, the French
Foreign Legion, and Lawrence of Arabia. This was a good
book. About the Haganah and the Stern Gang. He still regretted not going in '48. His mother had a very convenient heart
attack when he announced he was going to fight the Arabs. Very
convenient. One month later, a complete miraculous recovery.
He wondered how many of the bigmouths on this block would
have gone. It was terrible. The children of all those tough Jews
from South Philly and Strawberry Mansion moved up here and
became soft and squishy whiners. With Henry Wallace buttons.

Bunny had crossed her legs, and her skirt had slipped up
past her garters. The panorama made him gloomy. He surmised
that somewhere in the dim recesses of her dull mind she was
punishing him. Sweet and ducky. Bunny knew she had good
legs and was displaying what he was not going to get tonight. He
could peer right up to the shadowed triangle of her pink panties,
like a kid with his nose pressed against a bakery window. This
was a fine how-do-you-do: after all these years of marriage and
thousands of *shtips* he had to plan and scheme on making his
own wife, as if this were their first date in the parlor and her
father might barge in any minute.

He had always been crazy about those legs. Sometimes, he
sank to his knees when she crossed her legs that way on the
couch, and he tried to kiss her there, through the dress. She
would patiently wait him out and then push his head away.
Frowning. She would be cute if she did not wear that perpetual
frown. For everybody else, smiles, radiance, brightness, but
when she turned to him, her features stiffened as if she had
spotted a second cousin coming for a handout.

Without looking up from her magazine Bunny said, "There's a letter from your mother on the mantelpiece. From Florida. You should read it."

"Does it say anything?" he asked in a bored tone. She was obviously seeking to commence negotiations for a cease-fire.

"Why don't you read it yourself? It's your mother."

"I was only asking if she said anything important."

Bunny flipped a page. She flipped another page. Then a third. "She's thinking about changing hotels again. She says there are too many gossips in the hotel she's at, and they spend all day cutting each other, and she doesn't want to put with it."

"It gives her something to do. Every winter in Florida she changes hotels three times, and it's always either the gossips or the food." He looked up from his book. "Does this hotel cost more?"

"About the same. Six dollars more a week. I already wrote her out the check and wrote her a nice, long letter about the girls and mailed it. That's what I was doing this afternoon."

Auer sniffed. "Sure. 'Cause you want her to stay down there."

"Don't start," Bunny warned him.

"I wasn't starting."

"You were starting." She closed her *Life*. "You feel any better?"

"I felt fine when I came in here."

"Don't give me that. You stormed in here like a raging bull. I could tell by the way you dumped the box of groceries on the table."

"Let's forget it." He kneaded the flesh over the bridge of his nose. "I've got a miserable headache from that argument today. That was some mouth that woman had, like an unflushed toilet."

"Be more careful, Sam. I'm always afraid something will happen to you down there. I just wish you'd sell the store and get the hell out of there. I really wouldn't care if it meant less money. Sometimes, at nine, when the doorbell rings I wonder if it's you or the police arriving to inform me that something's happened to you on the way up Green Garden. I really get nervous."

His lips flattened complacently around his cigarette. Suddenly, out of nowhere, things were looking up. Her tone was unusually tender. Maybe he might get a little tonight, after all. It meant that he would have to prepare and take all the precautions. Not give her any valid excuses.

He pushed himself up from the easy chair and stifled a yawn. "Well, I'd better hit the hay. The alarm clock is already ringing in my ears." He stretched, and it was not till that moment that he realized how exhausted he was, how his nerves were twisted to the snapping point all day long with that window aggravation.

"That's another thing, Sam. Your hours are atrocious. You're up at five, and by the time you've digested your supper you're not in bed till midnight. You can't go on like this. This is no life for a person. It's not worth it, Sam."

Sympathy yet. Matters were definitely looking up on the sexual front. From the two-step landing he said, "I don't know, honey. Maybe I'll talk to your Uncle Joe about his offer to go in with him. I'll have to give it more serious thought. I've already locked the front door and put out the garbage. Why don't you come on up?"

As he climbed the stairs, he congratulated himself for mentioning her Uncle Joe's offer. That was a shrewd play, dangling that carrot. But now he regretted not having rinsed those few dishes. A major tactical blunder. Bunny was incapable of climbing into bed with dishes in the sink. Claimed they attracted roaches. Now those extra minutes she wasted puttering around the kitchen would provide her with the justification for collapsing into bed like a wall hit by a demolition ball. The prospects for a night of mad passion were dimming. He winced as he tiptoed on the top step, so as not to disturb the girls, and it screeched anyway, like the door creaking on "Inner Sanctum." These row houses were thrown up with about enough wood to build one sturdy model airplane.

Auer brushed his teeth three times to remove the taint of the salami, onion, and tomato sandwich he had for lunch. His Bunny was extremely finicky about odors. He blew into his palm. Toothpaste, at times, was insufficient for her delicate nostrils. Filling a glass with lukewarm water, he gargled Listerine. If he were going to make a serious effort to score tonight, it was best to cooperate as far as possible and cover all the loopholes while she banged the pots and pans around downstairs.

He sniffed at his armpits. For a normal woman they were possible, but Bunny was running for inspector-general. He quickly climbed out of his underwear and adjusted the shower flow to lukewarm. That was another of her pet gripes. If he took a hard, scalding shower—the kind he liked—she bitched that it steamed up the bathroom for hours and wilted her hairdo. He was going to block off her every escape route, give her absolutely no outs tonight.

Before climbing into bed, Auer laid out his socks and fresh underwear, so as not to wake her with screeching bureau drawers at dawn. He was more considerate than Bunny realized. As he slipped into his pajama bottoms, he paused to admire his physique in the dresser mirror. The face, only a mother could love, but that was one robust, hairy *bulvon* gleaming back at him. If the gut was too pronounced, it was a hard gut that gave off a solid, meaty ring, like a Sumo wrestler's mound. He dabbed more of Bunny's underarm deodorant on before slipping under the blankets. Another possible alibi snuffed out. Only his beard worried him now. He should have shaved, but that would have been gilding the lily too much, established a precedent.

Frost patterns offered weird decorations on the windowpanes. He huddled under his blankets and quilts, listening to the tinkling, swishing noises of her preparations in the bathroom: brushing, stroking, a mouthful of foam spit into the sink. The click of a lid. She was spreading that goop all over her cheeks. Part of a premeditated plan to discourage him. After a day like this, he deserved a piece. If the woman had any sensitivity at all, she would have sensed his need, but she was dragging it out in there on purpose. In the hope he would be snoring by the time she came in.

Before Steppie was born, they used to go at it all the time. But something went out of her after the second child. Now it went sourer every year. Half the time when he reached for her under the sheet, she would twitch him away and murmur, "I'm too tired. Leave me alone." But if he did not attempt to touch her the following morning, she would say "What's the matter, Sam? I wanted you last night."

Bunny could drive him nuts this way. Maybe that was what she was after, to have him taken off to Norristown in a strait-jacket. Or maybe not. She was tender and solicitous for those few seconds. Maybe she was preening herself to come sweeping in, dramatic and gorgeous in her pink negligee with the ruffles, and cuddle directly against him. Or else she would come dragging out in her shapeless yellow *shmatte*, flop into bed, and curdle into a lump. He had to await the verdict. . . .

The bathroom door opened, and Bunny was in her shapeless yellow rag. Definitely the *shmatte* treatment. The Lone Ranger did not ride tonight. She snapped off the lamp, scrambled quickly under the quilts, puffed and smacked her pillow, turned her back to him, and murmured "Good night."

"By whose standards?" he asked himself. He bit his lower lip in the darkness. He needed some relief. Some pleasure. Some reason for going on.

"Don't I even get a good-night kiss?" Auer ventured.

"Mmmm," Bunny answered. She twisted over, grabbed him roughly around the neck, kissed him hard, and rolled over again to repeat the "Good night."

Beyond his frosted windowpanes there was a streaked and

dreary sky over Oxford Circle, a view of ten houses exactly like his own. This must be all a part of God's master plan: Sam Auer was put on earth to sell pickled pigs' feet and hamhocks to the *hoishichs* for forty years and then conveniently drop dead so his future sons-in-law could buy homes in Merion and tour the Riviera.

Bunny was already breathing regularly, pretending she could fall asleep in less than a minute. It had all gone so sour. Bunny did not like to be kissed there. Thought it was dirty. She did not like to be touched. Said he became too rough with her delicate tissues. But the worst trick she had to really destroy him was to suddenly go slack when he was pounding away and enjoying himself, and mumble "Come already."

"Come already?" Sleep was nowhere near. Bunny dissipated all her energy keeping this morgue spotless, and he was overly agitated from his trip to Seventh Street. Other people had problems, too. How did Johnson—the sonofabitch, a vigorous broad-shouldered man like Johnson, who used to work with Barry in the quarry before he hit the bottle, how did Johnson rut with that puffy-elbowed mess he had in his bed?

According to Bunny, he was supposed to snore now and forget about it. Eat shit and call it honey. This could drag on indefinitely. He had to try. Rights which were not exercised were lost by attrition.

He reached over and rested his hand tentatively on Bunny's rump. Proof positive. Bloomers under the yellow *shmatte*. She had come to bed with malice aforethought. This was the clue to her disposition. When there was nothing underneath, it meant the moon was ripe.

Bunny squirmed away muttering, "Don't."

"Don't? Why don't? What am I—the milkman?"

"Just don't. I don't feel like it."

"Can I make an appointment for one of those rare occasions when you feel like it?"

She retreated toward her edge of the bed. "How am I supposed to get in the mood after all the rotten things you said at supper? Do you think those remarks were very conducive to romance?''

"Suddenly, you are Lana Turner and I am Clark Gable; we should have romance around here?''

"And I'm supposed to get romantic after a crack like that?''

He tossed his head from side to side on the pillow. "You were not romantic before the crack. Is there any statement I can make to change the tide? Perhaps I can go downstairs and get your copy of Walter Benton.''

"*Uch,*'' Bunny groaned.

"*Uch, uch, uch!*'' he mocked her. He must be firm. It was always better to try. Sometimes she was acquiescent, and sometimes she even warmed up to the fray.

Auer reached for her again, and Bunny rubbed her cheek away. "Don't paw at me, Sam, goddamn it. Your beard burns me, and I can't go outside the next day with my face all scratched up in the cold wind. You've got a chin like a Brillo pad.''

"People who have balls generally have beards,'' he raged. "What do you want, Bunny? You want the Blue Prince to float down on a pink cloud and throw a dickless, cotton candy fuck into you? I'm no Blue Prince. I'm just a man, and I've got a beard. You're driving me nuts.''

"I don't want anything from you. I just want to sleep now.''

"That's just dandy.''

Banging noisily, he opened his nightstand drawer and brought out his smoking equipment, the ashtray, cigarettes, and matches. Bunny hated for him to smoke in her bedroom, and especially in bed, but now he did not give a damn. He lit a Lucky as she deftly gathered the blankets over herself again. The flames flared and tinted eerie shadows in the dresser mirror. Yet nothing was eerie in this life. Life was mundane, and his varied from dull to unbearable. After he had spent thirteen hours in that cage, she fully proposed to go to sleep on him. Possibly if he sweet-talked her, apologized, apologized for breathing, beat on his breast for an hour proclaiming what a hairy, inconsiderate pig he was, she might relent and mutter, "All right, all right," and spread out to take her medicine. But she would make sure he got no pleasure out of it.

He truculently crushed out his cigarette, rubbed his palms dry, spun over in the snarled cocoon of sheets, blankets, and quilts, kicked and tore them away, and flung himself across his wife.

"Must you go on and on?" Bunny asked under him.

Gritting, he ignored the question, pushed up her yellow wool gown, and as he tugged her bloomers down, her nails sank into his chest. If anything, the resistance was more exciting than any cooperation might have been. He was really going to give it to her. She did not want him at all, and that released him from any obligation to be tender. He could push, twist, and grind for as long as he wanted, and eventually she might quicken to his thrusting, against her will.

"Goddamn you, you bastard!" Bunny said as he forced his way in.

He dug his fingers into her soft shanks and concentrated. This was home. This was his only refuge. Without this, the rest fell apart. The kids were an afterthought. One hardly seemed to have anything to do with the other. And after a while it was only the kids that kept people together. He was putting up with all this crap for his girls. He wanted Bunny to gasp, sigh, thrash, melt, respond to him, and she gave nothing, a dry well.

Probing, he assayed caresses she said she liked. He was strong inside her, and yet it was futile. He was unable to stir her. She was limp and her flesh like cold custard in his palms. Tears dampened his collarbone. Now she was whimpering.

All need faded, receded, shriveled away. Bunny had definitely proved her point. He retreated from her, smiled down to acknowledge her triumph. Immediately, she yanked at the blankets and shifted to her half of the bed.

Flakes were accumulating thickly on the panes, sealing off the night. It was as simple as that. Bunny granted him nothing when she was like this. She would not even lie there for a while, staring up at the sad, empty ceiling, contemplate the mess they were in.

He placed another Lucky between his lips and held the match till it almost burnt his fingertips, then flicked it into the ashtray. All she needed to find was ashes on her bedsheets in the morning, and he would not get laid till next Thanksgiving. For one second he closed his lids and saw himself yanking Bunny out of bed by her hair, slamming her against the dresser, clapping her mouth, banging her head against the door, kicking her down the stairs, and leaping down to land on top of her with his heels cracking her spine. Such was love.

Auer smoked his cigarette and wondered why people narrowed down their options so much. There were a billion women in this world, and he was supposed to be stuck with this one for the rest of his life. Why not Pauline Kozak? He remembered the way Pauline minced across Sixth Street this afternoon, in her tight skirt. Was Maddy getting his hands on that? No. Not likely. At seventeen Pauline was too developed for sweater squeezing and playing stinky finger in the movies. If she were putting out, it would be for one of those rich muff divers who waited for her in their Cadillacs on Glendolph Street. Besides, she was too fragile for Sam Auer. He was a bear, and a rugged *bulvon* like Sam Auer should have a strong, heavy-hipped bitch like Sophie Bitko.

Sometimes he imagined he was Starker, the boss. Starker chomping on his Corona Corona and waiting behind the wheel of his Cadillac at Eighth and Green Garden. Sophie hopped in, and as they drove down to Atlantic City he fondled her garters and her powerful thighs. For supper they had wine and split a Chateaubriand, and then took the elevator up to their suite on the twentieth floor. Sophie undressed for him, with the Atlantic Ocean gray and raging, storming on the horizon beyond the window. She had sturdy shoulders, high arrogant Polish cheekbones, and her flesh seemed to blossom softly as she stepped out of her black girdle.

Then shadows spoiled that vision. There was something

too hard and sophisticated about Sophie, a harsh "Show me" attitude. He might be too inept and clumsy for an experienced woman of her caliber.

It was strange. Right now, if he had his pick of any woman in the world, if he had a real choice, he would go after Mrs. Lewis from the schoolyard. A *shvartzeh*? He had never spoken to the woman, but he felt this strong pull from her. She was so prim and demure, but he had heard her laughter and knew she was intelligent. He imagined that tumbling into bed with Jeanette Lewis would be like snuggling with a jolly friend who would suddenly be passionate and never cross.

It was time to sleep. The alarm clock was set for five, and he had another thirteen hours coming up in the Congo tomorrow. He crushed out his cigarette and rubbed his chest. At thirty-four Sam Auer was a bull, a hard worker, in the prime of his life. There was no reason it should be so small and narrow. Maybe tomorrow he would talk to Jeanette Lewis. Or maybe tomorrow would be the day he finally had that cup of coffee at the diner, took a taxi to the bus station, and disappeared into the West.

PART TWO
PART TWO

Leah Dobry worked content after midnight, after all her men were tended to and asleep. She left the television set on, without the sound, and only occasionally glanced up from painting tiny features on ceramic figurines to frown at the posturing and posing of the actors on the hazy television screen. It was a choice between a better television set or another kiln, and she was going to get her oven in spite of her sons complaining about the lousy reception for their dumb ball games and boxing matches.

In her warm bathrobe and slippers, surrounded by her paints and brushes, clays and kilns, a pot of coffee on the hotplate to her left, this cramped, cluttered parlor was all she needed. She hummed opera and could pretend she was a great artist, a Mary Cassatt, and not just a dabbler with a knack for exquisite cheeks and lips and lashes. She could dream of the day when she finally got rid of her damn grocery trade and dedicated herself exclusively to the ceramics and antiques. It was a practical dream. She was doing much better. Just last week she sold three Marie Antoinettes and two Blue Boys. Now she hoped the city would let her stay here after renewal, give this building a historical plaque. With a historical plaque she could keep this corner, have a little antique shoppe in her declining years. When this neighborhood was renewed and became "Society Hill."

She was going to be alone. Her father, wheezing behind the partition, would pass on soon. At eighty-six, Daniel Radin was still rambunctious. If she turned her back for one minute the old man was out the store door, and the police might pick him up as far away as Girard Avenue or Market Street. She could never understand why men were so rambunctious. Maddy had that streak. He would graduate high school next year and he could not wait to be out of here. Herbie she would have for another eight years, and then she could start thinking about herself. She regretted moving to this corner. They were doing all right with the store at Glendolph and Cottonwood. But she let herself be persuaded to buy this place, take out a huge mortgage for the remodeling and repairs, and had never gotten out from under it, never escaped the crush of bills. Some people tried to make a move, and life stepped on them. If it were not for her ceramics. . . .

Leah let out a startled moan at the explosion of the shattering glass, and her arm swung out in a nervous reflex action, knocking over the jar with her small brushes and spilling turpentine on the floor.

Before she could push aside her worktable and rise, her older son, Maddy, was out of the rear bedroom like a shot and threw open the door between the parlor and the store. He was naked except for undershorts.

"Oh, jeez," he mumbled.

"Ours?" she asked anxiously.

"Take a look."

She stood by his side and was ashamed of her small twinge of relief as she passed through the gloom and darkness of her long store, saw that her own windows were untouched and that across Sixth it was the Auers again. She was ashamed of that flush of relief.

"The bastards," Maddy said.

"I'll call the police. You'd better call Sam."

Maddy quickly went to his room and put on a bathrobe. He returned to the store, picked his way through the jumbled labyrinth of Tiffany lamps and antique Victrolas in the rear. Leah called after him "Be careful. Don't go outside."

He took a dime from the cash register and went to the front phone booth. As he dialed Information to get the Auer number, he shook his head in commiseration. They had really done a job on Auer this time. It looked like a boulder had been hurled through that new window. Across Sixth, there seemed to be some movement in the shadows of the schoolyard fence. Dim movements. In a court of law he would have to testify that he had not seen but sensed a dim presence over there, a scraping of heels over ice, swift darting in the darkness toward Grenoble Street.

The few cars chugging down Sixth slowed at the sight of the shattered glass and then speeded up again. Information furnished him with the number, and he noticed the shade moving over at Grace's place. Fat Grace peeking out from behind her yellow window shade. That shade was always bright. They never slept over there.

Auer answered after only one ring, as if he had been lying awake next to his telephone. A surly "Hello."

"Sam? Maddy from across the street. Sorry to wake you, but I'm afraid I've got some bad news for you."

"What's the matter?"

"It would appear you have a broken window."

"I know," Auer snapped. "But I got it fixed this afternoon. You saw it. They put a new plate in."

"I know. But it would appear that somebody has just tossed a brick through the new one."

"What?"

"From where I'm sitting, which is in our front booth, they've used you for target practice again."

"Oh, my aching ass," Auer groaned up in Oxford Circle. "Did you see who did it, kid?"

"Nope. Just saw two shadows cutting down Sixth toward Grenoble."

"Were they *shvartzers*?"

"Couldn't tell, Sam. I'm not even sure I saw anything at all."

"Miserable, goddamn sonsofbitches," Auer moaned. "Goddamn their stinking hides. I just fit in a new one, and the cocksuckers already break it on me. I'll kill him when I get my hands on him."

"Just calling with the news, Sam. Don't slay the bearer of ill-tidings. I thought I'd save you a heart attack in the. . . ."

"Look, Maddy," Auer interrupted him. "Could you do me a big favor, kid? Call the station and have a squad car come around."

"My mom is already on the phone in the parlor doing that."

"Thanks. Could you sit there for me till the red car shows up, kid? I've got a couple of hundred bucks worth of merchandise in that window, and anybody could help themselves."

"I'll turn on the store lights here and hang around till either you or the squad car shows up, whichever gets here first. But I won't guarantee I'll rush outside with my sword to defend your gates if I see hordes of plunderers charging in."

"Do what you can for me, Maddy. Thanks. I'll be right down."

Auer hung up his phone and snapped on his night lamp. Bunny rolled over in her tangle of quilts and blankets and said, "What was that all about?"

"The miserable bastards threw another brick through the new window. I'm going to kill that sonofabitch Johnson tomorrow. I'll have to take the car and rush down there right now."

Bunny sat up quickly crossed her arms over her knees. He was already climbing into his trousers when she announced, "You can't take the car."

"What's that supposed to mean—I can't take my car?"

"Tomorrow it's my turn in the car pool. I don't dare miss it this week. To drive the kids to school."

"Car pool, shmarpool. Tell them it's an emergency. You can't make it. Emergencies happen."

"You'll have to call a cab," Bunny said stubbornly. "I had an emergency last week and couldn't make it. By the time I called all five mothers and got a replacement, and Norma got ready and got her car out, all the children were late for school. If I pull that trick again, they'll drop me from the car pool and Norma will never speak to me again."

"Screw Norma up the ass. I need my goddamn car."

"You can't take it!" Bunny screamed. "You think the whole world revolves around you and your goddamn store?"

"All right, all right," he mumbled, tugging the sweater down over his head. "We'll call a cab, and you don't go to the hairdresser this week to make up for the five-dollar cabfare."

"I'll make you a cup of coffee, Sam. If you're going out into the cold, you'll need a cup of coffee."

"Coffee I do not need, my dear. There are many things I need that I do not get, but coffee is not highest on my list."

"I'll make you a cup of coffee," Bunny repeated. She slipped into her lumpy bathrobe and hurried downstairs. He heard her snapping on the gas as he dialed Yellow Cab. Yellow Cab told him there would be a slight delay, twenty minutes to half an hour, but a cab would definitely be there.

Downstairs they sipped at their coffee in a sullen silence till Bunny glanced up and said, "Jewish husbands don't rape their wives."

"Bullshit. What's that? The Eleventh Commandment? I guess they forgot to circumcise me enough."

"I'll never forgive you for that, Sam."

"That makes three hundred and eighteen things you'll never forgive me for. When I reach a thousand do I get a prize?"

Another fight would have erupted, but a horn honked outside. The cab was early. Bunny kissed him at the door and warned him to be careful with the Johnsons. She told him to call as soon as anything definite developed, called out something else as he rushed through the bitter cold to the warmth of the taxi.

"Sixth and Cottonwood," Auer said, and the driver turned around to give him a funny look, forced him to repeat the address. They bumped over the rocky ice on Burtonrose Lane, and Auer lit a cigarette. He wondered why Bunny had admonished him to be careful. Surely she would be better off if he just keeled over and she collected the insurance. Though it was only ten grand. And whatever she got for Sixth and Cottonwood. Another twenty grand. How long could she get by with two kids on that? Three or four years at the most. After that ran out, what could she do, what was she worth? As a woman alone, she was worth maybe sixty bucks a week as a salesgirl at Gimbels. Maybe she would become a streetwalker? He grinned at the idea of Bunny entering a Locust Street bar, crossing her legs sexily on a stool, ordering a cocktail, casting a come-hither look at some traveling salesmen. If they arrested her, it should be for fraud, not prostitution. His wife should take better care of her investment. The dumb woman gave him such a rotten time, and yet without him she would be up shit's creek.

They sped down Roosevelt Boulevard, and Auer hated the bare trees and naked branches under a stark November sky, the muddy patches of brown snow. Trees and parks looked more depressing than factories and dump yards in winter. In fact, he knew he was never supposed to say it, but he had never liked the countryside. As a kid they made him go to camp in summer, and the very first day, surrounded by the bushes and trees, he was bored. The country was a drag, with those trees exactly alike, and the dumb camp counselor, Uncle Ed from Villanova College, took them on a nature exploration trip, showed them different leaves, traced the lines and veins, and told them there was a whole mysterious, marvelous world in a leaf, and he wanted them all to get enthusiastic about his leaf.

"How come you're heading downtown this time of night?" the driver asked. "I usually don't take calls down there at this hour."

"It's no pleasure trip," Auer assured him. "Some bastard threw a brick through my window last night. The cocksuckers threw one last night, and I got it fixed. They threw another tonight, and I don't know what the hell I'm going to do. I'm not sure the insurance covers it."

"One of them jigaboos," the cabby said with a dry Irish twang. "I used to live down there till they started crowding in. Right there by Third and Poplar. Used to be a place for decent people."

"No kidding. If you're from Third and Poplar, you must know Joe Gallagher."

"Gall?" The driver sniffed in amusement. "Sure I know

Gall. Went to St. Pete's together. Them sisters used to crack their yardsticks over Gall's knuckles and then come after me with the broken point. I know Gall.''

"You must know Zig then, too.''

The cabby snorted as if he had been reminded of an embarrassing incident in his past.

"That scrounge still around? I'd have thought somebody done him in by now. Dropped by that diner late at night for a hamburger, about two years ago. And there the sonofabitch was. Still shooting his mouth off in the rear booth.''

"Zig's still there. Still working in the brewery. Putting away his five quarts a shift.''

"If you're from Sixth and Cottonwood, I know people there, too. The Conlons?''

"Nine girls and two boys,'' Auer said proudly.

"Nine good-looking girls and two brothers. Had a fight with some kid from right there. Solly Radin? Punched Solly out all over Ludlow schoolyard.''

"Solly? Sure. His sister Leah owns the place across from me. A luncheonette and antique store. Solly's a dentist up in Mount Airy. Doing all right for himself.''

"That used to be a nice neighborhood. I was married right there in St. Augie's. Married a girl from Oriana Street. A shame about your window. I don't know how anybody can stick it out down there, man.''

"I'm just holding on by the skin of my teeth. Just about making it. If I could find a buyer I'd sell out in a minute, but ever since the City started talking about redevelopment and renewal nobody will touch the place with a ten-foot pole.''

"Sometimes, y'know, I get a fare all the way downtown to Market Street. On the way back, one of those people want me to drive them around your way. Or around Columbia Avenue. I have to tell them my flag is off. I'm off duty. It ain't worth it, buddy. I'd rather shag it back to Frankford empty than head into one of those places at night.''

"Too dangerous?'' Auer responded dutifully.

Within five minutes he was sorry he had rattled this man's cage. During the remainder of the slow, bumpy drive the cabby droned on about muggings, robberies, hopheads, drunken fares that refused to pay, cheap tippers, floozies that wanted him to be their pimp, and the cabby murdered last month by a woman, hit him with a steam iron hidden in her shopping bag. Auer found himself grunting at appropriate intervals. The same spiel from every hackie. He was in a stupor, estranged by the lateness of the hour. It was years since he was out this late, seen the streets deserted, free of traffic, the red lights flashing at every corner, with the driver rambling on monotonously about the dangers of pushing a hack.

They crossed Green Garden. Leah's store lights were off, but Auer saw the squad car in front of the school, the red searchbeam on its roof rotating with a garish glare. After all this nostalgic reminiscing about what this neck of the woods was like way back then, he had the irksome obligation to give the cabby a generous tip, a buck over the meter.

"Remember me to Zig and Gall," the cabby said as he pocketed the five dollars. "Tell them Mike Greary was asking for them, and I might catch their act some night at the diner."

"They'll be there," Auer replied as he got out.

Mike Greary shook his head once more at the sorry sight of the smashed window before driving off. Doors slammed on the patrol car. Auer did not recognize the two policemen approaching him across Cottonwood. He squinted hard to blot incipient tears. This time there was not enough glass left in the frame to spread newspaper over an opening. His new window was completely shattered except for jagged, triangular chunks in each corner and sharp chips sticking up from the bottom like stalagmites in a cave. Modern times. The glass was cheaper and broke more thoroughly.

"Are you the owner of this place?" the taller policeman asked.

"No, I like to take five-dollar cabs and admire busted windows in the middle of the night."

"We're just here to help, mister. There's no call to wise off at us. That won't help anybody."

"Since when am I supposed to help you out? If you guys patrolled these streets more effectively, there'd be less of this crap. Our taxes go up, and every year we get less service from you people. Every night I pass the diner the squad car is parked out there instead of cruising the streets. I guess it's safer in there than down by Zacky's or the Green Room."

"Let's calm down, Mister Auer," the shorter policeman said phlegmatically. "Calm down and we'll get along better. You have any idea who might have done this? If we don't have any eyewitnesses there's not much we can do about it, but if you have any ideas, we can drive around there and maybe shake them up a little."

"Sure I have an idea," Auer growled. "The slop over on Seventh Street. I slapped a kid's hand for stealing a piece of candy, and they threw a brick through my window. I didn't even bother calling the station to report it because I know how useless that is. I put in another, and they smash this one, too. The Johnsons. They're on Seventh Street, #424 Seventh, the miserable bastards."

The taller policeman tapped his club in his palm, glanced significantly at his partner. "Well, maybe it wasn't too smɐrt of you to slap that kid's hand, Mister Auer. I know I'd get pretty pissed off if I heard anybody laid a hand on one of my boys. I'd rather they'd call me, and I'd whop my boy myself, but if I heard anybody touched one I might get fairly angry."

"Sure," Auer snorted. "That's fine for you. You're probably trying to raise your kids as decent human beings. But you tell those people that you caught their kids stealing, and they tell you to go eat shit."

A rising burst of wind tore at the unprotected sheafs of paper and books in the window, spraying brown snow over his stock. Auer said, "Skip it. I can't stand here gabbing all night with the drizzle spoiling my merchandise. I want some action, or I'm going to have to call Doheny at the station tomorrow."

"Mister Auer," the shorter one said, "you can call the mayor, the governor, or the president, but we can't go banging on people's doors and accusing them of anything unless you give us a little bit more to go on. Did they admit to it, or brag about it, or did anybody see those people break your window last night?"

"Yeah, they'll admit to it. I can just picture them admitting it."

Both policemen shrugged in unison, as if it were a rehearsed act, and the taller was already turning as he said, "Well, we'll try to spend a little more time around this corner, but there's not much more we can do for you, Mister Auer. We're assigned a lot of territory to cover around here, and we can't turn ourselves into your personal night watchmen. . . ."

"Fine. Thanks a lot. That's what I thought you'd say. I'm the one under attack, the battle is here, these are the front lines, but you have lots of territory to cover and have to spread yourselves equally thin."

They chose to ignore his ranting, and he was still mumbling to himself as they drove off. He unlocked his front door, snapped on the lights, and gathered the supplies for temporary repairs. The battle was here, this was the Western Front, but they have to patrol the whole beat and dissipate their forces. Didn't the morons know that that was why Napoleon lost the Battle of Waterloo? Dumb Marshall Ney heard the cannon booming in the distance but stuck to original orders and didn't come to the rescue with the reserves.

Auer rubbed his palms and went to work. It took him three trips to get all his supplies outside: his step ladder, his rolls of brown wrapping paper, and two disks of black masking tape. After chipping away all remaining glass with his ball peen hammer and sweeping the slivers into the culvert, he ripped off wide strips of the wrapping paper and taped them over the frame. Four wide strips sealed off the window from bottom to top, and he decided to spread on three more layers to afford protection against the sharp, sporadic gusts of wind. He felt like a clown climbing up and down his stepladder, cursing at the difficulties in controlling the long strips of paper with the capricious winds whipping them around, and was sure that all the drivers slowing down to observe the spectacle of a man busying himself with such strange tasks at this hour had to be laughing at him. It was four A.M. before he finished picking the chips and slivers of glass out of his school supplies and candy counter. He went to the sofa in the parlor and stretched out with a cigarette, a cushion under his head. In the next room, his parents' old bedroom, there was a wide comfortable bed, but it was so close to dawn and opening time that it was hardly worthwhile sleeping. After short naps he usually woke up cranky and worse than ever.

Periodically, almost with the regularity of a metronome, there was a hacky coughing upstairs. Simmons, the old Negro in the second floor back. Time passed. Things changed. Negroes under the Auer roof. All of the rooms upstairs were let out to Negroes. Bunny wanted him to rent out this apartment, too. She thought it was an intolerable luxury and waste for him to keep his parents' old apartment behind the store: a whole parlor, a bedroom with bath, and the old kitchen in the rear. Once a month Bunny brought up that idea of putting up a plexiboard partition in the rear of the store for a toilet and a sink and sealing off this place, renting it out. She did not care whether he got his afternoon rest or not, or had a place to relax.

Simmons coughed again, and the wind was snapping against the mat of brown paper stretched across his window, slapping rhythmically like canvas sails crackling under ocean breezes. He remembered when the heavy, sticky black tape he just used was for covering a hardball and extracting a few more innings out of it, not for lashing down sheets of paper on a blustery night.

It was disconcerting being in this parlor at this hour. He was not sure whether it was exhaustion, but all of the familiar objects seemed to have sagged and faded. The television set was jarringly out of place, like a gold tooth in a mouthful of stained, decayed molars. It sat next to the floor-model Philco radio, which had once seemed so fantastically modern and now looked like an authentic antique, as much a relic as the wicker rocking chair next to it. In fact, all of the furniture back here, from the bulky wardrobe in the bedroom to the green-and-yellow metal table in the kitchen, he could give to Leah on consignment for her antiques. And strip the musty flower-pattern paper, already curling and warping, off the walls and send it up to the Art Museum. Genuine vintage wallpaper. . . .

The scraping of milk crates over ice woke him. He sprung up, angry with himself for having dozed. He had a headache, and the throbbing in the bridge of the nose indicated a good bout with a cold. The nap had been worse than no sleep at all, and there was a blemish on his cheek from the rough sofa fabric.

In the bathroom he shaved with a rusted blade and soap. His toothpaste tube was squeezed dry, and as he brushed his teeth in tepid water he thought about running over to Leah's for a can of Doctor Lyons' powder and some Gillettes. Then he wondered why he wanted to stock up. Was it for future reference, or was he planning on staying here?

Outside, the *Inquirer* man had once again missed the step with his bundle of papers. The edges were soiled. The boxes of pastry were untouched, and none of the milk bottles were frozen over, so that was some help. He started his urn of coffee and began a large pot of spaghetti sauce for his lunch hour. His customers ate proper sauce that simmered for at least four hours, and not that last-minute whiffy jiffy goop that Bunny served last night.

The bell tingled, and Beaumont entered for his coffee and Danish. The postman gazed at the mat of paper over the frame, still whipping and puffing like sails in a storm. He let his pouch slide off his shoulder, threw a leg over his usual stool, and said, "Couldn't get your window fixed yet, Sam?"

"Fixed yet? It was fixed yesterday noontime. The stinking

bastards heaved another brick. I had to come down here in the middle of the night and clean up the mess."

Beaumont pushed his cap back on his head and wobbled his chin in disbelief. "Now that's really something. I really think that's going too far."

"That makes two of us," Auer said as he minced the green peppers and onions to add to his sauce. He served Beaumont his coffee, and the postman repeated his story from yesterday morning with the same cast of white trash and vicious dog, and the same threat of retaliating with lumps of poisoned hamburger. That must have the one thrilling adventure of Beaumont's life, Auer concluded.

By eight he could no longer contain his nervousness. He searched for his insurance agent's home number in the telephone book and hit two wrong numbers first because there were four Milton Feinbergs listed and he could not remember the middle initial. Feinberg was naturally surly, and Auer apologized, saying, "I'm sorry to bother you, Milton, at your own home, at this hour of the morning before office hours, but I couldn't wait. We've got another problem."

"We've got no problems, Sam. I told you yesterday we're covering the window, and you should send us the bill. I'm pushing it through myself."

"That's exactly the problem. I got the window repaired like you said, and I mailed the bill yesterday. Last night the sonsofbitches threw another brick."

"Ouch!" Feinberg groaned out in Wynnfield. There was a pause, and he said, "The situation is getting impossible. I don't know how you can deal with people like that, Sam. I don't know how we can keep premium rates reasonable with conditions like this. That's our third window this month. . . ." Long, agonizing seconds slipped by, and the tone was firmer. "I'm afraid this one's going to be a bit more sticky, Sam."

"How so? I'm covered, aren't I?"

"Well," Feinberg murmured dubiously, "I checked through your policy yesterday. It stipulates that you're supposed to take reasonable and proper precautions. I don't recall you ever hanging any screens across your windows."

The bell tinkled in the store, and two customers were shuffling impatiently by the counter.

"What screens? From which hat do you pull this screens business?"

"The matter never came up before, Sam. You've seen the screens on the windows on Eighth Street. They're always having drunks stagger against them, or falling in, or heaving a rock through one so they can spend a warm winter in jail. Screens would have been a reasonable, proper precaution after what happened to you. I mean, we'll reimburse for the first item, but as for this second . . . Sam . . . this could go on and on, with no end to it. Do you follow me, Sam?"

"I don't want to follow you too far. The air gets thick. Why the hell didn't you clue me in on this screen thing yesterday? You never said one word about screens."

"Sam," Feinberg intoned gravely, "you are in business and supposed to do a little thinking for yourself. Nobody's going to do it for you. You have a head on your shoulders and a copy of your policy and should have read it carefully. We're with you all the way on this first window, but with this repeat performance I'm afraid you're on your own."

The bell tinkled, and one customer was leaving. Another entered. Auer gave his reflection in the parlor mirror a finger sign. "Fine. Very well. We'll continue this conversation when you're at your office. Good-bye."

He hung up and was close to saying he intended canceling all policies and giving his future business to Red Newman's kid, but he had not received the check for the first window yet, and it was safer to wait till it arrived. Then he would call this *faigele* up and tell him to eat a big hairy bucket of shit with extra helpings.

He rushed out to wait on trade, and when he was alone again he put his hands on his hips and frowned at the rustling mat of paper. It was pressed inward and curling under the force of the winds tearing down Sixth. The upper left-hand corner was already ripping and flapping loose. Feinberg was both correct and incorrect about the screens. Screens were adequate for accidents, stumbling bums, or a fresh kid tossing a stone, but useless against premeditated malicious mischief. Feinberg was correct on the other score, too; this brick-throwing tournament could go on and on, with no end to it.

After preparing bacon and eggs for a breakfast regular, he dialed Heinie Schmidt at the lumberyard. Schmidt was outraged when he heard what happened and promised him a special price for the wood, at cost. Thanking him and hanging up, Auer realized that he had ordered enough lumber to cover not only the Sixth Street side but his Cottonwood window and doorpane, too. Kneading his forehead with his knuckles, trying to drive his headache out, he phoned Manny's hardware store, and Manny promised to send him the best barbed wire he had in stock. Auer also ordered a safety lock for his parlor door to the street and bolts for the back door between his kitchen and the rear vestibule. He was digging in and would nail so much barbed wire over his apartment windows that not a snake could squeeze through without getting slashed to ribbons.

He waited on Pauline Kozak's fat mother. Mrs. Kozak would have preferred to patronize Leah, but she was too tubby to safely cross Sixth with all the rough ice on the cobbles. The helper arrived with Schmidt's shipment of discounted lumber, and Auer ripped away the mat of paper over his window. It again felt as though layers of live skin were peeled away to leave a shocking emptiness between his familiar fixtures and the incessant onslaught of traffic. Between gabby salesmen and customers, he went outside to his stepladder and nailed up the boards, board by board. Leah was observing him from behind the lamps and ceramics, and Fat Grace had rolled up her shade and was grinning with her toothless mouth at all his scurrying.

Auer could not shake the sensation that he was drifting through a nightmarish repetition of yesterday. The kids yelled on their way to school, wrestled, threw ice balls. He looked out for little Johnson, but he must have circled around to the Grenoble entrance again. Barry came in for his order, criticized the scoundrels on Seventh Street again, and sniffed at the boards nailed up and stacked waiting. The Tastykake man, the Freihofer breadman, and the *Daily News* man came in as the wooden barrier gradually rose, and yapped about muggings and burglaries, reminded him of Phil Basarov and the pistol-whipping at the taproom. The recess bell rang and Auer automatically peered through his Cottonwood window, searching for Mrs. Lewis in the yard. Apparently Jeanette was not on recess duty today.

With the last and highest board nailed into place, he carried his tool kit back inside and stacked his spare lumber behind the soda case. Turning, he blanched at the harsh aspect these boards lent to the store's interior. No light penetrating from Sixth Street, and the familiar static of traffic rumbling over cobbles was smothered and muffled. The store seemed to have shrunk, and from the inside the boards were rough and splintery. This silence was the worst he had heard since they shut off the motors on his troopship in midocean and they all sat tensely on deck, scanning the fog for periscopes.

He tossed his head, trying to shake off the mood. This was only a temporary situation, and he would prove them all wrong. He had detected the cloudy expression in their eyes. The *Daily News* man and the bread men had stared at the window being boarded up and looked away from him as if they feared bad luck was contagious.

In his pantry he pried the lid off a can of thick red paint remaining from last year's remodeling. He intended to show all these finks. They were yellow types who would cut out if they faced this kind of battle. Not Sam Auer. The Johnsons would find out who they were dealing with when he visited them again this afternoon. This time he would brook no back talk.

He kneaded the stiffened, paint-snarled brush against the rim of the can and then stirred the dull red paste till it was almost liquid again. Outside, Fat Grace and the drivers charging down

Sixth watched him spell out a defiant message in large, jagged, irregular letters on the raw lumber:

OPEN FOR BUSINESS

It looked like Mercurochrome daubed over bruised flesh, but no passerby could have doubts. This was a real attention-grabber. Now every jerk from Jersey could gawk as he zoomed down Sixth Street and know that Sam Auer was open for business and meant business, that no ten tribes of savages were going to drive him from his lands.

Big Vye came in for a quart of milk, and he asked her how Buzzy's appeal was going. Buzzy had killed a boy from the Project in a brawl at the Green Room, and the newspapers had made a big thing of it. Auer was immediately sorry he asked as tears welled in Vye's hazel eyes.

"Shit, Sam. They want to really do that boy in. You know my son, Sam. He was hardly ever in any trouble. But that boy from Twelfth Street kept on picking at him and said Buzzy had no heart, and you know how strong my Buzzy is. He banged that boy's head against that wall by accident, but the District Attorney is asking ten years. He don't deserve no ten years. That boy will never last ten years. . . ."

"That's a rough rap," Auer agreed.

Vye was so distraught she rushed out of the store without picking up her change. He studied the roll of her powerful buttocks under her skimpy blue skirt, and it was no wonder Buzzy was strong. Mama had picked up Peggy Moore like a rag doll to slam her against the electric factory wall. Yet sober, Vye was the sweetest thing on the block. One night, if he felt up to it, he would like to take her on, console that mama.

He went to the parlor and dialed his home number. It buzzed ten times, and he was tempted to hang up and dial again when Bunny responded with a breathless "Hello."

"I've been expecting your call all morning," he said with no introduction.

"Oh. I was in the bathroom."

"All morning?"

"No," she explained. "Just now. Is everything all right?"

"Everything is all screwed up. The insurance company balks at paying for a replacement of the replacement, so I've boarded up the front window until things settle down."

"You're closing the place up?" Bunny asked excitedly.

"*Was* he closing the place up?" he asked himself and nodded at his reflection in the mirror. The wife was right with it, ready to leap in there at the slightest opening.

"No. The boards are a provisional structure, till the storm blows over. When peace is restored I'll put in another window, but till then it's senseless. I've painted an 'Open for Business' sign on the boards outside."

"That won't look too nice," Bunny informed him.

"The main concern right now is not artistic effect."

"Get the hell out of that place, Sam. Take Joe's offer. Stop banging your head against a wall."

He winced as she used the same pleading, whining monotone she reserved for pushing that proposition three times a week.

"If I'm going to develop a hernia, I'll do it on my own time and at my own speed and without having to kiss your Uncle Joe's ass for small favors."

"What kiss his ass? He's offering you a steady high-paying job in his supermarket. He respects you, thinks you're a hard worker. In two years, he says, you'll be manager."

"Sure. They always dangle a carrot. Look, I don't like to give orders. I don't like to take orders. I prefer to be my own man."

"And such a man," Bunny said mockingly.

"Screw off."

He slammed the phone back on the hook, and for one second was ready to slam the whole contraption into the mirror. He took a cigarette to calm down and crushed the empty pack. A whole pack before noon. They were all that was keeping him going after an hour of sleep. Now he had to phone his kid brother at the office. It was shameful, the firstborn calling a kid brother, but he had no other recourse. The kid was so much sharper than he was, with the books at least. Central High, Penn, Wharton. This was the place for aid and advice in a bind.

An English accent chirping, "Good morning. Gamble, Gamble, Schoonover and Schwartz."

"Good morning. I would like to speak to Mr. Jerome Auer if I could."

"May I ask who's calling, please?"

Auer frowned nervously at his receiver. The chilling, cultured tone sliced right through him.

"Tell him, please, that it is his brother, Mr. Samuel Auer, who is calling, please."

"I believe Mr. Auer is in conference, Mr. Auer, but I'll check."

Plugs clicked on the switchboard, and Sam Auer took pride in having a younger brother who was not immediately available, shielded by receptionists with British accents, a brother who took business trips to California and Texas. He was transferred to another secretary, who made him declare that it was a dire emergency and a legal matter before he was gratified by a series of clicks and a peremptory "Auer here."

"Hello, stranger. How are you? This is Sam."

"Is that what you've called to find out? I have three clients in the conference room."

He was pleased by the vision of austerely attired Wasps gathered in conservative chambers around a polished oval table, waiting for his kid brother to enter with a folder and figure out income tax dodges and gimmicks for them.

"Jerry, I'm in a bind with the store."

"That's nothing new. Five years ago I told you to hold onto it. Two years ago I told you to get out while the getting's good. Do you want that in writing?"

"I can do without the sarcasm now, kid. I've got a lot of pressure on me."

"Quickly, Sam. In twenty-five words or less. Tell me exactly, clearly, and cogently what it is this time."

"Well, to make a long story short, I've had my window busted two nights running. The insurance company agreed to pay for the first, but they're balking at the second. They claim I should have put up screens."

"Where do I fit into this picture?"

Auer shrugged and hoped the gesture was conveyed through the wires. "Can't we sue them? I mean, an insurance policy should not be like a cherry, once it's used it's useless. Where I think we've got a case is, Feinberg never mentioned screens till afterward. The screens were after the fact. Could you take the case for me, kid? I'm in a real pickle. There's not enough money around here for me to be laying out for a new window every day of the week."

"Sam. . . ." From the tone Auer could predict what was coming. "I thought I instructed you not to call me at the office. Couldn't this have held till I was at home tonight?"

"I'm going nuts here, kid. I've boarded up the front, and it looks like hell."

"Sam, I have three hungry heirs in our conference room who are at each other's throats over a seven-hundred-thousand-dollar estate. If I don't get in there in two minutes there will be blood all over the rug, and Gamble, Gamble, Schoonover and Schwartz will be extremely perturbed at me. Call me tonight at home. Do me that favor."

"Give me an answer now, Jer. I'm cracking up. I can't run a business looking like a log cabin boarded up for the winter. Will you take my case?"

"I've told you before. As a policy, I will not touch these matters for relatives. It is not a wise policy to mix blood with business."

"Policy?" Auer exploded. "Since when am I a relative? This is Sam, remember? I'm the brother who had to charge out of the store to save your hide from the *shvas* in the schoolyard.

Remember? I'm the brother who left Southern and broke his balls lifting potato sacks on Second Street so you could finish Central and law school. What did they do—educate you so much you don't have any feelings left?''

"I'm grateful," Jerome Auer answered in a pained, weary voice. "If you need a loan, I'll give you a loan, because you're honest. I will continue to do your income tax forms, because they never taught you math at Southern. I'll even arrange your divorce from Bunny if you ever decide to go through with it. But I will not get mixed up with petty suits or litigation for you, because if I do, all my wife's dear relatives will be on my tail with eighty-six of their moronic problems. Do me a favor and sell that lousy store, Sam. Do that, and I'll handle the sale. Do you want to die down there selling penny pickles to the *shvas*?''

"It was not such a lousy store when it put you through Penn and Wharton.''

"It was fine then. It served its purpose, and this is a new era. Get with it, Sam. Harness makers have been replaced by auto mechanics. You're still bogged down in the thirties.''

"Sure, Jer. People served their purpose, too. It was a lousy store then, too, kid. 'Jerry is too busy studying to wait on trade.' Sam, the *shmuck*, can wait on trade. 'Now Jerry must get some fresh air because he's studied so hard.' Sam, the *shmuck*, can bring up the bags of coal from the cellar. Except when he had to dash outside and save Jerry from the bullies. So Jerry can grow up and become a hotshot lawyer with policies and relatives.''

"Now I'm the one going nuts," Jerome Auer groaned. "My secretary is signaling me frantically, and there's going to be a blowup in that conference room unless I get in there.''

"Let it blow. Hang up on me, or answer one question: Will you take my case or not?''

"No!" the voice cracked. "Take that job Bunny's uncle offered you and get out of that dead end. My secretary is ready to burst a blood vessel. Call me at home. Good-bye.''

Auer examined the dead receiver in his hands and sniffed. So Bunny had been campaigning, sneaking around his back, pushing her Uncle Joe's offer with Jerry. There they went again, trying to manipulate him. There was no way he would let them manipulate him.

Three customers were waiting in the store, but it was the shadowed front that smacked him in the face. Something would have to be done to alleviate the gloom, or his people would search for less depressing surroundings. He could paint those raw boards, Kemtone them a pale blue, and maybe tack up a few gay calendars and pinups to enliven the situation. The boards were ugly enough from the outside, but in here they made his store look like a mine or a bomb shelter.

After one-fifteen Auer went out to his front step and watched the children filling the schoolyard. Ostensibly, he was outside to search for Johnson, but he lingered on in the cold, relieved to be away from the dreariness of the interior. It had affected his steady customers. His spaghetti had been enthusiastically received, but his boys were not as animated and talkative today. They listened attentively to his story of taking a taxi down here in the middle of the night, but their eyes were overcast and he sensed their nervousness.

Mrs. Lewis came out of Leah's, laughing with the other Negro teachers. For the first time in five years he nodded to her. She pretended not to have noticed the greeting, and his eyes followed the group as they crossed Sixth. They entered the lobby, and he scowled as he saw Mrs. Lewis put her head close to Mrs. Bates's ear, whisper something. Both women laughed. That was nasty. He was only being civilized, and they made fun of him.

Manny's truck arrived as he was finishing the dishes, and he signed the bill for the spool of barbed wire and the locks. He carried his stepladder and tool kit outside and did his own work while Manny's men installed the locks. This house was oddly constructed; it had two side entrances on Cottonwood Street, steps to his apartment and steps for the rear entrance leading to the back stairwell and the second- and third-floor apartments.

As he worked diligently, nailing the strips of barbed wire around his window frames, he noticed how slowly and deliberately Manny's men were carrying out their tasks. Dillydallying, dragging it out, cheating Manny. That was typical of outside men. He had done the same thing. Everybody wanted to get out on that truck, outside and away from under the boss's thumb. But his brother and wife were plotting to stick Sam Auer under a boss's thumb again.

There was lots of barbed wire in this spool. Tough stuff. His shears could hardly clip it, and he had a strong grip. After lining the frames and ledges, he crisscrossed strips diagonally in a closely knit pattern. When he finished, he stepped back to admire his handiwork. These designs would win no beauty prizes, but his four side windows were safe: he was at least secure on his left flank.

He smoked a cigarette and gazed down Cottonwood toward Fifth. In the thirty-four years of his life this scene had not changed: the three-story jail-like school of yellow brick across the street, its wide concrete yard, the empty lot, two red brick houses where the Conlons and Shrafts used to live, and Starker's factory at the far corner. On this side, row houses down to Glendolph, then the Baptist Church stretching from Glendolph to Fifth. Past Fifth, Cottonwood came to a dead end and York Avenue cut in, with the whitewashed Russian Orthodox church blocking off the panorama. Bunny thought this area was horrible, but this was his life. He had his first piece in that schoolyard, when he took Rita Uzkoff one night against the wall where they always played handball. And no Johnsons were going to drive him out. Sam Auer would go when it suited him.

Again there was that weird sensation of repeating a nightmare as he adjusted his sign to indicate he would be back at four. It had warmed up, and the flat gray sky above was disintegrating into curling puffs tinged by blues. The brown and gray slush was backing up the sewers at every corner. Another bonfire at the icehouse, in an old oil drum. A rank stench of burning fur, cloth, and soiled fabrics. Next to Shor's taproom, Negro teen-agers were bopping to the jukebox in Morse's candy store. The icehouse gang had yanked the back seat from a wrecked Dodge abandoned on the lot and were using it for fuel, with the stuffed cotton smoking in the flames. Bowes, cuddling his guitar, eyes hidden behind unnecessary dark glasses, was sitting next to Sidonia on the rickety bench. Whenever Bowes needed extra change, he brought out his yellow cane, tin cup, and dark glasses and banged that guitar on a busy Market Street corner till the cops ran him off.

Sidonia winked at Auer, and the grocer made an obscene thrusting motion with his forearm to acknowledge the greeting. It was a shame, Auer mused. He once got along so well with those people. Everybody around here had gotten along. But he had seen the change in the schoolyard. Back in his day if two kids got in a fight, it was one against one; but now if a Negro fought a white kid, everybody piled on, or vice versa. That was bad.

Seventh was more animated today, bricks brighter, shades rolled up, people out. Auer saw Mutty Zackman's Cadillac turn the corner at Grenoble and sniffed in scorn. The local success story. From chicken plucker on Marshall Street to millionaire slumlord. For a kid that was a yellow punk and the worst athlete in the history of Thurston schoolyard. Mutty really had these *shvas* bamboozled. Ninety percent of the women on this block could knock Mutty on his ass, but Mutty was the big, tough terror with the convertible Cadillac and the daughter at Sarah Lawrence. One day she would live up there with the rich Gentiles on the Main Line and probably not talk too much about the properties on this block. A guy like Mutty made it hard for every other Jew.

He rang the bell at #424. When it brought no response, he signaled again with annoying longs and shorts. That failed to produce a stir inside, and he resorted to simply holding down his thumb till a window scraped open on the third floor. It was Luana, Johnson's oldest daughter. Only seventeen and already picked up at the Green Room for soliciting a colored detective.

"What you want?" she shouted down. "What the hell you leaning on that bell for?"

"Your father. I need a little conference with him."

Other windows were scraping open, and Luana Johnson called down, "He ain't here."

"Don't give me any of that bullshit. I can hear all kinds of creeping around inside."

"I told you he ain't here," Luana Johnson screamed shrilly. "Now get the fuck off that bell, or I'll call the police."

"A fat chance you'll call any police. To cart away a corpse, you'll call the police. You tell your father that I am aware of who is behind all this, and he'd better come round and talk to me. If I don't get results, I'll be the one calling the police and I'll have the whole pack of you put away."

"I ain't telling him nothing. You get the fuck off that step and stop bothering us, or I'm gonna spit on you."

Auer cupped his hands over his mouth and shouted, "Just try it. Go ahead and try it, you little slut."

Luana Johnson cleared her throat, drew in, and spat as Auer hopped down to the pavement. The green phlegm splattered over the step with a sharp smack. Auer pointed a finger at her. "Alright, you animal. Just tell your father I'm holding him responsible for whatever happens, and I'm not afraid of the whole pack of you. If he'd rather break rocks than collect a relief check, I'll be more than glad to oblige him."

"Oh, kiss my ass," she called down and yanked her window closed with a grating screech. The yellow shade followed it, rattled, and hung still.

As he slouched back up the block, Auer chuckled along with the spectators at this repetition of yesterday's confrontation. Sidonia gave him another raffish wink and said, "Well, how's Miss Bunny getting along, Mister Sam? I never see her around anymore. She used to help you out."

"You're right, Sidonia. My wife has become society since we moved up to Oxford Circle. She rarely ventures south of Wyoming Avenue nowadays."

"And how's your Momma?" Sidonia inquired.

"She's down in Florida, soaking up the sun."

"Florida's a mighty fine place," Sidonia murmured smoothly, and the icehouse gang laughed. Bowes cuddled his battered guitar and was gazing at Shor's taproom as if it had suddenly become fascinating.

"What's the matter, Bowes? Suddenly you don't know me no more?"

The guitarist snapped his head up, feigning shock and confusion, as if he had been lost in deep thought. "Why sure, Mister Sam. How you doing? How are the wife and children?"

"They're not starving, but that's no thanks to you, buddy. When are you going to drop by and see me about those thirty-seven dollars on the books? If I were charging you interest, you'd owe me a Coup de Ville by now."

"I was thinking about that, Mister Sam," Bowes announced brightly. "Just the other day I said to myself I'd better drop round and clear myself with Mister Sam. I was planning on seeing you next Thursday. That's when my boy sends money from the Army."

"I heard that story in September. Are you sure he hasn't fallen prisoner of war, Bowes?"

That brought a cackle from the icehouse gang, and Auer sniffed as he left them, satisfied to have produced a laugh if not any money. Almost against his will, he liked Bowes. At the Wednesday evening prayer meetings in the storefront church at Marshall Street, Bowes played a moving guitar. With the drums and bass to back him, Bowes sounded like a whole symphony orchestra. Auer stared at the crude crosses stenciled on the painted windows. Sometimes, when he locked up on Wednesday night, he was drawn here, a whole block out of his way, and listened outside to the music and singing, Preacher Barnes bellowing out his sermon. He hated to admit it, but sometimes they really got to him, really moved him. Perhaps he would ask Preacher Barnes to deliver a sermon on bricks and delinquent bills.

Maddy and tubby Herbert were playing chess amid the usual chaos as Sam entered Leah's. Her place looked like a mixture of café, art gallery, country market, junk shop, dry-goods bazaar, and secondhand bookstore recently hit by a cyclone. Behind her grocery partition the confusion swirled even thicker, with ceramics ovens, molds, battered Victrolas with horns, and china closets stuffed with costume jewelry. This was no way to run a business, Auer thought. Her dishes were unwashed, half a grocery order remained in cases blocking the booths, and these two intellectuals were too absorbed in their chess to attend a customer.

Maddy finally glanced up as Leah came in from the back apartment. Auer watched her attend to her father, asleep and snoring in his rocking chair. She managed to adjust the pillow behind his head without waking him. Daniel Radin had the same dull sheen as the oil portraits and junk that surrounded him.

"That's a cool printing job on the boards over there," Maddy said.

"People will get the idea, kid. I want our neighbors to understand that they can't run me off. Thanks for calling last night."

Maddy shrugged as if his contribution were only minimal. Little Herbert mumbled, "Trader Horn, holding out in his stockade."

Auer winced at the smart-aleck remark. At the age of ten, Herbert Dobry quoted extensively from Tolstoy and Shakespeare and had many other detestable traits. Auer said, "When are you going to slim down, Herbie? Maddy here used to be fatter than you are, but he's slimmed down and looks okay. I think he's transferred all his surplus to you."

"Leave him alone," Leah said, coming out from behind the soda fountain. "He'll be all right, too."

Pointing with his thumb to the boards across the street, Auer said, "What do I do, Leah? Your family's been in business around here longer than we have, and you've never run into anything like this."

"Maybe it's the way you treat people, Sam. You used to be well liked around here, but lately you have such bitterness in your eyes. God knows, I'm no saint, and I can get damn angry with my customers, and I let them know it, but . . . Sam, that contempt? Don't you think they can sense it? Where do we get it from? We're here at Sixth and Cottonwood; we're not Mr. and Mrs. Vanderbilt. I'm not saying you should go kiss their asses, but you have to treat people like human beings. . . ."

The boys winced as their mother used vulgarity, and Leah wrinkled her nose as an order to mind their own business.

"You can't get along with the colored?" she asked Auer. "Look, are the whites we have to deal with such wonderful bargains? Mr. and Mrs. Morris down the block, *shvartzers,* are fine people; you could eat off their floors, and their children are the politest in the neighborhood. If you had to spend the rest of your life on a desert island, would you rather be with the Morrises or with the Colemans down the block? The Colemans are white when they take a bath, but they could all drop dead tomorrow and it would improve my digestion."

"It's not likely I'll get washed up on a desert island this year. My problem is here and now. I might kill one of the sonsofbitches, and I'll be the one in court."

"So, your brother Jerry will defend you," she said in consolation, and Auer smiled bleakly at a vision of his brother visiting him in the cell and explaining, "I'd like to take your case, Sam, but that would set a dangerous precedent for the rest of the family to latch onto."

He showed Leah the latest pictures of Stephanie and Sheila he had in his wallet and then purchased blades, tooth powder, and shaving cream. It suddenly occurred to him that he needed fresh underwear, and he went over to her small counter and picked out three pairs of shorts, T-shirts, and black sox.

"That's such junky stuff," Leah said. "Why don't you go up to Marshall Street, Sam? You don't need that junk."

"Just something to tide me over. I'm going to stay down here a few nights. Till things cool down."

"The Forty Days of Musa Dagh," Herbert muttered.
"What?" Auer said.

Maddy, another pedantic type, smiled at his kid brother's snideness as Auer paid and then paused to give Herbert a painful pinch on the cheek that was supposed to be a paternal gesture.

Outside, Auer lit a cigarette and decided to take a walk around the block before returning to the dim interior of his store. He could almost hear the Dobrys talking about him, sense what critical remarks they were making. He suddenly chuckled at what Leah had said about the Morrises and the Colemans. The Colemans were the local disgrace, coalfield trash from Hazleton that had moved into Leah's old store at Glendolph, hung curtains in the windows like Gypsies. Nancy, the oldest daughter, was in trouble for marrying four sailors and collecting four allotment checks simultaneously from the government. Jimmy was in jail for car theft. Charlotte, the fourteen-year-old, was in the reformatory for sucking cocks on Ninth Street, and the peach of the clan was mother Marge, shacked up behind those curtains with two bums at the same time, the three of them always cursing and brawling, while her youngest batch of kids ran around the street with shitty diapers. Certainly the Morrises were preferable for a desert island. But nobody lived on a desert island. Nobody lived in a test tube. And the fact that there were scummy whites did not exonerate the Johnsons.

His stomach was churning as he reopened the store. He snapped on his lights early, and under the harsh glare of his shivering fluorescent tubes the boards seemed starker, straight from a mine shaft or a prison stockade. Now there was nothing to look forward to till Sophie Bitko hurried by at five-thirty. Then something pretty rugged coming up: When he told Bunny of his idea. When he called her later and explained that he intended to stay here tonight, a lookout, guarding his property. No doubt about it. Bunny would go right through the roof.

The shift whistle blew promptly at five-thirty, and Auer managed to be outside, sprinkling rock salt over the slush that was freezing up again in the early dusk. In seconds they were pouring out of that factory, jumping down from the loading platform, and Sophie Bitko came up the street like a lioness trailed by hyenas and drones. Nobody said a word to her. None forgot what had happened to Al Dominic. Auer regretted his own lack of boldness. Exhausted as he was, with just an hour of sleep last night, he wanted to intercept her, proposition this elegant, well-built woman who looked so imposing striding along in her high-heeled galoshes. He watched till she entered Leah's. One day he would walk right up to Sophie and offer one hundred bucks on the line. It would be worth that and more to see Sophie naked.

Those were his last agreeable thoughts for the evening. His stomach churned as closing time approached. He was exhausted. He tried to read his "Amazing Stories" and his eyes would not focus. It would be so much easier if he just followed his routine, just went home. And the later he called, the worse it would be. Especially if she had already started supper. If the pot was on, it would really be an aggravating circumstance.

He lit a cigarette for courage as he dialed his number. Both receivers were picked up, and he heard Bunny shouting for Sheila to hang up.

"I hope you haven't started supper," he began brightly.

"Something the matter again? You went to see the *shvartzers* again and gave them a final warning about the police?"

"*Ach,* it was the same garbage. 'Fuck you. Fuck me.' It's impossible to hold a civilized discussion around here. How are the girls?"

"Steppie's still running a slight temperature. You didn't look at her toity last night like I asked you to."

"Look, I have worse matters on my mind than Steppie's potty. You haven't started supper yet, have you?"

"I'm making a nice roast."

He made a fist at his reflection in the mirror. "Good. You can cut me a few slices and bring them when you drive down tomorrow. I'm planning on spending the night here."

"What?"

"If I leave, these miserable bastards are capable of burning the place down on me."

"You listen to me, mister. You get your little hide home. I've made a nice roast, and I'm not going to waste it because you've got a dumb idea in your head. I married a husband, and not a store. If I wanted a store, I'd have married Gimbel Brothers."

"Would you have turned your back on Gimbel Brothers, too?"

"Oh?" she said, as if the light had dawned. "So that's what's eating you? You're acting like an infant, Sam. I wasn't feeling well last night."

"You haven't been feeling well since I was demobilized, but that's beside the point. I have to protect this place. What kind of price could I get if I'm run off? Have you ever been to a fire sale?"

"I don't want to hear this. This is your home. This is where you should be tonight."

Auer was encouraged by the conciliatory note creeping into her tone and said, "Tomorrow I want you to drive down here with fresh shirts and underwear. And some work clothes. Nothing fancy. Just my work clothes. And my book about Israel. I left it on the mantelpiece."

"Forget it," Bunny said. "Just forget it. A man has a job where he comes home at night. You want clean underwear, you get your little butt on the El and sleep in your bed. Everything's in the drawer."

"Be reasonable," Auer pleaded.

"You be reasonable. I'm going to serve a slice of roast beef, mashed potatoes, and salad on the table by nine-thirty. If you're not here, the dish will just sit there till you do get home."

"I'll call in the morning," he said softly. "Kiss the girls good-night for me."

Auer remained on the couch for five minutes after hanging up. The bell over the door remained depressingly silent. His customers were not accustomed to him being open after eight.

Now Leah would accuse him of competing for the night trade. Let her. She had enjoyed a monopoly long enough, and this was only a temporary measure. He was merely staying open a little later to compensate for the business he lost with the ugly boards.

Bracing himself, he dialed Jerry's number. After perfunctory greetings Auer said, "I hope I'm not disturbing you again, kid. I wanted to apologize for giving you such a hard time at the office this morning."

"I'm in the middle of dinner, Sam. It's okay. We have an extension cord that reaches here to the dinner table."

"Yeah? Since when do you eat supper so late? I thought only I ate so late."

"My Bryn Mawr wife and her continental tastes," Jerry explained. "We don't like to sit down till the kids are bathed and in bed, anyway."

"So what do you intend doing for me, younger brother?"

"Absolutely nothing. You don't have a case, and if you did I wouldn't take it."

Auer lit a cigarette and slouched on the sofa, wearier after that harsh response. "You know, kid. I'm sitting in the parlor, here in our old house, and I could swear it's only yesterday. Any second I expect to hear Pop calling me from the store, or Sis yelling down to Mom is her dress finished pressing yet."

He heard his brother snapping at his wife, ordering Terri to be quiet, and then, "You know how long ago that was, Sam? You're talking ten, fifteen years ago. That's all very cozy, but Pop is never going to call you from the store again, and Sis is a married woman with three kids of her own out in Los Angeles. Take my advice. I'm tired of repeating it. I told you two years ago to get out."

"What do I get for it, kid? They talk about renewal. Not doing anything about it, just talking about it. There's a big article in the *Sunday Bulletin* with a map showing everything getting torn down from Independence Hall up to Girard Avenue and being rebuilt. All in the future. Meanwhile, the city plays it very shrewd. They don't condemn anything. They just drive down prices by calling this area a slum, even though there are lots of streets like Glendolph that are nicely kept up. Every time some jackass from City Hall comes around here with a notebook and glances at a corner and jots something down, property values fall by another five hundred."

"That should be your cue," Jerry said, chewing vigorously on what sounded like roast beef. "Take what you can get, and cut out while you can. Before the whole bottom drops out."

"Hell, no. I want to stay on. This neighborhood is going to become 'Society Hill.' It's going to be clean and prosperous again. I want to be able to buy this corner back and get the advantage from the change."

"I've told you," Jerry said wearily, "I've explained to you, it isn't going to work that way. Nobody is going to be allowed to buy their own property back. Everything is going to be razed flat. Doesn't it get through your thick skull, Sam? The whole idea is to get the *shvas* out of there and get white taxpayers to move back. That's the whole idea. You're bucking a tide that is much bigger than you are."

"That's not fair. I've stayed on here while the neighborhood changed, while everybody else flocked out to the suburbs. Why shouldn't I be allowed to rise with the new tide?"

Jerry made a noise of exasperation and said, "Cut. That's it, cut. Stop banging your head against a stone wall and cut out."

Auer sniffed. "That's what you did, wasn't it, kid? You grabbed what was here for the grabbing. It's funny. I've heard you brag about how you came from Sixth and Cottonwood, like to show how high you've risen in the world. All the way to Mount Airy. But I've never heard you mention to your classy friends how, when I was away in the Army, you let Pop wait on trade and carry up the bags of coal from the cellar with his bad heart because you were too busy studying to become a high-powered Philadelphia lawyer. You haven't risen in any world, Jerry. You are still a small and selfish man."

"Tell him to drop dead," Auer heard Terri saying in the

background. Jerry groaned, "You ruined my day at the office with your lecture. Now you have to ruin my dinner, too?"

"Oh, you poor boy," Auer said mockingly. "You want another lecture? I'll give you one on economics. Where's your check for Mom's rest in Florida? Sis has already sent her third, but you're two months behind. I mean, I know you don't have any more brother, but don't you have a mother, either? Or is paying bills punctually a thing for the peasants?"

"I'll send the check for Mom at the end of the week. Otherwise, I don't want to know from you, Sam. Don't bother to call. You were a thick kid, and you've grown up to be a dense, stubborn jerk. If you ever come to your senses again, let me know."

The bell tinkled over the front door. He went out to prepare hamburgers deluxe for three Negro teen-agers, and as they joked and elbowed each other at his counter, for the first time he experienced a pang of fear in his own store. He was alone here, in the dark, protected by police who arrived in time to cart away the corpses. Even Leah, who got along with everybody, had one attempted robbery and once woke up to find a young buck in her parlor. Her screams drove him off, but things happened in this city every night. Every morning there were items on the third page of the *Inquirer*.

Auer wheezed in relief when they paid for their hamburgers and left. Even skinny punks could be dangerous when it was three against one. It was obvious that if he were going to stay open late he would have to drop by Uncle Lou's pawnshop on Eighth Street tomorrow and get backing. Perhaps a blackjack. A blackjack next to the cash register, and if he had to visit the Johnsons again.

Conceding the last hour to Leah, he bolted his door at nine-thirty. To appease the snarling in his belly, he fixed a hoagie with salami, bologna, Swiss cheese, tomato, onion, lettuce, hot peppers, and olive oil. He opened a can of beer, picked up his "Amazing Stories," and carried all of his supplies back to the parlor. For noise he snapped on the television and then positioned himself on the sofa with his feet supported by the coffee table. Later, he could take up his position in the store. Traffic was still too heavy on Sixth Street for any rock throwing. Then, after eleven, he would hide out in the store and charge outside if he caught anybody skulking around.

Watching the television, munching at his hoagie, sipping at his beer, Auer suddenly chuckled with pleasure. It was relaxing being here without the girls squabbling and Bunny bitching. In the movies, whenever the snooty Main Line types had a spat with their wives, they went to their club. This grubby parlor was not exactly the Union League, but suddenly he felt like Spencer Tracy having a tiff with Katharine Hepburn.

The TV was idiotic, and biting deeply into his oily sandwich he flipped open his "Amazing Stories." The cover was again deceiving. In spite of the blond Valkyrie struggling with the green dinosaur, there was no Amazon tale inside. Those were his two favorite kinds of stories: "Thee Last Man on Earth" kind, and the ones where the brunette warrior girl knocks the hero down and leaps on top and rapes him, or says, "Come here, you." In real life, one was never so lucky. Most of the Amazons he knew weighed ninety pounds, and the big girls he knew were all sweetie pies.

His eyes were too tired to read, so he watched television. He would have changed channels, but it was too much trouble to get up. He shuddered. It was that fat Jewish schoolteacher comic again, making jokes about his momma in a Yiddish accent. Auer wished they would not put that crap on television, use all those Jewish sayings. Did those jerks up in New York actually believe they were loved over in West Virginia? They should have been with him that first Friday night in basic training when the Sarge barked, "All Jews, front and center." That was a chilling sound: "All Jews, front and center." And only four of them stood in front of all those hillbillies and wise guys from Jersey. Yet those *shmucks* on the screen acted as if the whole world thought that Jews were cute. They should ask his cracker buddies down at Fort Bragg, or the Irish on Oriana

Street, if they thought all these Yiddish sayings were cute. Or they could interview Bowes and the Johnsons on Seventh Street.

"The Star-Spangled Banner" woke him up. Two flies were circling over the hoagie crumbs, and his magazine had slipped to the floor. Wincing at the crick in his neck, he pushed himself up and snapped off the simmering static on the screen. It was time to take up his position, and he lit up a cigarette for energy. He rummaged through the back pantry for his monkey wrench, and then he carried the wicker rocking chair out to the dark store and set up a soda crate as a footrest. From this vantage point he was invisible from the street and could see the illuminated shade diagonally across in Fat Grace's window. Tonight, if there were any monkeying around, the sonsofbitches would have Sam Auer and a monkey wrench to contend with.

He had almost dozed again when he was startled by a scraping on the icy pavement, scuffling noises, like the soft swishing of sneakers. His grip tensed on the wrench, and the scratching outside ceased. Seconds of silence passed like heavy animals bumping by him in the night. Simmons coughed upstairs. Auer crept toward the front door and peered through the dirty glass. Sixth Street was empty down to the lumberyard at Grenoble. Cottonwood dark, except for the glare on Fat Grace's shade. Leah's nightlamp lent a mysterious glow to the statuettes in her window, the aura of relics gleaming in a shrine. He twitched as he imagined he saw a darting movement near the metal bars of the school fence running down Sixth. There seemed to be deeper splotches in the darkness, black gremlins dancing in the shadows. No forms took shape. He was so jumpy he was imagining all kinds of phantoms creeping around out there. A car came down Sixth Street, and its headlights swept along the fence. Nothing out there all the way down.

Making a blowing, rubbery sound of relief, he returned to the rocking chair and rested his feet on the soda crate again. He relinquished his grip on the wrench to light a cigarette and noticed that his hands were sweating. It was easy to go soft, easy to lose your manhood. He remembered a scene in front of the Chelsea Hotel last summer. A big husky individual forcing his wife out of the beach chair, pulling it away from her, saying, "I drove all the way down here, Myrna, and I deserve the beach chair." They tugged at it like two kids in a sandbox, and that was what homelife did to the finks on his block in Oxford Circle. They became like whining women with the rag on. In an emergency like this, they would all poop out.

The first crash came as if in a hideous nightmare, the pane on his front door shattering, the brick clanging against a fountain stool with a hollow ring, a horrible cobweb pattern in the remaining glass. Auer sprang up, gripping his wrench, ducked at the next crash as a brick shattered the Cottonwood window, falling glass knocking over pyramids of canned goods. More cans clattered to the floor as he charged for the front door, shoes crunching over glass chips, reverberations of shattered plates and toppling cans loud in his ears. Through the smashed glass he saw two boys racing down the far sidewalk on Sixth, past the lithographing establishment. Two were nothing. This was a war to the death. Two were nothing.

Without bothering to check for onrushing traffic, Auer hurled himself across Sixth, and a speeding car skidded and swerved to avoid hitting him as he raised his wrench above his head like a tomahawk. Now these sonsofbitches would learn that Sam Auer could run, move, run like he ran against West Catholic, charging right into Red Scoletti, run without blocking, plow right into that line and break their skulls.

They were cutting around the corner, and as he reached Grenoble he slipped on the ice, braking his fall against a fire alarm box and kicking over trash cans.

Five or six boys were swooping down on him from the shadows of the lumberyard wall. It was a trap. They had been staked out. The fuckers were ambushing him. He screamed, "C'mon, you sonsofbitches," and charged at them, swinging his wrench as they surrounded him in the middle of the street. A club streaked down at his skull, and he blocked it with the wrench, heard the crunch of metal against wood. A watery shriek erupted in his throat as a bicycle chain smashed him across the temple.

It was too quick. Under the dismal glow of the streetlamp on the far corner, it went too fast for him to recognize any of his assailants. He swung the heavy wrench and roared, "C'mon, you yellah bastards, let's go, let's go, let's go," his voice rising with fear and excitement to an almost feminine pitch as they darted in and out, attacked with chains, clubs, and sticks. The tallest was wielding a lead pipe, raising it again. Auer parried with his wrench, and there was a clang of steel against hollow lead, but Auer's grunt of triumph became a groan as a wooden club landed on his shoulder.

He backed up against the lumberyard fence. They were only punk kids, unable to concert their rush and attack together. Using the fence as a launching pad he kicked out, caught a short, stocky boy in the groin, heard his moan of "Ow, motherfucker" as he stumbled away in pain, and then Auer had the brief satisfaction of hearing an anguished shriek as his wrench crunched against a forearm and the tallest boy dropped the lead pipe. He paid for it immediately. A two-by-four slammed against his ear, and he was instantly woozy, lighter, swooning, almost relieved. He was being punched and kicked but was unable to feel the sticks and chains as the blinking, flashing stars danced before his eyes.

Auer did not go down. The pounding continued, and he had the strange sensation of being a spectator at this beating. Sticks and chains smacked his head and only seemed to strengthen his determination to stay up, not hit that pavement, where it would be all over. The wind roared in his ears and he was Gulliver with dark midgets swarming and dancing around him, trying to drag him to the Earth. Their blows were making him stronger, and he would catch his second wind, break through the line, shake off his tacklers, break into the open. He was too close to home for anything serious to happen. And this would soon be over.

A passing car saved him. A Pontiac paused under the glare of the streetlamp, and an unknown Good Samaritan was honking his horn. The boys began breaking away. The smallest took one final swing with his chain, wrapping it stingingly but ineffectually around Auer's wrist. He grasped it away from him as the rest scurried down Grenoble and were outlined briefly by the reddish glare from Zacky's sign at Seventh as they turned the corner at Marshall. The Pontiac sped off. The driver had done enough and did not wish to get further involved.

Auer rested with his back against the lumberyard wall. The stars, brilliant points, and squadrons of fireflies, slowed in their crazy orbits, were extinguished one by one. When he opened his eyes again, more constellations appeared. It felt as if his mind were knocked from his skull, floated, disconnected. The fight had not lasted two minutes, but he was staggering up Sixth Street as if he had endured a two-hour mortar bombardment. The damage report was coming in now. It was arriving from all quarters. He ran his fingers over the blood dripping from his temple and searing flashes streaked up his back and spread in a wide network of heat and pain. Each movement hurt now. During the flurry of combat he felt nothing, and now he realized that they must have given him eight or nine good solid knocks. Auer chuckled. The little bastards had done a good job on him. From the emptiness and ringing in his skull he might have a concussion.

The front door was banging open and shut with the wind. He was holding the wrench in his right hand and discovered that he was still stupidly dragging the chain along the ice with his dangling left hand. He flung it away as if it were a poisonous snake. The glass on his wristwatch was also shattered. A design that seemed to be a miniature reproduction of the smashed pattern of his door.

The lights went out in Leah's, but they were still burning in her second-floor front. Señora Gomez was staring down at him.

She was in a purple brassiere. For a full ten seconds they stared at each other, and then Señora Gomez pulled her shade down.

Auer kicked aside the cans of tomatoes and flipped on his fluorescent lights. Stacking cans could wait till later. The pressing task was to board up his windows, shore up his fortifications. In the grease-smoked mirror behind the cash register he saw spots of blood seeping through his white shirt and darker blood oozing from his scalp. He rinsed a fresh dish towel and fastened it pirate fashion around his head. A hospital could wait till he was finished. First he must strengthen the barricades. They might take an X ray of his skull, diagnose a concussion, keep him in bed. The place had to be sealed tight while he was away.

It took him thirty minutes to nail Heinie Schmidt's boards across the front door and Cottonwood window. The first time he climbed the ladder he saw stars again and almost toppled off, but he recovered and his breathing returned to normal. His teeth chattered as the damp, chill winds swept under his leather jacket. Simmons woke up with all the banging and hammering. The lights in the second-floor back went on, and Simmons called down, "What the hell's going on out there, Mister Sam?"

"Nothing, Simmons. Just boarding up my window. Go back to sleep."

The old man coughed, and the window scraped down. Auer blew at his freezing hands and balanced himself on the top rung of the ladder. His head was swelling, and every movement seemed to uncover hidden abrasions and welts. His hands were smeared with blood from touching his wounds. He snickered. The bastards had gotten him good, but he also got in a few licks. He must have broken the forearm of that skinny prick with the lead pipe.

A light snow was falling as he locked his front door. Inside it looked like a jail riot, but he could straighten up that mess in the morning. He hefted his wrench and blinked away the tears from the snow blowing into his eyes. He had to congratulate the fuckers. They had actually devised a plan to get him. They had spied on him and prepared an ambush. With tactics and strategy yet. And congratulate the police. After their big promise last night to do more cruising around his place, neither hide nor hair of them in all the time he was out here. This wrench was his only protection. Now he was walking around like Barry. Barry was always staggering around with some kind of club or weapon in his hands. Roaming around stewed on Saturday afternoon between Shor's and Zacky's and the Green Room, with a club or beer bottle in his hands.

There was a taxi parked by the telephone at the Sixth and Green Garden stand. As Auer drew nearer, wobbling over the slick black ice, the driver saw his blood-smeared cheeks and the wrench in his hands, hurried to turn on his motor.

Auer lurched forward and was able to open the door and dump himself inside before the driver could gun the cold engine. The driver spun around and snarled, "C'mon, buddy! Take off. Call yourself a red car. You're bleeding all over my goddamn rear seat."

"Take me to the Hahn."

"Look what you're doing," the cabby shouted. "You're dripping blood all over my new seat covers. Check out. I'm off duty."

"No shit," Auer said. "How about if I hit you with this wrench? Then you'll really be off duty."

The hackie measured his chances for chasing his passenger out with bluster against provoking him into using the wrench. Muttering, he decided to accept the fare. They bumped along Green Garden Avenue with no other vehicles on the wide, lonely street. Auer held his towel to his head and smiled as a hand reached up to adjust the rear-view mirror. He almost enjoyed all the hatred and fury ricocheting his way. Nice guy up there. Perhaps as a reward for his kindness, he should bash him anyway when they reached the hospital.

The taxi turned into the alley behind Hahnemann's

emergency ward, and Auer decided to forgo the lesson in basic manners and tip generously. The meter read eighty cents. He crumpled two one-dollar bills into a wad and dropped them on the front seat as he staggered out. The driver's mouth contorted, and Auer did not have to a be a lip reader to get the message. He raised his wrench as if to smash the windshield, and the cabby quickly backed up, blinding him with the headlights before swinging out of the alley.

Another shock inside. It was like a zoo. Walking wounded, sick, drunks in the dingy lobby, *shvartzers* sprawled out or sitting dejectedly on the benches. The pinched-faced secretary in the admissions cubicle refused to glance up and pecked away at the form in her typewriter. Somehow, he had imagined that he would be allowed to faint, and solicitous doctors and svelte nurses in crisp white uniforms would rush forward to catch him, conduct him to a rolling table with immaculate sheets, and whisk him away.

"Excuse me," Auer said, "I'm bleeding."

Irritated, the secretary poked her head out through the window in the cubicle and snapped, "Please be seated, will you. I'll be with you in a few minutes."

"Should I stop bleeding meanwhile?"

"I've only got two hands," the secretary rasped as if taking up an argument that started before he arrived. "Take a seat on the bench, and I'll call you in turn."

Auer slumped on the front bench, between two Negroes. He glanced around. Perhaps they had numbers, like at the meat counter in the supermarket. Most of the *shvartzers* and drunken white bums from Eighth Street were in worse shape than he was. This had to be the curfew crowd from the bars letting out at two. Business was probably better on the weekend. The waiting room managed to seem dirty and antiseptic all at the same time, stinking of sweat and blood and alcohol and ether. Brilliantly lit and yet dreary. In all the movies, hospitals were gleamingly modernistic like "Amazing Stories" covers, but this dump looked like Zacky's Employment Agency.

If he was lucky, this was a nightmare. A black woman was trying to get her husband to sit down, repeating and crooning, "C'mon, Hahr-old. Stop that Hahr-old. You gotta sit down, Hahr-old. You can't walk around like this, Hahr-old. This is a hospital, Hahr-old." Sure this was a nightmare. He had fallen asleep in the rocking chair in his store and would wake up shortly.

He became more certain it was a nightmare when the receptionist finally got to him and they began filling out the forms. Holding the towel to his head, with his nose throbbing and skull splitting, he was ready to strangle her.

"Do you have any insurance, Mr. Auer?"

"Yeah, I got something. My wife handles that."

"That's not very helpful."

"It don't matter. I'll pay cash."

"Is it Blue Cross?"

"Blue Cross, Blue Shield, Blue Shit, I don't know, lady."

"There's no call for vulgarity."

"There never is," Auer agreed. "Tell the doctor to wash out my mouth with soap when he gets to me. If he ever gets to me."

"You're a very difficult man to deal with, Mr. Auer."

By the City Hall clock it was four-fifteen when he came out of the Hahn. He shivered with the cold and lit up a cigarette. Nothing broken, no concussions, but his whole body was stung and smarting from the alcohol poured over him, and he felt like a pincushion or walking dart board, stitches all over the place and a big bandage on his head. At least he had a good doctor, a chatty *shvartzer* babbling on about the nightly rush hour, bashed skulls, knife wounds, ice-pick punctures, razor slashings, assuring him that this was a slow night, this was nothing.

Nothing? Auer stared up at the statue of William Penn on the City Hall tower. Nothing? Back in grade school they taught all that crap about the City of Brotherly Love, founded by William Penn and the Quakers to pray in peace, all planned with parks, the idea was to establish "a greene and rolling countrie towne." They had really messed it up, Willie boy. Old Willie would have another heart attack if he ever gave a gander at Seventh Street.

Auer walked down Cottonwood. As he passed the police station at Twelfth, he contemplated going in and reporting these incidents. And rejected the idea. All the police did anymore was keep score. The police had become like insurance policies, guaranteed money-back products, sensational free offers, and political platforms. In the end, all a man had was himself. Sam Auer was in an isolated fortress, and the *shvartzers* were like guerrillas out there in the jungle. Tomorrow he would have to buy himself some arms and weapons. It was already tomorrow.

The alarm clock had failed to wake him. He was in the throes of a nightmare, a woman cooing, "You gotta sit down, Hahr-old, this is a hospital, Hahr-old," and someone was knocking hard on the store door.

Auer sprang up and immediately regretted his rashness. His cuts stung under the bandages, and it felt as though scabs were broken and pus was trickling all over his arms and chest. The knob on top of his alarm was completely run down and emitted a tiny peep when he pushed it back in. There was another impatient rap on the door, and as Auer dashed to open it he saw that it was ten-past-seven on his Pepsi-Cola clock.

Beaumont, the mailman, was startled by his appearance, the gauze taped to his scalp, the unshaven cheeks and purple tincture around his wounds. He retreated a step as though fearing an attack when he saw the debris of smashed glass and cans scattered over the floor.

"Just a second. Good morning. I'm slightly behind schedule. I'll be right with you, Beaumont. Come on in."

The mailman seemed even more worried by the agitated gestures and the strange glint in the grocer's eyes. Shying away he said, "You don't have the coffee ready yet, Sam?"

"No. That's all right. Just a second," Auer spluttered.

"My schedule's a little out of whack. Everything will be all right. Come on in."

Beaumont hesitated and backed off the step. He mumbled apologetically, "That's all right, Sam. I can run up to the diner if you're tied up. I'll just run up to the diner this morning till you catch up."

"Wait a minute," Auer called after him, but Beaumont was already hurrying up Cottonwood with his leather pouch flapping. He refused to turn and was almost running as Auer repeated plaintively, "Wait a minute."

The freezing dawn bit into his scratched, naked shoulders. Auer spit into the dirty ice. There went another steady customer down the tube. He shook his head and quickly carried his milk crates, boxes of pastries, and bundles of paper inside. Before the next customer tinkled the bell over the door he rushed back to the apartment, washed, smeared deodorant under his armpits, and put on a fresh shirt. He started his urn of coffee, and losing Beaumont was beginning to depress him. Beaumont represented only a dime Danish and a nickel coffee, but that was ninety cents a week. He frowned. It was also forty-six dollars and eighty cents off his yearly gross.

All morning long he functioned automatically, straining his reserves of nervous energy, working with the clarity and wide-eyed emptiness of exhaustion. He felt alternately spry and limp, found himself committing inexcusable errors in mathematics. Between breakfast orders he managed to sweep the glass off the floor, pick the slivers out of the window, and stack the cans back into their symmetrical pyramids. After nine he had a short break and slipped outside with his red paint and brush to slash a crude "Open for Business" on the Cottonwood boards and a smaller "Open for Business" on the slats over his front door. To reaffirm this declaration, he took the two bricks that had smashed his windows and used them to hold the front door open. That let the cold in, but now all passersby could see that Sam Auer was holding fast.

With all the windows boarded up, there was a subtly softer

timbre in the acoustics of the school buzzers and bells, the yelling of the children at recess, the swish of the traffic clicking down Sixth Street. The pain of the bruises and cuts kept him going. At lunch none of his regulars seemed disturbed by the gloominess and shacklike atmosphere the boards gave to his luncheonette. His lamb stew was well received, and the banter at the counter had a loud and raucous echo to it, the hollowness of throngs shouting in a dank, high-domed railroad station. His lunch customers were fascinated by his description of the fight, the clubs and chains, and the rotten treatment at the hospital. They would not desert him. His people were workingmen who preferred a rough-and-ready atmosphere, a place where they could relax in their dirty overalls. Nothing too fancy would be successful around here.

In the afternoon he closed and headed down Cottonwood. To survive down here he needed a rod. The icehouse bench was empty, and he headed down Seventh to let the Johnsons know that Sam Auer was alive and kicking. No Johnsons were around, but the bums in front of Zacky's seemed intrigued by the bandages over his temple. One of the boys looked like a member of the ambush squad from last night, but it was hard to be sure. It was all too fast, dark, confusing.

The stench of the paperboard factory at Eighth and the railroad tracks assailed him with its nauseating mixture of pastes and horse marrow that reminded him of rancid cheese. Skid row began past the tracks. Three blocks of saloons, missions, flophouses, Army-Navy stores, and pawnshops for the derelicts. Once Eighth Street had not been this run-down. It once had decent restaurants, movies, and a burlesque hall, and the Sugar Bowl was a famous ice cream parlor patronized by the elite after the theater. Now the hoboes were found dead along the sidewalk in the morning, their bellies burnt with Sterno, and the greasy-spoon cafe at Eighth and Ridge was fined once a year for selling horsemeat hamburgers.

Since he was a kid he had walked this way downtown,

watched this stretch deteriorate, but today it was ugly beyond bearing. The dirty ice was splattered with broken bottles and the stains of last night's vomit. All the products displayed in the windows were designed to stick a finger in the throat: leather trusses, yellow crutches and canes, pink and gray surgical corsets, orthopedic foot gauze, dusty astrology pamphlets, syringes, jars of herbs and patent medicines, athletic supporters, plastic monsters' hands for party pranks, secondhand bonnets and used fur stoles, condoms, Sheiks, Trojans, French ticklers. Even the plastic mannequins in the haberdashery windows were freaky, wearing creepy smiles and moustaches, bad replicas of Brian Donlevy and Leslie Howard. But Feinberg was right: all these windows had bars or screens that folded out at closing time.

Drunks were already gathering by the Victory Mission. Every year they upped the price the bums had to pay for supper. The Mission made the winos squirm through a two-hour sermon, sing hymns to the organ music, and take a cold shower and dry off with paper towels before serving them nourishing, tasteless slop. Then came more singing.

Auer shuddered when he saw what men could sink to. These panhandlers slept with the roaches in their seventy-five-cent-a-night rooms, staggered around with brown or missing teeth, mouths reeking of rotgut, cheeks scabbed, trousers ripped at the knees, sucking cocks because no woman would go near them. He consoled himself with the thought that there were no Jews down here. Eighth Street was for hillbillies, Irishers, *shvartzers,* Poles. Today, a glimmer of fear. Maybe the safety net had disappeared. This afternoon Eighth Street seemed closer. What guarantee did he have? He unzipped his leather jacket and sniffed under his arm, exhaled quickly. Unshaved, unshowered, bandages growing dirty, he felt as grubby as any slob on the row today.

Lou Katz rose from his chair in the rear of the pawnshop as Auer entered. The wizened old man bellowed, "Sam! How are you? Sorry I asked. You look like hell. Bunny hit you with a frying pan?" He extended his hand over the counter, and the grip was powerful for a man of seventy. Lou was a distant relative of Bunny's, less than a cousin but referred to as an uncle. "You look shaky," Katz insisted. "Take a load off your mind."

Accepting the suggestion, Auer sagged into a cloth folding chair. He rubbed the cold sweat off his brow with his leather sleeve. The short walk had exhausted him. "Thanks, Lou. I'm not too steady."

"That, you didn't have to tell me. Is this a social call, or are you shopping for a casket, fella?"

"A gun, Lou. I'm shopping for a rod."

"To shoot Bunny? She's not worth the chair, Sam. Don't answer her back, and she'll settle down. That's how I handle my Molly. I play the strong, silent role, and she melts on me."

Lou was thin, quick, wiry. He wore the cynical smirk of an individual forced to hide high intelligence behind clownishness. Auer smiled wearily. "I'm not kidding. I need a gun. A heater."

"What for? Just like that, you come in here asking for a heater like you were John Garfield perhaps. How about a nice fishing rod?" Lou swept his arm toward the racks of fishing rods behind his knife counter. "I'm way overstocked with fishing rods. Lately everybody wants a killing rod, and nobody wants a fishing rod."

Auer recounted the events of the last three days, beginning with the penny pinwheel and ending with the brawl last night. As he finished, Lou said, "Sounds like you've got *tsouris,* kid. Generally, I'm willing to trade everybody their troubles for mine, but at this moment I prefer my headaches to yours."

"You'll sell me a gun then?"

Katz fixed his rimless spectacles over his sharp nose. "You're supposed to have a license for such accessories."

"I don't have time to go through the whole rigmarole. They could even attack me on the way back to the store, Lou. It's come to that. What are the chances without a license?"

"Hold on."

Katz went back to his safe. A minute later he returned with a pearl-handled .38. He placed it on the counter and said, "This is a hot little item. A *tunkele* unloaded it on me last week for a quick ten dollars. You'd be doing me a favor taking it off my hands."

"It's working?"

Katz opened his palms. "You're our killer. You tell me."

The bell over the door tinkled, and Katz had to attend to a Puerto Rican who came in to pawn his guitar. Auer was amused to hear Uncle Lou haggle in a barking pidgin Spanish with the Puerto Rican. As the argument dragged on, he lost interest and began examining the cutting tools and knives in the glass display counter. A man who wanted to slice somebody up had a variety to choose from: razors, machetes, paring knives, switchblades, bayonets, stilettos, black knives with engraved swastikas, one Japanese samurai blade. One night he might forget his pistol, might have to run out of the store on an errand. It was best to have something directly on his person. As a precaution he could use a switchblade handy in his back pocket.

The Puerto Rican boy stormed out with his guitar and slammed the door so hard Auer was sure the glass would crack. The bell continued jingling as the guitarist gave Katz a stiff-finger sign from the sidewalk. Lou shrugged it off and returned with his hands in his pocket. Tossing his head he said, "The Latin lover claims I was trying to buy his soul for five dollars. I told him fifty cents for his soul and five dollars for his guitar." Pointing with his chin at the collection of guitars hanging in the window, he said, "Look at all those dreams hanging there, Sam. It looks like a bunch of corpses hanging up there, rotting in my window."

Auer did not hear that. He was absorbed by the fascinating and mysterious knives.

"What do you get for switchblades, Lou?"

"Thinking of buying a birthday present for the girls?"

"No, it's for me. I need something in case I'm attacked in an emergency."

Katz paused, and gloom spread over his sharp, gnarled face. He said, "Sam, when things are so bad that you need a gun and a knife, you don't need a gun and a knife, you need a real estate agent. That's not the Taj Mahal you're defending."

"It's where I make my living."

"You'll make a living anywhere. You're never going to starve, Sam."

"Thanks for the free advice. Meanwhile, three kids came into the store last night, and I was sure they were going to jump me. A pistol I can keep behind the cash register, but I'd like something on me at all times."

Twitching with anger, Katz stalked behind the counter and began pulling out the velvet cases of knives. He spread them over the glass counter and gestured expansively. "Take your pick. Keep an open door, and all kinds of nuts walk in. What kind of knife were you planning on this season?"

"Something in a switchblade," Auer answered in the same flat vein.

Katz snatched a black-handled blade with silver trimming from a case and tossed it to Auer, who caught it with both hands.

"Try that one, Sam. All my knowledgeable customers seem to prefer that model. Very popular. Handy for rumbles, cutting your girl friend's face, leaving around for the children. Don't be a jerk!" Katz shouted suddenly. "Forget the damn knife."

Auer pressed the button and recoiled as the blade snapped out with a distinct, efficient click. It was a beautiful instrument, balanced, tempered steel. He ran his fingers down the sharp edge, tested the point with his thumb till the skin pinked.

"Sam, you've seen lots of fights around here. Curse and the man curses you back. Throw a punch, and more punches are thrown. Pick up a bottle, and the other guy picks up a bottle. You get a gun, and you're upping the ante way over your level."

"How much, Lou?"

"Take them!" Katz said angrily. He pulled a box of bullets out from under the counter. "Take this, too. Do you think I would sell a fine boy like you this shit? Such articles I don't sell friends and relatives. If you came in for cyanide, I'd give it to you but I wouldn't sell it to you."

Auer reached for his wallet. "It's too much. I'd rather pay."

"Put your damn money away. You're too stubborn to hear reason. I'd chase you right out of here, except you'd just go buy this poison off some other *gonif* on this block."

Auer showed him the latest snapshots of Sheila and Stephanie, and Lou assured him that they were raving beauties. He advised him to visit a physician for his health and a psychiatrist for his head. Auer tried to thank him again, and Lou dismissed the gratitude.

"A dope. You're a dope. I supply you with razors to cut your throat, and you want to thank me. *Trug, gezeunte heit,* Sam. Use them in good health. Just don't come complaining to me when you get killed."

Lou was getting on, Auer concluded, as he walked toward Race Street. At seventy, Lou still had moments of sharpness and then these senile contradictions. First Lou was more than delighted to unload the hot .38 on him, and then he gets all shook up because of the knife. Senile contradictions.

His belly growled, and he was only a block away from Chinatown, at Ninth and Race. He could almost taste the bowl of wonton soup, two egg rolls with hot mustard, and mint tea. A hilarious thought struck him. He and Bunny always ate at the Jewish-Chinese restaurant. There were about ten Chinese restaurants along Race Street, and each catered to a different clientele. All the Italians from South Philly went to one spot, and right under the Shanghai was a chop-suey joint reserved for the *shvas*. The tolerance posters on the El wanted everybody to get together, but even to eat their shrimp chow mein people separated.

The patrolman across Race squinted, and Auer faded toward Franklin Square. He did not look back. These guys could smell fishy business. With the black stubble on his chin, the bandage and purple swelling, the leather jacket, he looked like he had just hopped off a boxcar. Worse, he suddenly realized; if they should suddenly give him a quick shakedown, he had a switchblade and a hot pistol.

Chilly as it was, bums were on the benches in Franklin Square, chins resting on their chests. It was illegal for them to lie down. If they stretched out, the park guards prodded them with billy clubs. At Sixth and Vine, lines of bums were forming in front of the Sunday Breakfast Association. Auer waited for the red light and stared at the towers of the Delaware River Bridge. An impressive bridge. An impressive feat of engineering, that suspension bridge. A hell of an entrance to a city. Thousands of cars poured off that bridge in the morning, and the first thing people saw was the barren park and lines of hoboes in front of the Sunday Breakfast Association.

Fat Grace waved to him as he reopened the store and lodged his bricks against the door. She shook her head in commiseration for his bandaged head and boarded windows. Fat Grace knew. Without ever leaving the room, she was on to everything that happened around here. The social workers were always trying to pump Grace and Leah about which women on relief had men visiting them, but neither squealed. It was after four, and he had missed his afternoon rush again. If he did not watch out, he would lose his coffee-break rush permanently. A pattern broken was a pattern broken.

Auer went to the parlor and dialed his home number. Bunny became immediately testy when he attempted to describe his misery. Incredibly, she cut him off and announced that she believed none of it.

"What do you mean, you don't believe me? Come down here and look at my stitches and the bandages on my head. Then you'll believe me."

"You know what I think, Sam?"

"What? What do you think?" he demanded to know.

"I think you've got a woman down there."

"My aching ass."

"I think you're playing around with some tramp."

"Sure. I'm Errol Flynn. I've got them lined up around the block."

After a cold pause she asked, "You really got hurt?"

"I've been in misery all day, honey. Even when I washed the dishes my arms stung in the water from all the cuts and scratches."

"You sound pretty lively over the phone."

"You should see me. I'm a mess, honey."

"You ought to take better care of yourself, Sam. You know you haven't provided well enough for the girls and me for you to go off and get yourself killed."

"Hey!" Auer shouted. "How about worrying about me for once? I'm the one who's hurting for once."

"I am worried about you," she said in a more conciliatory tone. "That's why I want you to come home right this minute. Close up the place, and take a cab. If you're that hurt, you should take a cab."

"I can't. I'm just going to spend a few more nights down here. Till things blow over. Drive down tomorrow, and bring my clothes."

"Sam," she said threateningly, "I am going to make fresh mashed potatoes. And a fresh salad. But I am going to serve the roast from last night, with gravy. It's going to be on the table at nine-thirty. If you are not here to eat it, you can just as well stay down there permanently for all I care."

He slammed the phone down. For one second he wished he were Plastic Man, streaking through the telephone wires and emerging through the receiver in Oxford Circle to strangle her.

Their argument made him worse for the remainder of the evening. He asked for little out of life and was denied that little. With the boards up, he missed Sophie Bitko going by and only caught Pauline Kozak for one second through the opened door. Between ringing up sales on his cash register, he was compulsively fondling his new pistol and the switchblade in his back pocket. In just a few hours he had already acquired a bad nervous mannerism.

In the morning his eyes creaked open as the alarm rang. His stitches were smarting and he was sore all over, sore, stiff, bruised. That was some walloping he had taken, and Bunny did not even believe him. His back hurt from the buttons on the naked mattress. He was so exhausted when he flopped into bed last night he had not bothered to lay a sheet down, and just pulled two wool blankets over him. The pistol and switchblade were on the nightstand, handy in case anybody snipped through the barbed wire. He looked at the yellow bricks of the school through the barbed wire crisscrossing the bedroom windows. Strangely, he felt closer to his dear father. How many times had his old man woke up on this rack, stared out at those yellow bricks, and just wished to turn over and sleep. Now he needed a cigarette but was afraid to move, afraid of the pain surging and rushing to fresh sectors. Bracing, Auer reached for his cigarette, and after the pain and stinging lashed through him, he smiled. He could make the day. He was a tough cookie and could make the day.

Shaved and showered, by seven he was completely ready for the postman: the floor was swept, coffee perking, and the supplies in. By seven-twenty he had to concede that Beaumont was permanently lost to the diner.

"Up his," Auer said aloud. "Small loss."

He placed his bricks at the door to enjoy the light snow falling, airy flakes drifting down leisurely and gathering over the grimy clumps of ice. The boards were not affecting him as badly this morning. The fresh wind blowing into the store was invigorating. All of his customers entered stamping their shoes and boots, ruddy and exhilarated, as they cursed the weather. All kinds of encouraging signs. He called Manny's and ordered new fluorescent tubes. Even without windows, by installing a double row of bright lights around the rim of the grocery shelves, his business could be gay and cheery inside.

The brisk weather stimulated appetites: the messenger from Starker's came in with an unusually large lunch order, nineteen sandwiches and twenty-three coffees. All of his counter regulars scarfed down his Friday clam chowder and creamed tuna with noodles. Then the helper from Manny's arrived and worked all afternoon, nailing in fixtures, climbing up and down the ladder, and joking with him about the place looking like a stockade. He liked the animation, and when they snapped on the brilliant new fluorescents, he was curiously pleased by the clash between his white fixtures and the raw boards. Auer raised a finger. Screw the Johnsons. Sam Auer would gut it out.

The euphoria did not wear off till he made a quick trip over to Doc's pharmacy at Seventh and Green Garden in the evening. With his pistol in one jacket pocket and the knife in the other, he hurried through the dirty slush. Doc Fine, though no particular friend of the family, attended all of the Auer funerals. The pharmacist glanced at the bandage peeking out from under his cap and said, "I heard you got jumped, Sam."

"I got in a few, too."

"They get you bad?"

"Nothing broken."

"You want some aspirins?"

Doc raised an eyebrow as Auer brought out five ten-dollar bills and asked for a fifty-dollar money order, made out to Mrs. Bunny Auer.

"For a token and a transfer you can deliver it yourself, Sam."

"You working for the PTC, or you sell money orders?"

"Problems at the hearth."

"Now you're writing a book."

Doc took out the pad of forms from under the counter. "Sure, I sell money orders all the time. They go to Alabama, North Carolina, Kentucky. Except for a few hillbillies, you're the first white man who's asked me for a money order in years."

Auer shrugged. When he had nothing to say, he said nothing.

The pharmacist inserted a sheet of carbon between the forms and lowered his voice. "I had a tip, Sam. You probably know it, but I got this tip. You're right about the Johnsons. At least about the window breaking. About the attack on you, I haven't got firm information yet. I'll let you know."

"Thanks," Auer said indifferently.

"I've had a lot of trouble with the *schlech* myself. Whenever they bring a prescription in, I feel like adding a few drops of arsenic."

"You could do me that favor," Auer said. He went to the magazine rack while the druggist rambled on about his problems with the berrypickers, shoplifting, ten tubes of lipstick stolen a week, people ordering prescriptions and never showing up for them, demanding dangerous drugs without a prescription, ringing his bell in the middle of the night to ask for bandages and adhesive tape. The drug addicts demanding needles, Syrettes, morphine. It was rough on this corner, too. . . .

Auer let him babble and grunted occasionally as he selected the sexiest girlie and adventure magazines from the rack. Some girlie photos and pinups could enliven and camouflage the boards, alleviate some of that starkness. As he flipped the pages, the pictures shocked him. Before the war, such poses would never have been allowed. Whores smiling under their legs and pointing their silk-covered asses at the reader.

He kept five and included an *Ebony* magazine with pictures of sedate tan girls in decent bathing suits. For his *shvartzer* customers. So they shouldn't complain.

"You'll work it out," Doc assured him as he paid for the magazines. "Bunny's a fine girl, and you've got two lovely daughters. I remember when Bunny was a kid, came in here for milkshakes and told me about her crush on you, Sam. She told me how you'd pass her store on Marshall Street with Dutch Radin and your *shaygetz* buddies Zig and Gall, and she'd be sitting outside with her mother and father, hoping you'd give her a break and nod her way. But you never did, and her mother would say never mind, you'd settle down. You were just passing through your wild stage. . . ."

"Very romantic," Auer thought as he returned to the store. Here he had all this romance in his life that he never knew about. He brought out his scissors and Scotch tape and began snipping photos of the women in the most provocative positions and frilliest bloomers. The five magazines provided him with enough photos to cover all of the blank boards. Most of the females had hard, mean, vapid faces, but one girl was so beautiful she hurt him. She gave him a sinking pain in the chest and a wish to die. Roberta. She was a pert brunette in a white slip. An impudent smile. He had accidentally cut off her last name, and all he had was Roberta. He ran his fingers over the glossy paper, caressed her snub nose. It was unfair. A woman had such power over a man, and when he fell into her clutches she really gave it to him.

In spite of a steady flow of kids coming in for Cokes and hamburgers, he closed early to watch the fights from the Garden. As he nestled on the couch, sipping his beer, munching on a salami sandwich, a sonorous belch escaped him. He saluted his reflection in the mirror with the beer bottle. It was a pleasure to enjoy this freedom to belch in peace. Bunny would have made a Hollywood production out of it and ordered him to go to the doctor to see whether he had cancer of the intestines. Perhaps the Johnsons had done him a favor, arranging this vacation for him. About the only thing he missed right now was that half hour after supper when the girls climbed all over him and fought for his attention. That was quite satisfying. They were going to be classy chicks. He was going to send them to Bryn Mawr or Radcliffe, and he would not mind if they were ashamed of him. After all, he had been ashamed of his own father—of his gruff, immigrant ways and thick accent—so he could let his girls be a little ashamed of Sam Auer. They were what it was all about. One thing he would not do: he would never tell them how hard he worked, or how much he sacrificed for them. Kids did not want to hear that crap. You brought a child into the world to love it. Because it became so hard to love another adult human being. So it hardly mattered whether the girls loved back.

Before sleeping, he made another trip into the store. He struck a match and held it up to Roberta. She still hovered before his eyes as he stretched out on the bed, this time with a sheet. There was no comparing her to the other sluts in their laces and girdles in those pinups. It had been six years since he touched another woman, since he was mustered out. He chuckled in the darkness. If he was on a vacation, he should have an adventure. Bunny had accused him of messing around with a tramp down here. That was like practically giving him a license.

He began counting on his fingers, establishing his priorities: Sophie Bitko first, of course. Pauline Kozak. Jeanette Lewis. And there was so much local talent. Maggie May. Peggy Moore. Big Vye if he was feeling brave, and Señora Gomez from Leah's second-floor front. With that purple brassiere. He moistened his lips. What tits.

He slept heavily till a scratching and scraping outside woke him in deepest night. The headlights of a car on Cottonwood Street brightened the shades and gleamed in the tips of the barbed wire, lent a silvery sheen to the steel blade on the nightstand. He would have reached for it but was so exhausted he felt as though he were sewn into a sack. He plummeted back into darkness.

Saturday was his main grocery day. Customers came in for their weekly orders and paid a part of the bill on the books. After their orders the bill was even higher. Four of the five roomers came down to pay their weekly rent and, miraculously, Albert from the third-floor front even made up one week's back rent. Several of the women seemed offended by his collages of pinups, but the men made jokes, went over to examine the fold-outs, studied them hard, as if they were touring the art museum. Barry said, "Hell, Sam. That stuff you hung up there is way better looking than the streets anyway. If I had to be in here, I'd much rather look at this pussy than no schoolyard."

Twinges of jealousy pricked Auer as he saw Barry grinning at Roberta. Roberta was his and his alone.

Later in the afternoon he locked the door and phoned Bunny. It had already become a routine, practically a ritual, with their scripts from a radio serial. The Fibber McGee and Molly Show. She absolutely and positively refused to drive down with fresh clothes. His clean underwear was in his drawer. Moreover, she was running short of cash.

"I sent a money order," Auer explained.

"A what?"

"A money order. Last night. It should get there by Monday."

"I think you've gone crazy, Sam."

"Why not? It's no fun being sane."

"The girls were asking for you. They can't understand what's going on. What am I supposed to tell the girls?"

"Tell them I love them very much and that I'll be home sometime next week. Things should have quieted down by then. Unless you all want to drive down here tomorrow, and we can go out for dinner in the afternoon. To the Ambassador or the Capitol on Girard Avenue."

"I'll do no such thing. You're just looking for another pretext to get me to bring your clothes."

"How come you're so clever about some things and so dense about others?"

It was a triumph of sorts. This time it was Bunny who hung up first.

He closed at ten, rinsed out all his dirty laundry in the bathtub, and headed over to the diner. Zig and Gall were holed up in their usual booth, and Auer could not resist the temptation to show off his pistol and switchblade. He immediately regretted the weakness, as they began kidding him and passed the weapons around to the other customers. Zig started calling him, "Bad-ass Sam, the gun-and-knife man," and they all picked up on it. Yet Auer enjoyed his brief notoriety as they gathered around to hear about the ambush of the lumberyard, and how he took on seven spades with a monkey wrench.

Moony insisted on inviting him to a drink, and they all tramped through the snow to Hymie's Bar at Fourth and Grenoble. It was the same kind of crew but from a younger generation in there, drinking boilermakers and playing the pinball machines and darts for side bets. Auer was not exactly comfortable in there. Zig and Gall were in their middle thirties, just like he was, but they still hung around with these smart-aleck kids in their twenties.

In the back booth the Duke had everybody cracking up with his educated dirty stories where he mixed highfalutin scientific phrases with scummy ideas, and that was all the Duke retained from two years at Temple University. Zig was always trying to imitate the Duke's style but could never carry it off, did not have the education to pull it off. Again Auer was embarrassed as Zig told the crowd in Hymie's about the pistol and switchblade, and he had to bring them out. The chant was picked up: "Bad-ass Sam, the gun-and-knife man." Auer won at darts and wondered what Sheila and Steppie would say about "Bad-ass Sam, the gun-and-knife man." The image of puzzled disapproval on their faces led him to reject the gang's invitation to tag along to Slovak Hall when Hymie's closed at two.

A lull the following week. With all of his bustling, Auer forgot about the Johnsons. They became a vague annoyance beyond the horizon of his immediate concerns. He was mainly worried about sprucing up the face of the store. The naked boards were already warping and smudged dark by the harsh weather. With another month of sleet and storm they would look like shriveled gray driftwood, and his investment was sliding down the drain. He imagined how much a prospective buyer would pay for the "goodwill" evinced by these swelling boards.

Tuesday morning he called Barry over, and after sharp

haggling Barry agreed to help paint the outside of the store for forty dollars. Barry had access to a scaffold and another stepladder. Auer called Manny's and ordered enough paint to cover not only the boarded windows but the surrounding bricks, the sandstone step, the wood framework, the carved cornices, and the entire exterior around to the rear door on Cottonwood. The weather was with them, blustery but dry, and Barry, sober for once, proved to be steady and reliable.

Auer took off whatever time he could to help Barry paint, spread the dropcloth on the pavement, and move the scaffold from position to position. They used stencils to trace "Open for Business" in cream white on the front door and both boarded windows. Barry was extremely careful, taking pride in his work. He motioned often to Fat Grace, seeking her approbation for the splendid job he was doing.

Auer was so pleased with the results that he gave Barry an extra five, and another five to run up to the State Store and bring back a fifth of rye. After a few shots and toasts with Barry, he went outside in his shirtsleeves, crossed Cottonwood to the school, and with his fists on his hips admired the way the blue contrasted so sharply with the white "Open for Business" in neatly blocked letters. He crossed diagonally to Leah's sidewalk and shook his head in appreciation of the notable improvement. His place, with regular glass, was only a rundown luncheonette with flyspecked, cluttered windows. With the royal blue paint it had suddenly acquired character, a distinctive, compelling character. Every driver using Sixth Street craned his neck and was forced to notice the place.

Leah came out and told him it looked alright as a stopgap measure. Bunny, that evening, further dampened his enthusiasm. She said, "That's very nice. You threw more money away painting over your boards. That's really going to fool a buyer. If you could find anybody fool enough to sink money into that quicksand."

"Why do you do this to me?"

"What do I do to you? You sent me a money order. Perhaps what I need is a court order."

"Why do you do this to me?" Auer repeated. "I'm down here fighting for our livelihood, to stay above water. Other women, when their man is on the front lines, when he's surrounded, they're right behind him loading the musket for him. I, when I turn around, instead of finding support, my woman loading my musket, I see a knife upraised for me."

"Suddenly I married Daniel Boone," Bunny said laconically.

"What kind of crack is that?"

"Nothing. I wrote your mother and told her how irrationally you've been acting."

"That's a dirty trick. Why did you want to drag her into this?"

"Don't you think she should know her son is acting like a madman?"

"She can't do anything about this down there. This will only make her sick with worry and spoil her vacation. You know what you are, Bunny? You're a snake. You can't get your way up here, so you have to spit your venom all the way down to Florida."

Another victory of sorts. She clicked off. Those were the rules of the latest game: whoever hung up first had lost.

Auer remained on the sofa and was more determined than ever to make better use of his respite. He deserved a reward for all he had been through. Zig and Gall were encouraging him to hold fast. It was not completely disinterested support, because as they said it they were scarfing down his sandwiches and whiskey, reminiscing about Rita Uzkoff and the good old days. Zig and Gall also agreed that the blue paint job gave more class and character to the store, and Zig had mentioned the possibility of bringing three women around for a party. He had met these three tramps at this cocktail lounge on Girard Avenue, and they might be persuaded to drop in for a small orgy. Both he and Gall had scoffed because Zig was such a terrible bullshitter, but they did not come down too hard, because there was just a chance the Polack might actually have something this time.

On Friday morning it snowed again, accumulating thick and fast in graceful drifts and unsullied planes over the schoolyard and empty lot. He left the front door open, spread newspapers at the entrance, and turned on his double fluorescent tubes. He discovered that he was growing accustomed to the loss of daily peeks at Sophie and Pauline and Mrs. Lewis. Roberta more than compensated for it. He had Roberta and the voluptuous sluts in their merry-widows and red nylons all day long. With luck, Zig might come through with that party in back with those three tramps from Girard Avenue.

In the evening he went to Doc's to send another money order to Bunny. It was again an odd sensation, writing his own address on a form. He felt removed from himself, distant, as when he sent letters to Sixth and Cottonwood from Europe during the war. Doc gave him some more cheap advice, and then Auer headed down Seventh, which had a clearer path through the frozen muck and slush. Next to Shor's taproom, teen-agers were bopping in Hank Morse's candy store. Hank Morse was the first Negro to buy a small business around here. Morse had returned from the Army with an attractive German redhead, and Auer often paused when he passed that candy store to glance at the woman. Instead of Ulla Morse behind the counter, he saw Junior Johnson bopping near the jukebox. There was a plaster cast on his left forearm.

During that ambush the boy that got the wrench on the forearm was lean and lanky, just like Junior Johnson, or so it appeared in all the confusion and darkness. Auer glared at the scene. He had been through all this suffering, was still all stitched up, with a scar on his skull, and there was Junior Johnson, sipping on a Coke and getting his cast autographed by a pretty black girl in a fuzzy blue sweater. She must have written something amusing, because Johnson showed the autograph to the two boys in suede jackets and everybody laughed. Auer reached up and touched the scar knitting over his scalp. He was alive merely because a Good Samaritan in a Pontiac had stopped to honk his horn. Otherwise, those seven-against-one with their club and chains would have beaten him to death. Now they could have such a good time on Friday night as though nothing had happened.

Worry spread across Hank Morse's face as he saw Sam Auer enter his candy store. Morse knew Auer was not dropping in for a pack of fried pork skins. He said, "How's it going, Sam? I'd appreciate it if there weren't any trouble in my establishment."

"It's all cool, Hank. Not going to be any trouble. Just want to talk to somebody." He turned to Junior Johnson, who had managed to ignore the intrusion and was pretending to study the selection on the jukebox. "All right, Johnson. You know I'm here. You can come off it."

Johnson spun around in his loose, floppy cubavera, with the sleeves rolled up past the cast, and snapped, "So what's all that, I'm here? What's all that action—I'm here?"

"I'd like to know where you got that cast, boy."

"At the hospital. You know? You need a cast, you can buy one right up there at the Northern Liberties, Mister Sam."

"Don't give me any of that crap," Auer said, advancing. "You tell me how you got that cast or you might need one for the other arm."

The dancers between them withdrew to leave an open field. Johnson tossed his head diffidently. "Sheee. What's that to you? That ain't none of your business. I slipped and hurt my arm on the ice on Monday. You can ask anybody around here. James here took me to the Northern Liberties Hospital. You can ask him. Didn't you, James? In your own car."

"That's right," James Hughes said quickly. Auer waved his arm to dismiss the witness and said, "No need for both of you to lie. I think you broke it last Wednesday night on Grenoble Street. I think your arm was hit by a monkey wrench."

"Oh, man," Johnson groaned, denying the ridiculous accusation. "Last Wednesday night I was at the movies. I was right up there at the Astor, and we seen *Sands of Iwo Jima*. James here was with me. Wasn't you, James?"

James Hughes nodded sincerely. Auer said, "Sure, he was probably with you all the way. When you broke my windows, and all you little bastards jumped me."

"Man," Johnson shouted in anguish, "I wasn't in on that. You can ask my father and mother."

"Yeah, and if I believed them I'd have more holes in my head."

"You calling my father and mother a liar?" Johnson said and stepped forward menacingly.

Auer flicked at the dirty cast, covered with initials and scrawled obscenities. It was a light movement, as if he were flicking off a fly, but the other teen-agers moaned in protest, and Johnson shrieked, "You hurt my arm! You hurt my arm, you sonofabitch. Get off me, I'll kill you!"

Folding his arms across his chest, Auer sniffed, "Yeah, you're a real tough guy. When it's seven on one with clubs and chains, you're fucking Beau Jack."

Backing up behind the pinball machine, Johnson said, "That wasn't me. That was them guys from Callowhill Street. The Ninth Street gang. I can't mess around no more. I'm out on probation, and I mess around they'll send me back to the farm."

"The Ninth Street gang, huh? Well, you tell your father that I'm gonna hold him personally responsible for the future exploits of the Ninth Street gang. If the Ninth Street gang is once again seen on Sixth Street, all kinds of shit will fly at #424 Seventh Street."

"How we gonna hold them over there?" Johnson complained.

"Never mind. Tell your father to come around and see me, talk to me, man to man. I want to thrash this out and put an end to this mess."

The crowd around him murmured in anger as Auer stopped by the cash register to talk to Morse.

"I'm sorry to barge into your place like this, Hank, and cause this ruckus, but I have to put an end to this shit."

"I know how you feel, Sam. My windows ain't made of steel, either. Sorry about your troubles."

On the way over to Hymie's Bar, Auer zipped up his leather jacket and concluded that Morse was probably sincere in that expression of sympathy. As a *shvartzer*, Morse might want to stick by his brothers, but as a businessman he had to realize that once the rocks started flying nobody was immune. They really gave it to each other. The cleaning ladies getting off the #47 trolley on Green Garden Avenue, after a day of scrubbing floors uptown, were always getting their purses snatched, always by another *shvartzer*.

Zig and Gall were in the rear booth at Hymie's. He told them about his run-in with Junior Johnson, and Zig reached across the table and gave him a supercilious pat on the shoulder.

"That's my boy—hard-ass Sam, the gun-and-switchblade man. That's the way I like to hear you sound off, Sambo. You must stand up to these coons and say, "Blivvah, don't fuck with my bazaar. My family's been trading that Samuel Sandler salami for two generations, and I root for the Birmingham Barons, so stay peaceful, or I'll piss on your pickled pig's feet."

Zig's handsome Slavic features dissolved with laughter. He thought he was hilarious and tossed his head till his blond pompadour hung loosely over his ear. The dart players came over to enjoy the tirade, and Zig snapped his fingers at the owner and shouted, "Hyman! Hey, Hyman! Set up my man Sambo with a double of your choicest slivovitz. Sambo just told off some junior nightrider and needs a bracer before he heads back to the stockade. Old Sambo left Bunny and the bambinos safe up north and painted the shop in blue-and-white Palestine colors, bought himself a snub-nosed .38 and a switchblade for his close-in work, so the man needs fortification, Hyman. Put it on my man Gall's tab."

They all thought Zig was a riot tonight. Auer sipped at the double shot Hymie served him, and Zig made a thrusting motion with his forearm. "Now you listen to the straight word, Sambo Auer, because I shit you not. You gotta hang in there, Gunga Din. You are not just protecting the mortgage on that shop. You are carrying the flag for all us settlers who will not let the invading Ashantis drive us off the turf."

Encouraged by the laughter of the kids around the bowling machine, Zig kept on mouthing off long after his inspiration had run out. Auer grew irritated as his buddy forced the wild talk without producing too much humor. It was Gall who finally broke in and said, "Have you got the goods, man? It's Friday night, Zig. What's with those three snatch you've been promising?"

"Not tonight," Zig answered expansively, as if it were only a temporary setback. "I chatted with them three pigs this afternoon, and they are locked into a pecuniary proposition, probably with three great Danes at a B'nai Brith smoker. But they were extremely sympathetic to Sambo's case when I told them how he wasn't getting any nooky lately because his regular supply refused to drive downtown with laundered BVD's. They said they'd try to catch us next Wednesday."

Next Wednesday. Even as a kid, Zig was perpetually promising women, parties, deals that never came through. Now he was a part of the inventory here and at the diner, but he claimed to be leading this fabulous existence where he was constantly making cocktail waitresses, meeting boxers and celebrities, catching shows and nightclub acts. Nobody could figure out when all this was supposed to take place because Zig was either in here or at the diner every night of the week.

Reconciled to the fact that Zig had nothing lined up, Auer paid for one round of drinks and trudged the three blocks back to his corner. The TV offered nothing but garbage, and he felt lonely and restless as he undressed. Simmons coughed upstairs. Every two minutes, like Chinese water torture. Auer shivered in his cocoon of blankets and felt a tingling and soreness in his throat, hot flushes at the nape of the neck. The last cigarette he smoked had a funny flavor, and that meant for sure he had a cold coming on. He was peeved at Zig for exciting him with promises of free whores coming in here and stripping down in his parlor.

There was squabbling outside, in front of Grace's. Car doors slamming. People arguing about going into Grace's or driving over to Jersey and continuing to drink in a club. More car-door slamming. He heard Big Vye threatening to punch Barry in the mouth if he did not leave her man George alone. Shouts of "Fuck you," and "Get the hell upstairs!"

He trembled with his fever and decided that it was really horrible down here. Tomorrow, Sunday, he could go home. Face the music. But it was a shame that he had not taken advantage of his temporary freedom. Tomorrow night he could go over to Zacky's or the Green Room, and for ten bucks he could bring a woman back here. But he would not do it. He would go home. Why desecrate the bed where his parents had slept for forty years? Jeanette Lewis would be another matter. That would be no desecration. He closed his eyes to sleep.

During the night he twisted over once and reached for his switchblade. A chipping, sloshing noise out on Cottonwood disturbed him. The murmuring and scratching continued, but just as he was about to rise and investigate the commotion it ceased. He lit a cigarette, ears straining, and decided that it must have been the snow plow or the Sanitation Department arriving early. Tomorrow he would go home.

In the morning Auer sensed something wrong the second he drew the bolt and attempted to pull open his boarded door. There was a momentary tug of resistance, a cracking sound, and his eyes widened with horror as he saw the black, sticky asphalt mixed with dirt and pebbles that had been dumped on his front step.

A groan escaped him, and his eyes instantly clouded with tears. He jumped over the goop on his step, and it took him a second to recover his balance on the ice. He shuddered at the mess they had made and had the dry heaves. He would have vomited if there was anything in him.

The front of his store was a horrible smeared blotch stretching all the way around to the side door on Cottonwood. He was trembling, but not from the cold. The Johnsons had thrown buckets of a weak yellow paint solution against the boarded windows, tossed more buckets of black tar over the yellow slop, and the whole mess had been smeared and mixed together with rags. Some of them were still stuck and frozen stiffly in the mess, giving the effect of toilet paper in the droppings of a sick man. He looked down, and the mucous-colored paste had stained the ice where the wall met the pavement.

For a moment he was dizzy with shock. He felt empty, as though he were a shell or a balloon that could float away into the white, frigid sky beyond the school roof. They had defiled and ruined his beautiful blue paint job. Since dawn the drivers racing down Sixth had been gaping at this nauseating babyshit splattered over his gleaming blue paint job.

With nothing in his mind, Auer went to his back apartment, put on his leather jacket, and picked up his pistol and knife.

Leah was already opened, preparing her urn of coffee, as he entered the store, She said, "I was going to call and wake you up, Sam, but I thought I'd better let you sleep late. I knew you'd feel bad enough when you saw it."

"How much do you charge for baseball bats?"

"Have you called the police?" she said, as though she had not heard the question.

"I've already called the police. For a few nights they cruise around, and then they get bored with the same block."

"Sam, I'll call the police. I'll call Harry Lipofsky. Lipofsky will light a fire under Doheny, and you'll get better protection."

"What do you get for baseball bats?"

"It's not the season. I don't sell baseball bats when it isn't the season."

"It's the season," Auer said. He pulled a five-dollar bill

from his pocket and dropped it on the counter as he grabbed a baseball bat from her window.

Leah rushed out of the store after him, calling for him to come back as he marched up Cottonwood with the bat over his shoulder. Her son Maddy was chipping a path through the ice. He straightened up and said, "I saw what they. . . ."

Auer brushed by, and Maddy, after hesitating for a few seconds, ignored his mother's frantic motioning for him to return to the store and followed Auer up Cottonwood.

Smoke rose from a bonfire of broken furniture in front of the icehouse, and Auer was taking short, practice half-swings, as if loosening up before stepping into the batting cage. Sidonia and Bowes were warming their hands over the fire while two boys loaded the wagon, covering the cakes of ice with brown burlap. Maddy stayed at the corner in front of Shor's as Auer marched down Seventh. Bowes and Sidonia nodded to Maddy, who was a popular boy in the neighborhood. The three of them watched Auer climb the steps at #424 and shook their heads in agreement.

A full minute passed with Auer pressing down on the buzzer. He saw it was futile and suddenly stepped back, reared back, and took a wild swing at the tin plate on the door. The hollow explosion reverberated up and down the block. Green and yellow shades were going up. Roomers were poking their heads out the windows. Auer took another swing with the bat, and the metal dented. He cupped his hands to his mouth and yelled, "Johnson, you yellah cocksucker, come on down and bring your fucking little bastards with you."

A window screeched open on the third floor. A brown hand came out holding a teakettle. Auer jumped back as a stream of boiling water spilled down on him. Most of it missed, and the steam hissed noisily on the iced pavement.

Auer rushed up the steps bellowing, "You black motherfucker, I will kill your ass." He began to swing in a steady rhythm, like a logger felling a tree, with the sound of metal bending and wood splintering. He was aiming lower, trying to smash the doorknob. Tramps had gathered on the street to enjoy the action and the pounding of the bat against the door, like the cannonading of distant artillery. Auer was taking huge, sweeping cuts, had the door loose on its hinges, till with one last swing he miscalculated and the tip hit the bricks, snapping the bat off at the handle.

The street was silent as he examined the splintered handle. He chuckled and tossed it away. His eyes were glazed as he came up Seventh. People moved out of his path. Not a word was said as he went by. They granted him the respect given to those who are beyond words or reason. People on Seventh had seen men with these eyes before and knew what they meant.

PART THREE

Those ghastly stains on the boarded-up windows were potent advertising. During the month of December, his store was crowded with many unfamiliar supporters. For a while the business flourished. Word spread for miles around that Sam Auer was "holding out against the niggers." The abominations on his walls and step became a badge of honor. People would walk six blocks or more to patronize his place or drive down from as far away as Kensington or Lehigh Avenue.

He had a new clientele: members of the congregation from the Baptist church, hillbillies from across Green Garden, Poles from York Avenue, the Irish from Oriana Street, bums from the rooming houses up Sixth. They flocked to his store and winked at him, gave him victory signs. Workers from the Starker cabinet factory—Italians from South Philly and old Germans from Jersey—those with cars, men who had been strictly lunch customers, suddenly made large twenty- and thirty-dollar grocery orders to show their support. At night he received calls from strangers who wanted to rant about the "niggers" for hours. It seemed that every freak and racist nut in town had heard about the battle at Sixth and Cottonwood and wanted to drop by and spew out his hatred. There was even an anonymous contribution in the mail, a ten-dollar bill with an unsigned note full of Ku Klux Klan language that gave Sam a chill.

That was the sour touch. At the height of that brief and unnatural prosperity, he felt queasy at the music of the cash register. He had read enough science fiction and novels to realize that these grim, embittered people were converting him into a symbol of their frustration, were using him to strike back at the *shvartzers*. And he also realized that these Ukrainians who walked all the way down from Glendolph and Fairmount or these Irish who drove down from Fishtown were the kind of people who had little love for Jews either. It just happened to be the Negroes who were up against it this month. The Romanians from Third Street who would walk through the sleet to patronize him would be just as delighted to participate in a pogrom. There was no elation as he bustled around the store, filling out their large orders. It was no fun being a symbol. He was bothered by the way most Negroes in the neighborhood stopped entering his store. They never even looked at him anymore. They knew what was going on, why cars were showing up from Lehigh Avenue and Eighteenth and Green, people making special trips to shop at his dump. It disturbed Auer. He had been raised here, went to school with many of these Negroes, regarded many as friends, and now he was almost an invisible man when he walked up Cottonwood. Except for a few like Barry or Bowes who had exhausted all other lines of credit, no self-respecting Negro would enter his establishment.

The prosperity did not last long. January came, a cold and bitter January, and the support faded. People might make those gestures two or three times, but put enough ice and snow on the streets and they returned to their regular habits. The workers from Starker's did not repeat their large grocery orders; their wives did the shopping in their own neighborhoods. Worse, many of the new customers he acquired were just as bad with their bills as his *shvartzers* had ever been. There were shrewd types exploiting the situation. They had latched onto this racial thing because they had used up their credit in every other store in the area.

February arrived, and Auer felt stained. He was walking down Glendolph Street, returning from his nightly coffee at the diner, and he felt he had been contaminated by his ordeals, and more so by the way this mess had temporarily turned to his advantage. All that talk he had heard and spouting off about the "nigger" gave him the sensation of having bathed in a toilet these last few months.

In front of the Kozak house Pauline was chatting with

Maddy Dobry and his buddy Steve Kraft. Auer wondered why she still bothered with kids. The Kozaks were moving out. Mrs. Kozak said they were moving to a duplex up in Frankford.

"Hi, Sam," Pauline said.

"Hi, kid."

The boys nodded, and as Auer reached the corner he heard the three kids laugh. He was becoming the neighborhood crank, a character. Bad-ass Sam, the gun-and-knife man. And Maddy was a wiseacre, one of those Central High wise guys with a flip remark for everybody.

There were sounds of stumbling against furniture and angry shouts in the curtained storefront apartment at Cottonwood. Auer grimaced. His new customers, the Colemans, were living it up in there, knocking each other around. Trash, white trash, in the old Radin store. Everything was changing around here. The Baptist Church across the street had just been sold to a Negro congregation. They would take occupancy soon, and that would mean another slice off his business.

Auer hesitated for a moment. Yesterday Marge Coleman had intimated that he should drop by—for a sandwich or a drink. He glanced back. The three kids were watching him, and he had to continue on his way. There was something shameful about sniffing around a Marge Coleman. She reminded him of how once in Europe, when he was feeling low, he went with a huge fat whore and was disgusted with himself afterward.

Back in his apartment Auer turned on the television and thought about her offer again. In the afternoon she had waited till the place cleared out so she could chitchat with him. She lingered over her coffee and positioned herself on his first stool so that he had to brush by her when he went behind the counter. And he noted that she was careless about the way her dress crept up over her heavy thighs. He was washing his dishes and Marge said, "You know, I admire you, Sam."

"That's nice to hear."

"I've always claimed that you people were goddamn

smart. You're not one of the smart ones, but I like your guts. Where I come from a woman likes a man with plenty of guts. Those useless boozehounds I'm cooking for wouldn't have stood up against the niggers the way you did."

"I'm sort of tired of the subject."

"It must get pretty lonely for you down here without the missus."

"It gets lonely," he agreed. "But I don't miss the aggravation."

Marge toyed with the hem of her skirt. She scratched at a brown imperfection above her knee. Seeing him stare she grinned at him coyly, and her grin became bolder as she said, "I can't see how Bunny would let a nice guy like you alone down here. A handsome hunk of man like you, Sam. I'd never leave you alone down here if I was Bunny. Not with all these loose women around here." Marge dimpled girlishly. "I've always heard that you people treat your women kinda' nice. Especially on the money side of it."

For one insane second he had been tempted to lock his door and invite her back to the apartment, but he sensed she would want about a week of free groceries for one quick roll back there. Her ponderous breasts were very available in the loose blouse, and he could have just reached out and cupped them, but he stopped. The woman was simply too oily. She needed to be blotted dry with a slice of white bread. He began to add up her bill, and the disappointment spread across her face. To get her revenge she waddled out with an accentuated hitch of her hips, as if to taunt him with what he was missing.

Now he missed it. He sipped at his beer and glared dumbly at the television screen, the women skating around the roller derby rink, hardfaced broads bumping and elbowing each other, snarling and grimacing on the hazy screen. Now he regretted it, regretted not having locked the door and brought Marge back here. Auer chuckled. Eventually he regretted all of his rational impulses. In the big load of novels he brought home from

Leary's used-book store, all the characters were spontaneous, and here he was spending ninety percent of his time thinking about missed opportunities.

The telephone rang. He let it ring. That would be Bunny, and he knew exactly what she had to say, so why bother to listen to it. For a month now she had been harping on the divorce, how he had deserted her, the neighbors in Oxford Circle gossiping how his daughters were asking for him, the letters his mother wrote from Florida stating that she would straighten everything out once she returned home. Even the ringing took on a whining, insistent quality. It reminded him of her voice: Radio Red Flag. He envisioned her frustration at the other end of the line, all that exasperation up in Oxford Circle.

On the fifteenth ring he picked up the receiver.

"You don't answer the phone anymore?" Bunny began. "So what happened? I'm cut down to forty dollars? Your children don't have to eat anymore?"

He was silent, and Bunny said, "You've got nothing to say for yourself. Your family doesn't rate anymore? You want us to take in washing up here?"

"Why not?" Auer asked calmly. "That's what happens around here. The colored women don't treat their men right, the men take off, and they take in washing. Why do you get an exemption?"

"If you have no feelings for me, think about your daughters."

"That's all I think about. If it were just you, I'd have sent forty scorpions in the envelope, and not forty dollars. Business has been terrible this last month. Don't you understand?"

"I don't understand anything anymore, Sam. I think you're ill. I've talked to your mother and sister, and they tell me they can't get through to you either. I think you must be going out of your mind down there."

"If I am, it's no wonder. Suddenly you're so hot and heavy on the line with my mother and sister. Money is in short supply, so you have to make all kinds of long-distance calls to my mother in Florida and my sister Sylvia in California. Before you couldn't stand her, she had a big mouth, and now you have to make ten-dollar calls to California."

"I thought maybe Sylvia could talk some sense to you."

"How could she talk sense to me? She's a moron, too."

"Tonight I'm a moron? Last week it was honey and darling, and you were practically on your knees, tried to rape me."

"Yes, precisely. If you had half a brain and behaved like a human being, I'd be up in Oxford Circle this very minute, and you could be nagging me up there. If you had half a brain, you would have taken my hand, gone to the bedroom with me, pulled up your dress, and we could have made love and made peace between us."

"That's all you were worried about? I drive all the way down there, had to pay for a baby-sitter, for a serious discussion about our future, the future of our children, and all you could think to do was start grabbing and pawing at me."

This time she won. He hung up. Two points for Bunny. With nervous, jerky movements, he ripped the cellophane wrapper from a fresh pack of Luckies. The Roller Derby women were still circling the track with their phony ferocity, knocking each other against the rails. He glared at the telephone, anticipating another ring. It was woman's weapon. God gave them tits and asses, and the AT&T supplied them with the telephone.

He winced as it rang again. Touching the humid plastic was a detestable sensation. This was their chief means of torture. His mother calling collect from Florida; Sylvia calling from Los Angeles. Thank God he was on such bad terms with Jerry. But everybody else had a horn in his ear. Uncle Lou calling. Uncle Joe. Even the rabbi called and wished to make an appointment. The *shmuck* rabbi with his dumpy wife and faggy kids does not wish to interfere but he wishes to make an appointment. Nobody called and said, "Hey, Sam, I've got two tickets for the Warriors game." The telephone was mostly for wives, bill collectors, and idiots.

Auer reached down and wrapped the phone wire around his

fist. There was not one person in this world he wished to hear from again. He tugged, and relief flowed up his arm as the infuriating racket ceased. Silence descended upon his parlor like a messenger of death. There had been another flow in his groin, almost a sexual sensation, when that wire was tugged from its socket. It felt as though a limb was amputated and the severed nerves were still tingling in the ether.

He was not certain why, but it seemed that he had done something which set him apart from other men, a deed bordering on the sacrilegious. Nobody else he knew was capable of tearing the wires out of the wall like that, cutting off his links with the outside. It was like crossing some kind of Rubicon with a hazy destination. He let the wire slip from his fingers to the floor.

The following evening, toying with the unraveling threads of the wire, he momentarily regretted ripping it from the wall. There were still two voices he wished to hear: Sheila's and Stephanie's. He traced the wire slowly across his lips, kissing his daughters by a strange remote control.

Stretched out flat on the sofa, he stared up at the ceiling and remembered the hours he had spent on this sofa as a child. The house was sagging, and the cracks were so much deeper. In those days the ceiling, with its white paper pasted over rough plaster, was his own personal, huge, square universe. It was a great rectangular ocean with continents, islands, peninsulas, and archipelagos ringing the landmasses. As a child, sprawled in this spot, he imagined that he was an explorer in an open sailboat, upside down, crossing these broad white seas and reaching dangerous, mysterious shores. He gave romantic names like Mylania and Saharun to all the splotches and figures created by the fissures up there. Sometimes he reversed the geography: the seas became the lands, and what had been islands became huge lakes.

There were tears in his lashes, and Auer spoke out loud over the television static: "I don't want to do this, God. I'll try to be a good father and a good provider. I'll try to pay the mortgage and send fifty dollars every week. I swear to you that I will never let my little girls suffer. I feel like a louse for abandoning them, but you only gave me one life and I can't take Bunny anymore. Any pain, any misery, any accidents or illnesses you might have in store for my girls—give them to me, I'll take them all, but don't make me go back."

Saturday came, and he had sixty-two dollars in cash. Sending Bunny fifty meant asking for another extension with his wholesalers. He was on the downward spiral, from down to further down. As his grocery business petered out, with hardly any Negroes coming in, he often failed to order certain items. They would be just the items his customers asked for, and that would be another customer lost, one more for Leah or Red Newman. One by one, all of his steadies were dropping off.

He sent Bunny the fifty and immediately regretted the rashness. But after sealing the envelope, he was too ashamed to ask Doc for another form and ten dollars back. With the remaining twelve dollars in his pocket, he strolled over to Hymie's for a beer. The crowd greeted him with the same, "Bad-ass Sam, the gun-and-knife man." It irritated him. He wondered how these scrounges could go on and on, never getting bored with themselves, drinking the same drinks, playing the same records to death on the jukebox, cursing when they tilted the pinball machine, using the same nicknames: Zig's younger brother had to be "Zig Two," and Gall's "Gall the Man," and Sam Auer was now and forevermore "Bad-ass Sam, the gun-and-knife man."

He drank his beers and kidded back, but they made him feel old in Hymie's. They talked about boxers, street fights, barroom brawls, and never threw a punch. They yakked about broads and went on for hours about Pauline Kozak's legs or black Maggie May's figure, the days when Rita Uzkoff gave them hand jobs in the front row of the Astor Theater, sex all the

time—and except a whore they paid for, they got laid maybe
once a year.

Zig started up with his three tramps again. According to
Zig, they were still hot to trot but were having difficulties fitting
a freebee into their tight schedules. Gall said maybe they would
not be needed at all. He had talked to McGloughlin, the real boss
down at the union hall, and McGloughlin said that seamen were
needed for the long run to Korea, the long haul across the
Pacific. It meant lots of overtime, dangerous-duty pay east of
Saipan, and Gall prattled on about geisha girls, communal
baths, tricky massages where they tickled the balls, and the
chance to see whether it was really horizontal. Gall was going to
fix it up. Zig would start out on deck as an O.S., and Sam could
sign on as a messman or second cook. Auer just stared at him.

March blustered down Sixth Street wet and windy, and
Auer hardly seemed to care that his business was going to pot.
Every week there were more legal documents from Bunny for
him to sign: insurance papers, deeds, titles, mortgage papers,
court decrees. He signed them all without reading the fine print.
The legal documents were exactly like his telephone; they
never contained anything he wished to read, hear, or know
about. His blank forms arrived from the Internal Revenue Service, and he tore the envelope up, smiled as the pieces fluttered
into his garbage can. Let them hire the accountants and calcu-
late how much he owed and send him a bill. He would not even
mind paying the interest and fines, but he would not let them
steal the hours from his life, stick their hands in his pocket, and
give his earnings away to the bums in front of Shor's, the scum
in Zacky's, the parasites in the Green Room, and all the whores
across the street fucking all afternoon and producing more
bastards for the relief rolls. He hoped an IRS agent showed up,
so he could check out Lou Katz's .38. If they locked him up in
jail, he would no longer have this weight on his shoulders, no
longer have to think, make decisions, meet responsibilities.

He sent Bunny her money order every Saturday night. It meant he would be short for his bills on Monday morning, but he was fascinated with the process. He was sinking, eating into his capital, and was an interested observer studying this curious form of self-destruction. He smiled when he saw Marge Coleman enter the store. That was the residue of the new clientele of his great prosperity in December, when he had all that support to "hold out against the niggers." She was carrying a slice of home-baked apple pie. Maybe she would also have something against her hundred-dollar outstanding bill.

"You like apple pie, Sam? Them boozehounds down there were going to eat the whole thing, but I reserved a slice for you. It's still warm."

"Looks pretty good, Marge. Smells good, too."

"I thought you needed something to cheer you up. You've been looking so run-down lately."

"I am," he agreed. "Very." He added a tired wheeze to evoke more sympathy.

"I hate to see such a nice guy like you get a raw deal. Y'know, Hazleton, where I come from, we know how to treat a good man right."

Auer was amused by the hypocrisy. He had heard this woman outcurse a crew of swabbies behind the curtains of that storefront apartment. And now her voice was like taffy.

"I'll bet it's been a long time since you had a hot, home-cooked meal," Marge murmured. Her breasts pressed into his back as she leaned over him to put the dish of apple pie on the counter. She gave off an odor of pomades and talcum powder over dried sweat, but it had been months since he touched a woman.

"I usually eat what I make for my lunch trade. It's not much fun cooking for yourself alone."

"I know. It must be terrible. You should come over to our place sometimes. Everybody likes my roast chicken and dumplings."

From the shrewd glint in her eyes, Marge was offering more than chicken and dumplings. Auer pursed his lips, as though considering the invitation, and Marge said, "And if you don't like my cooking, maybe you'd like one of my daughters'."

"Which one?" he blurted out quickly and was immediately embarrassed by the way he bit her hook.

"Joanie's . . . or maybe Charlene's?"

"I thought Joan was in jail," Auer said dubiously.

"Nah," Marge sniffed. "She was sprung Tuesday. They didn't have nothing on Joanie. They couldn't make it stick."

Marge helped herself to a loaf of bread, five tins of sardines, a jar of olives, and two cans of peanuts as he ate her apple pie, and then she brushed by him, a good brush with the hip, as she got a bag from under his counter.

"Think about that invitation, Sam."

"Yeah, I will. Sounds nice."

"Put these on the bill, will you?"

"I'll mark it down."

Marge stunned him by abruptly spinning around and posing in the doorway, giving him a languid gaze as though she were Rita Hayworth with a rose in her teeth. It was hilarious and creepy, yet it stirred him. A bleak sun gleamed through her flimsy dress, outlining her strong legs. That sight bothered him for the rest of the afternoon. He found it irritating that even a raunchy, unappealing woman like Marge Coleman had the power to disturb him and take advantage of him.

Zig and Gall rang his side doorbell at ten. Auer observed that, as usual, their hands were empty. He made hoagie sandwiches for everybody and drank a beer while they finished off his Seagram's. They watched the fights on television, moaned and hissed at the slow jabbing and shuffling from Madison Square Garden, and reminisced about their own battles in the schoolyard. Gall once again bragged about the afternoon he dropped Solly Radin with one punch after a basketball game at Christ's Church. Auer smiled behind his beer can, recalling the night the taxi driver drove him down here from Oxford Circle and bragged about how he decked Solly up at Ludlow schoolyard. Now Solly was a rich dentist in Mount Airy and crapped on all of them.

"You think you're still in shape?" Gall asked. "Can you still go, Sam?"

Auer flexed his bulging biceps as an answer. He knew he could pin either of these two bimbos to a wall, but he reached down to smack his gut. "I don't know. I'm no fullback anymore. They'd have to play me as stationary guard."

"Hell, man. You'd better get with it. I've been talking to McGloughlin, and McGloughlin says things should be breaking pretty soon. We might be on our way to Japan, Sambo. You've got to be able to take care of yourself out there. If you're a messman, those characters out there will give you *mucho* shit. Half them guys get like old women about their food on long trips, griping all the time, shoving dishes back. If the cook screws up a meal, you catch all the shit, not the cook. Zig and me will be around to give a hand, but you'll have to pull your part on the line, Sambo."

Zig sat up. "That's right, Sambo. The Three Musketeers. All for one, and all up theirs. Phhfft." Zig made a nasty noise and thrust out his forearm stiffly. "The Three Musketeers from the Green Garden Diner out there on the seven wide seas."

Auer compared the size of his meaty fist to Zig's. He was amused by the way Zig sat erect to hide his thickening torso, and the way Gall sought to tuck his soft belly under his belt. All three of them were washed up, and this palaver about brawling on a ship was silly. What would Sheila and Stephanie say about their father rolling around on a deck? He had no illusions. Any kid in halfway good shape could pick him apart.

Zig indicated the screen with his chin. "Look at them slouches, Sam. They think they're wrestlers. You ought to go that route. You can deck yourself out with a blue-and-white robe with a Star of David on the back and come on strong at the

Arena as 'Battling Auer, the Hebrew Whale.' You're getting big enough. They'll just bounce off that pouch you're sporting, and maybe you can get Manischewitz Wineries to sponsor your career.''

Auer was close to snapping back about their own porkiness, but he let Zig ramble on about his future career as a pro wrestler, the big gates he could draw at the Arena. Auer wished they would just get out. He was reading a good book, *Smoke* by Turgenev, and wanted to get back to it. Lately he had been reading Russian novels like peanut butter. He glanced around, and his parlor was a mess. Maybe once a week he made an effort to straighten up back here, but the three rooms were musty with the lingering sourness of unwashed ashtrays and used air. It hit him, when he came in from the winds of the street, that his apartment had come to smell like the hallway of #424 the day little Brenda Jackson opened the door for him.

Zig was rinsing his teeth with a sip of the Seven-and-Seven. His broad face brightened with a sneer. ''Yeah, Sambo. I was conversing with those three tramps, and they swore they're coming through this time. Next Sunday. They cleaned up at a convention in Atlantic City, and now they're inclined to spread some charity. I promised food, so maybe Sambo can whip us up a little roast, with some cool red wine. . . .''

''Right,'' Gall agreed. ''First the feast and then the fucking.''

''Slow, boy,'' Zig commanded in his superior tone. ''Whoa, you know how the deal works with these tramps. If they are tramps all week long, they have to be treated like the Queen of the Cherry Festival on Sunday night. Finesse, if you're capable of it, you Irish crotchgrabber.''

''Have you ever seen these women?'' Auer asked Gallagher, breaking in on the tirade.

Gall was about to exclaim ''Yes'' when he twisted around and stared questioningly at Zig. ''No, I ain't seen them, but what's that supposed to mean? Zig's got them lined up, ain't he?''

"Does he? I would hardly believe them if I saw them now."

Zig, face darkening, pointed his thumb at his chest and said, "What are these strange noises, Sambo? What is this you are coming up with?"

"You know how long you've been stringing us along with your three tramps, Zig? Since December. And that's no lie. You started this B.S. back in December. And since December you've been sponging around here and handing out your pathetic B.S."

"Man!" Zig's cheeks were crimson, and his brow reddening under his blond pompadour. "That's an ingrate for you. Me and Gall thought we were doing you a favor, coming in here to keep you company. You think it was easy to put up with the stench of this pigpen? With that store boarded up and you wallowing back here, it's a wonder the municipal manure department doesn't throw a padlock on this coop. And this is the thanks we get? I was going to arrange three women, and you turn around and spray your skunkshit on us."

"Three women!" Auer scoffed. "I'll bet you almost believe it yourself by now. If you know three women, it's your mother and two fat aunts. You might even believe you have three women lined up. I'll tell you what happened. Probably one time you talked to three women up on Girard Avenue, and since then you've built this whole thing up in your mind. Nothing's changed, Zig. You pulled this same shit when you were a kid. Always copping out with the excuses."

Both guests shot up, blanching. Auer smiled up at them, almost hoping they would attack. It came to him very clearly that he and Zig were great lifelong friends who had probably despised each other since kindergarten.

"Have you ever heard such crap?" Zig asked Gall. He was shaking his head as if he had finally perceived the depths of mankind's baseness. "We do this slob a favor, we waste our valuable time in this pigsty, and he's been sweating it out because he thinks we ate too many of his greasy sandwiches and drank his cheap whiskey? Man, Sambo. You shall bring your cash register in here and keep a running tab on your invites."

Gall opened the side door, and his face was rubbery with confusion. He mumbled, "Yeah, Sam, that's pretty low."

"You're fuckin-A right it's low," Zig said, still nodding as if absorbing the full impact of this treachery. "C'mon, Gall, let's blast out of this outhouse before we choke on the air. The guys over at Hymie's will be interested to hear what a cheap prick Sambo turned out to be."

Auer gave them a mocking salute. "Shoot down there, Zig. If you need free booze, go suck Hymie's bar rag."

Zig snarled and slammed the door.

The humming resounded for several seconds, and there was a sudden roar from the crowd on the television screen. Auer closed his eyes and wondered how he could have been buddies with those two scrounges for so many years when they really hated each other's guts all this time. Gall probably despised Zig, too, probably would like to kill him. Force of habit had to be the conclusion. Probably most marriages and friendships stuck from force of habit, and a man could go from city to city, street to street, and have a new wife and different friends in each place, and it would make no difference at all. Probably all the books and movies where people were tied and locked and knotted to each other were all lies. He was supposed to care about so many things but, except for his two daughters, he would not give a damn if they dropped atom bombs all over the place.

Without Zig and Gall sponging every night, he began closing at nine and took long walks with the pistol and switchblade in his jacket pockets. Invariably, he went by the Johnson house on Seventh Street. Not once could he catch Johnson outside. The Negro berrypickers watched Auer pass with a dull glint of anticipation in their eyes. A rainy April began, but not even the heavy downpours could hold him in that parlor after a day in the gloom and artificial brightness of the store. Some evenings he wandered aimlessly, and other nights he left the store with a specific destination in mind. He trudged down Sixth to Lombard for a hot dog with mustard and sauerkraut at Levis's or walked to the Y at Broad and Pine to peek through the gym windows at the young girls playing badminton, their breasts bouncing under white blouses. For three nights in a row he went to Allinger's poolroom at Thirteenth and Market to watch the pool sharks practice, run rack after rack, take their trick shots and bank shots, and he listened to the talk about fabulous matches in the past, one-ball matches for a hundred dollars a game, thousands of dollars riding on one shot. After his third evening at Allinger's he was too tired to walk home and ended up in the all-night Family Movie across the street, saw a triple feature of two John Wayne marine movies and *Destry Rides Again*.

It poured the following evening. In his old Army raincoat he walked all the way downtown again and spent three dollars worth of nickels in the pinball alley at Fifteenth and Market. As he was leaving, he saw Charlotte Coleman, Marge's prettiest daughter, in the orangeade stand next door. Charlotte was laughing it up with two pimple-faced swabbies, and Auer decided not to wave to her. At fifteen Charlotte had already had one case of the clap and one of syph.

The rain stopped, and he was hungry. He went up Benjamin Franklin Parkway, past all the fountains and famous museums, the Logan Library, the Rodin Museum, remembering the class excursions as a kid, the teachers herding them through these places. Everybody got one day of culture. This was the Philadelphia on the postcards. The Johnson kids probably got their day of culture, too. He cut through the park, lost himself briefly in the forest and came out of the darkness at Strawberry Mansion, ate a Pat's steak at Thirty-Third Street. His thigh muscles were stiff and wobbly after that hike, and he took a taxi back to Sixth and Cottonwood.

Nobody got in his way on those long, nocturnal strolls. He could walk through the toughest neighborhoods, Columbia Avenue, South Street, practically inviting hoods and muggers to jump him, so he could whip out his pistol, have an excuse. Nobody said beans two. Troublemakers never wanted trouble with a man who would be delighted to find it. Addictions came and went quickly. For five nights in a row he headed for the poolroom at Sixth and Girard and lost money he could hardly afford at One Ball. One night he went to the rock 'n' roll clubs of Thirteenth and Locust and watched the sharp Italian girls shaking their asses cool, tough South Philly style. That experiment was not repeated. He knew he had no business in those places. Sitting at that bar, among all those sharpies, he stood out as a creep or a sex maniac. But his boredom grew so thick that the following evening he entered the Victory Mission on Eighth Street to hear the sermon for the bums, just to see what it was like. In minutes he discovered that there was a boredom greater and more terrible than the boredom of patrolling empty streets. He rose and tried to slip out quietly, but all the winos shushed him and grumbled at the disturbance, and the preacher gave him a nasty look from the pulpit.

On the walk home it occurred to him that he was not living up to his potential. From his reading he had decided that he was a yeoman type. Nature had designed him to be a yeoman. If he lived up to his potential, he could be something like a bos'n on a ship, a sergeant in the Army, or a foreman in a factory. None of these prospects seemed particularly fascinating. All that effort, just to be normal. And when he reviewed his fantasies, not even the fantasies really grabbed him on close inspection. It might seem great being a Hollywood producer for a while, having all those luscious young starlets come into your office and spread out, but eventually even that would get repetitious. Or when he thought about actually being President of the United States. Dictator might be fun for a while, but the President had all that fighting with Congress, and a man in that position was a worse prisoner than he was now, could not even peek at a pretty ass without fourteen photographers catching him with his hand in the cookie jar. Essentially, Auer decided, the problem was that life was irrevocably boring. The only thing that would make life interesting again would be an atomic war. It would be horrible, of course, millions dead, misery, all kinds of mutants and freaks and humanoids scavenging around in the rubble, but life would definitely become interesting again. Even Philadelphia would be interesting after an atomic war. It would be fascinating watching what would happen with everything wrecked and smashed. The people would form different tribes and bands in every neighborhood, and suddenly all those finks on his block in Oxford Circle would need guys like Sam Auer to captain one of the Hebrew tribes. There would be a Roman tribe down by Snyder Avenue, the Cossacks out in Frankford, the Hibernians in Fishtown, the Teutons over by Girard College, front lines and barricades across Olney Avenue. The *shvartzers* would probably take over Fairmount Park, and there would be drums and campfires along the Schuylkill. They would probably all go back to worshiping Babalú. And Sam Auer would suddenly be the man in demand. With his own tent. Bunny returning from the well with a jug on her head.

He returned to his parlor. He was tired of being Sam Auer, of having the same memories, a memory for that corner or this corner, what he thought when he crossed the bridge and contemplated suicide, or looking at Leah's second floor and thinking of Señora Gomez and her purple brassiere. If he was finally going to face up to his life, he could begin with cleaning up the apartment, scrub the rings off the bathtub, mop the floor in the luncheonette. It could be a great, all-encompassing program for coming back, step by step, a practical plan, a little at a time. He could spruce up the parlor, change the sheets on the bed, cut down on his food, stop drinking, and go up to the *shvitz* at Seventh and Girard and let a Turkish bath steam the grease out of his system. He could straighten up the shelves in the store, rip down those degrading pinups, scrub out the icebox. Point by point there were a hundred things he could do to bring himself back: sweep the sidewalk out front, sweep the upstairs halls and stairs, scour his lunchmeat slicer, clip his fingernails and get a decent haircut. If he did these minor things diligently, item by item, he could build up his reserves and strength to attack the larger, significant problems and make the important decisions.

He could buy a suit, take the El to Oxford Circle, see the girls, and arrange matters with Bunny—without quarreling. Then, with all that out of the way, he could bring in an agent and put this place up for sale. Merely mulling over these plans, making up lists of prospects, gave him a warm sensation of well-being and hope.

Auer slumped on the couch. He was goddamn miserable. He was crawling inside his skin. After a cigarette, as if in a trance, he went to the store. Striking a match, he studied his photo of Roberta in the pale, mellow light. She could almost make him swoon. He had to control a yearning to melt and rub his cheek against the glossy paper. She had a snub nose and slim, elegant arms. In this pose he could not see it, but he could visualize her soft, delicious bottom.

The match burned his fingertips. He flicked it away. Almost blind, self-hypnotized, he took the photo down and carried it to the bathroom. He lowered his trousers and shorts, plopped down on the toilet seat, and cleared his throat to spit in his palm.

An odd thought occurred to him. She was alive. If she were alive, she had to be somewhere at this very moment. She was probably out in California. At this very moment some agent or Hollywood producer was running his hand over her knee in a candle-lit restaurant. She was not one of the impossible goddesses on the cover of "Amazing Stories" but a live person, so why should he grovel, admit to this ultimate defeat, humiliate himself this way?

Auer crumpled the photo in his fist. He rose and tucked his erection back into his shorts, zipped up his trousers. If he started flogging himself again he would never get that testimonial dinner at the Warwick with John B. Kelly and the mayor. Tossing the crumpled paper into the toilet bowl, he winked at his reflection in the medicine cabinet mirror. Sam Auer still had something left.

He wondered when he would receive his reward. In his mind there had always been a direct connection between virtuous conduct and changing luck or a payoff. Reading became his new obsession. Some nights he would read till dawn and stagger into the store, wondering how he would make the day, and then returning to his novel between customers. He read *Smoke* again and went to Leary's to get everything they had by Turgenev. On the night that Maddy Dobry knocked at his side door he was absorbed in *Fathers and Sons*.

Auer opened the door and immediately sensed that something was wrong. The boy on the steps did not have to say a word or explain anything; it was all in his face. Instead of the habitual stance of the drugstore cowboy, he seemed grave and respectful.

"You have a call in our front booth, Sam."

Auer saw the boy wince at the disorder in the parlor, the litter of ashtrays and paper dishes on the coffee table. The features immediately froze into a mask of seriousness again.

"I thought I told your mother that I didn't want to be disturbed with any more calls. I gave Leah specific instructions weeks ago that if I got calls, she was to tell them my lights were out and I wasn't in."

"This one I think is pretty urgent, Sam. It's Bunny. She sounded pretty shook up." Maddy paused and said, "I'd answer it if I were you."

"OK, I'll be right over. But in the future I just wish that Leah would follow my instructions."

If it was Sheila or Steppie he would cut his throat. He would slit it from ear to ear. That would be the proper punishment for his leaving them. His scalp was tingling again. They were always skating near the top of the stairs. Steppie might have tumbled right down.

He slipped into his lightweight jacket and armed himself with his cigarettes, wallet, switchblade, and knife. He snorted at all these precautions. Just to cross the street he required an arsenal. Maybe he was a worrywart. Bunny might only have a message she wished to relay from her lawyer. Another bill she wanted him to shell out for. They had argued about dancing lessons for the girls.

Maddy and Herbert resumed their chess game as Auer entered the store. Leah was in the rear, massaging her father's neck as he dozed amid the clutter of lamps and antiques. With her chin Leah indicated the front booth. Auer snatched up the telephone, praying that Bunny would hit him with a repetition of old complaints.

"What is it now?" he began.

"Sam, I. . . ."

"You got your fifty, right? The mortgage payment was made, right? I sent the checks for the insurance. What is it now?"

"Sam, I've got something to tell you. . . ."

"You've always got something to tell me," he cut her off.

"I got a call."

"Sure, sure. You're always getting calls. You and Jerry are on the phone all the time now. You could never get along before, and all of a sudden you've found common ground, the killing ground where you stomp all over me."

"Will you stop?" Bunny screamed. "Will you stop? I got a call from Jerry. Your mother's dead. She passed away."

Auer shivered. He shivered because a wave of relief had washed through him. From her tone he was sure it was one of the girls, and he squinted away tears at the thought that he felt relief it was only his mother. He glanced back. Leah had joined her sons at the table, and the chess game went on. He lit a cigarette before asking, "When did it happen?"

"Jerry said tonight, at supper. She just keeled over in the hotel dining room."

"Should I make the arrangements?"

Bunny was crying. Probably she felt guilty. She was always so relieved when his mother went to Florida for the winter.

"Should I make the arrangements?" Auer repeated.

"Jerry is making the arrangements. He wants you to call

him. Her body will be flown up here, and the services will be held on Sunday, with the burial afterward. Sylvia will be flying in from California on Saturday."

"Where are the services?"

"The funeral home on Broad Street. The one we always use."

"Why did Jerry want me to call him?"

"I don't know. I guess he wants to discuss what price casket and matters like that. It's your family. I don't want to get involved. And he wanted to make sure you wore a suit to the funeral. He had reports that you were dressing very shabbily lately."

Auer inhaled on his cigarette and thought for a moment.

"Tell him if he's afraid his brother will embarrass him with his big-shot friends, just let me know and I won't be at the services."

There was a gasp up in Oxford Circle, and Bunny said, "What do you mean you're not going to the funeral? It's your mother. You have to be there to pay your respects."

"I don't pay respects to my mother by being there. Funerals are for the living. Will Mom know? Will she hear the rabbi speaking over her? Will she be peeking over some cloud to check who's attending her funeral?"

"I've never heard of anything like this. Sylvia is flying all the way in from Los Angeles. Don't you want to see your sister?"

"Exactly. A big social event. She runs off to California and writes maybe once a year. If I see them cry, I may vomit all over the funeral parlor. Bunny, I hate your fucking guts, but you did put up with Mom these last five years. Jerry could not be bothered. Once a month was too much for him to drive over and take her out for a drive on a Sunday afternoon. And Sylvia? She will show up like the Girl of the Golden West and do a scene from *La Boheme* for us. Skip it. There should be more love for the living and less tears for the departed."

"What shall I tell the girls, Sam?" Bunny was sobbing.

"They're going to be at their grandmother's funeral, and their father won't be there. The other is between you and your brother and sister, and I don't want to get mixed up in it, but what should I tell your daughters?"

"Don't take them. Get a baby-sitter and leave them home. There's nothing but clay in that casket. There's no need for the girls to see that scene when they're so young. Let somebody escape that morbidity."

"You've become a monster, Sam. I think I should send a psychiatrist down there to examine you."

"I probably need a psychiatrist. If I spent twelve years married to you, it's proof I'm a sick individual. Kiss the girls for me. Good-bye."

The Dobrys remained silent as he came out of the booth. They waited for him to make the announcement, though they were already well aware of the news.

"My mother died yesterday. The funeral is on Sunday."

Daniel Radin's eyes opened, widened in triumph, as if it were a miraculous achievement to see light again. Sometimes he was totally lucid. He stretched out his arms and said, "She was a good woman. She and my Sara never got along, but she was a good woman."

Herbert advanced a pawn, and Leah glared at her two sons for their cruel impassiveness. She rose and said, "Is there anything I can do to help, Sam? Tell Bunny and Jerry that if there's anything they need, just to call me."

Little Herbert glowered unhappily at Maddy. Their mother was the inveterate volunteer, and he was opposed to her constantly extending herself all over the map for every dog in the streets. Auer smiled at the fat child, and then up at the grim portrait of Daniel Radin in the back of the store. In three generations the Radins had gone from rock to this putty.

"You want a drink?" Leah asked solicitously. "I've got a bottle of Kummel back there, and you could probably use a good stiff shot."

Auer rubbed his hands over his cheeks, kneaded his fore-
head with his knuckles, spoke through the hands over his face.
"No, thanks. I'll be all right. It was expected. It's no shock.
I knew when I saw the expression on Maddy's face. . . ."

"If you want to sit down for a while . . . ," Leah
suggested.

"Thanks."

Without another word, Auer spun around and left them. As
the door closed, Herbert slid an attacking rook across the
chessboard and mumbled, "Since when do we have to send out
to call white people to the phone? He can't pay his phone bills
over there?"

Maddy chuckled at his brother's premature misanthropy,
and Leah snapped, "Shut your smart mouths, both of you. A
man's mother dies, and you have to continue your chess like
two cold-fish philosophers. How I ever brought two such heart-
less bastards into the world, I'll never know."

Out on Leah's step, Auer stared mutely at the boards over
his front window. Not for a million dollars could he go back
inside now, be alone in that parlor, her parlor, infested with
memories.

He straightened his shoulders and headed up Sixth. The
lights of the oncoming cars made him blink, and he was unable
to cry. Bunny, a bickering daughter-in-law, had managed to
shed many tears over the phone, and he merely felt . . . he was
not sure what he felt. Like a drunk hit by a car and too stunned to
see stars. Maybe Bunny was shrewd in her dense fashion.
Maybe Bunny, realized, without thinking it through, that with
his mother gone, her one last chance was gone. With his mother
gone, there was no one left to bump heads together, no one left
to reproach him, no one he had to be good for, explain to, justify
himself.

The darkened synagogue at Green Street. Sold. Closed. Its
gardens were leprous, untended jungles, thick roots and vines,
sharp brown blades and unhealthy green leaves on the shrubs.

Maybe Bunny and his mother were in league from the first, allies in plotting out his rotten groove. When he was fifteen. He caught them putting their heads together upstairs. On Yom Kippur. His father dragged him to this synagogue, twisted his ear, slapped his mouth, because he said he would rather go to school and not miss his junior varsity football practice. He sat below, with the men, in an agony of boredom, repeating Hebrew chants that he knew by heart and did not understand. Then the excited, listless lull as they began calling out the annual contributions. Everybody stirred and all ears were cocked as Goldman came down the aisle, repeating out loud the sums whispered to him, the crowd mumbling comments about the size of the offering, with the ten witnesses up front memorizing the pledges because nothing could be written down on a holy day.

Goldman always began with the Schiffs, shouting, "Mr. and Mrs. Schiff, five hundred dollars!" and Shachter repeated, "Mr. and Mrs. Schiff, five hundred dollars." "Mr. and Mrs. Neufeld, four hundred dollars!" and Shachter droning, "Mr. and Mrs. Neufeld, four hundred dollars." "Mr. and Mrs. Berman, five hundred dollars!" Everybody sneered. Millionaires like the Bermans with a flourishing trucking business could easily go a thousand. "Mr. and Mrs. Glass, four hundred dollars!" More sneers. A fortune that black marketeer made in green stamps and red stamps in '43. "Mr. and Mrs. Spiegelbird, three hundred dollars!" The Spiegelbirds, up one from last year? Uh-oh, better check the books in the City Water Department. "Mr. and Mrs. Beck, three hundred dollars!" Down one from last year, but the Becks could still afford two weeks in the Poconos. "Mr. and Mrs. Dvorkin, three hundred dollars!" Max must have had a good day at the track. "Mr. and Mrs. Hartman, two hundred dollars!" So business was bad on Brown Street. "Mr. and Mrs. Fox, two hundred dollars!" Schoolteachers were poorly paid. "Dr. and Mrs. Glick, four hundred dollars!" Shachter raised his voice, "Dr. and Mrs. Glick, four hundred dollars!"

All heads together in the balcony, the buzzing lower meaning that the women were really saying something nasty up there. The oldest Glick boy had dropped out of dentistry school to marry a redheaded *shiksa* waitress, was driving a cab.

Goldman leaned over them, and Simon Auer held up two fingers. Goldman was taken aback, sought confirmation, and Simon showed the two fingers again. Goldman shouted, "Mr. and Mrs. Simon Auer, two hundred dollars!" Shachter was also surprised but composed himself and, in a booming voice to give them extra credit, shouted "Mr. and Mrs. Simon Auer, two hundred dollars!" as the men on the benches stirred and the women upstairs fluttered. The Auers were one-hundred-dollar donors, small fry, and today they stepped into a higher league. The rabbi nodded, and men twisted around on their benches to examine Simon Auer and his sons Jerry and Sam in their new blue suits. Upstairs, the gossips craned their necks to admire Jenny Auer, while her husband accepted winks from some of his big-shot wholesalers from Marshall Street. Simon Auer could not resist the temptation to sneak up one sly glance at his wife and exchange triumphant twinkles with her.

Sam Auer, Southern's next fullback, squirmed in agony. Upstairs, his mother was chatting with Bunny Stein's mother. Cute little Bunny was pouting, cheeks drawn with pain, also bored mindless. Bunny was too dumb to get into Girls' High; she was going to William Penn. Jenny Auer and Mrs. Stein were getting thicker up there. Suddenly, Bunny's mother was pointing down at him. He could read her lips. "You see. What do you mean there are no boys? There's a nice boy." Little Bunny shut her eyes in misery, twisted away in embarrassment, but he could read her lips, too. "Mother, how could you?"

They had picked him out right then. He was speared like a fish in a tank. That was why women were segregated from men in an Orthodox synagogue. They were upstairs in the balconies so they could examine the crop on the benches below with their fathers, pick out the right provider for their daughters, evaluate the stock, make a deal with the boy's mother. He had seen these same women select a carp from the tanks in the fresh fish store at

Marshall and Poplar. Their eyes narrowed as the carp flitted about. They pointed a finger and said, "That one." The fish was scooped out with a net, tossed onto the wood block, the cleaver raised, the yellow fish eyes blink, splat, the head chopped off, cold blood oozing from the raw white spiny flesh.

Bunny Stein and Sam Auer never had a chance. Their mothers put their heads together up in that balcony, and they were sold down the river. He was scooped out of the tank, set aside for future use, ticketed for delivery to Bunny when they were both ripe.

The neon sign of the pool hall at Sixth and Girard flickered defectively. Perhaps Bunny was right. Maybe he was a monster? His mother was dead, and instead of mourning her, going to his brother's home, he was resenting her plotting with Anna Stein in that balcony twenty years ago, assigning him to Bunny as if he were the fifth prize at the state fair.

Once she shamed him into tears. She told him to bring up fifty bags of coal from the cellar. It smelled like a snowstorm, and he answered no, he had no time, the team was picking him up for a football game out in Strawberry Mansion, real tackle on a regulation field with goalposts. She grabbed his arm and said that his father could not climb the cellar steps twenty-five times with two twenty-pound bags of coal. It was going to snow. People would need coal to heat their rooms. Just then the gang showed up outside, all suited up, calling for him to come along. He said, "Let Jerry do it when he comes back from his music lesson." She said, "Jerry won't be back from his music lesson for hours yet." They argued back and forth, and the gang gave up on him, headed down Cottonwood to take the bus on Ridge Avenue. She grabbed his arm and said, "If you don't do it, your father will climb those steps. You know how stubborn he is. You're just like him, but you have no heart."

He broke away from his mother's grip and escaped, dashed down Cottonwood, caught up with the team at Eleventh. Out in the Mansion he had the greatest day of his life. Before it started snowing, he ran back two kickoffs for touchdowns and scored two more touchdowns from scrimmage, ripping off eight and nine yards with every carry. Before the field got too slushy in the third quarter, they were leading the Tioga Tigers forty-six to eighteen. On the bus back, Zig and Gall tried to deride his exploits, but Solly Radin said, "Bullshit, Sam. You played a great game. I kept the statistics and you picked up more yardage than both teams put together."

When he returned to the store, there were nineteen bags of coal in the window. He brushed the snow from his shoulders and said, "Did Jerry bring them up?"

"Jerry? I brought them up. I brought up thirty, and we've already sold eleven. But I couldn't take them two at a time, so I had to make thirty trips. I hope you're satisfied with yourself now. Just don't tell your father."

"Why didn't you wait till Jerry got back?" he screamed. "Is he the goddamn Prince of Wales, he don't work around here?"

"Never mind, Sam. Never mind. Don't use that language on me, and don't tell your father."

He broke out crying, and she pulled him down so that her arm wrapped around his neck. "You're no good in school, Sam. You bring back a report card like a graveyard. Learn to work. That's what you'll have to learn. My back hurts, but I'm used to that, too. Learn to work, baby."

The customers leaving the dairy restaurant at Seventh saw tears trickling down his unshaven cheeks. He hurried on. He had become a slob in his stained tan jacket, the shirt hanging loosely from his trousers. Too many people from Marshall Street knew him around here. The tears were flowing freely as he thought of that shriveled body in some vault down in Florida. Once it was so strong it could make thirty trips down to that dark, dank cellar, place the bags of Blue Reading Coal on the sidewalk, push up that last, high dangerous step, and present him with the bags of coal stacked in the window when he returned. To spoil the flush of his glory. To turn his glory into shame.

There was a Tarzan double feature at the Astor Movies. Auer fished sixty-five cents out of his pocket for a ticket. He had to get off the streets and sit down, or fall on his face. The cashier seemed surprised when he tapped on the glass.

"The first picture is already over, and *Tarzan and the Leopard Woman* already started, mister."

She was frightened by the tear streaks on his cheeks and the wildness in his red eyes. He thrust the coins through the slot and said, "I know it by heart."

Inside, he sat in a nearly empty section. A boy was thrusting his hand under a girl's skirts across the aisle. Auer brushed the dried tears from his lids with his arm. Nothing had changed. The girl was squirming, forcing the hand back. He remembered when the gang piled in here and searched for Rita Uzkoff. Rita Uzkoff gave the best hand job in town. Fat Rita stationed herself up front, used her Kensington High sweater as a cover, and maybe jerked off the whole team plus the subs during a matinee. They went down there one-by-one and played with her tits while Rita got that stroke going below. She was a good sport and only got pissed off when a guy didn't say he was coming and stained her sweater. Once his mother caught him talking to Rita in front of Doc Fine's pharmacy and said, "Who was that, Sam? Pocahontas or the Queen of Sheba?"

Auer chuckled aloud, and two spectators turned around to glare and several people nearly shushed him. He glanced around and wondered why people would demand quiet to see such a stupid movie. These Tarzan movies were all alike. The evil white man invades the jungle and fucks around with the natives, disturbing their customs and trying to steal their jewels or ivory idols. Jane, the stupid twat and a very poor judge of character, always wants Tarzan to aid the expedition because there are good white men, scientists or archaeologists, with worthy purposes. Tarzan resists, and Jane insists. Then Boy gets kidnapped, and Cheetah has to point which way they took him. Tarzan swings through the trees to rescue Boy, the good scientist gets his herbs, and the bad guys get sucked into the

quicksand. The movie always ends with the good scientist saying, "Why, thank you, Tarzan," and everybody laughs as
Cheetah does something cute.

The tears were rolling down his cheeks again. What shit.
Here this was supposed to be deepest Africa, and they don't
even use real *shvartzers*. All the natives up there looked like
Mexicans or Hawaiians. He laughed. The poor *shvas* really got
screwed. Negroes could not even get jobs playing Negroes in
movies. If they were running short on them, they should set
up a casting office down at Sixth and Cottonwood. There were
plenty to spare down his way. They got screwed all over the
place. Almost all the boxers were black now, but in the comic
strips the world champ was Joe Palooka, and in the movies it
was Kirk Douglas. . . .

A flashlight was shined in his face. The usher wanted to
know what the commotion was all about. Auer waved him
away, motioned for him to just go away, rose threateningly, and
the usher withdrew.

He tried to concentrate. It was impossible. The degenerate,
perverted, moneygrubbing morons in Hollywood never made a
movie right. In the novels Tarzan was complex, spoke impecca-
ble English and fluent French. Jane was from Baltimore, and
Tarzan Lord Greystoke had his private army, the Waziris, tall
and noble *shvartzers* who did not wear top hats. But those muff
divers out in Hollywood always messed up those great plots
because they believed everybody was dense and ignorant. . . . His mother was in a box, and he had time to worry
about Joe Palooka and the Waziris.

Auer stood up. "Thank you very much, Tarzan."

The temperature had not fallen outside. A pastel sky and
sweet spring night mocked his sadness. He ordered his belly to
stop rumbling and lowering him to thinking about physical
needs. The Ambassador Dairy Restaurant at Seventh was still
open, but he could not enter in this state. The excuse that his
mother had died was not valid; he had been grubby for months.

It was seven blocks down to Green Garden, and once it

seemed shorter because this was his neck of the woods and he knew every sign, every landmark, a thousand people in these three-story red brick houses. Before they were run out. Now it seemed longer. Now it seemed like a dark gauntlet. There went old Tarzan swinging around in a Hollywood backlot, and there was probably not a village in Africa to match his way for violence.

A dismal glow penetrated Fat Grace's shade when he reached his corner. It was still too early to go into that parlor and try to sleep. He crossed Sixth and hovered outside the window, listening to the clicking of chips, muffled curses, the shuffling of cards. Fingering the roll of bills in his pocket, he reviewed his financial situation. With eighteen different expenses and bills due on Monday, he could never hope to be clear this month. And another extraordinary expense this month. His third for the casket and funeral. His third for the hearse. And maybe his third for the airfare, unless Jerry was picking up the whole freight. Maybe this was an inspiration, a gentle nudge from Lady Luck.

A lizard curled through his heart as he entered the dingy vestibule. The hair on his forearms crawled. He realized that it was weird that he should experience this terror. This ghastly apartment building had sat catty-corner to his own house since he was born. It was probably the first thing he saw when they brought him home from the hospital, and in school he sketched this place. The building looked like it was designed by a child, shaped like a cigar box standing on end and covered with a rough cement whitewash, with a rusty exterior fire escape on Cottonwood. And this was the first time he had entered this fetid lobby.

He knocked softly on Fat Grace's door. The clicking of chips ceased immediately.

"Who the hell is that?" Grace snarled angrily.

"Sam Auer," he whispered, mouth close to the door. People might be awake upstairs. "Sam, from across the street."

Wicker screeched in relief as Fat Grace rose from her chair. The others inside were mumbling. Grace left the chain in its slot

and opened the door only a crack. Over her head Auer saw
Barry, Winston the runner, and three more unknown Negroes in
the game at the kitchen table. Big Vye was sleeping off a drunk
on the couch, her powerful thighs gleaming through a white
sheet.

"What you want here, Mister Sam?" Grace whispered
conspiratorially.

Auer cleared his throat. Her face was terribly marked and
had the texture of a black pumpkin with brilliant eyes for
Halloween.

"Sit in on the game."

"Since when you play poker?" she asked gruffly.

"Since tonight. I played all the time in the Army."

"Get on. This ain't no place for you. Miss Bunny kick your
ass all over the street she knew you were sneaking around here.
Go home and sleep it off."

"I'm not drunk," Auer said humbly. "Just feel like playing."

"Let the fucking man in already," Barry called from the
table. "Sam's our neighbor. If he's itching for action, he gotta
fucking right just like anybody fucking else around here."

Grace's lips puckered with disgust as she removed the
chain. Auer nodded uncomfortably at the strangers around the
table. They eyed him dubiously till Barry said, "Sam, these are
all friends. Nelson, Jonesie, and George Skinner. George
Skinner just got out of the Army. And Winston here is our local
pride and joy."

"How's it going, Winston?" Auer said as they moved their
chairs to make room for him at the table. Cokes were being
mixed with Grace's home brew. The vats were upstairs with
holes cut in the floor, and the spigot was hidden behind her coal
heater. Every year Grace paid her fine and went back to her
cooking.

"These boys are from Twelfth and Poplar, the Project,"
Barry explained. "Mister Sam is my old friend. Did business
with his father, too. We use chips, Sam. Regular chips like a

goddamn casino." Barry shuffled the cards expertly and continued, "A cheap crowd tonight, Sam. Yellow chip a dime, red twenty. Blue's thirty cents. Hardly enough to cover my costs here. Have to use chips to keep the 'poh-lees' happy. Rough me up everytime they need 'cee-gar' money. I think those blue shirts give them itchy palms. Like a disease." Barry continued shuffling. "Ten dollars' worth of 'cee-gar' money a week, and I'm Father Divine. I thought they was here early when you knocked, Sam."

"We playing poker, or did we drive over here to hear you shoot your goddamn mouth off, Barry?" George Skinner asked. Auer thought that Skinner was a fine-looking individual. With his bearing and trimmed mustache he was probably a master sergeant in the Army.

"How many chips to start off with, Mister Sam?"

"I'll start with twenty and end up with all of yours," Auer said confidently. The others looked dubious.

Five-card open or five-card stud, dealer calling, were the games. Auer won the second hand big and was ahead for thirty minutes before he started going down. Nelson, Jonesie, and Skinner from the Project acted more amicably once he began to lose. Barry sat in and withdrew one blue chip from every pot as the service charge. Barry and Grace also made more money by selling paper cups of the Coke and home brew for thirty-five cents.

As he got into the swing of it, Auer enjoyed himself. He snapped his fingers and groaned and wisecracked with the rest of them, laughed at Winston's cool, sarcastic humor. He hardly cared when he ran out of chips. Twenty dollars was cheap to escape himself, to escape from thinking. He bought another twenty dollars' worth of chips, wanted a larger nut, to bump and bluff. Tears suddenly flashed in Auer's eyes. He was thinking about his mother and Rita Uzkoff. "Who was that, Sam? Pocahontas or the Queen of Sheba?" He smiled, and the tears erupted against his will. Auer realized that the men around the table probably thought he was tearing because he was losing money. He blinked the tears away quickly and said nothing. It would have been more embarrassing to explain that his mother was dead, that he had dropped in here on the off-chance he could pick up enough money to pay for his third of the casket.

Barry pushed the stack of his chips his way, and as Auer counted them his eyes also took in the dramatic curve of Vye's behind under the sheet. Skinner noticed his interest in that direction and said, "You appreciate that stuff?"

"It's not bad, from here."

"Just got back from Italy," Skinner said with a deep sigh. "Don't know what the hell I came back to this town for. That was all right over there."

"I was over that way," Auer said laconically, fanning his cards. "It had things."

"Some fine-looking stuff over there. I still can't figure out why I came back to this town. This is a tough town to make it in."

"Everybody does, though," Auer said and tossed down two cards. "And then nobody can figure out why."

"The Aquarium. The Planetarium. Rowing on the Schuylkill River," Winston murmured suavely. "Fairmount Park is pretty in the spring."

They all laughed, and Big Vye stirred on the couch. She sat up abruptly and then shook herself violently. It was like a big black bear coming out of hibernation. Tears rolled down her cheeks, and Auer said, "What's the matter, girl? Buzzy?"

Vye rose and swept down her skirt angrily. Hands shaking, she lit up a cigarette before saying, "Sure, Buzzy. I went to visit my boy today, Sam. They want to kill that boy. You knew Buzzy, Sam. He had a temper, but he never fucked with nobody. Buzzy was a nice boy, and that motherfucking mean judge gave him seven to ten. He ain't never gonna make seven years in that place."

"Do you think they want him to?" Nelson asked her "You think their main concern is to feed some nigger sonofabitch for seven whole years? Waste the taxpayers' money, honey?

Seventy-eight cents a day to feed some black sonofabitch for seven years. That's money, honey."

"Shut up," Vye snapped at Nelson. She wiped the last tear from her eye and turned to Auer. "They hope to do that boy in, Sam. You know they don't separate no fags from no normal people in there, and Buzzy's just eighteen. Buzzy was almost bawling behind that screen today. He's too big a boy to be bawling. Them fags are after his ass. The fairies tried to jump him in the shower, and he fought his way out, but he says they'll get him next time. He says they got this big one called the Queen Bee that bosses the place, and the only reason they ain't raped him yet is the Queen Bee picked him out for his own. The Queen Bee promised he was gonna get him transferred to his block and then he'd get him. He told Buzz once he was down his way he'd better never sleep."

"Why doesn't Buzzy tell the guards or the warden?" Auer suggested, and everyone at the table laughed. He joined in, as he recalled just how much cooperation he had received from the police, how they patrolled his corner, in his vendetta with the Johnsons.

"You don't understand the rules," Winston assured him patronizingly. "Everybody likes peace, Sam. Peace on Earth. Even the screws like peace. So they let the Queen Bee buzz and suck in his sweet juices, and that pack helps to run the show and keep the lid on for them. That's one hard, fast rule in any society, Sam. Nobody wants bad headlines."

Auer lost again, his two kings squelched by three puny fours. Vye gulped down her mulekick straight, without any Coke, and passed the cup to Barry. Winston nodded, indicating he would pay for it. Jonesie looked up and said, "Buzzy will learn, honey. What Buzzy gotta do is hurt one sonofabitch real hard, Vye. Real, real hard. I don't mean hit him, I mean hurt him. That's what I learned to do in Alabama. About my second day on the farm, the Kangaroo comes round to tell me the guards only think they run the place, that the Kangaroo runs the place. And I had to get initiated."

Jones pointed to the neat scar under his eye, running to the bridge of his nose. "Initiated, you see? So they initiated me. Whomped me with rakes and garden hoes. . . . The next day the cracker guard says, 'Hey, Jones! You look like you fell down, boy. You'd better be more careful, boy. We wouldn't want to have to throw you into the hole for mahl-lingering on the job, Jonesie. You miss all the sunshine if you're in the hole, boy!' "

The card players chuckled, and Auer joined in as Jones outlined his scar again.

" 'Mahl-lingering,' that man said. But I seen New Orleans Smith in the afternoon. Smith smoking a cigarette while the rest of us are breaking our backs on our knees. And New Orleans says, 'How'd you like your initiation, Jones?' and I said 'I liked it like this, motherfucker!' and I drove my hoe handle into his nuts. He squealed like a woman and went right down. Ten minutes later the Kangaroo circle me with their hoes, and I told them, 'C'mon, I'll die, and I'll die, and I'll die cause this fucking life ain't worth shit, but I'll kill any sonofabitch that comes near me, so don't come on unless you're ready to go all the way and die with me. . . .' "

George Skinner rolled the toothpick around on his lips and saw that Jones was close to tears. He said, "Play cards, Jonesie, play cards."

Vye sipped at her mulekick, let it burn her tongue and seep down. She shook her head at Auer again. "Buzzy shouldn't even be in there, Sam. You know why they threw his ass in there. It's a black ass."

Tossing away a seven off a pair on the chance for an inside straight, Auer said philosophically, "It came at a bad time, Vye. All the papers were up in arms for what those colored boys did to that Chinese student near the University of Pennsylvania."

"Buzzy killed that boy in a fair fight, and that boy started it, picking at Buzzy. You know damn well that if Buzzy wasn't no nigger he'd be upstairs now, sleeping in his own bed. You think they'd lock up Leah's boy across the street for the same thing? You believe if Maddy accidentally killed a boy in a fair fist fight they'd lay seven to ten on him? Shit, baby. Miss Leah'd get on her phone and call her brother Harold, and Harold would call all his judge golf friends, and Maddy would be out on the street on probation, just like everyone else. Once her brother Harold got in on it, the goddamn cops would send Maddy home with an ice cream cone."

"Man," Nelson moaned, "is this a poker game, or is this the court of goddamn last appeals? We ain't gonna spring Buzzy with all the lah-dee-dahing in this room. Call the governor, Vye honey. Catch him around Christmas time when he's in a good mood."

Auer was down to his last chips on the table. He was forced to dip into his pocket for a dollar to see Jones's bump. Jones spread out a hand with three nines, and Auer rose, saying, "Looks like I've had it." His gaze fell on Big Vye, and his Adam's Apple twitched involuntarily. Vye was such a magnificent beast, heavy, but as attractive as Peggy Moore or Maggie May. He blotted away an incipient tear. His mother in a box in Florida, and this was what he thought about.

Barry removed a blue chip from Jones's pot and said, "You just had a streak of bad luck in there, Sam. You gotta get the cards in this game. A man can't do much in poker unless he occasionally gets the cards."

"You are positively a goddamn philosopher," Winston told the old man. "It has been many years—since Sunday School—that I have heard such words of wisdom for free."

"Why don't you come back Saturday night?" Barry suggested. "Your luck might change Saturday. Pots are usually bigger. Give you a chance to recoup."

Auer lit his Lucky and spoke through a cloud of smoke. "Maybe I will. I generally win at poker."

"You'll shit," Fat Grace called in from the bedroom. "I don't want to see your ass in here again, Sam. You scratch on my door again, I'll slam you with a frying pan. I can tell from my window your store ain't doing shit these days, so you just better hold onto your money. You play poker like a fool."

"Don't pay her no mind," Barry calmly advised Auer. "All these fuckin' women are the same. Money, money, money from a man, but they don't want him to enjoy his own, no way. Try us Saturday. I've watched winners leave my table with a clean thousand."

Auer wondered why, with all this money circulating, Barry was so bad with his bills. He said nothing and merely answered, "I'll see you all," with false cheerfulness. They mumbled good-byes and nodded him through the door.

As he paused for one moment in the rank lobby, there was a burst of laughter in there. That was for him, of course. The three gamblers from the Project and Winston the numbers writer had to classify him as a pigeon. That was their prerogative. He had played his cards like a real sucker. How did anybody wreck a pair of sevens to draw for an inside straight?

Nothing had changed on Cottonwood Street. His mother was still dead. His headache throbbed as the humidity trickled in his sinuses. Just as he fitted his key into his lock, the luminous dials on his wristwatch glinted, the glass face still shattered from the brawl. It was two o'clock. He removed the key and stood motionless on the side step. It was late, but he felt absolutely no inclination whatsoever to go inside. To what purpose? His last pleasure in there was to gaze at Roberta, and he had crumpled up her photo in the only victory he had scored lately. He could not sleep now. Something more had to happen. If he tried to sleep, he would only toss on his bed, torture himself with old guilts, his mother lugging thirty bags of coal up from the cellar, or how he felt like a louse, so relieved, when every winter he put his mother on the train for Florida. Now she got to come back in a plane. There had to be something more tonight, or he would bang his head against the wall in there.

His shoulders hunched as he straggled down Cottonwood toward Glendolph. He felt like a wounded ape, or the first or last man on earth. Under the dull sky this familiar landscape seemed vaguely mysterious, the empty schoolyard, the rock-strewn lot, the wood factory ruins from a desolate and silent planet.

He lit another cigarette and hesitated in front of the Coleman's glass door. It was amusing how he attempted to be devious with himself. Like the diner for a cup of coffee was really his destination when he started this way. If a patrol car passed, they would nab him as a prowler for hovering near this door. He still hated change. Leah had moved down to Sixth from this corner over five years ago, and he still expected to find old Sara Radin here, and not the Colemans outside in summer on milk crates and benches, sucking on bottles of beer and fried chicken, looking like a pack of Neanderthals munching bones in front of their cave. The size of the pack constantly fluctuated, with the children shuttling back and forth between reformatories and "homes," and cousins coming and going from Hazelton.

Auer rapped lightly on the door. The glass pane still bore the Phillies cigar advertisement from the Radin days. Inside, a squirming and scuffling, a rustling of sheets and squeaking of bedsprings. It sounded like weasels bumping around in a warren. A man's voice snarled, "Get away from that door, you goddamn nigger, or I'll be out there with my .22."

The threat made Auer giggle. That was Bill, a terrible coward. Marge often chased him around the block swinging a broomstick. Of all people, Bill was threatening to come out with a .22. If anybody came out, it would be Marge, almost as formidable a horse as Big Vye.

Auer knocked harder on the wood frame. More shuffling and murmuring inside. As he anticipated, it was Marge who tugged the curtain aside and peeked out at him. She released the bolt immediately, and his heart thumped, more with fear and disgust than any desire.

"Sam, what's the matter?"

"I needed to talk to you." He sensed that it sounded idiotic, but what else could he say to a woman at two in the morning?

"What about?" The question had an instant cunning edge. She opened the door wider, so he could see her transparent nightgown.

Auer kneaded his lips, trying to formulate a reply. Her shapeless nightgown was even less appealing than Bunny's old yellow *shmatte*. Marge saved him from his embarrassment by saying, "I can't do anything tonight, Sam. Not tonight."

"What's the matter?"

"I'm growing tomatoes."

"Oh."

"I'll try to catch you Sunday, Sam. Honest, I'll come by the store. If you want me to visit you in back, just say the word."

"Okay. Come by Sunday."

Marge rewarded him with a quick, salacious grin that curved her Gypsy mouth. She closed the door gently, and Auer was relieved. The constricting sensation of imminent diarrhea subsided. When she said she was growing tomatoes, his terror vanished. He made an honorable attempt and was not responsible for her condition. Now he could sleep in peace.

He was halfway down the block when he heard a sibilant, demanding, "Sam."

Turning around, he saw that Marge had come out with a man's overcoat thrown over her nightgown. His heart began pounding again as she hurried toward him, with her high heels clopping loosely on the brick pavement and a rabbit's-foot key chain jingling in her hand.

Marge said breathlessly, "Thanks for stopping, Sam. I was thinking. . . ."

"What?"

Marge caressed his hair with a curiously maternal gesture. "I might be growing tomatoes, but there's still some other things I could do for you."

"What do you mean?" He was stammering, and ashamed of his nervousness.

"You know, Sam. Don't be naïve on me."

He was surprised, not only by what she intimated but by her use of the word "naïve." It was jarring to hear a crass hillbilly like Marge use a cultured word like "naïve." She took his hand as though silence signified assent and moved him along toward his steps. Auer was amused at how the woman always took over once it definitely got down to sex. He made his bold play, knocked at her door at two in the morning, and now she was the boss.

Price was not discussed till they were in the parlor. Marge removed the bulky overcoat, and he gloomily observed that she fitted in with the run-down condition of his apartment. Her breasts, with enormous brown nipples, sagged under the nightdress, and her hair was matted with strands as thick as shoelaces. Marge hugged him, legs powerful under layers of fat, strong to support her belly. When she brought his hands up to her pendulous breasts, they seemed to overflow his fingers like cold, soggy custard. He moved his chin to deflect her kiss, and desire was completely absent. After so much frustration he was bumbling and dead.

"It'll cost," Marge whispered, with sharp teeth nipping at his earlobe.

His arm circled her thick waist. "Not too much, Marge."

"Ten dollars."

"I'm low on cash. I don't have it," he pleaded. Her raw smell of rumpled bedsheets was in his nostrils. No bath could cure it. The rawness was internal, oozed from her as it had from Rita Uzkoff, the Queen of Sheba.

Marge used her tongue expertly in his ear, darting and swishing through every fold and crevice. "Eight, Sam, eight. I need eight bucks. Joanie has to go for her shots tomorrow."

His hands slithered down to her massive buttocks. She was working hard thighs against his groin, thrusting like a hostess in a dime-a-dance hall. "Can't we take it off the bill, Marge? I'd give it to you, but I've only got six to open the store tomorrow morning. You owe me over a hundred on the bill."

"Take six off the bill and give me four, Sam. I need at least four," she said desperately. "Four won't break you."

Fumbling with his belt buckle, they moved into his bedroom by mutual consent. He was furious at the spectacle he made of himself by stumbling around as he climbed out of his trousers. When he stretched out on the bed, he was irked to note that he had forgotten to remove his green socks. With the green socks down there, he looked like a huge, hairy elf, and it was too embarrassing to reach down and remove them with Marge standing over him. Whipping the nightdress over her head, she plopped down on the mattress, springs screeching. She nudged him with her hip and murmured, "Move over a little, would you, honey."

Auer obeyed, shifting toward the wall, imagining that the riveting of his heart against his ribs was thunderous in the darkened room. Marge soothed his chest and belly with a cool palm. "You're sure a handsome hunk of man, Sam."

"I'm fat now. I got this roll around the waist, and I can't work it off."

She pinched him playfully. "Nah, you're beautiful, honey. You got nice broad shoulders. And a big nose. The nose didn't lie, honey."

They both laughed. Her smooth belly, shaped like a distended medicine ball, rippled into an intricate mass of wrinkles as she twisted around. He found it shocking that Marge Coleman, a neighborhood sow, should be giving him an expert, professional workover, knew her business, how to French, starting off at the nipples and licking her way down the line of the abdomen, just like a real call girl. He concluded that she must have made her living at it before her body thickened, at a roadhouse in the coal region. He was useless, limp, less than useless, yet her practiced lips were extracting respect. Marge came up again and slowly grazed her hanging breasts and nipples over his chest. It was all ridiculous. After months of abstinence, the big trip to her store, the thumping heart, the stench of sacrilege on the bed, he was crapping on an altar with no pleasure whatsoever, with only a wish to get it over with and get her out of here. He needed no woman to do this to him; he wanted a woman to worship—clean, gorgeous, like Sophie in her black galoshes, Mrs. Lewis, even Bunny in her green tailored suit. Roberta, rising from her kneeling position, extending her arms to him, offering herself. . . .

He opened his eyes to discover Marge Coleman's wide hump covered by dingy bloomers, stringy black hair hanging over her head, obscuring her swishing. It was spoiled as it happened, seared forever in his brain by his mother's voice in the void. "What are you doing, Shem? What are you doing, poor baby? Why do you do this to yourself?"

When the alarm rang in the morning, Auer twisted over to discover that his last cigarette of the night had rolled out of the ashtray and burned a stain on his nightstand, next to his pistol and switchblade. Bunny would have gone out of her skull. So would his mother. Who could no longer do that because she was dead.

He had a nasty hangover from the white lightning, one more valid excuse for remaining in bed. Out of respect he was not supposed to open the store. He was supposed to sit *shiva*, to mourn. Mourning? He had really lived it up last night, went off on a tear. A unique way of sitting *shiva*, losing sixty-one dollars in poker and catching a blow job off your friendly neighborhood whore. The Tarzan movie. He forgot the Tarzan movie.

This bed felt too good. Anything this good had to be immoral. He examined his hands. They were his father's hands now, the hands of a butcher. It was strange but, as of today, he was more the world. With both the old folks gone, Sam Auer became the world, Daddy, the one-and-only Auer. He was responsible for the state of the world, and there were no more elders around to turn to for advice, a loan, a push, a pat on the head. A horrible thought. A man was never totally free and mature till both his parents were dead.

Out of respect for his parents, he should remain closed and venerate her memory, but that was precisely what he did not wish to do: remember. Nor did he wish to walk the streets and look at strangers. Nor could he remain in this bed. From the dresser his parents were staring at him from the old-fashioned brown-tinted photo in its pearl frame. Jenny Auer in a black velvet dress with a white lace collar. His old man stiff and erect in a pinstripe and a dangling watch chain. Such dignity. Such solidity. They had watched Marge give him the blow job last night.

Auer opened the store. After nine, Larry Hermans, his wholesale grocery salesman came in. He wondered why Hermans expressed no condolences. Hermans looked like the kind of boy who read the obituary column first thing in the morning *Inquirer*. Hermans talked about the spring Richie Ashburn was having for the Phillies and then got down to business. He rested his elbows on the lunch counter, tapped the tips of his fingers together.

"We're not making it, Sam."

"You had to tell me that? You don't collect no consultant's fee. That I knew without a survey."

The grocery salesman wore the face of a pathologist charged with reading off an unfavorable report. With his bow tie Hermans attempted to be distinctive, but it merely accentuated the softness of his double chin.

"I don't like to hit you like this when things are going bad, but Pearlman called me into his office this morning and told me this was it. You're into us for over eight hundred dollars, Sam. Pearlman wants to know how long we're supposed to carry you."

"You're asking me, or you're telling me?"

"I guess I'm telling you," Hermans explained gloomily.

"That's sweet, kid. Forty years good, four or five months bad, all bad."

"You're oversimplifying, Sam. We've been very patient with you. Pearlman has a soft spot in his heart for your father."

"I should hope so. We dealt with your firm for over forty years. Now I have a little trouble with the community, and you want to pull the rug out from under me. Where is the good faith and integrity? We weathered the Depression with your firm, and now that I'm having my own personal depression all the rats are fighting for the honor of being the first off the ship."

"Sam, please. Listen to me. It's not me. You think it's

me?'' Hermans touched his lapel as if to guarantee his sincerity. "Pearlman says he can't see any way out. He can't see the end of it. You yourself used the word 'community.' Pearlman also said 'community.' This morning, in his office, he told me that he had decided to check out the reports for himself and drove by this corner, and it looked like the 'community disgrace.' That no wonder you couldn't pay your bills. I tried to argue him out of it, but he wouldn't hear from it.''

"I'll bet you argued with him, kid. I can really hear you standing on your hind legs and defending me to Pearlman.''

Hermans opened his palms, and Auer wondered why a boy who was born here, who spoke accentless English, who was a graduate of Northeast High and had years in at Temple, should still use these ghetto gestures.

"How hard could I defend you, Sam? Be reasonable. You think I like turning the screws on an old friend and customer? But look around you. Let's be frank. I don't relish entering here anymore. This place looks—and smells—like the community disgrace. How can you operate here? Since the windows were boarded up, this corner looks like a sharecropper's shack. And look at yourself, Sam. You used to be such a neat, clean individual, and now, sometimes I think you wear the same shirt from week to week. Pearlman is right. If we extend more credit to you, we're throwing good money after bad. You've become a losing proposition, Sam.''

"Things will settle down. Give me a few. . . .''

"It's not that simple,'' Hermans cut him off. "Pearlman has pressures on him, too, you know.''

"What kind of pressures? I thought the only pressure he felt was in his pocketbook.''

"Pressures,'' Hermans assured him. "There are subtle pressures at work here. Mister Silverman, the principal of the school across the street, has called him to complain.''

"I'll be a sonofabitch!'' Auer exclaimed.

"No, no,'' Hermans said quickly, flinching back. "Not just Silverman. Many of the other grocers and merchants and businessmen in this area are unhappy with this situation. They say that you've become a focal point of tensions."

"Has Leah been complaining?" Auer demanded to know.

"No," Hermans said wearily, "Leah has not said a word. Leah said she could never say one word against you ever, because it was your father who pulled her brother Harold off the trolley track and saved his other leg; otherwise both would have been cut off. Not Leah. But I assure you that many others have insinuated they just wished that you would sell out and move away, lower the level of tensions."

"Fuck 'em."

"That seems to be your attitude toward everything these days, Sam." Hermans stepped off the stool and began zippering up his briefcase. "But this is it. Pearlman says strictly cash. Not one more cent of credit till the bill comes down, the boards come down, the windows go up, and you're cleaned up like a *mensh* again."

With the water in the sink splashing noisily over his breakfast dishes, Auer watched Larry Hermans pause in the open doorway. Hermans obviously wished to depart on an amiable, optimistic note.

"How's your mother, Sam?"

"She's dead," Auer called back to him.

"That's great. Tell her I was asking for her. Give her my regards."

"I will," Auer said. After the salesman had gone, he added, "Eventually. Eventually, I will give her your regards." The boy could not help it. He had said it in a loud, clear voice, but people did not hear. Nobody listened. Maybe Hermans deserved sympathy. Auer chuckled. Hermans could never be "a focal point of tension." That was a great honor. Six months ago he was a *shmuck* grocer, and now he had risen to this elevated status of "focal point of tension." Whereas Hermans was such a flop as a human being, he did not even know he was a failure, made out of squishy cheese and papier mâché, finished off by a haberdasher clearing off his back rack of seconds.

His own brother Jerry? What was Jerry? Could Jerry ever be a focal point of tension? Jerry could make a million bucks and buy the PSFS building, and he would still be cheese. But maybe Hermans and Jerry were actually happy and thought they were the way they should be, or should be the way they were.

Barry entered and had consoling remarks about the poker losses last night, invited him for another round tomorrow night, on Saturday. Auer made him pay cash for his ten-dollar order, for once certain this bastard had cash in his pocket.

The recess bell rang, and Auer sauntered outside with his broom to sweep the sidewalk toward Glendolph. He looked at the windows of the school administrative offices. If he caught that finky little cocksucker Silverman outside, he might give him a few in the chops. Then he would really be "a focal point of tension." That was no way to treat a *landsman,* calling up and trying to get his creditors to put the squeeze on him. Silverman, of course, had it made. Playing big white daddy to three hundred little blackies, with his job security, and he could go eat lunch at the Oyster House every day and pretend he was an executive.

Auer paused with his broom. He was lucky today. Mrs. Lewis was on recess duty. She had admirable taste in clothes. On this warm May morning she was lovely in an olive green skirt, mint green blouse, and dark green high-heeled shoes. She was separating two boys but doing it good-naturedly, like an older sister, laughing. This was a woman he could marry. For this woman he could go to night school, learn another trade, change his shirt twice a day. Of course, his mother, who was not yet in her grave, would spin in her grave if she ever saw him walk down the aisle with a Negress on his arm, but he would not give a shit—this woman he could marry. He could not remember seeing her out of sorts or sulky. That, too, could be a public pose. Bunny also put on a good show in public. Under her own roof, Mrs. Lewis might be a bitch on wheels. Only her husband would know, and her husband died four years ago, in a military jeep accident in Japan.

During the afternoon Auer blinked away more tears. It was too late now. He could never carry up those thirty bags of coal from the cellar for her. And what would she say to his latest idea, the drastic solution, to reestablish his credit and restock his shelves, slap another mortgage on this place, take out a loan? That would undo her husband's main accomplishment. His father was so grim and serious. His life was so narrow: the store, the newspapers, and the synagogue. A huge, long grind of a life: work, the newspapers, and the *shul*. Only once had he seen his father totally happy. The old man became so exhilarated he became tipsy on Southern Comfort.

All the neighbors dropped in for the celebration in the parlor: Daniel and Sara Radin, Harry Lipofsky the ward-heeler, the Newmans from Eighth Street, the Conlons came in with their five oldest daughters, for the strudel and knishes. The parlor was packed, and his father, that stolid, somber man, got drunk for the only time in his life. He had gutted it out for forty years for that moment, survived a razor-slashed arm from a drunk, a knock on the head from a robber, bad bills, a fire upstairs, the Depression, all to invite his neighbors in for a toast with the *schnapps* and light a Corona Corona, apply the tip to the mortgage, while everybody cheered and applauded as his misery went up in smoke. And his father, who never said a word, shocked everybody with the toast: "Let us drink to America, a land where a man can burn a mortgage. A land where a man can become free and clear."

In the evening Auer closed, still sickened by the thought of the solution he was considering. To slap a new mortgage on this corner was decay, degeneration, sliding backward. He could not tear down his father's main achievement, with his mother not yet in her grave.

Bowes was strumming his guitar in front of the icehouse, had a small audience. Auer was tempted to drift over there and enjoy that unique style he had with a sliding spoon and thimble on two fingers, but that, sadly, was out. Bowes owed him money and would think he was stopping by to dun him. It would sour his guitar.

Hundreds of eyes were on him as he went down Seventh.

With the warm May night, all the roomers were on their steps, drinking beer and listening to portable radios. A hundred times he had come down this street over the last few months, his finger wrapped around the trigger of the pistol in this jacket pocket. A few of the berrypickers nodded but most stared right through him.

He rang the bell at #424, and there was no answer. His finger was on the trigger, and if Johnson answered the door he intended to shoot right through the jacket, like they did in the movies. He would not mind dying tonight. They could bury him next to his mother on Sunday.

"Nobody there," Maggie May called from the bench in front of #422.

"All the Johnsons out?"

"Like I said," Maggie May snapped, "ain't nobody home. They all went to a party over her sister's house out by Lancaster Avenue."

"Lou Johnson not around?"

"Sheee. He ain't been around for a while. Working down in Delaware or Maryland or somewhere."

"Thanks."

He stared at Maggie's good legs and concluded that she was lying. Lou Johnson working?

Late-model cars lined the block around Zacky's. Many of the Negroes who made it out of the neighborhood still drove down here on Friday and Saturday because of the jukebox and the atmosphere, or to show off their finery to their brothers who had not made it. Auer pushed through the swinging doors, and the place was seething inside, the Friday night crowd laughing, dancing, three deep at the bar, jukebox roaring, red lightbulbs flashing. It was like a quick snapshot of the Inferno, black skins purple under the red glare and wild gyrations to the pounding beat of "Do the Hucklebuck."

As he made a tour of the long rectangular bar, searching for Lou Johnson, it occurred to him that this was the first time he had ever entered this joint. He had been in the employment agency next door a few times, to dun people on payoff night, but he had never entered this bar before. It looked lively, and a few of the women were not bad, one or two knockouts.

The customers were eyeing him back as he made that slow tour. Those from not around here gathered that a rough-looking white his size, with a bulge in his jacket pocket, strolling so nonchalantly around Zacky's, had to be a plainclothesman or a holy fool.

No Lou Johnson. Auer headed up Eighth Street. It was jumping on a Friday night. The swallows were back from Capistrano. All the bums who fled south when the snow fell were flocking back with their toothless gums and scabby noses, sprawled out in front of the hock shops and barber colleges. He was worried because no bum was sticking his paw out for a dime. A year ago, if he walked up this street, they grabbed him and said, ''C'mon, Billy, give an old sailor a nickel for a beer,'' and tonight he was totally unmolested.

When he reached the corner of Eighth and Race, Auer decided against continuing on to the Horn and Hardart's downtown and going to a movie afterward. If he looked that shabby, it was better to hide out around here. He went down Race Street to Chinatown and had another decision to make. Usually, he went upstairs to the Shanghai for his won ton soup and egg rolls, but the Shanghai might have people he knew from Oxford Circle or Marshall Street. He was not dressed for the Shanghai tonight.

He entered the Moonglow, the chop-suey joint under the Shanghai, and was the only white in the place. The Chinese waiter gave him a funny look, and the other patrons, all well-dressed Negroes, definitely resented his intrusion. Fortunately, there was a copy of the *Daily News* on the table next to him, and he hid behind it while he ate his spare ribs and fried rice, left with half the portions remaining on the serving trays.

On another spontaneous impulse, he entered the Troc Burlesque. It was not in his mind as he left the Moonglow, but he did not know what to do with himself. Arch Street was so empty, all the way up to Broad. He did not want to join the other geeks prowling around downtown.

When he pulled out his money, the cashier said, "You've already missed half the show, bud."

"That's okay. I've seen it before."

The cashier gave him a surprised look and then lowered his voice. "Give me a buck and go ahead in. It's okay."

Auer understood the kindness of the gesture when he saw the cashier pocket the dollar and make a signal to the ticket taker. Sports all over. Sam Auer was a freak because he was so honest with money. A freak who went to burlesque halls while his mother rested in a box. He wondered whether the body had arrived or was still en route.

The audience was whistling in derision as the Trockettes high-kicked their way offstage. That, at least, had not changed over the last twenty years. The Trockettes were supposed to be a chorus line, and they danced with as much precision as a centipede stricken with palsy. He slouched lower as the top banana came on stage, stuck one hand deep in his pocket, threw out his other like an operatic tenor, and sang, "Oh, sweet mystery of life, at last I've found you!"

The whole gang used to pile in here with false I.D.'s when they were kids. Zig and Gall and Dutch Radin and Moony. They competed for who could make the dirtiest catcall or shout the filthiest thing at the strippers. They always said they were going to the Teddy Roosevelt Opera Company, and their parents knew full well that stood for the TROC. Probably everybody else in the gang went home and played with themselves like he did, remembering the way the stripper wiggled her behind.

The audience was roaring at a skit, a skit he had seen twenty years ago, the top banana as doctor and two busty chorus girls as a nurse and a patient. Nothing had changed. The audience whooped as Miss Ann Smith, the stripper with a college education, swept out onstage in a black academic robe and tassled black cap on her head. She bowed and circled with the book in her hand, curtsied primly, stuck out one long, beautiful leg from the gown, and then danced around stage to the beat of "Night Train." The crowd went wild as she suddenly spun around, flipped up the gown, and pointed her red silk-covered ass at them. They cheered, whistled, shouted for her to take it all off. Auer felt sick. All these punk college kids in West Chester and Temple jackets, all these bums from Franklin Square and traveling salesmen, and lonely perverts. This was such a stupid, hypocritical society. It permitted this shit but closed up all the whorehouses. This was legal because nothing happened. All the shit was retained in the mind. Between the legs, forbidden; between the ears, fine.

Miss Ann Smith twitched her butt muscles at the audience and was grinning at them under her legs. She was removing her pasties and attaching some kind of gadget to her nipples. As she swung around, Auer saw badminton birdies suspended from strings attached to plugs. The audience applauded and whistled at her feat of getting both birdies swinging and rotating in opposite directions with perfect control of her pectorals. Auer wondered why she did that, why they would want her to do that, why they would applaud such an idiotic trick, why they would want to use and abuse a beautiful woman in this manner? Was that supposed to be appealing artistically or sexually exciting? Auer covered his face with his hands, but the tears trickled through his fingers. He had two beautiful daughters. Girls without a father, without a man around the house, often went wrong. He would die ten thousand deaths in hell before he would ever let his Sheila or Stephanie go astray, end up on a stage like this, making these disgusting shrieks in front of this zoo. No sacrifice was too great to prevent that or the chance of it. No sacrifice. He would call Bunny and ask her to take him back.

Auer stepped on other spectators' toes as he rose and forced his way down the row, strode up the aisle to get out of this place. On Arch Street, in the emptiness, he was tempted to call Bunny and beg her to take him back. If he could eat shit and call it honey for eleven years, he could do it for another eleven years. He shook himself violently, and then realized how over-wrought he was and how emotional he was being. He was trying to please his mother, the memory of his mother, but she would not be peeking down from a cloud and observing that he was a good boy. Fat chance of his daughters ending up at the Troc with Bunny to train them. All Bunny needed was the money, honey, and they would be proper Jewish girls, batting it out like mad in the back seat, the diamond engagement ring, the shower, the reception at "D" and the Boulevard with the combo playing the "Wedding Samba," the whole dreary *shmeer*. It was Sam Auer he had to worry about. It was much more likely that Sam Auer would end up as a regular customer at the Troc than that his daughters would appear as performers there. Perhaps that was why men held onto their children, to keep from going down the tube themselves.

He would leave it up to them. On the way back to Sixth and Cottonwood he determined that he would leave it up to them. He had been the good son, even though she loved Jerry and Sylvia more, Sylvia because she was a beauty, and Jerry be-cause he was a brilliant scholar. He would sit *shiva* by himself. His mourning was his alone. The rest was for public consump-tion. But if Jerry and Sylvia called, he would go to the funeral, even if it meant a fight.

When he reached his steps, he was about to put his key in the lock, but a sultry breeze traced across his cheek. He glanced toward Glendolph. Marge Coleman was a pig, but now that he had a taste of her, knew what she could do, what she was capable of, she had power over him. Even though he had show-ered in steamy water for fifteen minutes after she left, brushed his teeth twice, she had power over him.

He walked down Cottonwood and rapped on her door. She answered it in her bathrobe, and a knowing smile creased her lips.

"What can I do for you, Sam?"

"You still growing tomatoes?"

"A six-day crop, every month."

"Too bad."
"There's still the other, Sam."
"Four cash and six off the bill."
"Six cash and four off the bill."
"Okay."

Two of his roomers avoided him on Saturday, and three of his regular grocery customers did not come in to pay their weekly bills. By late afternoon he resigned himself to the fact that all were aboard who were coming aboard, and he locked up to go to his barber on Fairmount Avenue. He needed a haircut in case Jerry and Sylvia called and wanted him at the funeral. People had stared at him all day. His mother's obituary had appeared in the *Bulletin* and the *Inquirer*. A small notice. Charity work for the Deborah.

There was one Puerto Rican in the chair, and one other man ahead of him. Shumsky, the proprieter, examined him disapprovingly as the bell tinkled over his head.

"Haven't seen you in a long time, Sam. It must be two months."

"I'm faithful to you, Irving. I haven't had a haircut in two months."

Auer slumped down heavily in the chair next to the magazine rack. He recognized the other customer: Maury, a plumber from Brown Street. Irving Shumsky said, "Heard about your mother, Sam. Read about it in the *Bulletin*. Very sorry to hear about it."

"Everybody reads the *Bulletin*." Auer reached for a stack of magazines. Shumsky had an exotic collection of books and magazines. Instead of normal publications like *Collier's* or the *Saturday Evening Post*, Shumsky had subscriptions to the *Daily Worker*, socialist weeklies, magazines about cultural life in Russia and Chinese peasants, and books by Ring Lardner, Jr. and Howard Fast. Auer flipped through a back-dated issue of the *Daily Worker*, and Shumsky rested his scissors for a moment.

"Come to get a haircut for the funeral."

"Maybe. I don't know whether I'm invited yet."

Shumsky gave him a look. Then Auer was surprised to hear Shumsky speak Spanish to the Puerto Rican. The Latin seemed to be giving detailed instructions about his sideburns. With his dramatically etched sideburns, black pompadour, and sharply traced features, he looked like Aquaman or Submariner from "Marvel Comics."

Maury said, "Where you pick up the *spañol*, Irving?"

"My family went to Argentina before we came here. I spent eight years down there as a kid."

"That's down by Rio, ain't it?"

"No, Rio is Brazil. Argentina is Buenos Aires," Shumsky explained patiently.

"Lots of *putas* down there," Maury said. "I was on a tanker to Tahm-peeko during the war. Place crawling with *putas*. That's the only word I learned. *Puta* and *cerveza. Cerveza* means beer."

The Puerto Rican scowled, imagining they were mocking him. Auer decided to forgive Maury his ignorance. Half the men on his old block in Oxford Circle would have mixed up Buenos Aires and Rio, too. College graduates, and they read nothing. College graduates, and they had the conversation of stock clerks. He reached for a copy of the *Daily Worker* and smiled at the cartoon on the front page: an evil Uncle Sam distributing rifles to skeletons in Nazi uniforms. Old Irving never gave up. He still dreamed of seeing the Red Army march down Market Street on May Day.

With his head resting against the wall Auer dozed, exhausted by the emotional drain of the last two days. Shumsky prodded him back to consciousness. The shop was empty, and Auer, embarrassed by the way he had passed out, rose awkwardly and took his place on the chair.

"Just a trim. And raise the sideburns."

"A trim? To give you just a trim, I'll need sheep shears." Shumsky fingered his thick black hair, tugging tentatively at a tuft, and said, "At least it's clean for once. How come?"

"A woman gave me a shampoo last night. She insisted."

"It's still no go with Bunny?" Shumsky asked, clicking busily with his scissors.

"Nope. Still troubles."

"You've got all kinds of troubles. Harry Lipofsky was telling me how several businessmen down your way were putting pressure on him to get you to move out. And Maddy Dobry was telling me how you carry a pistol and a switchblade."

"The whole world comes to you, doesn't it, barber? You stay here ten hours a day, and you know more about what's going on than WCAU."

"It isn't just what people tell me. It's because I read."

"So I read, too."

"What?" Shumsky said scoffingly. "What? What do you read?"

"I just finished *Smoke*. Now I'm reading *Fathers and Sons*."

"You?" Shumsky spluttered. "You are reading Turgenev?"

"Sure. Since I left home, I must have read fifty books."

"I remember when you only read *Amazing Stories*."

"Even 'Amazing Stories' were better than that fantastic crap you've got over there."

"If you read and digested some of that literature over there, you would have a better understanding of what's been happening to you. Of the objective material and historical process behind it."

"What's there to understand, Shumsky? The *shvartzers* toss bricks through my windows. I don't need to hire Sam Spade to tell me that."

"If you could open your mind for once, you might see that it's an integral part of the system, Sam. Hatred is fomented among the races so that the attention of the workingman will be diverted from his true problems."

"There's no need to foment it. It's a very natural thing. Whenever people mix, one screws and one gets screwed."

"Do you think things like this could happen to you in Russia?"

"Of course not. I could never own a store in Russia."

"Boy, they've really got you brainwashed, Sam. You've got all the answers. You don't want to know nothing from nothing."

"If I'm brainwashed, what are you? What kind of robot reads that crap over there? Russia this and Russia that. Fuck Russia. I shit on Russia."

"This place is so wonderful? Look what they're doing to you. This place is dry. Look at the milkmen. In Argentina the milkmen wore colorful berets. They put wreaths on their horses and decorated their wagons. Here, it's all so dry. In Argentina, it was colorful."

"You like Argentina, they got boats leaving every day."

"I'm too old to start over. My Milton is graduating high school, and my Marvin is at Penn."

"So what are you complaining about? Where else does a *putzy* one-chair barbershop produce enough extra to send a boy to the University of Pennsylvania?"

"I'm paying through the nose for it. It costs me a fortune."

"With that nose you can afford it," Auer said and chuckled at his own comeback. "If Marvin were smarter, he could have won a scholarship. My brother Jerry won a full mayorality scholarship, and the tuition didn't cost us a cent."

Auer winced as the clippers bit too deeply into the nape of his neck. Shumsky said, "Bones for the dogs. They eat the meat, they toss us the bones. And we're supposed to sit up, scrape, bow, say thank you. They've got you well trained, Sam. They take all the choice cuts and leave you down there at Sixth and Cottonwood, fighting it out with the *shvartzers* for the leftovers. And all you know how to do is bark like a trained dog, defending your masters' interests."

Auer snorted. "And you say I've got all the answers."

"In Russia. . . ."

"What is ths crap with Russia?" Auer cut him off. "I'm from here. I'm from Sixth and Cottonwood, six blocks north of

Independence Hall. When I go home from here, I pass the big sign: 'Visit the house where Poe wrote *The Raven*.' What's Russia to me?''

"And this is your Utopia?'' Shumsky scoffed, digging in with his clippers.

"It's no Utopia, but think where we came from. Go take a walk over to that Cossack Hall. Look at those faces in there when they get drunk. A few glasses of vodka, and they're all ready to light the torches. That's where we came from. The only thing that stops them is that such things are not done here.''

"They're all fascists. They were Whites, czarists. They escaped.''

"They escaped. We escaped. They have their faces. We have our faces. Given the opportunity, they would gladly smash our faces and light the torches. And if those torches are ever lit, you know why they'll be lit? Because mockeys like you don't know to kiss the ground you walk on.''

Shumsky stepped back and said. "You are an ignoramus.''

"Fine,'' Auer said, rising. He ripped off the napkin around his neck and removed the barber's apron. "I'm an ignoramus. How much do I owe you?''

"I'm not finished.''

"You're finished. Skip it. I'll get it finished at Glass's.''

"I don't want your money. I can't do business with people who can't hold an intellectual conversation without turning into wild animals.''

Auer peeled off two one-dollar bills and said, "You charge a buck. Here's a bonus. The other dollar is a contribution toward your boat ticket.'' He crushed the bills and dropped them on the hair-covered floor as he stalked out.

It was twenty-to-six and, still fulminating against Shumsky, Auer hurried to Glass's barbershop at Fourth and Grenoble, only to discover that Glass had closed a little early. There were barbershops on Girard Avenue, but by the time he took a taxi to Girard they would all be closed, too.

Grumbling, he returned home and attempted to repair the

damage with his small curving cuticle scissors. Using the medicine cabinet mirror and a small hand mirror, he attempted to straighten out the ragged edges and cursed at his reflection for not keeping better scissors around the house. Bunny, for all her faults, had scissors.

After five minutes of clipping and snipping, his head was more uneven and chopped than before. This was his punishment for losing his temper. Lately he was becoming the most truculent bastard in town, a regular snap case. With all this careful and meticulous trimming, he was emerging as a lopsided porcupine. He was down to a choppy crewcut with irregular tufts sticking out like stubborn sage and cactus. He made one last attempt to achieve some sort of balance and checked the results. None too cool. He suddenly hurled the scissors into the bathtub and slammed the medicine cabinet door closed so hard that the mirror broke and a line divided his disfigured head. The scissors had bounced up and landed in the toilet bowl. He fished them out. It did not matter. The head could last till Monday, and if he went to the funeral tomorrow he would wear a hat anyway.

He reopened the store and, with the warm Saturday night, sold a lot of soda water, packets of Kool-Aid, and lemons for lemonade. Between customers he stayed outside on the step and glared at the Thurston School looming over him in the darkness. On a hot night like this he could have made a fortune on beer, but Mrs. Silverman had maneuvered to deny both his place and Leah's beer licenses because they were too close to the school. Silverman fought the waiver on the ordinance, the prissy shit-ass. It was against the law. How ducky! As if the kids did not walk exactly two blocks and see the same bums staggering out of Shor's or the Green Room. As if a law could protect these kids from anything. At six years old they knew everything. At twelve the girls were getting wall-jobbed up the alley. The City Council should be in the Astor Movie to hear the kids roar and hoot whenever one of the characters on the screen made a noble speech or gesture.

The light was on behind Big Grace's shade. Auer checked

to see whether Leah or her sons were looking, gathered up the day's take from his cash register, leaving behind just twenty to open up with tomorrow, and hurried across Sixth. With any luck he could make up for Thursday and come out ahead.

Auer winced. Somebody had pissed in the vestibule. With these open doorways, anybody dropped in. He knocked, and the shuffling of cards and clicking stopped. This time it was Barry who opened a careful two inches. Barry grinned. "Come to try your luck again, Sam? I knew you'd be back. Saw the bug bite you Thursday night."

Winston was there, dressed sharply as usual in a suede wraparound. The expensive Saturday night clothes of the other three Negroes around the card table made Auer flinch. Their sleek suits, lustrous neckties, golden cuff links, and white-on-white shirts contrasted sharply with the defeated furniture and stacks of dirty dishes on the cupboard. Peggy Moore was sprawled on the bed in the next room, her long black legs under a red slip.

"I don't want you in here," Grace said roughly.

Two of the strange Negroes tensed, and the biggest was about to rise when Grace signaled for him to take it easy and rasped, "What you getting your balls in an uproar for, Cleve? He's all right. I just don't want him sitting in and letting you nasty motherfuckers take his money away. Go home, Sàm."

Barry snorted at her domineering attitude and poured more Four Roses into his paper cup. He filled another cup for Auer and slid it across the table as Auer took a green kitchen chair. "You hear that fat bitch talk, Sam. Sometimes I don't know who the hell she thinks she is."

From the sofa, with her eyes closed, Grace murmured, "I sit down on your skinny ass you'll know who the fuck I am."

"That's a cool head," Winston said to Auer. "A very unique style."

"Yeah, I got in an argument with the barber and stormed out," Auer explained. "Then I tried to trim it myself, and it didn't come off too good."

"I'd say that," Cleveland agreed.

"You're looking pretty sharp, though, Winston," Auer said.

Winston fingered the lapel of his suede wraparound. "This is nigger upward mobility, Sam. I used to be a part-time burglar, and now I am an affluent numbers writer. With any luck I'll die the king of vice."

Everybody around the table chuckled, and Barry said, "How many chips you'll be needing, Sam? Start you off with twenty for starters? Everything's a quarter tonight."

"Twenty will be all I need to clean up tonight."

Barry winked, as if dismissing these pretensions, and slid four stacks of quarter chips across the table, guiding them through the maze of ashtrays, cups, and bottles. He scooped up Auer's two ten-dollar bills and tucked them into his shirt pocket as though they were gone forever. "Oh, my," he exclaimed. "I forgot the fucking introductions. This, gentlemen, is Mister Sam from across the way. Owns that store over there looks like an Indian fort. Mister Sam, this is Cleve, this one here is Willard, and this ugly-looking one is Calvin Jones. Looks like the fucking vice squad, don't he?"

Calvin Jones, a burly Negro in a gray pinstripe, shrugged indifferently, and from his broken nose and marked cheeks Auer would have bet he had much to do with the vice squad without ever belonging to it.

The card playing began, and Auer was irritated with himself as he again played like a real fish, recklessly, bluffing with low pairs, trying for inside straights, imagining that with bullheaded tactics he could reverse the tide. He was also aware that Barry was exploiting him, manipulating him, pouring him free drinks under the guise of friendship.

"I heard your mama died, Sam," Grace said from the sofa, her eyes still closed. "Little Herbert across the street told me the funeral's tomorrow."

Cleveland, Jones, and Willard eyed him inquisitively, as if wondering why he were playing cards at a time like this.

Auer said, "Little Herbert has a big mouth."

"Your mama was a nice woman," Grace intoned. It was like the bowels of a great distant black mountain speaking.

"Thanks, girl. I thought so, too."

"Whoof," Grace moaned. "She wasn't like Leah's mother. That was a mean old lady. I hated to go into Leah's store and see her mean old face. And with Miss Leah so nice, she go down to Glendolph five times a day, clean her up, give her her needles, and old Sara say, 'You hope I die, don't you? You can't wait till I die.' And Miss Leah come back crying."

"Leah's all right," Barry said. "I told every motherfucker around here that if he messes with Leah's store he'll have me to deal with."

Calvin Jones tossed three cards, signaled for three more, and said, "Well, that ain't too much danger to worry about."

"Yeah," Barry said calmly. "There are four dead sonsof-bitches in the graveyard thought the same thing."

"Four?" Willard squinted as if trying to recall something. "The last time you told it, it was five."

"Well," Barry said, shrugging. "Your mother passed by the cemetery, and one of my victims got up to trail after her hot ass."

Everybody laughed, and Auer joined in, noticing that Willard made absolutely no move to show he was offended. For a small, wiry man in his late fifties, Barry commanded a lot of respect on these streets. Younger, bigger men backed off because they knew Barry went all the way.

"I'm gonna die soon myself," Grace announced. "The doctor was here this afternoon and told me I was carrying too much weight for my heart. Said I better slim down to three hundred pounds."

They roared again, and the rolls of fat shook and quivered on Fat Grace's arms. Barry said, "Sheee. You ain't gonna die, bitch. The good die young, so your black ass'll hang on to two hundred."

"Nope. That's what the doctor told me," Grace said with

sudden seriousness. "They're gonna back up a Mack truck to haul my carcass out of here. Then, who'll cook and watch after you, Barry, you dumb cocksucker, you?"

"Ain't no problem at all," Barry assured her. "There're all kinds of alleycats waiting for you to kick off so'un they can get their hands on me. The day you dead, the line will stretch to Marshall Street. Peggy back there is just waiting for your ass to be out of the way so she can come sliding in here like Jackie Robinson into home plate."

With her heavy lids hiding her hazel eyes, Grace moved her huge head slowly. "Listen to that fool talk. I'd like to see you run with Peggy Moore, boy. She is too fast for your ass, Barry."

The card players glanced back at Peggy Moore. She was sleeping like an angel, apparently nothing under her red slip. Auer was struck by the long sweep of her arms. Peggy had the arms of a fashion model. Ridiculously enough, he could envision her removing elegant high pink cotton gloves as she swirled around in a clinging gown. That was especially ridiculous when he recalled all those jabs and hooks she threw the night of her brawl with Big Vye.

"You still running with Peggy?" Auer asked Winston.

"She still holds a warm spot in my affections, but we have gone our separate ways, Sam. Mostly I have this redhead from Temple University these days. She thinks it's very daring socializing with someone of my pigmentation. I'm afraid I might show up in one of her term papers."

"Play cards," Cleveland said.

On the next hand Willard's pair of aces lost to Auer's triple fours. As Auer scooped in one of the few pots he had won, Willard said, "You went to that Thurston School across the street?"

"About two hundred years ago." Auer offered the deck to be cut.

"Yeah," Willard mused, "I got you placed now. I was two years behind you. In Miss Miller's class."

"Room 303," Auer said as he dealt. "She's long gone. Where you living now?"

"Over by West Philly. I remember your father now, too, man. Grabbed me once and accused me of stealing a tennis ball from the window. That man shook me and shook me till I thought my teeth was gonna shake loose."

Willard's friends appeared distracted, but Auer detected the menace creeping into his tone. Auer began scratching his ribs, near his jacket pocket. "Well, did you steal it?"

Willard ignored the question and continued, "I always swore I was gonna get that man one day. Then we moved out to West Philly, and I went to another school."

Auer held his five cards in one hand and began scratching his ribs inside his jacket pocket, while the others played their cards with a strained nonchalance.

"I saw that store tonight, all boarded up, and that's what I best remembered about this neighborhood—the way that old man grabbed my ear and shook me. I still resent that. I don't resent much, but that man had no right to shake me that way, you know what I mean?"

Cleveland, eyeing the bulge in Auer's pocket, smiled at Calvin Jones and said to Willard, "He must have really shook you hard 'cause your fucking brain came loose. You sound like you want to mess with the sonofabitch, here, and you can't even see that artillery in his pocket."

"It wouldn't be too advisable to mess with Sam," Winston said smoothly. "Sam is a tough cookie. Took on seven kids down there by Sixth and Grenoble one night and came out of it alive. Even broke a few arms."

Auer nodded at Winston in appreciation. It was a strange note. Those were the first words of praise that had come in his direction for many months, from anybody.

"Besides," Barry said, "you want to fuck with Sam, you got to get past me first."

"Oh, shit," Calvin Jones said. "Now he's gonna tell us about those four or fourteen people he killed again."

The moment of tension dissolved into laughter, and Willard relaxed into a less bellicose posture. Auer removed his hand from his pocket and scratched his neck. It was like playing with a new gang in the schoolyard or entering a new bar. A man had to establish who he was, and then everybody could relax.

By two in the morning Auer was eighty dollars down. He cashed in his remaining chips and excused himself. As he rose, he gave one last look at Peggy Moore on the bed, obviously sleeping off some narcotic. Grace had often let women use that bed in there, charged two bucks for the room. Several years ago she arranged dates between Negroes and Mrs. Ramble, the white trash who lived in Leah's second-floor back.

Winston said, "Just a second, Sam, I'd like to talk to you about a matter. Outside."

Auer thought he was going to offer him Peggy, but when they got to the step Winston said, "You've been having a streak of bad luck, Sam."

"Thanks for speaking up for me in there, Winston."

"You interested in getting in a game where you don't lose?"

"I don't get you."

Winston lowered his voice. "Well, I may be moving on to better things. I may. Nothing sure yet. But my bankers would be interested in somebody to cover this territory. A reliable person, with a good head for figures."

After a second of perplexity Auer said, "You mean, write book?"

"Something like that. There could even be heavier action—once you got established."

Auer paused to light a cigarette. "I don't know. I've never thought about it."

"Start thinking about it. No hurry yet. Just think about it."

"Thanks, Winston."

The sharply dressed gambler gave him an encouraging pat on the shoulder, and Auer decided that Winston was definitely all right as he crossed Sixth. The burden of the eighty dollars he had just lost was slightly relieved. Slightly. One hundred and forty bucks in two nights of gambling. Sam Auer was a real ace. At least he had the thing about the funeral expenses straight in his head. Why had he been so concerned about his third? A funeral home was not like a cafeteria, where you had to pay before you ate. In business, the bills came after the fact. And if he was a bit late with his third, Sylvia and Jerry were always late with their thirds for Florida. His big deal little kid brother. The kid jerked off every time he went to the bathroom till he was old enough to vote for Truman.

Auer undressed in the darkness. He still did not believe that she was dead. The call had come three nights ago, Thursday, and it seemed like an eternity since Thursday. The only way to prove it was to go to the funeral tomorrow and watch them lower the casket into the ground. Even then he would not believe it. If they called tomorrow and insisted, he would go to the funeral. And try not to provoke any fights. He closed his eyes and saw Miss Ann Smith, the stripper with a college education. Miss Ann Smith and her swinging birdies.

The sun glinting on the tips of the barbed wire lifted his lids, and he blinked at the shattered crystal on his wristwatch. It was eight-thirty, and today, on the very day of the funeral, he could stay closed. Out of respect for the neighbors. The neighbors.

He chose not to turn on his fluorescent lights and prepared himself a cup of coffee in the darkened store. Cars bumped over the cobbles beyond his boards. The undertone only seemed to accentuate the silence. He had never listened to the silence before, studied it, concentrated on it. It was there behind everything.

Auer shaved and showered. The freaky-looking hair he could do nothing about, but he would be wearing a cap anyway. He dressed in old, stained denims and a sweatshirt. If they called, he could quickly change into his good suit and tie. They would have to call. It was impossible to conduct the funeral without the oldest son present. He might go anyway. If only to see Sheila and Stephanie. So long since he had seen them. Bunny refused to drive down here, nor would she let him visit the house till all the legal questions were settled.

He snapped on the television and listened to a Baptist choir from Georgia. The chorus gave way to a strident minister preaching a sermon. It was futile switching channels. At this hour all the channels had some priest, some pastor, some rabbi bleating and roaring and wheezing in that unctuous voice that was supposed to sound religious and pushed the button for automatic boredom. What did it all amount to? Be good, be good, be good. Be like who? Like cartoon characters? Joe Palooka or Terry and the Pirates. They were good and pure. Outside the door was the real world, and what did the grandeur of God or the solemnity of death have to do with that whining on the TV screen or that droning "Mr. and Mrs. Glass, two hundred dollars! Mr. and Mrs. Birnbaum, three hundred dollars! Mr. and Mrs. Dorf, fifty dollars! Mr. and Mrs. Dorf, fifty dollars!"

He went outside with his beach chair and newspapers, wanted Leah to be sure and see him when they called so she could send Maddy or Herbert to fetch him. It was a beautiful Sunday, a beautiful day for a funeral. It would be beautiful at the cemetery. He would behave himself and let all bygones be bygones for a while. It would sure be nice to see Sylvia after five years. They had never gotten along, but she was still his sister.

Cars were rushing past, speeding down Sixth. Half of them would take the left turn at Race, cross the bridge, and head for the shore. The Sunday drive. Sunday had been Bunny's favorite day for torturing him. She had the full day to work on him and made the most of it, doing a wash load or annoying him with the vacuum while he tried to read the papers, and demanding to know by what right he parked on his fat ass and read the papers when she had to straighten up the house. And he invariably snarled back something about why the hell she had to screw around with the house on the only day he had to relax. Then came the drive. She nagged at him to get ready, and an hour later she was still futzing around with the kids, arguing with them about what to wear, and then snapping at him for no reason.

Then they all piled into the car, and he had to drive them to Bucks County to be bored at some antique or flower show, or over to Bala Cynwyd to gape at the mansions of the rich, or around Fairmount Park to watch the *shvartzers* picnicking, while the girls scrambled back and forth in the back seat, scratching each other, Bunny scolding Mom for not disciplining them or getting peeved if Mom so much as tapped their hands. And finally the grand finalé, ending up at the Hot Shoppe on Broad Street, with Steppie in the high chair, harried waitresses, Mom picking at her food, making faces, Bunny complaining she never got to eat her own supper she was so busy attending to the girls. Then Steppie knocks over her glass, and Bunny gets peeved at the waitress for giving her a look when she asks for more napkins. Those were his Sundays. He would rather be a bum sitting in Franklin Square than endure those Sundays again.

Leah was coming out of her store with Maddy and Herbert, the boys in dark blue suits and Leah in a black dress. She gave him a puzzled look and called out, "You want a lift, Sam? We're going to take a taxi."

Controlling the shudder lancing through him, gripping the arms of his beach chair, he called back, "No, thanks."

"Okay, we'll see you there."

Leah gave him another puzzled expression and then continued up Sixth with the boys. He saw Maddy give Herbert a small punch on the arm, obviously for saying something sarcastic, and Leah telling Maddy to leave him alone. The three of them entered a yellow cab at the stand at Sixth and Green Garden. He shuddered again, remembering the night he had to threaten the driver with his wrench.

Auer gathered up his beach chair, newspapers, coffee cup, and cigarettes and carried them inside. Now if they called, nobody would be in Leah's store to fetch him to the booth. He threw himself down on the sofa and for five seconds thrashed out of control with his arms around his head. He refused to cry.

No more tears. He would not go to their fucking funeral because it was not for his mother. Funerals were for the living. There were no respects to pay because he did not respect them. A daughter who flies back after five years, after writing about once a year. A son like Jerry, who could never be bothered. Screw them. Fuck them. Let all the hypocrites howl. It took strength to be "a focal point of tension."

He put on his jacket and tucked his pistol and switchblade into his pocket. Outside, as he crossed Sixth, the shade in Grace's window was pulled aside, and Barry was beckoning to him.

"Hey, Sam! Sam, my man! C'mon over here!"

Suddenly they were old buddies from the Army, Auer thought. And so what? Barry was about as trustworthy as Zig and Gall, which was not saying much, but he had hung around with Zig and Gall for thirty years before telling them to pack it in.

"I wanted to invite you for a Sunday taste," Barry said from the window. "C'mon in, Sam."

"What, want to lubricate my losses?"

"No card game. Just a friendly little Sunday taste. Don't be so mean, Sam."

Auer went rhrough the smelly vestibule, and Barry opened the door. Grace was still asleep in the back room, looked like an enormous loaf of pumpernickel under the pink spread. George Skinner and Cleveland were at the table and toasted Auer with their paper cups. They were his favorite people from the two card games. He was practically at his club.

"A man tries to be your friend, and you don't half let him," Barry said. "You're too hard a man, Sam. I'm going to treat you to some real James Beam."

Auer sagged onto the sofa, and Barry poured him a generous shot in a paper cup. He wondered why Barry still hid his bottle in a brown paper bag. There was no statute against drinking in the sanctity of the home.

"Y'know, the goddamn people around here don't do right

by this man," Barry told Skinner and Cleveland. "You know that sonofabitch, Lou Johnson, over by Seventh Street?"

"Yeah, I know him," Cleveland said. "I don't want to know him, but I know him."

"That Johnson had his boys throw bricks through this man's windows. That ain't right. That ain't no way to teach children. I mean, Sam here is, you know . . . white, and we're, well, you know; but Sam, he's been around here all his, you know, I mean, everybody around here, you know, it ain't never, I mean . . . shit. Nobody should act like that."

"Well, get his ass," Cleveland said. "I never liked that man. He comes sniffing around Twelfth and Poplar, him and that fat wife of his'n, and we told him to stay clear. We didn't need his kind at Twelfth and Poplar."

"I've gone after him," Auer said. "Can't even catch him in. He's always away, or they won't answer the door."

"Well, get him when he comes back," Cleveland said.

"He's been away?"

"Hell, yeah. Working down in Maryland or somewhere. If his ass was around, his ass would be in Zacky's. I'll let you know when he gets back. You can use that thing you got in your pocket to cross-ventilate him."

Skinner snapped on the radio, and they heard the voice of By Saam announcing the pregame lineups at Shibe Park.

"How's Sam gonna do that?" Barry asked. "This man got two cute daughters. How's he gonna shoot Johnson? They'll put him over there on Fairmount Avenue in the same cell with Buzzy. I like this man, Sam. I'd put my hand down on the Route 43 trolley car tracks for this man." He swung around. "You want me to do Johnson for you, Sam? When he gets back, I'll lay a bottle up by the cocksucker's head."

"Why, thank you, Barry," Auer said, and they all laughed and slapped their knees.

Skinner pushed himself up from the kitchen table to grab the fifth and refill all the cups. They were quickly gone, and everybody had another. By the second inning the Cincinnati

Reds were leading the Phillies four to nothing, and they had finished the Beam and broken open a Calvert. Auer was feeling warm and looser inside. Nothing seemed to count. He was flaunting every rule in the book, and no lightning bolt crashed down to char him to a cinder. Of what use was a God who did not reward and punish? He swished the Calvert through his teeth. A wake should be joyous. Grief proved that people did not believe in an afterlife. That was why they cried; this shit was all there was. The only thing he was missing was seeing what kind of chintzy spread Jerry and Terri laid out for the crowd from the cemetery. Their icebox door creaked like Inner Sanctum, but whenever they dropped by with their three brats, Aladdin was supposed to produce a magic feast.

Grace loomed in the doorway, yawning to reveal almost toothless gums. She was wider than the doorframe. Rapidly blinking away cobwebs, she said, "What the hell you doing here, Sam?"

"I'm listening to the ball game."

"That's nice," Grace said, squeezing through the door sideways and brushing against both frames. "That's real nice. Miss Leah went and closed her store to go to your mama's own funeral, and you're in here drinking with these bums? You ain't shit, Sam. I mean, you ain't shit."

"Don't come down on the man," Barry shouted back at her. "What the hell you care? You stick your big nose into everybody's business, bitch. Can't you figure out that Sam don't want to think about it? That's why he's here. He wants to be here with his friends and drink, and forget about it. I know his feelings."

"Well, he ain't gonna set his ass here while I'm here," Grace roared. "Sam! You get your ass out of here and take a taxi to your own mama's funeral. Go on. Get the fuck out of here!"

Skinner and Cleveland chuckled at Auer's difficulties in rising from the sofa. The blended whiskey had hit him on an empty gut, and he could not recall ever having been this woozy.

"You better wash up first!"Fat Grace raged. "You're a terrible sight. Go across to your place, put your head under a cold shower, and then put on a suit. If I could get through the door, I'd drag you over there and dress you proper. You get over there, and I'll have Cleveland drive you to the cemetery."

"How the fuck Cleveland gonna drive him to no cemetery?" Barry shouted at Grace. "He's so goddamn drunk he couldn't get no key into the ignition. How you like the cops to stop their asses on Broad Street?"

"Put some hair around that ignition, and Cleve'll get his key in," Skinner said.

Auer clenched, resisting a wave of hysteria preparing to sweep over him. If he visualized that scene too clearly, saw it in his mind, he might collapse in a giggling fit on the floor. He saw Barry, Skinner, Cleveland, Grace, and Sam Auer staggering into the cemetery, pushing the other mourners aside to see the casket being lowered into the ground. And then piling back into the car and driving up to Jerry's house, elbowing all his aunts and uncles aside to get to the corned beef and potato salad. It was horrible and ludicrous, but why not? These were the neighbors. His mother had lived her entire life around here except for the last five years. Who else were the neighbors? Not the people from Oxford Circle who knew her only as a pathetic old lady. The Auers were from Sixth and Cottonwood, and these were the neighbors.

Grace ordered him to get out. Auer stumbled through the vestibule and on the front step pulled himself unnaturally erect, then winced as he heard Grace raising hell with the boys inside. He laughed. Fat Grace was a *balebooseh*, a total woman.

The blended whiskeys had dilated his pupils, and the raw contours of his homeland struck back at him with stunning power. Sprigs of brownish grass sprouting through the cobbles on Cottonwood. Leah's long side fence tilting toward him, crowned with thick barbed wire. Thickly meshed screens over her windows. A voluntary concentration camp. No singing from the storefront church at Marshall and Cottonwood. He could use some of that good, powerful Wednesday night singing. He sang. . . .

> "Through this world of toil and cares,
> If I stumble, Lord, who cares . . ."

The pavement swayed and pitched as he headed down Sixth. It was littered with yesterday's newspapers and chips of broken beer bottles. Sunday in Philadelphia. The distant towers of William Penn atop City Hall and the PSFS skyscraper. Why was this Sunday different from all other Sundays? Because on this Sunday they were burying his mother. Otherwise, it was exactly like every other Sunday. If a man could defeat Sunday, he triumphed over life. On those Sunday drives with Bunny, picking a destination always alleviated the tension. Five Points. Wissahickon Creek. Cherry's in the Mansion. The Zoo. The Zoo was always an excellent last resort. As long as there was a specific destination, there was less tension.

He needed to eat. The whiskey was sloshing around in his empty belly like bilge water in the hull of a rotting ship. As he slouched past Franklin Square, he could taste a Levis's hot dog. Down at Sixth and Lombard. A seeded roll. Tangy pickle. Hot mustard. A cherry phosphate. Even Franklin Square was deserted today, more squirrels on the grass than bums on the benches. He glanced without interest at the towers of the Delaware River Bridge. If this were a normal Sunday, he would be driving back from the shore with Bunny and Mom, the kids squabbling in the back seat. This society had been designed by a fiend. Five days a week people worked at jobs they mostly hated, and then they swarmed to the shore and swarmed back and ended up honking their horns in traffic jams on Admiral Wilson Boulevard.

Sixth Street was empty up to Market, wholesale houses and businesses closed for Sunday. He wondered whether Jerry was giving her a proper funeral. Before she took the train to Miami, she became very specific about a proper burial. A casket with no nails, only wooden pegs. A shroud made by old women out of pure linen. It was unlikely that Jerry would worry about such details. Jerry was a modern man and above such rituals. Sophisticated. What replaced ritual? Sewing machines?

"*Yis-ga-dahl-vi-yis-ka-dash-shi-may-rah-baw*," Auer recited. It had such power. Such raw power. A sonorous and powerful chant to conclude and honor a life on earth. He wished, he wished, he wished they were kids again, walking down to Levis's for a hot dog, Jerry and he quizzing each other on sports or geography: what did Harry Heilman hit in 1925, what was the capital of Australia? And as smart as Jerry was, he always lost those quizzes to Sam.

Market Street was empty all the way down to City Hall. Today he wanted life, and the city had none to offer. There were a few people waiting for a trolley in front of the Earle Theater at Eleventh Street. A few adolescents playing the pinball machine in the Dewey's orangeade stand across Market. Auer shut his eyes. This was all so shabby. They had let this historic area get so run-down. Up the street was Independence Hall. Three blocks over was Betsy Ross's house, and yet they had let this section become so grubby. There was the big plan. In a few years this was all supposed to be torn down and be replaced by a park and a mall. Big deal. It would probably make this stretch even deader. They would replace all these secondhand bookstores and shoe jobbers with a park. Perhaps if they arranged a population exchange, they might accomplish something.

As he reached the corner of Sixth and Chestnut, he observed two busloads of tourists running around Independence Hall. Their chartered buses were parked farther down the block. Auer chuckled and lit a cigarette. They were all foreigners in funny-looking suits, all very pompous, the posers assuming stiff postures, and the picture takers crouching and stooping with their cameras to get in both the subjects and the statue of George Washington.

Near the buses were three official-looking Americans who seemed to be running the show, looked like a bunch of Scoutmasters trying to herd the foreigners back on the buses. From City Hall, probably. Maybe worse. Maybe Washington. Brought these foreigners over here to show them how great things were. Shit, he had just paid his taxes last month, and this was what they spent the money for—to bring these creeps over here and show them the Cradle of Liberty. Why the hell didn't they take them a few blocks up the street to Eighth and Race or Seventh and Cottonwood? See his boarded-up store? "We hold these truths to be self-evident." Bullshit. "That all men are created equal." Bullshit. Who believed it? A man read that speech six blocks up the street, they would nail his ass to a mailbox.

Auer scowled as he recognized the babble of voices across Chestnut Street as German. Deutsch, no less. Deutsch. Maybe the S.S. had rented the place for its annual reunion? First the U.S. kicked their asses, and then brought the bastards over here to show we were nice folks.

He cupped his hands around his mouth and called, "*Yah, Yah! Jawohl,* Fritz! *Jawohl,* Hans! *Achtung!*"

Several of the tourists were staring at him. They were all bulky types, thick, like a delegation of bill collectors or labor leaders. They were discussing him, pointing at him, and a few were poising their cameras. Like maybe he was picturesque. The Deutsch tourists wanted a shot of a typical American bum, hair screwed up and drunk, on the afternoon they buried his mother. He would give them an action shot.

Auer raised his arm in a Nazi salute. "*Sieg Heil,* motherfuckers!"

His audience was getting bigger. All of them were unslinging their cameras now, flocking to get in on the action. The guides were signaling them frantically, and the bus drivers were honking their horns. A fat tourist in a gray suit and a red Bavarian cap had got down on one knee to take his shot.

"You want something?" Auer shouted. He reached down and cupped his groin. "Latch onto this, baby."

The red car screeched as it was halfway across Sixth Street. Auer winced as it immediately went into reverse and pulled back to stop about twenty feet behind him. He nodded his head knowledgeably. That was just like these cocksuckers: never around when he needed them and had to show up just as he was having a little fun. They were staring at the back of his neck. More bullshit. He had every right to stand here if he pleased and catch this goofy scene. He spent four years in the U.S. Army fighting for this building and the right to stand where he damn pleased. He was just having a little fun.

Somebody beeped a horn. Probably the cops. He resolved not to look back. That was exactly what the sonsofbitches wanted. If he returned their gaze, it was tantamount to an admission that he was guilty of a misdemeanor, and he was guilty of absolutely nothing. Perhaps of making an obscene gesture in a public place. This was just like the cops. When the bricks were flying through his window and he was getting stomped on Grenoble Street, they were having coffee at the diner, but they had nothing better to do on a boring Sunday afternoon than bug an honest citizen. Now the American guides were pleading with the Krauts to get back in the buses, but the Krauts were too interested in this scene.

Feigning a casual air, he lit a cigarette, but slowly, inexorably, with an almost physical pain tightening his neck muscles, he glanced back over his shoulder at the patrol car.

He had won. He had forced them to make the first move, not let them get away with shooing him along without saying anything, scoot him out of here with just their presence. The cop behind the wheel was crooking his finger, so Auer had already won a moral victory. And they were up the creek anyway. With all those foreigners with cameras across Chestnut, they could not try any rough stuff.

He approached the car coolly, nonchalantly, making them

sweat it out. The thing to be with cops was debonair, casual, puff slowly on the cigarette.

"Aren't you a long way from Eighth and Race, buddy?" the driver asked.

"I'm not from Eighth and Race, I'm from Sixth and Cottonwood."

"I didn't ask where you were from," the driver snapped. The other cop was getting out of the car. The driver was getting out of the car. Auer stepped back, but he was not going to let these snide bastards intimidate him. He was an established businessman going for a hot dog at Levis's.

"Franklin Square's back that way," the bigger cop said.

"I'm going the other way," Auer said, pointing south with his thumb. "For a hot dog."

"Well, maybe you better just do that," the driver said. "You're not too decently dressed to be around here."

"Decently dressed? I thought as long as my ass was covered and my fly was zipped I was decently dressed."

"Let's see some I.D.," the taller cop said.

"There ain't no such thing. My kid brother is a lawyer. He told me that nobody has to show an identity in the United States."

"That's it, Mac." The driver wheezed in resignation. "Hop in the back."

"Bullshit," Auer said, stepping back. "I ain't going nowhere."

The expression on the driver's face went through a series of transitions beginning with shock and ending with rage. He repeated, "Hop in back, buddy. That's it. The rear seat."

The other cop was brandishing his club, and Auer retreated, throwing up his arms. Across Chestnut, flashbulbs were popping in front of Independence Hall. The cars driving down Sixth slowed up to watch the action.

"What is it with you guys?" Auer spluttered. "What the hell's the matter with you?" he pleaded as they tried to grab him, the shouts of the tourists loud in his ears. He broke free, and they were circling him with their clubs. Out of the corner of his eye he saw one of the guides holding his hands over his face, while the foreigners gesticulated and several were trying to reload their cameras.

"Been living it up today, huh?" the driver said, poising and waving his club, "Tied yourself a few on, and it's made you frisky."

"C'mon, man," Auer complained. "Leave me alone, will you? What is it with you guys? Get off me."

The driver rushed in, and Auer pushed him off. As the cop fell back, he tugged at the tan jacket, ripping the pocket. Auer felt his heart freeze with horror as the pistol spilled out and clattered on the sidewalk.

"Hoo!" the driver bellowed. Auer saw the nightstick coming at his head. With his forearm he blocked the downward arc, pain lashing through his arm, shouts in his ears, and then a bigger pain in his skull, a distant sound of "thwap" sagging his knees, another explosion near his temple, an enormous wave of agony fusing with the first, rushing together, mingling into a red screen fading into blackness.

A slap across the mouth revived him. They were dragging him out of the car, twisting his foot as they rushed him up the steps, dragging him, shoving, pushing, jostling him along.

They yanked off his belt, whipping it through the loops, shoved him against the wall. They had ripped the back of his trousers pulling the switchblade from his pocket. Lights were glaring over him. Harsh, blinding lights. They were rushing him down the hall to the bullpen, going to toss him in there with all the drunks sprawled on the floor.

The barred doors clanged open, and he felt himself being hurled against the wall. His arms came up just in time to protect his face from being smashed against the rough plaster, and he paid for it with a banged elbow. After a few seconds of supporting himself against the wall, he slowly slid down the rough plaster like ice cream melting off a cone. As he reached the floor, he turned over, rested his head between his knees, not wanting to examine his surroundings.

It hurt all over. He could not remember hurting like this since high school, a gym class, climbing the rope, the rope coming loose from its mooring and him falling thirty feet to the mats below, slamming onto the mats. They had pulled off his shoes, and his palms and head were smeared with blood. His ears were ringing, and he felt like he had a concussion. They had no right to rough up anybody this way. No right. He suddenly chuckled in his misery. He had taken a worse beating from the cops than from the gang on Grenoble Street.

When he looked up a few minutes later, he saw there were five or six whites in the lockup with him, all the rest were black. The Sunday crowd. Pulled out of speakeasies, picked up on corners, squatting around him on the floor with their heads in their arms. One big Negro was taking a crap on the seatless toilet bowl, and the drunks were moaning and mumbling, dribbling at the mouth, walking in circles, cursing. His nose wrinkled at the stench of unwashed feet and dirty socks without shoes. It was worse than the stink of the man on the toilet bowl.

Auer watched a turnkey tap his club over the fingers of a young Negro who had gripped the outside bars. Two more Negroes were dragged down the hall, were being frisked with their heads down and their hands up against the wall.

He closed his eyes. They had no right to treat a man this way. He had only been heading down to Levis's for a hot dog and gotten a little out of line, and now there was blood dripping from his scalp and his collarbone felt broken.

When he opened his eyes again, he saw Jonesie from Thursday night's card game smiling and nodding to him from the far end of the lockup. Auer returned the greeting with a small twist of his hand and attempted to smile, but his lips did not quite make it. That was funny. He had buddies down here. It was like the club.

He fought to stop the tear, but it leaked out anyway, mixed with the dried blood on his cheek. He was going to have to call Jerry and tell Jerry to come down here and bail him out of Mocco. All the friends and relatives at the funeral reception, the whole city, would know that Sam Auer was in the tank with all these blacks.

PART FOUR

PART FOUR

Mutty Zackman was annoyed at the roasting he was getting off the newspapers. Zeke, his chauffeur, was also annoying him with that humming in the front seat. He gave the bartender a break, let him escape from behind the bar for a few hours, and Zeke had to croon even though he knew it irritated his boss, when he hummed along with that crappy rhythm and blues. As if they did not have that crap blaring away all day and night.

"Knock it off, will you?" Zacky snapped.

The driver reached forward and turned off his radio.

"That's better. That crap gets to me."

"No sweat, Mutt."

Zacky sank lower in the rear seat of his Cadillac convertible and let the sun pound down on his face. He wanted to write a letter to the papers, but his lawyers advised him to say absolutely nothing. A reply would only fuel it. In a few months, with the usual sealed brown envelopes, it would all blow over till the next time snotty reporters scratched around for a sensational issue. The papers never gave both sides of any issue. It was easy to write exposés of Zackman, Baron of Zackmanville, with thousands of violations of the housing code in his ninety properties. The papers neglected to mention the difficulties in renting rooms to ex-sharecroppers who pawned his fire extinguishers for a pint of whiskey, chopped up the banisters and stripping on the stairs for firewood, stole the light bulbs from the halls for their own rooms, clogged the hall toilets with clothespins, never paid the last bill, and vanished in the night.

His own daughter was not very objective for a college student. Shana called him from Sarah Lawrence to inform him, quite pompously, that she was reading the series of articles and was ashamed of the name Zackman. Also, that he was not even a capitalist bloodsucker but a feudal vampire. Also, that he was notorious. One of the illiterates at the social welfare center where she did volunteer work in Harlem had asked if she were related to the famous Mutty Zackman of Philadelphia. And she had said no.

Zacky smiled with his eyes closed. He sort of liked the idea of being notorious. It was a step up for a boy who began life plucking chickens on Marshall Street, slitting throats, draining their blood in a bucket. So forty years later he could have an aristocrat at Sarah Lawrence who was educated enough to call her daddy a feudal vampire. Unfortunately, they forgot to teach Shana to cancel her charge accounts at Sak's and Peck and Peck's, which sent monthly bills to the feudal vampire. He himself had never owned a garment that was not flawed, mended, or a hand-me-down till the age of twenty-four. What that was like they could not teach at Sarah Lawrence. And with all the arguments they had on Shana's vacations, she had never been able to answer him one question: if he could make it, why not everybody else? Zeke was humming again, and it was lulling him to sleep.

A sudden bump over a brick woke him, and they were on Seventh Street. He saw Sam Auer coming out of Shor's with two quarts of beer.

"Pull over," Zacky said. Often, when feeling low, he was given to impetuous outbursts of generosity. A bum hit him for a dime, and he slipped him a dollar bill, just to catch his reaction. Charity by checks and mail deprived him of the personal pleasure of seeing the joy on the recipient's face.

The Cadillac turned into the curb. Zacky called, "Sam. Hey, Auer, come here for a minute."

Auer paused and thrust out his lower lip in recognition of the honor of being summoned by the Baron of Zackmanville. All by himself, Zacky was putting this place on the map.

"How's Jerry, kid?"

The "kid" Auer found strange. In his entire life he had not exchanged fifty words with Mutty Zackman.

"Haven't seen him for a while."

"I heard he had to go bail for you at Mocco."

"He went on his own. I never called him."

"Had you in there for a week, didn't they? Until they straightened out that matter about the pistol?"

Auer shrugged. "Eight days."

"Things haven't been going too good for you, fellah. I understand you've been catching a hard time from the *dreck* on my block."

Auer glanced at Big Zeke. The driver was impassive or unaware of the meaning of the word *dreck*.

"You bring these people around here, Mutt, and we have to deal with them."

"I don't bring anyone around anywhere, kid. I rent rooms. You've been reading that series in the papers? The reporters smear me on the front page, but they don't answer one question: they don't say where else a poor man can get a roof over his head for eight bucks a week."

"Maybe they should erect you a monument for public service, Mutt."

Big Zeke strained not to grin in the front seat. Zackman slowly relit his dead cigar. He had stopped to give this *zhlub* good news and received unwarranted guff. It was obviously impossible to supply a misfit with good news.

"Medals, I don't need. Anytime the city wants to take these properties off my hands, I'll be more than glad to sell out. I stopped to tell you your troubles were over," Zackman said. The idea had occurred to him only thirty seconds ago, when he saw Auer coming out of Shor's. Now it seemed like an excellent idea. "I've had reports on your troubles with the Johnsons. Johnson is coming back next week. I'm going to throw the sonsofbitches out before the old man gets back."

"Don't do me any favors, Zacky."

Zackman tossed his head in bewilderment. Some people were beyond help. "You don't get me, kid. You'll be able to take down your boards, and put in windows again. That should not be a cause for giving me lip."

"Nah. I shouldn't give you lip, Mutt. You're a generous guy. The women tell me that when you're in a good mood you let them wash your steps and knock three bucks off the bill."

Zeke hunched his broad shoulders to restrain his laughter, and Zackman looked up in sorrow. It had been so long since anyone spoke to him this way he had to assume the grocer was deranged. "Sam," he said, "try prosperity for a while. I stop to tell you I'm taking the heat off you, and you bite my head off. Now that you say it, maybe I am doing it for me. If I let them get away with that shit around your corner, who knows where it might end?"

Auer had no answer for that. Zackman, perplexed by his blank expression, studied the grocer for a moment and motioned to Zeke.

"Let's go. This man is in another world."

The Cadillac rolled down Seventh, interrupting a stickball game, and Auer returned to the shade of his store. It was too hot to snap on the double lights. He drank his beer in the shadows, staring at the two bricks holding his door open for the sunlight. It was a little late for anybody to wave a magic wand and make everything all better. It was no longer a question of windows or boards. Lou Johnson owed him. And like old Jonesie in that cell: You must hurt a man real hard one time once to clarify matters. Lou Johnson owed him for the stink in here when he returned to this store after eight days downtown, the moldy bread and the sour milk. Johnson owed him for the battered fingers on his left hand when he started to rattle the bars, demand his rights, and the turnkey bashed his fingers with a nightstick. Perhaps when Lou Johnson's body was lying in a gutter with a few broken bones, matters could go back to normal. Meanwhile, normal was a whole new ball game.

In the evening he stuck his new switchblade in his jacket pocket and strolled over to Seventh Street. Just in case Johnson returned early from Maryland. He missed his pistol, which had been confiscated. Lou Katz had said it was hot but never that hot, used to kill a druggist on Porter Street last year. It had really given Jerry the chance to lord it over him. So now the whole city knew that Sam Auer was a jailbird who made obscene gestures in public places and staggered around drunk with a hot pistol.

Auer fingered his torn pocket, poorly mended after that altercation with the law. His heels were run-down, his watch crystal cracked, everything about him was ragged or battered. If he were a ship, he would put into port for overhaul and repairs. About the only thing working properly for him lately was his joint. Marge Coleman could give him the testimonial dinner. Since leaving the can, he had been banging her almost every night and almost developing an affection. Till last night when she pulled that crap. He was sleeping afterward, peaceful as a baby, and the bitch sneaks into the store. He might never have caught her if a car had not run over a bottle on Cottonwood Street, popping it with a loud explosion. Red-handed he caught her. Marge had managed to get the cash register open without ringing the bell and had pocketed sixty bucks cash. What a woman! When he threw her out, practically knocking her down the side steps, instead of getting angry she said, "If you don't want me no more, Sam, I can send around Charlotte or Joanie. . . ." What a woman.

The sidewalks were moist from late afternoon showers, and the berrypickers had spread newspapers on their steps to protect their bottoms. Bowes was entertaining a bunch of people with his guitar at #422, using that sliding spoon and thimble style. The music stopped as Auer climbed the steps and rang the bell at #424.

"They ain't there, if that's who you're looking for," Maggie May said.

"Where they at?" Auer asked.

"They all got moved out this afternoon."

"So fast?" Auer felt his heart sink, as when he accidentally knocked over a knicknack when he was a kid.

"About five this afternoon. Big Zeke and two other 'n Zacky's men went in there, told them to clear out. Linda Johnson was screaming that it was against the law in this state to evict a family without no notice. Zeke said they'd better move, or they'd get the living shit kicked out of them."

"Just like that?"

"Yeah, Sam. They got a man from the stable on Glendolph Street with a horse and wagon, loaded it up, and took off with all the kids sitting on top of the mattresses and blankets."

The others on the steps cackled at the recollection of the wagon and green-manged horse clattering down Seventh with banging pots and pans, eight or nine kids holding tight to the blankets and furniture, while mean strangers with their cars parked in front of Zacky's honked their horns and startled the horse so that it bolted and galloped over the cobbles, with all the pots and pans rattling and bumping wildly.

Auer came down the steps and examined Maggie May's good legs before asking, "Any idea where they moved to?"

Silence. It was not customary to give out that kind of information. Nobody leaving this neighborhood had a forwarding address. Auer said, "Bowes, you hated their fucking guts. Where did the bastards move to?"

"Heard something about Ninteenth and Thompson, Sam. Didn't get no exact number."

"One other thing," Maggie May said. "Linda Johnson wanted to give you a message."

"She did, eh?"

"Yeah. She said this wasn't the end of it. She said you could forget about putting windows back in. That one night you'd get it."

"One night I'd get it? I didn't know she was hot for my pants," Auer said, and all the berrypickers on the steps laughed at the crude humor.

In the morning Auer stared at his switchblade on the nightstand. Out of sheer force of habit he had unclicked it and left it next to the ashtray. It was Sunday and the Johnsons felt very far away. Those threats had not impressed him. They were loser-type threats, the kind a kid made when he left the schoolyard with a bleeding nose and said, "I'll be back with my buddies." And everybody knew Johnson had no buddies, no backing. Sam Auer had won this one. He had survived. Auer squirmed under the sheets and felt little satisfaction. If anything, he was agitated, irritated, at odds with himself. A bad period might be ending, but he felt exactly as though he had survived his own funeral, as though he had died, was carted away, laid in the casket, heard the crying and the eulogy, was driven to the cemetery, and lowered into the ground. At the last minute, after everybody dropped their stone on him, he had opened the casket, taken a taxi home, and reported into his regular job the next morning—where everything was exactly the same and totally different.

Today was his visitation rights. Every other Sunday was the temporary arrangement. They called it the Orphan's Court, but it was the father who ended up as the orphan. With the television on loud enough for him to hear the hymns and spirituals in the bathroom, he shaved and showered. He dressed in his best outfit, pressed slacks and a matching sport shirt, and at the last minute put his switchblade in his pocket. He sensed that it was a strange tool to take along to exercise his custody rights.

When he reached the corner of Sixth and Green Garden, instead of turning right and heading for the El, he turned left and faded toward Broad Street, toward the railroad bridge with its three tunnels on Ninth. He was not sure that he could repeat that ordeal. Two weeks ago he exercised his "rights." It was stiff and rigid, with little of the joy he had anticipated. The neighbors were outside on their folding chairs, gaping as he came up the block loaded down with presents for the girls. Their heads went together after he passed. There he went, the drunk with the hot pistol, beaten up and thrown in the drunk tank the afternoon of his mother's funeral.

Inside the house it was worse. Bunny had the girls decked out in their prettiest clothes, and she herself was attractive in a blue summer frock, all brisk and crisp. But she would not let him borrow his own car for a drive. He offered to take the girls to a movie and they checked through the entertainment section. The girls had already seen every movie in the area.

Then they did not want to go for a walk, so he was trapped in the parlor while Bunny seethed upstairs. After his initial pleasure of seeing how they were growing, their delight with his gifts, the girls became restless. He heard himself sounding like a stodgy uncle to his own daughters: "How are you doing in school, Steppie? You're looking so mature, Sheila. Come and sit on Daddy's lap, Steppie. You don't want to sit on Daddy's lap?" They ended up playing Monopoly.

Walking down his block afterward, a few of the old neighbors nodding, most shunning him, and waiting for his bus in the dusk, he had felt like an intruder up there, like a porter or handyman who spent the day cleaning a basement and was supposed to leave the neighborhood before nightfall. Sam Auer no longer had any business in Oxford Circle, that saccharine-sweet world where people played gin rummy on their front lawns and advised you to buy IBM.

Auer took the subway at Broad Street and got off at Lehigh. He pinched the roll of blubber around his belly and decided to walk up to Shibe Park and call Bunny from there. But once he was inside the baseball stadium and installed in his seat, he changed his mind. He bought a hot dog and a scorecard and thought to hell with Bunny. If she could be that much of a constipated bitch, not to even let him use his own car, he could be a hard-nosed bastard and let her sweat it out for once.

By the third inning he found his stance intolerable and was fidgeting in his seat. To punish Bunny, he was making the girls suffer. They were probably all dolled up, getting restless, and their father was a swine.

There were protests as he pushed his way down the row, several spectators missing a sharp single to right as he brushed by. He hurried to a phone booth and dialed his old number.

"Where the hell are you?" Bunny snapped.

"I'm sorry, I got tied up with some business down here."

"Do you know the girls have been all dressed up and

waiting for two hours. You said you were taking them to *Fantasia* today.''

"I couldn't help it. I couldn't break away.''

"Damn it, Sam. We could have driven to Atlantic City today.''

"How? You never drive that far.''

"We had an invitation.''

"From who?''

"That's none of your business, Sam.''

"From a man?''

"That's certainly none of your business.''

A bat cracked, and there was a roar from inside the stadium. Bunny said, "Are you at the racetrack, Sam?''

"No,'' he explained quickly. "That's the television.''

"If this is the way you're going to behave, I'm going to talk to the lawyers about your custody rights. This is totally irresponsible.''

"It won't happen again.''

"What can I tell the girls? They've been cooped up here for two hours waiting for you.''

"I'm sorry. It won't happen again.''

"I'm calling the judge tomorrow. Good-bye.''

It felt eerie, surrealistic, leaving the stadium early, alone, without the crowd. Even while screwing Marge, he had that sensation of not being there. Another weird notion had been torturing him. That maybe this was real life. Since he was a kid, he had wondered what happened to characters after the book or movie was over. Like real life began after it said "The End.'' Like, suppose Romeo and Juliet had worked things out and not fouled it up with the timing and the poison. Twenty years later Juliet would be a fat Italian mama, and Romeo would be cutting off slices on the side, and they would probably be yapping at each other like Bunny and Sam Auer.

At Lehigh he turned down Broad and saw two colored teen-agers shadowboxing on the far corner. In *Ring* magazine Philly always had five or six world champions listed. This one town could produce more champions than entire continents. Sunday afternoon had to be the training grounds, the mental training grounds. They could hone their killer instincts on these deadly, quiet Sunday afternoons. Temple University locked. Closed car salesrooms. About the only businesses that seemed to be operating were the funeral parlors. All the way down to City Hall he could not see ten people on the sidewalks. Drivers in cars he did not count. If they were in a car, they had joined the conspiracy of dullness.

At the corner of Thompson he thought about walking up to Nineteenth and checking to see whether the Johnsons had really moved that way. He lit a cigarette and touched his switchblade. That would also be a phony play. He decided he had lost all interest in the Johnsons. In novels characters always had these driving, grinding, endless obsessions, and he often felt like shouting, "Why don't you get off it already? Cut out the crap." The Johnsons were such a pathetic pack. Killing Lou Johnson would be doing him too much of a favor. Perhaps Lou Johnson had done him a favor? The Johnsons had kept things stirred up this year and precipitated the breakup of his lousy marriage. They had made his life much more interesting. Auer shook his head. Nope. That was also a lot of bullshit, too. He wished none of this had ever happened. He wished that he could arrive at his store back in November and find his window just fine.

The cashier in the Horn and Hardart at Broad and Locust was amused by his dinner selection: four weiners, three servings of baked beans, two helpings of cole slaw, and a baked apple with cream. Because of the heat wave they had stopped making his favorite chocolate whipped cream cake early this year.

He carried his tray to a spot near the window and tried to ignore the lady twisting her lips at the adjacent table. In this heat she was wearing two sweaters and a wool babushka. The Sunday afternoon crowd. All the geeks and freaks seemed to emerge from the woodwork on Sunday. All the downtown cafeterias had these people talking to themselves, arguing with invisible enemies, twitching, suddenly scowling at strangers and then returning to their private hells. Or maybe it only seemed there were more out on Sunday because all of the so-called normal people were home with their families, so the lonely weirdos stood out more vividly. He doused more hot mustard on his baked beans and wondered whether he was destined to join the ranks of all the lonely creeps sitting around him. That was the big mystery: did they realize they were creeps, or did they believe they were just fine and dandy? If it happened to him, would he be aware of it? Or would he be sitting here mumbling about the Johnsons and Bunny and taxes and the Communists without realizing he had slipped over the edge. Would he be sitting here planning his testimonial dinner at the Warwick Hotel with Mac McGuire, Nate Benn, Congressman Green, and the Polish-American Mummers' Day String Band playing "Oh, Them Golden Slippers."

He broke out laughing and cut it off as several of the creeps at surrounding tables glared at him.

On the long walk back to Sixth and Cottonwood he wondered whether it was life in general, Philadelphia, Sunday evening, Sam Auer, or a combination and mixture of the four elements that made him wish to slit his throat. As horrible and sickening as skid row was during the week, Eighth and Race took on new depths of misery and squalor on Sunday evening when all the saloons were closed. It was a free country, and a man could vote for either Eisenhower or Stevenson, but neither could do much about Sunday evenings.

He turned the key in his lock and glanced toward Glendolph Street. Now he was sorry he had tossed Marge Coleman out. It hardly mattered that she was a treacherous bitch who tried to rob him in his sleep. Not when he felt low like this and could use those strong legs around him to dream. In fact, the fact that she was a treacherous bitch only made her more interesting.

His latest "Amazing Stories" awaited him. He was laying off serious novels for a while. The good books were only more skillfully deceptive, Vaseline against the tedium. He snapped on the television, and the best it had to offer was "What's My Line?"

Auer installed himself on the sofa with a beer and gave the panelists on "What's My Line?" the Italian finger sign. It was truly an outrage. Thousands a week they earned for being such drippy clods. A man worked five, six days, had a day off, and they entertained him with this mindless shit. Maybe that was a part of the system. The masses had to be kept mesmerized and apathetic, or else they might ask dangerous questions—like why did Sunday night have to be so boring? To keep the factory chimneys belching smoke, the masses had to be glued to their TV sets with bated breath to see whether the goosey panelists can guess the identity of the mystery celebrity guest who uses a falsetto to confuse them.

With a groan of rage, Auer threw his "Amazing Stories" across the parlor and rose from the sofa. He felt so strong and frustrated he could burst the bonds of his skin and break out bleeding from every pore. He abruptly flexed his biceps and examined himself in the mirror. It was a bull there. He spoke aloud: "Goddamn it, you're strong, Sam. You're tough, and you're a great fucker. You don't know two men who could have put up with the shit you've been through these last seven months. So why let these motherfuckers defeat you? All day long you've been telling yourself you're dead. Great. The dead are free. A dead man doesn't have to worry about anything. From now on, you can be a lot more bold and daring."

The temperature was over ninety on Monday. A glorious June afternoon. It was going to be one stinking hot summer, Auer thought, as he came out with his broom at five-thirty. The schoolyard was crowded, two softball games going on simultaneously from either end with the outfield mixing in the middle, farther down the basketball courts swarming with future stars. Down the block Marge Coleman was skipping rope with her younger daughters, shockingly agile for a woman of her size, her rolls and tits bouncing under a dirty black satin dress. Up Cottonwood, at Marshall, they had opened the fire hydrant, and fifty kids were screaming and shouting in the spray.

He swept his sidewalk diligently, digging the straw broom into the cracks, and waited for that five-thirty buzzer to sound. The second hand galloped under his smashed crystal, and he smiled because it was almost like a countdown for the atomic bomb. His heart was thumping, and he wondered whether he could live up to that brave speech he made last night.

At five-thirty on the button the buzzer sounded, and the workers in Starker's began pouring out of the two doors, men in gray and green uniforms jumping off the loading platform, women clanging down the metal stairs. Nothing could hold them inside that place on a steaming day like this. In ten seconds Sophie Bitko came around the corner of Fifth Street, in a white blouse and red skirt. Auer resumed sweeping and admired her progress up Cottonwood. Even at this distance Sophie was special, a sight to behold, the breeze blowing into her, outlining a shocking "V" in her tight red skirt and her high bosom, all kinds of motion and movement under that blouse and skirt, a whole symphony coming up Cottonwood Street with her blond hair blowing wildly.

As Sophie passed the school front steps, Auer called, "Miss Bitko, could I please speak to. . . ."

Instantly, he was ashamed of his performance. Like a *klutz*, he had let his voice falter and break. Several of the Starker workers gaped at him. For one terrifying second he imagined Sophie intended to ignore his shout and continue to Leah's, but instead she gave him a quizzical look and approached him across Cottonwood. He felt Simmons's eyes on his neck from the second-floor back. Grace was watching from her window. She mumbled something to Big Vye, sitting on the bench under her. A few of the older boys in the schoolyard leered at the sway of Sophie's red skirt as she picked her way through the cobbles.

"Yes, Mr. Auer?" Sophie said and confused Auer with her amiable, sunny tone. He had expected a brash, hard voice.

"I've been meaning to speak to you. . . ."

Up close she was smaller than he imagined her. In his fantasies he had blown Sophie up into an Amazonian goddess, and yet she barely came up to his nose in her high heels. She was older, too, with heavy cosmetics to hide tired eyes, and a pink powder heavily caked over her red lips obscured a few faint blond hairs.

"Is there something the matter? You look kind of ill, Mr. Auer."

Maybe he was ill. Wind whistled in his eardrums, and he seemed to be toppling from a distant ledge. Only the "Mister" penetrated. "Mister," as though he were a total stranger. He had done so many things to this woman in dreams, while she ignored his existence. Now he was discovering that he was some kind of nut, a neurotic who was close to collapsing, with little girls playing hopscotch ten yards down the sidewalk.

Sophie gathered up her pocketbook and said, "I'm in a bit of a hurry, Mr. Auer. If it's anything to do with the plant, could you call me at the office tomorrow?"

"It has nothing to do with the factory, Miss Bitko . . . Sophie."

Her eyebrows arched at being addressed so familiarly. Auer stared at the intricate harnessing of her slip and brassiere under the translucent white blouse. He pondered what would happen if he simply reached out and put his hands on those breasts: the onlookers would gasp, the ground would tremble, Sophie would yelp and break away, and a squad car would be around here in three minutes flat.

"I'm really in a bit of a rush. I'll miss my appointment at the hairdresser's."

Auer cleared his throat. "I guess you've been told many times that you're an extremely attractive woman. . . Sophie."

The confidence faded in midsentence as her eyes narrowed,

as if from the very first word she comprehended or was getting it now.

"It's always nice to hear, Mr. Auer." She slid her pocket-book strap further up her shoulder. "Now, if you'll excuse me." He almost reached out to stop her, felt as though he were stepping over a ledge. His ears were closing, to block out the words from his own mouth. "Do you ever need any extra money, Sophie?"

"I beg your pardon." Her face wrinkled as though he were a dog mess on the sidewalk she was stepping aside to avoid.

"One hundred bucks to come inside and spend two hours with me," he blurted out before she could escape.

It was done. He had said it. It was too late to retract. Come what may, he had come out with it and wheezed in relief as the knot in his temple loosened. Marge Coleman was staring from Glendolph Street. Big Vye was conferring with Fat Grace at the window. The kids in the schoolyard roared as the batter smashed a long drive. Sophie Bitko was already across Sixth Street. She glanced around to give him a look distilled of disgust and fear before hurrying into Leah's.

Auer went inside and immediately began washing the dishes remaining in the sink. The slippery glasses eluded his grasp in the cold soapy water, and with his nervousness he chipped one against the faucet. He dropped it into the trashcan and was glad he had tried to prove his point. Zig or Gall or those big-mouthed lice in Hymie's would never have had the guts for a play like that. For years they had been rhapsodizing about Sophie's frame, but they were too chicken to even nod her way. If he caught it, he caught it. He was going to live up to that speech he made last night.

Later, watching clowns throwing cream pies on television, he told himself that he was in for it. Retribution would come for such temerity. Such audacity produced repercussions. When Sophie mentioned this to old man Starker, if Starker got wind of his attempt to proposition his kept woman, the retaliation would be swift and cruel. Old man Starker did not mess around. Ask Al

Dominic over at RCA. Auer stared at the comic with the cream pies. About the best he could hope for was that Sophie would not squeal, that she would be too embarrassed to report the matter to Starker.

When the health inspectors came in on an unscheduled visit the following morning, Auer looked up from his *Daily News* and said, "Sophie has a big mouth."

None of the usual affability. They were men on a mission. Auer watched their diffidence as they filled a test tube with dishwater and began mumbling about microbe counts and amoebic dysentery. McGraw searched around with his flashlight under the sink and stood up to jot down a few notations about defective plumbing. Vanessi mentioned something about coffee, and Auer thought, "Screw them. If his dishes were full of germs, they could pay a dime for their dysentery just like everybody else."

With his arms folded across his chest, he watched them write a poem about the boarded-up windows, and then they consulted in lowered voices about the racy pinups. That also merited a few lines.

McGraw probed with his flashlight behind the soda case and suddenly stood erect. "Hey, Charlie! Get a load of this."

The other inspector, Vanessi, crouched, examined the spot, and rose shaking his head. "That's some rat hole down there, Sam."

"You discovering America, Charlie? This whole neighborhood's got more rats than Carter got liver pills."

They exchanged glances and started scribbling away. Next came the icebox. McGraw sniffed, called Vanessi over, and they both agreed they could detect a faint odor of gas escaping. They were waiting for him to argue, but he remained silent. It was too fascinating watching these jackals in action. They obviously intended nailing his ass to the wall, so arguing would only provoke them into discovering more violations and infractions. The crunch was on. It was as simple as that. Usually, these two-bit pikers were fixed up with a promise to be a little more hygienic and a ten-dollar *shmeer.* From Leah across the street, they extracted merchandise, zipping up one of her ceramic statuettes in their briefcases, saying, "This will look nice on my wife's breakfront." There was something in the air today which warned him not to make any offers, that these cheap chiselers were waiting to pounce on him.

Vanessi handed him a carbon of their checklist, and they were waiting for him to make a protest or an offer. McGraw said, "Y'know, you've really let things slide around here, Sam. We don't like to crack down like this, but you've got to hold up your end, too."

"If I do, somebody will stick a shaft in it."

McGraw touched the carbon copy. "You want to dispute any of them. There's an appeals board downtown."

"I'd suggest you'd better get cracking," Vanessi said. "There are a lot of things to fix up here."

"Strange that we've all been able to live with them before."

They both stirred as if he had offended them and they intended to return and uncover a few more violations, but they changed their minds and left.

Before noon Issacs, the weights-and-measurements man, was in to check his scale and slap a violation on him, even though the red line was slightly off in the customer's favor. Braidman, the building inspector, toured the cellar and upstairs halls and apartments to discover thirty-seven violations of the Municipal Code. Three vultures before lunch. Auer wondered what the hell Sophie had told Starker last night—that he cornholed her against the kerosene drum? He studied the list Braidman handed him and said, "I see. I am Rockefeller, and this is Colonial Williamsburg you want me to restore."

"You're trying to make me the heavy, Sam. You weren't born yesterday. If it wasn't me, it'd be somebody else, and they'd really rake you over. So don't make me the heavy."

"I get you, Henry. You want to act like a prick and keep your white hat, too."

"If that's your attitude, I don't see how we can work together anymore."

"When did we work together? Because you had your hand in my pocket, we were partners?"

The inspector tucked his briefcase under his arm as though he were a real college-graduated engineer and not a civil service drone with a night-school certificate. Braidman was about to say something, but he thought better of it and departed.

Auer snatched up the three reports and read Braidman's checklist: defective pipes, radiators, rats, staircase, . . . He crumpled the reports, squeezed them into a tight wad, and tossed it into the wastecan. This had become his method for dealing with notices, bills, claims, and subpoenas. That really screwed up all the lappers who lived by paper. They could drag him to court. The courts were screwed up, too, clogged with backlogs of cases, and it took years for a case to come to trial.

Covering his head with his arms, he laid his cheek on the counter. God had heard him the other day, heard that bold speech, and cut him down right off. God sure used miserable instruments to display his wrath. Three drones from City Hall. In that light it was funny. When the bricks were smashing his windows, the government was spread thin, but suddenly it had all this spare personnel assigned to hounding Sam Auer.

The bell rang, and Auer remembered it was the last day of classes. Thurston let out early today. He went outside to watch the children pouring out of the exits, shoving and yelling with glee. Bullies were chasing after small fry and two girls were entwined in a headlock and rolling over the concrete. Back in his time the last day of classes was for settling scores. Promises were made in April and May: "I'm gonna get you in June!"

Kids were snapping their pencils and dropping their composition books down the culvert. A bunch was chanting, "No more pencils, no more books, no more teachers' dirty looks."

Jeanette Lewis was coming down the front steps, alone. Since when did he have luck coming to him? She was having difficulties controlling her pocketbook, suit jacket, and a cardboard box full of folders, portfolios, and books. Auer rushed across Cottonwood, smiling broadly, knowing that she had to walk all the way to her trolley stop at Eighth and Green Garden with the heavy box.

"Here, here, let me take that."

Worry suffused her face. "There's really no need. . ."

"No trouble at all. You can't lug this heavy box all the way up there. It's my pleasure. Just a minute, I'll lock my front door and we'll go."

He left her with her jaw moving with unvoiced protest and jogged boyishly across Cottonwood, her carton in his arms to prevent her escaping. She was obliged to follow him across the street and stand there while he locked his door. Silverman came out of the school and registered surprise at finding the two of them together. Mrs. Lewis gave Silverman a small, wan wave of farewell, and said, "I really don't think you should put yourself out like this."

"No bother at all," he said too loudly, explosively, and bent down to retrieve the box before she could recover it. "I always close up around this time and go for a little fresh air. It's my pleasure, Mrs. . . ."

"Jeanette," she supplied after a pause.

From the wistful look she directed at Leah's he guessed that she wished to drop in there and say good-bye for the summer. He moved as if to cross with her, but she gently guided him toward Green Garden, and he gathered that she was reluctant about being seen with him on Cottonwood, so many kids dashing around, Sidonia and his whole crew stationed at the icehouse.

Shifting the box in his arms, he smiled at the tattered compositions, drawings, thumbtacks, old performance sheets, a potted plant, and the romantic Frank Yerby novel she was reading. He saw her turn her head at the sight of Maggie May snoring on the step at #523, sleeping with her head against the door and her dress up so that all the drivers on Sixth could see her good thighs.

"This is really too kind of you," Mrs. Lewis said as they waited for the light.

"It's nothing. Sincerely, I always go for a stroll around now."

She led him across Green Garden, and he suspected she was choosing the far sidewalk because there were fewer pedestrians out. The kids in front of the bank had gone bug-eyed at the sight of them together, and several drivers speeding down Sixth felt obliged to do a double take. "So what are you planning on doing with your summer vacation . . . Jeanette?" He winced at his own stilted voice coming out with a stilted question.

"Work my head off," she answered merrily. "I'm enrolled for two advanced courses at Temple to get my master's. And I'll be a playground director in the afternoons, blowing a dumb whistle after kids."

"Still hitting those books, hunh?"

"Sure need to. That degree means another two hundred a year. I've been taking credits every summer for three years now."

"Where did you do your undergraduate work?" He was displaying his familiarity with the terminology.

"Oh, some dinky little place down South you probably never heard of."

"Did you run track for your college?"

Jeanette Lewis tossed her head up and laughed gaily in the middle of Marshall Street. "My secret is out," she announced to the sky. "I ran the hurdles. As hippy as I am now, I can't imagine how you could have guessed that, Mister . . . Sam."

"You have that about you."

"Well, how could you tell?" she demanded to know in a friendly tone. He was confused by her naturalness. He was the stiff here.

"By your calves. You have muscular-attractive calves."

The good humor drained from her face. He hoped he had not stuck his foot in it by mentioning her calves. Legs were a personal, intimate topic, and he had just admitted he had been peeking at hers.

"They'd have to be a lot more muscular than they are now to get my secretary's spread over the bar," Jeanette Lewis said nostalgically, and he was relieved. If she could mention her secretary's spread he had not gone too far by mentioning her legs. She smiled up at him and said, "That was longer ago than I care to remember. I was anchor girl on the relay team, but I was such a skinny little thing carrying that baton. Must have put on thirty pounds since then."

"On you, they look good," he murmured, assaying another gallantry. It had gone too far. She quickly changed the subject, asking, "What are your plans for the summer? I hope you're planning on putting windows back in. Those boards are such an eyesore. But I guess you know that."

"They're up in the air. I've been kicking around the idea of selling the store and moving to California."

"That sounds nice. Your wife and children will love it out there."

He cleared his throat. "They wouldn't be going with me. We're in the stages of getting a divorce. I'd be traveling out there myself." His heart rose in his chest. "Unless I could find somebody to go with me."

"I'm sorry to hear that. Especially when there are children involved."

The big Negro crowbarring a tire in front of the vulcanizing shop at Franklin and Green Garden thrust out his lips in amusement at seeing them together. They refrained from speaking till they were out of his earshot. Auer shifted the box again. "It's a wonder that an attractive widow like yourself hasn't married again. It's been around five years since your husband died in Japan?"

The glint in her eyes indicated she was intrigued at this revelation that he had been gossiping about her personal life with someone. He could not explain that he had once discussed her with Leah, and Leah said it was a shame that a lovely woman like Mrs. Lewis could not find a man. Suitable men were in short supply for an educated colored woman like Mrs. Lewis, and so she went from unhappy affair to unhappy affair with bartenders and musicians and colored policemen.

"I've had my offers but I guess I'm too picky and choosy, Sam. To tell the truth, my first didn't work out too well. We fought like cats and dogs, poor guy. If you get burned once you're not too anxious to jump back into the fire."

They had reached the corner of Eighth and Green Garden. Auer peered up the tracks. Her trolley was in sight of Girard Avenue. He had at best two, three minutes before it scooped her up and carried her out of his life for the next three months, or maybe forever.

"Let me take that box now, please. Your arms surely must be aching after carrying it all this way." Her hand touched his wrist as she attempted to take the carton, and they both pulled back quickly.

The trolley was stopping at Poplar for passengers. Auer stared at the cinnamon tint of her pale skin. This close to him, she was much more appealing than Sophie Bitko, had none of that hardness or brassiness. She was looking directly into his eyes, and Auer said, "Do you ever go out with white men, Jeanette?"

"I have, but I wouldn't like to get involved with anything like that again," she responded calmly. "It gets too complicated and hardly worth the effort. I especially wouldn't get involved with a married man with children. Not while there's a chance he might return to his family."

"There's not the slightest chance of that. I've always thought you were a very lovely and fine person, Jeanette."

The trolley was stopping at Parrish. She could no longer look him in the eye. She murmured, "I'm very flattered, but. . . ."

"I'd like to take you out for dinner. To get to know you. No funny business. . . ."

She smiled again. "Well, there's not much sense in seeing a person unless there's at least the chance of 'funny business,' "

"Then there could be funny business," Auer said quickly.

"Could I have your phone number? I checked through the book, and you don't have a number listed, and the operator refused to give it out."

"I had it unlisted because I was getting annoying calls."

The trolley was not stopping at Fairmount Avenue. It was aiming directly at them. He relinquished his grip on the carton.

"Not even dinner?"

"I'm afraid not, really. I'm keeping company with someone right now."

"Anything serious?"

"*Comme ci, comme ça,*" she said with a fluttering motion of her hand against the box. The trolley halted to discharge two passengers at Green Street. Auer took the box again as she opened her purse to fumble around for a token. There were three other people at the corner, and they stirred in discomfort at being present at this intimate scene.

"I don't want to wish you any bad luck," he whispered, "but if anything happens during the summer, if you should get lonely or feel like going out for a cup of coffee, give me a call at Leah's phone booth. Don't say no now. Just think about it." The trolley doors sprang open, and the other three people boarded. Auer took her elbow to assist her up the high step and handed her the carton again.

"I'll think about it," she promised with a brisk, business-like smile. A second went by, and the conductor frowned at the delay. Jeanette Lewis said something else, which Auer did not hear as the doors snapped shut in his face.

He watched the trolley rumble down the tracks, rush by Cottonwood, and stop with a jerk at Grenoble. For a few seconds there, he thought he had her going, melting, giving in. With another few minutes to work on her, he might have broken her resistance. He would never know.

Back behind his sink he began to measure the dimensions of his crassness. He was becoming like the proverbial man in the joke who could not make out in a whorehouse with a fistful of fifties. Two up and two down. About the only woman left in the neighborhood he had not propositioned was Fat Grace. Maybe he could go scratch around old Rita Uzkoff's house on Oriana Street and see if the Queen of Sheba still gave hand jobs. It was funny, he was offering to run off to the West Coast with Jeanette and she would not even go for a cup of coffee with him.

It came to him slowly, he resisted the notion, but he had to acknowledge that he had been snubbed. And rightly so. He was a *zhlub* grocer who asked out a schoolteacher and got a thumbs-down. He was a *grubyahn* who dropped out of Southern arrogantly asking out a woman obtaining her master's degree, and imagining that his whiteness made up the difference. That was arrogance, imagining that a white corner grocer was preferable to a colored mailman. For his whiteness. As if it were such a great honor to belong to the same race as Zig and Gall and Marge Coleman.

God had probably taken notice of his speech the other night. Heard all that temerity. This was what a Sam Auer got for peeking over the fence or through the cracks. If he actually went over the fence, there was a kick in the head and a kick in the balls awaiting him. When it came to women, what did he deserve? A Maggie May was much more his speed. A fine body. In a red dress, from the rear, she could win the next Miss Philadelphia contest. And if her face was battered and she sprawled drunk on steps so every driver racing down Sixth could see her thighs, that only meant she was in Sam Auer's league.

Closing at ten, he tucked his switchblade in his back pocket and went outside with no destination in mind.

Big Vye beckoned to him from the bench under Grace's window. He straggled across Sixth, figuring Vye would hit him for four bits for a taste at Shor's. She was alone and had to be hurting for a taste on a hot night like this.

"You heard about Maddy, Sam?"

"What about him?" Auer sat down heavily on the bench

next to Vye and indicated the darkened store with his chin. "Leah hardly talks to me anymore. She doesn't like some of my guests."

"You didn't hear what happened last night?" Vye asked him, as if amazed at his ignorance.

"I'm shut off from polite society," Auer said sarcastically. "And I had my own troubles today."

"Hell, Maddy's in it deep. Herbie told me. You know Steve, that rough boy Maddy runs with?"

"The painter? The one who painted the picture of Leah's father?"

"That's the one. Him and Maddy really messed up. Last night in South Philly there was a fight at this graduation party, and this boy picked on Maddy, and Maddy hit him. So this boy comes back with a whole big gang, with one big guy to tear Maddy apart. And Steve offered to fight the big guy, and they went outside, had it out on the street, and Steve killed the big guy."

"Killed? Jesus Christ!"

"It was in the papers," Vye assured him. "The late *Bulletin*. He died this afternoon."

Auer whistled. "Killed him? I was too busy to read the paper today."

"According to Herbert, Steve knocked this big guy down and then kicked him in the head."

"Woof. Leah told me she was worried about Maddy hanging around with that kid, but I never figured them for a fuck-off play like that."

Vye reached over and took a cigarette and matches from his shirt pocket. She lit up before saying, "Nothing they can't get out of. They're bookin' Steve on murder and Maddy as some kinda' accomplice but Leah got her brother Harold at the station, and you know Harold ain't gonna let his nephew get fucked up too bad. I wish I had a Harold for my Buzzy. He wouldn't be in there for no seven to ten."

"Seventeen is a fucked-up age," Auer said.

"They is all fucked-up ages," Vye assured him gloomily.

"Seventeen is the worst, girl. I remember when I was seventeen, fighting all the time, punching Jerry, arguing with my Sis, my father, shouting at my mother. One day I got so pissed off at my family, I picked up our table radio and threw it through the window. Chips of glass hit Jim Sibronsky's sister out on Cottonwood Street, and the Sibronskys wanted to sue my old man for a thousand bucks."

"What's that supposed to prove?" Vye said, "You're twice seventeen now, and you're twice as fucked-up." She took the last swig from her bottle of beer. "How'd you make out with Sophie yesterday?"

"We were just passing the time of day."

"Sheeee. . . . And that little redhead today? Got a nice little movement to her black ass for a schoolteacher."

"You've really been keeping tabs on me, haven't you, baby?"

"You've been all over the street, Sam. Just like horseshit." In the dull haze from the streetlamp he watched her scratch her plump knee. Vye, with all her bulk, was a damn attractive woman, and sober she was a sweetie pie. Their eyes met, the gazes locked for a second, and Vye gave him an amiable poke with her elbow.

"Seems like you're still catting around, Sam. Why don't you run up to Marge's? You were getting that steady."

"Had to drop her. Bitch tried to hit my till."

He stared at her hard again, smiling, hit her with a double whammy like Sidonia used to say.

"I wouldn't mind taking you up some time, Sam, but you know I'm staying with George Wilson now. I don't want to be unfair to George. You wouldn't want me to be unfair to George, would you?"

"Nah," Auer said mockingly. "I'm a nice guy. I wouldn't want you to be unfair to George."

They both laughed, and Vye gave him a harder poke with that elbow. "You're a bad sonofabitch. Head on around to the

Green Room or Zacky's, Sam. All kinds a' women in there be glad to spread for a few bucks."

"Doesn't sound like a bad idea," Auer answered pleasantly, rising from the bench. "I might just do that."

"How about sporting a lady to a taste at Shor's?" Vye said. It came out as an oblique afterthought.

"George might not take too kindly to anybody sporting his woman to a drink, no?"

"C'mon, don't be a cheap bastard, baby. George don't get home from the rug plant till one o'clock, and I'm thirsty right now, baby."

Auer paid his toll of fifty cents and drifted up Cottonwood. Zacky's sounded like a good suggestion. The establishment had no doorman to exclude prospective patrons without neckties. It was no big move. Hymie's at Fourth and Grenoble was off limits for him, so he was merely sliding over to Seventh and Grenoble.

The chorus was stamping its feet and clapping hands, reaching high for chilling, thrilling notes in the storefront church at Marshall Street. The Wednesday night meeting on Tuesday this week, and Bowes pounding away on his electric guitar. Auer lit a cigarette and paused to listen. He loved this shit. Up in front of the icehouse there was a lively crap game going on. The red cars just rolled on by.

He turned down sweltering Seventh and had to admit that he liked it here. It throbbed and reeked of boiled cabbage, dirt, and sex, kids sucking popsicles, boxing and bopping to the music of the portable radios. You were not supposed to like this filth and noise and confusion, but he preferred this to his block in Oxford Circle. For him. Not for anybody else. He belonged here, and in no other place in this world would he truly belong. On this whole vast planet this was the only stretch where he would ever be totally at home. Anywhere else he would always be a transplanted fish in a foreign pond. He did not want to be one of those guys sitting in a bar in a strange town, talking about back home, talking about people nobody knew or cared about.

No particular attention was paid as he entered Zacky's and

took a seat near the cash register. It was slow and sluggish, even for a moneyless Tuesday night. There were maybe fifteen customers around the huge, rectangular bar. Except for Lenny, the driver for the oil burner place on Marshall Street, he was the only white. Lenny could hardly be called white, either. Lenny was what Zig and Gall used to call a jigman. There were three or four around the neighborhoood, hanging out mostly at the Green Room, guys who had dropped out of white society and were shacked up with colored women. The Negroes despised them and gave them a rough time, a worse time than they gave the redhead Hank Morse brought back from Europe.

Big Zeke said, "Since when you come around here, Sam?"

"It's a free country, I hear tell."

"I've heard that rumor," Zeke agreed with a shrug. "What'll it be?"

Auer studied the greasy signs on the wall. "I'll try the Zacky's forty-nine-cents special." It promised a shot of blended whiskey with a draught beer chaser.

The bartender said something which was drowned out as the jukebox blasted out a raucous rhythm and blues number, attacking all the drinkers from three strategically located loudspeakers. The drink was served, and Auer pivoted on his stool to admire Peggy Moore carrying on behind the jukebox, snapping her fingers and shaking her hips to the lyrics of "Sixty Minute Man." He could rock and roll it for about twenty minutes.

Peggy, spinning around, saw him appreciating her efforts. She pointed her index finger and thumb, cocked as if aiming a pistol, and gave the other women near the jukebox a wave of "too-da-loo" as she exaggerated the swing of her hips and plopped down on the stool next to him.

"Fancy meeting you here, Samuel Auer. Whatcha' doin' in this dump, baby?"

She turned her knee against him, and her breath was sweet on gin-and-tonics. Auer said, "Heard you got more for your money in this joint, and I've got a fair thirst."

"That makes two of us, baby. You *are* going to set a lady up with a cocktail, aren't you?"

Auer indicated Peggy with his thumb. Zeke glared disapprovingly, and Peggy stuck her tongue out at the bartender.

"You saw what the man told you, fool. Don't go making no mean faces at me."

Zeke examined the ceiling unhappily and then reached for his bottles of gin and tonic. Peggy said, "You heard about Maddy?"

"Yeah, Vye was saying something."

"I just talked to Barry. He told me Maddy's already out, but they're holding his buddy for second-degree murder."

"Since when is Barry the big legal expert?"

"Hell, Barry knows more about judges, juries, and lawyers than Perry Mason."

Zeke slid away two quarters and returned one penny. Peggy raised her glass, and they traded evil, knowing grins.

"You still at the laundry, Peggy?"

"Hell no," she said, laughing. "I quit that place a month ago. What the hell I want to work in that sweathole? After they get through taking out the taxes, the Social Security, and my carfare and lunch money, wasn't enough left over to keep a pair of panties on my back end."

"What you doing for money then?" he asked solicitously.

"Various things. I'm not starving yet."

Auer lit a cigarette, drew in, exhaled.

"Y'know, my apartment in back is in a mess. It could use a woman's touch."

"Un-unh," Peggy said. "That's what you had in mind. You need a few floors washed."

"Yeah. Among other things." He shook his head. This girl knew not only the score but who had rigged the game.

"Let's concentrate on the 'other things.' I mean, I don't want to be wasting no time down on my knees, scrubbing floors, if all you really wanted to do was fuck, baby. You get me, Sam?"

"I get you, Peggy."

They had one more round of drinks before Peggy said, "No sense waiting around for the future, Sam. I could be dead and in my grave before the future arrives."

Peggy went over to the jukebox and made some wisecracks to her girl friends that produced a lot of laughter before she returned to take his hand and guide him out the door. Always, they took over, he noted. There was no route that could get them to his apartment without fifty neighbors spotting them and flipping. Within twenty minutes Bunny's phone would be short-circuited by all of the local storekeepers trying to reach her simultaneously. So let it happen, he thought. With the good opinion of the world plus one token, he could get to League Island.

Like a merry schoolgirl Peggy swung his arm as they headed up Seventh. The berrypickers stared, and Peggy began singing "Take the rain from April showers."

"Good voice," Auer said.

"Oh, I'm talented, Sam. As you will find out."

Sidonia glanced up. "Swing loose, children, swing loose."

Peggy wrapped her arm around Auer's waist and said, "Nobody knows, and he won't tell, so mum's the word, Sidonia sweetheart."

She squeezed Auer's hand, and as they passed the congregation coming out of the storefront church, their heads turning, Peggy whispered, "Don't fret, Sam. If anybody asks tomorrow, you can tell them that you had me over to scrub some floors."

"I don't give a shit."

"You're a rugged individualist, ain't you, Sam?"

"Why not. I'm my own man."

"Who else would have you, honey?"

As he opened the side door, Peggy whistled, not in appreciation, at the mess in his parlor. She stepped inside and whistled again. "Y'know, I really do believe you need a girl to straighten up around here more than you need a piece of ass. This is one terrible sight."

"Well, I've been living alone with no woman around, so I've sort of let things slide."

"You were bringing fat-ass Marge Coleman in here. Why didn't you get her to clean this mess up?"

"You were onto that, too?"

"I thought I heard that on the Walter Winchell Show. Sam Auer, dot dot dot, is screwing Marge, dash dash dash, Coleman." She kicked a bottle aside and said, "You got anything to drink around here, baby?"

"Some beer in the store. I finished off my fifth of rye at supper tonight."

"That wasn't too thoughtful of you," Peggy complained. "I could use another shot. Go into the store and get us some beer, and I'll go into the bedroom and get comfortable. I've got a mind to clean up this mess right now, but I guess it can wait till morning."

Auer squinted, wondering why she believed she would be here in the morning. This was not the proper moment to argue the point.

"Don't strip down yet. Wait till I get back, so I can watch you undress."

"Go on ahead," she commanded playfully and pushed him toward the store.

When he returned to the bedroom with provisions, he was disappointed to discover that Peggy had disobeyed him and was stretched out, completely naked, her clothes draped carelessly over the squat oak bureau.

"Hi, baby," she said as he placed the beer and cigarettes on the nightstand. Climbing out of his trousers, he studied her lithe, athletic figure, the blue-black skin enhancing the definition of her washboard torso. He dropped his undershorts over her nylons and smiled down again. He certainly had been wasting a lot of time, all these months of celibacy and agony, when there were so many fine things around this way.

They shared a beer, and then Peggy turned to do him a Marge Coleman type favor, but he did not need that. He took her, and her legs clamped high around his back. Their loving seemed to him strangely bland and innocent after having battled with Marge Coleman on this bed. Supporting himself on his elbows so as not to crush her with his massive torso, he moved inside Peggy slowly and deliberately, imposing his rhythm. Her response was chaste, affectionate, with none of Marge's thrashing, scratching, biting, filthy squealing and vile orders whispered in his ear.

Peggy had a vague smile on her lips. Her eyes opened, dull and shadowed, as his mouth sought hers, and the long, moist kiss was flavored with salt, tobacco, gin and sweet lemons, more romantic than passionate. Her arms were growing fierce and strong on his neck, she was trembling under him. He was liberated, absent, calm, could go on till dawn with her haunches gathered in his hands, floating with the confidence of a long-distance swimmer. Peggy was stirring, her torso muscles bunching hard, tightening into a knot that suddenly loosened as she melted and her sharp tremor racked through him.

"Oh, thank you."

"That's all right," Auer said.

Now he could pursue his own pleasure while she ground against him to no avail. This was how he liked them, how he wanted her. Once he moved a woman, he was relaxed, uncoiled, and no matter what she did to him or threw at him, he could hang on past her. A woman's gasp made him masterful and arrogant, and now he could dream, ride high above Peggy and dream of Jeanette Lewis, sedate, demure, a trolley door snapping in his face. . . .

"You sure throw a mean one," Peggy told him when they were finished.

"You did it for me," Auer said calmly. "It all depends on the woman. With some I'm no good at all. You ever go out with a white guy before?"

"Sure. A couple hundred of them. Don't you remember I got picked up in that raid over by the foundry? That's all that ever came to that place—white men."

Auer smiled as he recalled his amazement two years ago when a real brothel was uncovered a block away, over the foundry, behind the lot. He, who had lived around here all his life, knew nothing about it. The newspapers played it down because the raid pulled in several executives from the electronics plant and chocolate factory on Fifth Street. Maggie May went to jail for six months and McMann, the cop on the beat, said it was a lunch-hour service with a plush furnished apartment and a well-stocked bar, right on top of the old foundry.

"All kinds of white men," Peggy said in retrospect.

"I meant for . . . like love. Not money."

"I don't know how much love there was, but I once fooled around with Maddy, one day when I was cleaning Leah's apartment."

"Hey, now," Auer said, chuckling. "Maddy. The kid's all right. I didn't think he had it in him."

"I just got my skirt back down in time when Leah opened the door, but didn't fool her any. That's why Leah never had me back no more to do her place."

"Hardly seems fair."

Peggy pulled the sheet up over her legs, tucked the pillow under her head like a child, and rose to give him a quick, affectionate kiss. "You okay, Sam? I'm going to sleep."

"I'm okay."

He lit a cigarette and decided he was not yet enough of a hard-nosed bastard to hand her ten and tell her to get out if she really preferred to sleep right now. She could spend the night. Peggy existed that way, drifting from room to room, no man ever lasting for her. No life at all.

With her eyes closed and her hands tucked cherubically under her cheek, she said, "You're probably gonna catch some hell tomorrow, Sam."

He crushed out the cigarette. "I know."

The aroma of bacon frying woke him in the morning. Movements out in the store. From the squat bureau, his parents were observing him in that brown-tinted photo. A portrait. They were bold. Nobody dared to pose for a photo like that anymore. Stand right up with those powerful stolid faces, determined chins up, shoulders back, chests puffed, demand respect for their dignity and values. They were like figures in a quaint historical pageant.

Auer reached for his trousers and said, "Sorry, Pop. What you did doesn't work anymore. It's not even respected. Stick it out forty years with the same woman, gut out forty years of work, and people laugh at your ass. It's a whole new ball game, Pop."

Peggy had already brought in the bundles of newspapers, the crates of milk, and the boxes of doughnuts. The bacon and eggs were crackling away on the grill. Moving her little butt, Auer noted. Really pushing it. That was all right, too. He liked people who played their role hard, and this morning she was Miss Good Housekeeping of 1952, moving her frisky little tail behind that counter, with a dish towel around her waist as an apron.

He accepted her peck on the cheek and then a deep kiss, a few whispered words about how much she had loved last night, before they sat down with their coffee and eggs at the counter.

Barry was their first customer of the morning, and it was Peggy who got up to wait on him. From his bleary eyes, old Barry had probably been up all night, but they were not so bleary as not to immediately widen with total appreciation of the situation.

"Mm-mmn," Barry mumbled.

"Mm-mmn, your ass," Peggy said.

Auer chewed on his bacon and eggs and enjoyed the comedy. Barry stacked five items on the counter, and as Peggy put them in a bag, he said, "You can just add this on."

"No way. Fork up or put 'em back."

"What you mean, woman? You take over this place?" He spun around and appealed to Auer with his expression.

"She's a minority shareholder."

Grumbling under his breath, Barry produced dollar bills. Auer totaled up his bill, Peggy took the two dollars, rang it up on the cash register, and returned thirty cents.

"Sheee," Barry grumbled on the way out the door. Except for the one beat that his heart skipped when he saw Peggy's black hand dip into his cash register, Auer enjoyed that scene. He flipped to the sports pages and sipped at his coffee. Glancing around, he smiled at Grace's ugly building. There should be a waterfall over there. This was like a damn honeymoon. She was freshly showered, with a red ribbon in her hair, humming as she poured him another cup of coffee. Peggy, sensing he was pleased, winked, and they both laughed.

It all proceeded naturally. After breakfast Peggy went for her clothes at the room she was sharing with Maggie May on Marshall Street. She returned with one battered suitcase and a shopping bag full of cosmetics and *True Confessions* magazines. For the rest of the afternoon she washed floors, dusted the venetian blinds, swept out cobwebs, scoured the bathroom, and evacuated four large cardboard containers of trash from the apartment. At the three-thirty coffee break Heinie Schmidt's eyes bulged as he saw Auer give Peggy at pat on the rear, and she responded with a quick kiss to his neck. Children from the schoolyard dashed in to check the rumor, gaped at them for a second, and rushed out to spread the word. Customers who had not been in for months showed up, satisfying a malignant curiosity, and hurried away as if to report an attack of the plague. Auer found their reactions hilarious. The only disturbing moment came after supper when Peggy tore down all of his pinups and covered his boards with old red Christmas wrapping paper. He felt himself bridling like Barry when he grumbled about a woman taking over.

By the following afternoon every shopowner from Second Street to Broad and from Franklin Square to Columbia Avenue knew the story. The breadmen and newspaper drivers were effective couriers. Sam Auer, the maniac who back around

Christmas "was holding out against the niggers," had moved a colored prostitute into his place. He was shacking up with a black whore who was waiting on trade. Up in Oxford Circle, Mrs. Bunny Auer, after hearing reports from five different sources, left her phone off the hook.

When Herbert waddled into the store, Auer already knew his mission before he could mumble, "It's your brother Jerry in our front phone booth. He says he wants to speak to you immediately."

"I'll bet he does. Tell Jerry it's not my policy to answer unsolicited phone calls. If he has anything important to say, he can drive by here and say it himself. Otherwise, I'm incommunicado."

Herbert shrugged indifferently and shuffled out. Ten minutes later he shuffled back in and mumbled. "It's your Uncle Joe this time. He sounds agitated."

"Give him the same message."

Herbert slouched out, and Peggy, washing dishes behind the counter, sniffed in awe. "Woof. That's some keister Herby's packing there. I remember when Maddy was fat, but he never got that five-by-five."

A minute later, as though the invocation of his name had automatically conjured him up, Maddy poked his head through the door. "C'mon, Sam. Give us a break, will you? We're running a regular unpaid pony express for you, and it's tying up our booth. It's your wife this time."

"What are you doing out of jail, killer? I thought they locked you up and threw away the key."

"Personal cognizance," Maddy said with the expertise of a hardened criminal. "C'mon, Sam. Get over there and take your medicine."

"Whatcha' say?" Peggy called out gaily from the sink.

"Whatcha' say yourself, baby doll?" Maddy responded in the same sarcastic vein. "Looking all domesticated in that apron back there."

Auer said, "Is your mother over there, kid?"

"You think I'd be inviting you over there if she were? She's off on another antiques expedition to Bucks County."

"I'll be back in five minutes," Auer told his new helper. "I might as well get them off my ear."

He followed Maddy across Sixth and entered the cool shade of his rival's store. As usual, Daniel was snoring on his rocking chair, and Herbert was contributing little to the general welfare. With thirty cases of an unpacked grocery order cluttering up the floor, he was munching on a sandwich and reading *Great Expectations*.

Bunny's penetrating voice attacked his eardrum before he quite had the phone in position.

"Sam, tell me it isn't true what I hear, or I'll go crazy up here. Every time I place the phone back on the hook it rings."

"Pull the wire out."

She spluttered something, and he held the phone away, let her rattle in the distance for over a minute. It was strange. She already sounded like a voice from the past. The deep past. The strident voice of a querulous unfavorite aunt that could not bring herself to realize that an errant nephew had grown up.

"So what's all this to you?" he asked when she finally paused.

"Are you insane? Aren't you through torturing me yet, you hairy pig?"

"I don't see how I'm torturing you," Auer said calmly. "As long as you get your check on time, we have nothing more to do with each other."

"What about your daughters, you bastard? What do you think it will do to those poor girls when they learn their father is shacking up with a nigger whore?"

"Use your sweetness and wisdom on them," Auer suggested. "Be wise, sweet, kind, gentle. Explain it to them. Teach them tolerance."

"You miserable sonofabitch. You're doing this to hurt me,

and you don't care how much it hurts them. How do you think it will affect them when they're old enough to understand?''

"You've already told me they're mature and sophisticated for their ages, and fully understand about our impending divorce. When the proper time comes, I'll explain about this, too.''

"What makes you think you're going to see your daughters again? I'd be deathly afraid to let them out of my sight for a minute with somebody acting as crazy as you are.''

"What makes you think you'll ever see another cent off me if you deny me access my next custody day?''

"Good God, you've really become a bastard." There was a faint trace of admiration in the statement.

"Maybe I have,'' Auer conceded. "I'm trying it on for size.''

Bunny's tone abruptly changed again, became sisterly and intimate as she said, "That's the best you can do for yourself, Sam? The best you can do for yourself is a *shvartzeh kurva?*''

"She's a lot better company than you are. You whined all day. So far she hums all day. For Sixth and Cottonwood society I don't need much more.''

"Drop dead. Do me a favor, get a bone stuck in your throat, and drop dead.'' The phone clicked.

Hatred and malevolence still seemed to be emanating from the phone. It was frightening what time could do. Once he had actually loved that woman, could not wait to get home to Bunny.

He lit a cigarette as he emerged from the booth and said, "What's the story with you, kid? We hear you're a big murderer now.''

"Oh, man, it's a mess. A couple of months ago I got in a fight with this punk up at the Hot Shoppe on Broad Street. Almost two punches thrown. More of a mouth fight than a fistfight. And he promised to get me. I threw the best punch and broke open most of his pimples. So Monday night he spots me at this graduation party on Porter Street down in South Philly, and he comes back a half hour later with ten guys and Jerry Simone.''

''Jerry Simone? Is that the guy who used to play football for Southern?''

"The very same."

"Christ, he's almost as old as I am. And the guy weighed around two-twenty back then. What was he doing screwing around with you teen-agers?''

"Yeah, that was my thought, too, Sam. So my buddy, Steve, offered to fight Simone one-on-one, and it was really funny. As big as he was, Simone couldn't fight at all. Steve only weighs one-sixty, but he picked Simone apart from the outside, and the guy started charging at him like a bull. Then he tried to tackle Steve and bite him, and Steve shook him off and kicked him in the head before he could get up. That was it. Simone just lay there.''

"That's known as screwing the moose, Maddy."

"It sure is. So far it's Steve for manslaughter and me for accessory or something.''

"Your Uncle Harold going to defend you?"

"Fat chance. Harold's a tax specialist. Wouldn't soil his hands on anything as mundane as murder. It would divert him from his sacred task of defending the rich against the poor. He's assigned me this young guy who just graduated law school from his office. I guess I'm supposed to be part of his on-the-job training.''

Auer opened the door and said, "You're a smart kid, Maddy. Give my regards to your mother."

"I better not tell her you were in here, or she'll make me spray the place with DDT. You went on her shit list for Marge Coleman, and then Sophie had a few things to say, and when you moved Peggy in yesterday she went through the roof.''

"Well, we both know what she has against Peggy," Auer said and enjoyed the way the boy blanched. He shut the door and crossed Sixth, shaking his head at the thought of a bull like

Jerry Simone, over thirty, crashing a high school graduation party and throwing his weight around. This was a strange city. Adolescence for guys like Zig and Gall and Simone seemed to stretch out till they approached forty. Philadelphia was full of guys like that. He himself had only recently begun to feel like a man. Not getting married, not having children, not killing a few Germans had done that for him. Only in these last few months had he felt himself solidifying, growing denser, becoming Sam Auer. And to everybody else he probably looked like a buffoon.

Peggy had a big bundle of laundry wrapped in a sheet, sitting on the soda case. As he entered she said, "What the hell you been doing for clean clothes, Sam?"

"Oh, I've just generally dumped 'em in the bathtub, sprinkled on soap powder, and let 'em soak. Then ran the shower over them."

"Uch," she groaned. "These are raunchy. Your underwear is like cardboard. Give me a few bucks, and I'll take this crap up to the laundromat."

He slipped her a few dollars, and she gave him a nasty, swishing kiss in the ear before trudging out the door with the heavy bundle over her shoulder. This was very nice, he decided. It did not mean a thing, it would go nowhere, but it would be nice for a while, like making love to a woman on a raft slowly loosing its air in the middle of the ocean.

That first week together they went to the movies almost every night. They finished off the cinemas on lower Market Street, and then Peggy insisted on catching the Dracula double feature at the Booker in the Project. Auer thought he was the only white man in there, till they met Lenny and his girl on the way out. Lenny invited them for drinks at the Green Room, and the two couples danced and drank till closing time.

The following evening Peggy wanted a banana split. They went to the Sugar Bowl on Eighth Street, and Peggy asked why he was so glum. He assured her it was nothing and meanwhile wondered how he would get out of this hole: he missed his girls, his business was a shambles, the lowest scum on the street looked down on him, and every day the mail brought new deadlines and threats from City Hall. Since Peggy moved in, not a white came into his store, and the more refined colored were equally scandalized.

"You sorry about us, baby?" Peggy asked.

"No, I'm not sorry."

"You were looking so pitiful there, I didn't know what to think."

"Ah, I was thinking about guys like Heinie Schmidt who won't come in anymore because you're there. Or all the people who are cutting me dead. And a big shot like Starker pulling all those strings to smash me. And I'm suddenly glad I'm not one of them. I don't know what I am yet. I could still become anything."

"I don't get you, Sam."

"That's okay, baby. Let's go to the Green Room."

Auer was still floating in that vague and nebulous trance when Harry Lipofsky, the ward heeler, stood in his doorway. His lunch hour had been nothing. Empty stools. There was a notice on Starker's bulletin board that his place had been condemned by the Board of Health, which was not technically true, but could he sue? Auer looked up from his sink and said, "To what do I owe the honor, Harry? Registering people early this year?"

Lipofsky hurried to a stool, craned his neck to assure that Peggy was not within earshot, and then leaned over the counter.

"It doesn't look good. It doesn't look nice at all."

"What's the whispering for? Speak up, Lipofsky."

"It doesn't look nice at all," Lipofsky repeated in the same desperate whisper.

"What's that supposed to mean?"

"It's none of my business, but I've been a friend of the family for a long time now, and perhaps that's why I was chosen to relay this on to you. This is an outrageous situation. Bunny must be eating her heart out."

"Who has chosen you to relay which message?"

"Don't be cagey. I've known you since you crawled around this store in wet diapers. We've been receiving all kinds of complaints about this situation."

"Father Divine has been complaining?"

Lipofsky raised a hand, as if imploring support from the ceiling. "Go ahead. Be a wise guy. Be flippant. You don't know. This morning I got a call from Doheny. . . ."

"Doheny, no less. Since when does a police captain have jurisdiction over my bed?"

"Ah-hah," Lipofsky exclaimed triumphantly. "So you do know what I'm talking about, don't you?"

"Sure. And you can tell whoever sent you, they can kiss my ass. In Wanamaker's window. On the Juniper Street side."

"Sam, Sam," Lipofsky said soothingly. "Be reasonable. Who are you? Ask yourself that one question. Let's face it. Who are you? What are you fighting against? Do you think you can defy the entire community with impunity? You've been a focal point of tension around here. First you stir up racial strife and then you bring this unfortunate girl into your home. Do you think I like talking like this to a man whose father I sat next to in synagogue for thirty years? You have drawn a great deal of attention to yourself. It has not, I assure you, been favorable attention. You may not realize it, of course, but on the statute books of the State of Pennsylvania there are laws against fornication outside of marriage and. . . ."

"Yeah? What do they say about jerking off? You've got an ordinance to cover jerking off?"

"It's on the books, Sam."

"It'd be funny if they tried to apply it," Auer said, chuckling at the vision of three army divisions surrounding the city and herding hundreds of thousands of fornicators into Frankling Field and makeshift concentration camps.

"To you it's just a joke, eh? You don't realize what serious trouble you're in."

"I'd say I realize that. And these are no joke," Auer reached for the stack of bills and letters over the keys of his cash register. He began dealing out the notices and threats as if they were cards. "Board of Health, Weights and Measurements, Building Code violations. And there also seems to be some bureaucratic confusion here. On the one hand, my building may be condemned, and today I got this last letter indicating a reappraisal of value, and the property taxes are going up. They should coordinate those things a bit better."

Lipofsky bit on his cigar. "That was a wonderful brainstorm you had there, kid. Trying to put the make on Starker's secretary. That one took the prize."

Auer pushed the letters and notices at him. "Stop worrying so much about my love life and tell me what you can do about all this. You've had my family's vote for forty years, Harry. Plus a few padded votes from upstairs."

"You think I can go up against Starker, Sam? For years he's been threatening to shut his plant down and move it to New Jersey. That would mean a loss in tax base and a loss of about three hundred jobs for the city. You know what he said downtown? That the streets around here had become too unsafe. That his secretary couldn't even walk down the street without being molested. Too much clout, Sam."

"You deliver about one thousand votes to the party, Harry, maybe five hundred of them legal. Doesn't that give you any clout?"

"What kind of horseshit you talking now?"

Auer laughed. "I'm talking about calling up the *Bulletin* and *Inquirer,* so they can check the voting rolls. You've got thirty names registered as voting out of my place. This must be a very healthy building. Nobody ever dies here."

"You're talking a lot of horseshit. This verges on slander, Sam."

"Or I might have the reporters around with photographers on Election Day, when you stick your hand through the curtain and push the drunks to make sure they pull the right lever."

"You're definitely verging on slander," Lipofsky said, rising from the stool.

"So sue me." Auer extended his arms to take in the store, the depleted shelves, the Christmas wrapping paper over the oppressive boards, the decrepit fixtures. "Sue me and take this off my hands as a judgment. That would really be a judgment on you, you *mumser*."

Lipofsky marched indignantly to the door and spun around. "Zacky told me you'd gone off the deep end, and now I believe him. The next stop for you is Norristown, boy. You're headed straight for the boobyhouse."

Auer winked at him. "There's probably a lot of nice people up in Norristown."

Totally mystified by these reactions, Lipofsky wobbled his loose chin and fled across Sixth Street, muttering under his breath about people going off the deep end.

It seemed to be the general consensus, Auer noted behind his counter. The verdict of the community was that he had gone off the deep end. Yet he felt strangely calm. And solid. Strong. As if he had not even begun to tap his resources, as if every blow and knock were just making him stronger. He stared at his depleted shelves. It would be easy to restock them. All he had to do was slap another mortgage on this joint and put in a few thousand bucks for repairs. He could outlast Starker, too, with all his clout. They would see who had the staying power. Some of those colored businesses on Ridge Avenue hung on for years, candy stores struggling along year after year with a jar of pickles, a soda case, and a rack of fried pork skins. Of course, those stores were only a front for numbers writing operations.

Auer went directly back to the bedroom. Peggy had picked up this irritating habit of napping every afternoon. She was a sweet kid but the worst kind of drunk, an easy drunk. With the second gin she became slushy and disconnected, and then she just knocked them back and had to sleep ten hours. He touched her shoulder more roughly than he had intended to.

"What's the matter, baby?"

"What's Winston's phone number?"

"Which Winston?"

"Your old Winston."

"If he's still there it's MA 9-8563."

"Put on a dress and get in the store. I've got to go up the corner and make a call."

She blinked her eyes in disbelief and pulled the sheet back over her head. From under the white sheet he heard a muffled mumble of "I'm sleepy, baby. I'll be out there by and by."

Irritated, he locked the store and walked to the phone at the corner of Sixth and Green Garden. Miraculously, it was working. It was usually jammed and had cost him a lot of dimes since he stopped using Leah's booth. A woman answered, and Auer gave his name and asked for Winston. The sunshine came right through the wires.

"How's it going, Sam baby. Funny thing. I was just thinking about passing down your way."

"Glad to hear that. Hope I'm not interrupting anything."

"Ten minutes ago you would have. Interrupting a lady's term paper, y'know. Heard you picked up a little company yourself."

"One of your old flames."

"A nice girl, but all her drinking puts out the fire. Hope she doesn't pull that on you."

"What about that proposition you mentioned? Still open?"

"I'm going to be seeing people in about an hour. I could bring them by your place, and you can talk directly."

"If you don't mind my asking, Winston, how come you're so generous with me? What's in it for you?"

"That ain't really none of your business, Sam, but I'll tell you anyway. I'm being promoted to more expensive items, and my people want somebody to cover my old book. A store's the best place for that. Everybody comes into a store."

"What kind of items?"

"Imported products."

"I gotcha."

Two hours later Winston came into the store with two sharply dressed white men, Italians from South Philly. Winston introduced them as Glenn and Vince. Auer brought out beers all around. He could sense that his dingy place at first repelled them but that they liked him personally, especially when it was established that he had played fullback for Southern and that Vince and he had a lot of friends in common down by Snyder Avenue. For a few minutes Winston was the outsider, as Vince and Auer bartered anecdotes about candy store toughs and agreed that it was amazing that a hardrock like Jerry Simone could let himself be killed by a seventeen-year-old kid.

Glenn cut the amenities short by saying, "Winston tells us you're a steady, reliable man. How's your mathematics?"

"I keep straight books," Auer said.

"That's always a problem," Vince said. He was a handsome, muscular man of about twenty-eight; his sport shirt opened to the waist to reveal a hairy chest and a gold crucifix. He cracked his knuckles, more of a nervous mannerism than a threat, as he explained, "A lot of bookies, storekeepers, don't find a seventy-thirty split fair. How do you find it, Sam?"

"Well, it's not the most generous split that ever came down the pike."

"Think of it this way, Sam. We're taking all the risks. The payoff on a hit comes out of our end. And you also generally get a fat tip when somebody makes a big hit. Also, you gotta figure it helps your business. Everybody comes in here to lay a dime or quarter down, they buy a loaf of bread, a quart of milk, that's all yours."

"That goes down," Auer agreed.

"Problem is," Glenn cut in "some people try to get funny.

Hold back slips. Hold back money. Want to take our odds and become their own banker. You read about people like that in the newspapers. Body in a lot. Body found behind the counter in their store."

"Sam ain't gonna pull none of that shit," Winston assured them. "I've known this man all my life, and I can vouch for him."

"There's one other thing that comes out of your end," Vince said. "Forty a week for McCann, out of your end. McCann gets to keep twenty, and twenty goes to Doheny at the station."

"Doheny's on the take?" Auer said with genuine surprise.

"Are you kidding?" Vince said. "Doheny's got a big family. Us wops and the micks have lots of kids, Sam. You can't hardly expect the city to take care of all of them."

"Doheny on the take. That's funny."

"What's so funny about it?" Glenn asked.

"Nothing you'd understand."

Peggy pushed the curtain aside and was about to enter the store. She immediately sensed that a business conference was taking place, gave Winston a wave of greeting, and closed the curtain. Vince and Glenn stared at the curtain but said nothing. Auer guessed that they might have had some comment about spades if Winston were not there.

"That's it, then," Vince said, rising from the stool. "As of tomorrow your territory is Willow to Green Garden and everything from Fifth to Eighth. People want to play, they come to you. You got penny carbon paper books, or I can start you out with a box I've got in the trunk of our car, Sam?"

"Thanks, I'll take them. My regular wholesale confectionery man carries them, so I can pick up a load off him."

"They all carry them," Glenn said. "Snuff, Bull Durham, and penny pads. That's what keeps the economy going."

Auer went out to the car with them to get his box of penny books, and Winston said, "I'll go spread the word, Sam, drop by Shor's and Zacky's and the Green Room and tell them you're taking over for me.''

"Winston, you're a goddamn prince," Auer said, and they all laughed. Hands were shook firmly and Auer stayed outside after they left, watching the softball game in the schoolyard. They had left him with a good feeling. He liked the way those guys did business. All straight. Clear. No B.S. Man to man. For the last seven months all he had heard was whining and sniveling and people whining that they did not make the rules, were merely enforcing them. Glenn and Vince had definitely left him with a good feeling.

Over dinner Peggy told him she wanted to see the Joan Crawford–Bette Davis double feature at the Astor. He had no particular desire to catch all that heavy emoting. His mind was swirling with mathematical calculations, multiplications, new vistas that might be opening up. Also, he was not looking forward to all the stares he would get around Marshall Street and Girard Avenue, where so many people knew the Auers. But Peggy had made him an excellent supper, spaghetti with hot sausage, and deserved a reward, and he was elated anyway, seething with an uncontrollable excitement. He wondered whether he could actually beat them all. The old "focal point of tension" might ram it up all of them.

Dusk looming over the river had tinted the clouds purple, and on this sweltering, humid evening everybody was out on their steps. With his arm around Peggy's waist, Auer walked up Sixth and nodded at the shopkeepers who had known him since childhood. None acknowledged his greetings. Most stared right through him, as if he were glass. Peggy was in her bright green dress, and he was sure she was accentuating the wriggle of her hips as an invitation to those gaping at them to kiss her backside. The colored boys playing basketball in the twilight of the Kearny schoolyard stopped to watch them drift by. It seemed to Auer that time had slowed down, and they were floating through a misty sea with the sky closing above the reflection of darkening waters. Across the street was the day nursery where, before she gave it up to take care of her mother, Leah had been superintendent. Leah was like a sentimental relic of the old days, like that photo of his parents. She was lucky, he thought. She did not know the world was a dark place. Or what it would take to survive in the future.

Peggy said, "I want to stop by Rose's dress shop on Marshall Street and try this dress on."

Auer looked down at her. "You testing me, baby?"

"Maybe," she conceded. "You nervous about being seen with me? You got all your people on Marshall Street."

"Their good opinion never put much money in my pocket."

"You getting to love me, Sam?"

"I'm thinking about it."

She pinched his wrist, and they both laughed. At Parrish they turned left and then went up Marshall. He loved these blocks on Marshall up to Girard. This was the only exotic, colorful spot in the whole city, all the stands and stalls with junk and dry goods, toys and fruit, the smell of bakeries and delicatessens, roasting peanuts, fresh fish, and chicken coops. The babble and swarming of all the Hungarians and Puerto Ricans, Kalmucks, and Ukrainian women from Third Street with their leather shopping bags. Each store had its aroma, sauerkraut and green tomatoes in barrels, sawdust on the floors, powdered sugar, baking bread, onions frying. This street was scheduled for renewal, too. Bunny had hated this chaos, dreamed about getting to that sterile block in Oxford Circle, dreamed about shopping in bland supermarkets where the chickens were already dead and wrapped in cellophane.

He was getting the other side of it tonight, could catch their comments in Russian, Yiddish, German, Romanian, as they spotted his hand in Peggy's. Everybody on Marshall Street was a social commentator, and this was a bit too advanced for them.

It was a shame there was so little pity to spare. So little margin. These were all immigrants and the children of immigrants, but from the sneers and looks, he could be passing in review for the Cabots and the Lodges.

Fortunately, Rose's was closed. Auer took Peggy by the arm and led her firmly away from the millinery shop she tried to enter. As they took seats in the Astor, the audience cheered for the Bugs Bunny cartoon flashing on the screen. Bugs was munching on a carrot, and Auer slouched low in his seat. An enormous exhaustion seeped through him, and he realized how nervous he had been this afternoon. Of course, he had kept up a good front, things were cool, but Vince and Glenn were not Zig and Gall. They talked quite casually about bodies found in empty lots and behind store counters. Not to impress him. Just to explain the ground rules. He had a franchise in a different league now.

When his head shot up, Joan Crawford was getting another comeuppance. Bette Davis had already got her comeuppance. How about Genghis Khan? Genghis Khan never got a come-uppance. Auer lit a cigarette, and when a woman in back protested, he said, "Fuck off." Then he sank lower in his seat to enjoy his smoke. They were speechifying on the screen. Joan was getting hers. He was fed up with the movies. Peggy had dragged him to every movie within walking distance, and he had concluded they were all phony. The great novels he read were false because they made existence too interesting, but the movies were worse because they were basically religious. All little sermonettes preaching that success was hollow, big shots suffered too, you should sacrifice for your buddies and human-ity, that money wasn't everything, that if the librarian will just take off her glasses and apply the proper makeup she is really Elizabeth Taylor, that crime does not pay, that convicts are nicer than guards, that a guy is a killer because he didn't have a puppy when he was a kid, and that immigrants were picturesque and colorful. All of this horseshit ground out by directors, writers, and producers around pools in Beverly Hills, guys who would sell their mother to the Bulgarian Army to get a notch ahead. . . .

He laughed, and Peggy said, "What you snickering about?"

"I couldn't begin to tell you."

"You don't like the movie?"

"I love it. Fucking ducky. Only problem is, Joan looks like she could punch out any of her leading men."

"Shhh," somebody in the rear whispered.

"Sit on it," Auer snapped back.

"What you so angry for Sam?" Peggy said meekly.

"I'm angry at having watched this crap all my life."

"You want to leave?"

"Say 'shazam,' baby."

They walked down Franklin Street hand in hand, Peggy singing "April Showers," and Auer thought about the pictures he had seen about Philadelphia. Always some socialites on the Main Line, veddy veddy rich, pushing each other into pools or flinging goblets of champagne in each other's faces in the big dramatic scenes. Philly was mostly two million Italians, Jews, Irishmen, and Negroes getting up to go to work at seven every morning, and he could not quite envision Big Vye flinging her champagne goblet in Barry's face.

"Whatcha' smilin' at?" Peggy said.

"Nothing much."

"You hardly ever talk, Sam."

"Nothing to say right now. I'm checking back on everything I ever thought."

"You seem so sad."

He put his hand on her bottom and enjoyed the wiggle and roll of her soft cheeks till she shook it off.

"You can take care of that later."

"I'll try and do that little thing," she said gaily and kissed his shoulder.

They entered the Green Room, and Peggy immediately

ruined the moment by letting out an exuberant yell of "Johnny! Johnny Hunter! Hey, now."

The customers on the barstools watched Peggy rush to the rear booth to give the hug of a long-lost friend to a moustached Negro in an Ike jacket and fatigue trousers. They held the embrace, and Peggy was babbling excitedly as Auer folded his arms across his chest. With the lighter V-shaped patches on the sleeves where sergeants' stripes had been snipped away and his scuffed combat boots, John Hunter was obviously recently mustered out and quite drunk. Around here lots of the boys wore bits and snatches of their uniforms for years after their discharge. The sergeant excused himself to his buddies in the booth and was coolly letting himself be dragged forward for an introduction by a vivacious Peggy. She wore her most devilish grin as she said, "Johnny, I want you to meet Sam here. I'm staying with Sam these days. Sam . . . Johnny."

Auer found himself involved in a quick, stupid test of grips, and Hunter abruptly drew his chin in, squinted in recognition, and said, "I think I already know you. But I'll bet you don't remember who I am."

"Hunter, John Hunter?" Auer chewed it around. "Sounds familiar."

"Fuckin-A, daddy. We've met before. We met hard. You were backfield for Southern, and I was starting end for Bok Vocational."

"That's going back some, John."

"Yeah, Southern was supposed to roll right over us, with you leading the way, and I brought you down every time you tried to sweep around my end. Remember that?"

"No shit," Auer said. He frowned, concentrating, flipping through his mental files for the clippings that were almost memorized by heart. Southern had smashed Bok about 40–0, and he ran for three touchdowns that day. "I guess the other guys didn't give you much support, John."

"You don't remember me, eh?"

"Yeah, I've got you pegged now. Sure. You used to live next door to Alvin Brown on Callowhill Street. And I ran right through you twice that game. Whatcha' been doing since then? Turned pro?"

Hunter held out his arms for an inspection of his disheveled army uniform. "I was making a career of the Army till this cracker captain got me on some kinda' black market shit. Same shit a lot of other cats were messing around with. So I told 'em to shove it, y'know what I mean? Just got back from Deutschland. Your family still got that store over there?"

"I'm running it myself now," Auer said gravely. "They both passed on."

"That does happen," Hunter conceded. He wrapped his arm possessively around Peggy's shoulder. "And what's the story with Miss Moore? What does Miss Moore have to say for herself."

"More of the same. More of the same, only more so."

Poking a finger at Auer's beltline, Hunter said, "You put on some pounds there, daddy. You used to be quite the trim fellah, Sam."

"I ain't running for Mister Universe anymore, John." He patted his gut, still hard. "You seemed to have stayed in fair shape."

"All that exercise in Deutschland, daddy. I'll tell you, they've got some wicked pussy on that continent. All them *fräuleins* can wear a man down to nothing."

"Sit down and have a drink with us," Auer suggested.

"Why don't you have a drink at the bar?" Peggy cut in. "I just want to chat with Johnny for a few minutes, Sam. Find out what's happening in his young life. I ain't seen this boy since the end of the war, and we were real sweet on each other a long time back."

"Yeah, let me borrow her for a few minutes," Hunter said glibly. "I'll send her right on back. If I remember rightly, this woman drinks way too fast for any man to stay up with her, so I'll let you carry the heavy part of her bill."

Peggy nudged Hunter with her elbow for that remark and then took his arm. "I'll be right back, Sam. You order yourself a drink at the bar, and I'll be right along, honey."

The old sarge winked, and Auer was not sure whether it was a wink of collusion between two men of the world at the general flightiness of women, or the condescending wink of a smoothie who had just lifted a girl from a sap with a whole barroom looking on.

Sy Green, the bartender, served him a Seven-and-Seven and his usual bag of peanuts. Auer thought about stuffing some change into the jukebox but did not feel like walking across the room and being stared at. He had already been made to appear foolish. His reflection in the grease-smeared, flyspecked mirror behind the bar was dour enough.

In the heat, the "Red Dynamite" offered on the mirror sign seemed to be the popular drink: a wine cooler laced with rum. That seemed to be the main goal in the Green Room—get stupefied as cheaply and quickly as possible.

Peggy yelped with laughter at some remark made in the rear booth, and Auer could only hope he was not the butt of the joke. He sipped at his Seven-and-Seven and remembered the night, after the Booker, when they came in here with Lenny and that Pocahontas he shacked up with, and he had wondered how Lenny could take all that crap off an ugly black squaw. Now he was taking it. He turned on his stool and watched Peggy having such a gay time with the four losers in the back booth. So far she had been pretty nice to have around the house, but she had to be one really dumb cunt to pull this shit on him.

"Another, Sam?" Sy Green said, indicating the empty glass. "Hit it."

Sy poured him a generous shot and said, "Winston told me you're taking over for him. Put a buck on 417 in the box for me."

"Got no slips on me."

"I trust you. Do it on a napkin."

Auer scribbled a 417 in a lopsided square, added a G for his own memory.

"How's business?" Sy asked.

"It will improve."

"She used to hustle out of here, y'know."

"I'm rehabilitating her. It appears she's backsliding tonight."

"Give her a wallop."

"I may just do that."

The jukebox had been activated, and Auer listened to the lyrics as Sy went to attend to another customer. He smiled at the "The Story of Love." She had to be one dumb cunt. Today he was off on this great new venture, had just written his first number, thirty cents his way, and she pulls a dumb stunt like this.

One drink later he was ready to swing off his stool and walk out, go home and dump her crap on the doorstep, when an arm curled around his waist and Peggy murmured, "Let's go, baby." Auer signaled to Sy for his check, and the bartender said, "Cover it with the other, Sam, okay?"

From the rear booth John Hunter awarded Auer a semimilitary salute, and Auer responded with a casual nod.

Over Green Garden the summer sky was chalky and swollen with rain clouds. Lightning danced on the river, beyond the El tracks. One more flash of lightning would lance open the sky and unleash the downpour. Peggy held his hand and was quiet till they reached Cottonwood.

"You pissed at me, Sam?"

He said nothing.

"I figured you were. I hadn't seen that boy in so long, honey. You ain't got no call to be pissed at me. He was just telling me all about Europe and everything. All about Germany."

Auer lit a cigarette, glanced at her.

"Don't be this way." She tugged at his arm. "That boy never meant anything to me at all. We were just messing around back there. I don't have any romantic interest at all in John Hunter."

She was still protesting her innocence, using that vocabulary from *True Confessions* Magazine, when he opened the side door and they entered the parlor, just escaping the first drop of rain. The left side of her face flattened under the force of his slap, and Peggy crumbled to the floor. He jerked her back to her feet and gave her two more slaps before hurling her across the room, so that she banged her knee against the coffee table before the sofa broke her fall.

Auer lit another cigarette off the butt and placed the butt in the ashtray on the radio. Undumped. The parlor was getting scruffy again. Hardly here two weeks, and those high standards of housekeeping declined.

Still crying her hands over her face on the sofa, between sobs Peggy managed to say, "Why'd you have to do that? You didn't have to hit me that hard."

"The next time I'll break your fucking head in. You got that?"

"I got it."

"The next time your ass will be out of here so fast you'll never know what hit you. You got that, too?"

Between sobs, she nodded in agreement.

Auer went to the store icebox for a few bottles of beer. Peggy was still whimpering and shuddering on the sofa when he returned to the parlor. He said, "Why don't you knock off that shit, already? Go in the store and heat up more of that spaghetti and sausage. Serve in the back kitchen."

He opened his bottle of beer and plopped down at the white metal table in the back kitchen. It had been a real pleasure to bop Peggy that way. A definite tingle had gone up his arm. Now he was sorry that he had not given Bunny a good bop in about the third year of their marriage. Of course, she would have probably thrown him out of the house for it, but that would have set matters right or spared him the misery of the next eight years. He sipped at his beer and was feeling much better. If he took no crap off the entire world, why should he take it off a woman?

Peggy brought in his dish of spaghetti and sausage, and he

liberally sprinkled in Tabasco sauce and pinches of salt and pepper. His parents had never learned to use salt and pepper shakers. They had this partitioned old stone mug, brought from the old country, and in another twenty years it could probably be a collector's item. The four-legged stove, the wood icebox, most of these kitchen furnishings could probably fit in well with Leah's antiques.

Across the table Peggy gave one long last sigh that swelled her bosom, and she seemed to be recovered. He watched her sip at her beer and unwrap the sweet roll she had brought for herself. In this kitchen, where his father had lit the Friday night candles, she looked about as natural as a visitor from Pluto or Uranus. Tomorrow her face would be swollen and bruised. He reached out to touch her cheek, and the tears flared in her eyes again.

"You're so mean, Sam."

"That's wrong. I'm the nicest guy in the world. Just don't mess around."

Tilting her head, she pressed her cheek against his hand and said, "You didn't have to hit me that hard. My knee is all hurt, too."

"I'll try to make up for it later."

In spite of the loving before they slept, it began to sour after that incident at the Green Room. Peggy did not get up till eleven the next morning, and when she finally made her appearance it was to have a quick jelly doughnut and coffee and ask for seven dollars to buy that dress in Rose's window on Marshall Street. She promised to be back before two, to wash the lunch dishes, but did not return till after five, without the dress, shuffling torpidly, and the odor of Sen-Sen on her breath.

Auer might have slapped her again, but he was too busy and elated to lay down the law at that moment. Winston had done a thorough job of advertising the new franchise. On this, the very first day, he had written over thirty-six dollars in numbers, mostly in dimes and quarters, but with a few dollar bets also, and each and every one of those customers had picked up a couple of grocery items or bought a soda, along with laying down his nickel or quarter. When Glenn and Vince came in and saw the sheet he had drawn up, aside from the milk bottle full of coins and slips, Vince said, "That's good. You keep good books, Sam."

Glenn studied the total at the bottom of the sheet. "Your take is down a lot from Winston's."

Vince gave Glenn a light backhanded tap on the arm. "That's to be expected, man. What do you want from Sam? It's his first day on the job, and the people around here are used to dealing with Winston's black face and not his white face. They have to develop confidence in Sam. Just wait till somebody gets a nice hit, and then they'll be swarming in here. The take will go right back up."

It went exactly as Vince said. Two days later, Bowes the guitarist hit for thirty-five cents on 771. A one-hundred-forty-dollar payoff. The news shot through the neighborhood, and Auer say his store crowded for the first time in memory. Half the berrypickers from Seventh Street poured in to put down from a dime to a dollar, believing that luck was contagious. Auer set up a rule. Anybody who wanted to play had to buy some groceries—cash. To those who protested, he explained that he wanted no trouble with the police, so nobody could leave the store with empty hands.

Bowes brought along three friends the following afternoon to witness that one-hundred-forty-dollar payoff. Auer handed him eighty-three dollars and sixty-seven cents. The look of joy faded from the old black's face, and he wailed, "What the hell is this, Mister Sam?"

"You've got sixty-six dollars and thirty-three cents in my books, Bowes. I'm not asking for any tip. I'm just subtracting what you already owe me."

"C'mon, Mister Sam," Bowes wailed in a high-pitched, breaking voice. "That ain't right. What for you want to spoil my great thing for like this?"

Auer let him sweat it out for a few seconds and then handed him the other sixty-six dollars and thirty-three cents he had waiting in another envelope. "Okay, Bowes. We won't mix the one with the other. Now I want to see how you treat me."

Bowes snatched up the envelope, checked the contents, thrust a twenty-dollar bill back at Auer, and said, "You're all right, Mister Sam. Goddamn it, you're all right."

He was practically dancing with glee as he went out the door with his three buddies, and for the remainder of the hot afternoon the icehouse gang had a party at Shor's with Bowes buying, the party only ending when Sidonia knocked Lenny off a stool, bringing in the red cars. But the word had gone out. Mister Sam was all right. All that trouble back in December, those cars showing up, was forgotten.

Auer told the story of Bowes dancing out the door to Vince and Glenn when they arrived for the milk bottle that evening. In just a few days they had come to seem like close friends. They generally needed something cool after a day of driving around picking up milk bottles at plants and stores, and Auer had learned to prepare Vince's favorite drink, a wine punch with lots of ice, lemons, and oranges. Glenn cackled at his description of how Bowes had sweated before he received the other sixty-six dollars, and Vince said, "You were telling us you might not be able to hold onto this place, Sam. That's a shame. Your take is coming up there. You're doing better than Winston did."

"Yeah. Well, I'm getting a lot of white players Winston never had. All these guys from the wood factory down the street coming in for lunch, dropping a quarter or fifty cents."

"Yeah," Vince said, sipping at his wine punch. "It'd be a shame to lose this corner. This could be a very lucrative location. Not just for this penny-ante shit but for bigger things. How come you might lose it?"

Auer went to the cash register and brought back all of the letters, notices, warnings from all the departments in City Hall which had descended on him. He spread them out on the counter, saying, "The same wood factory up the street. The owner forbid the workers to come in here, posting a sign saying this place was condemned by the Board of Health. They're coming back anyway now, to put their money down."

"What's the bastard on you for?" Glenn asked.

"Ah, he's got this very sharp blond secretary. Probably needs knee pads and a broom handle to keep her in line. I talked to her one afternoon, you know, tried to put the make on her, and the next day the whole roof caved in. Everybody but the mayor was in here."

Vince nudged Glenn with his elbow. "How do you like that shit, man? A straight guy like Sam just talks to a chick, and they want to screw him like this. That's a real crock, ain't it?"

"Yeah." Glenn agreed. "I can see the guy sending a gunsel, or a couple of guys around to like rough you up a little, but all this crap here is really unfair."

Auer stared oddly at Glenn as Vince began to make a stack of the notices and warnings on the counter and said, "Let me take these with me. I can't guarantee anything, but I can talk to people who know other people, and maybe they can straighten this out for you."

"If it's any bother . . . ," Auer hesitated.

"Nah, man," Vince said. "A straight guy like you, Sam? You should have told us about this before. If you need something, ask. I can't guarantee anything, but we can always see. . . ."

Auer did not know what they did. He only knew that no further letters and warnings arrived from City Hall. Except one advising that the tax-readjustment had been in error, and his property taxes were being reinstated at the lower level. He read the letter and laughed. They never taught it this way in his high school civics course.

With his luck changing, Auer went to Fat Grace's that evening. He had one hundred dollars in his pocket that he felt he could lose with total equanimity. It was one hundred to spare, and he just wanted to play cards. Naturally, he won. Relaxed, laughing, there was no more of that throwing away a pair of sevens to draw for an inside straight. Cleve, Nelson, Barry, and Skinner looked on unhappily as he raked in every second or third pot, and by one A.M. they were all cleaned out.

As a sport, he gave Nelson back thirty dollars when he moaned that he needed it for his rent or his old lady would kill him, but before they could all start moaning he invited Barry, Skinner, and Cleveland to his place for a drink. None of Grace's home brew. Two bottles of real Johnny Walker from the State Store.

Grace said, "Why don't you just get your old ass in bed, Barry. You run out at this hour, you always get in trouble."

"Get off my ass, bitch. My friend Sam is kind enough to offer his hospitality, so I'm going to cross the street and enjoy his hospitality. That's logical, ain't it?"

They all agreed it sounded logical and shuffled across the street. Peggy woke up, always ready to join a party, and brought in the paper cups, ice cubes, and bags of pretzels. Drinks were poured all around, and Barry proposed the first toast. He raised his paper cup and said, "Goddamn Sam, you're all right."

"Yeah," Auer agreed, "I'll have to confess. I'm all right."

"Ain't he all right, Cleve?" Barry demanded to know. "And you can vouch for him, Peggy. You live with the man, and he treats you fine. And you too, Skinner."

The other two men nodded, depressed by their losses. Barry shook his head in admiration and assured them, "I mean this. I'm not just saying this to hear myself talk."

"It'd be the first time," Peggy said dryly.

"Don't shit me now, girl," Barry snapped. "Because I will tell you why this man is all right. Sam is all right because he knows what it's all about. Don't you, Sam?"

"It took me a while, but I learned."

"Your're fuckin-A right, you learned. And I'll tell you how you learned. You got conked on the head, and there's nothing like getting conked on the skull to clear up what's going on inside. You see them stars for a while, but when them stars settle down, everything becomes bright and clear. Jonesie told me about how you looked when they tossed you into Mocco. One sorry sight. You had just graduated from the school of hard knocks."

They laughed, and Barry nodded in appreciation of his own wittiness. "But you were lucky, Sam. They really don't know how to work over a man in Mocco. You ought to try Wilmington, Delaware, when you get the chance. That's the town. I mean, I had cops whip shit out of me in Raleigh, Memphis, Florida, and Kentucky, but Wilmington, Delaware, they do it up brown." Barry shook a head as though he still had fond memories of the guards' technical skill. "Man, they threw me in that cell, my pants were coming down, they worked over my belly, they chopped my head, they were so good they had me going up the wall instead of down to the floor. I pissed blood for a week. Those boys earned their pay. So that's how I know there's nothing like getting hit on the head to clear the mind and open the eyes."

"That's what made you so smart, huh?" Peggy said. "Getting knocked on the head so many times?"

"Me?" Barry pointed his thumb at his chest. "I ain't smart. I'm not even all here. Did you know that, George Skinner? I'm not even all here. Sometimes I sit there for an hour, just sit there, and when I look up I wonder where I've been and what the hell I was thinking. I know I must have been thinking something, but I can't remember what it was."

"You're probably better off not remembering," Cleveland said.

"Shit, I don't know. Only thing I know is, Sam is all right. That's an unusual thing. A goddamn white man who knows what it's all about."

His guests dawdled on till after the Johnny Walker was finished, but long before that Auer had grown weary of the testimonials to what a grand fellow he was, and how different from all the other bastards around here. He guessed they were hoping for another flask to miraculously appear, and finally had to inform them the well was dry and half-usher and half-shove them out the door.

Peggy had already passed out on the bed. He climbed over her long legs and nudged her so she would stop snoring. If she was awake, they could have celebrated his winnings, three-twenty minus thirty, with a piece. Lately, he had really been letting her get away with a lot. She slept late, hardly helped him in the store, drifting in and out at odd hours, constantly hitting him for money to head over to Shor's for a taste, and he would have shaped her up if he had not been so excited and busy in the store.

He wondered whether she was messing around with Hunter during those long disappearances in the afternoon. If she was he hardly cared. It was easy to see why Winston dumped her now. Too much of a lush to care about sex. It must have been a real torture for her to be a prostitute. The way his business was picking up, he would soon be able to afford a lot better than Peggy on his bed. Till then, she was a convenience. As long as she kept the house straight, was docile during the day and available at night, he hardly cared what she did. It made no difference at all.

On Saturday afternoon Peggy persuaded him to close for a few hours and use part of his poker windfall to shop for new clothes downtown. It did not require much persuasion because he had been planning on showing up well dressed for the court hearing and rubbing a bit of his new prosperity in Bunny's face.

They walked to Himmelhoch's haberdashery, past Eighth and Race, and he let Peggy select a suede jacket with a wraparound belt for him. Building around the suede jacket, Peggy picked out a pair of mauve slacks, a chocolate sports shirt, alligator shoes, and a matching high-brimmed hat to complete the outfit.

"It's very smart," Himmelhoch assured him, smoothing the lines of the shoulders.

Auer cocked the hat at a more jaunty angle. Evaluating the total effect in the three mirrors, he was aware that this rakish getup would work against his interests at the hearing. His best bet to cop a plea would be to show up threadbare and poormouth the judges to get lower support payments, but he was not that concerned with playing this deal cool. Nobody had ever called Sam Auer cheap or chintzy. He wanted his daughters safe and comfortable and would pay through the nose, but he also wanted to show Bunny a new Sam Auer, show that bitch he was doing all right.

"Shall we wrap these up?" Himmelhoch asked hopefully.

"I'm thinking," Auer said. He fingered the suede lapels. These threads were too loud, too South Street, but maybe they fitted in with his new calling. Vince and Glenn were sharp dressers. He knew they respected him for his toughness but also thought he was a slob. If he was going to be associating with guys like Glenn and Vince, he was going to have to change his image. There was no reason that life could not open up for him. Once he dumped Peggy, he could get a car, move out a little, catch up on all he had missed by being such a goody-goody boy for so long. That did not mean he would skimp on his girls. What he wanted to do was drive up to that house on Sunday, dazzle his girls, be stylish and vibrant, take them out in the car, and make Bunny look frumpy and dowdy.

"If it's a check, we need three identifications," Himmelhoch said.

"Cash. If you can throw a cuff on these trousers, it's cash, and I'll wear the whole ensemble out."

Catering to a cash customer, they stitched up the cuffs in less than twenty minutes. Meanwhile, he let Peggy buy a brilliant scarlet dress as a reward for her patience. She chose to wear it out, and if the bums and pawnshop owners had stared before, it was nothing compared to the sensation they caused flouncing back up Eighth with Peggy shaking her hips, swinging the shopping bag with their old clothes, and stopping in a parody of a model's pose to admire her reflection in every hockshop window.

Peggy wanted to drop by Zacky's for a midafternoon pick-up, needed to show off her new dress. Auer begged off and gave her five dollars, told her to be back for supper. He walked down Cottonwood and food Maddy plinking on his guitar on Leah's side step. Auer stopped to listen with a trace of derision on his lips. This Maddy suddenly thought he was Bowes, trying to bang out blues. The boy abruptly placed his hands over the frets and said, "Those are mighty violent togs you're sporting there, Amos Auer."

Auer flicked lint from his lapel. "Like them? Picked them up on Eighth Street."

"I didn't think it was Bond Street."

"How's the murder trial going, killer? You and your buddies going to cop a plea? I see you coming home dirty every day from the rubber factory."

"It keeps on getting postponed. Now it's on the docket for late September."

"That will sort of mess you up on starting college?"

"I'm not sure I'm going. I can't see myself singing boolah-boolah out in California if my best buddy is in jail for a mess I got him into."

"California? I'll really envy you if you get out to California. You go to college, kid. Otherwise you'll end up a dummy like me."

"You're doing okay, Sporting Life. You've got the busiest corner in town these days."

"Things have turned around," Auer said as he moved to leave.

"They sure have, Sam. Put a quarter on zero-zero-zero for me."

Auer sniffed and crossed Sixth to open his store. Since business had picked up so much, he hated to be away from it. Before, while it was sinking, he had closed it to wander the streets, but now his mind was constantly doing mathematical calculations, multiplications, his brain swirling with figures and fantasies of wealth. He had never signed any contract that stipulated he had to remain small-time his entire life. Glenn and Vince had hinted at much more lucrative fields.

Peggy showed up after midnight, pounding loudly on the side door instead of using her key. He opened it to discover that her new dress was already ripped at the sleeve, and that she had brought along a pack of riffraff from Zacky's.

"What's all this?"

There were six or seven milling around outside, a few he knew and several strangers. Peggy said, "I've brought them along for another drink. They're all friends of mine, Sam."

"Weren't you supposed to be back to make supper?"

"I'm sorry, Sam. I got tied up. I had to drive out to Strawberry Mansion."

"You had to, eh?" He looked over her shoulder at the crowd she had brought along. "Sorry, we're all dry around here." The lie came glibly. "Barry was here and needed the last of my stuff over his place."

He waited patiently as the crowd on the sidewalk argued as to whether to drive over to a club in Camden or go to Barber John's after-hours joint in the Project. Peggy touched his arm. "You mind if I go along with them? It's hard for me to sleep when it's so hot like this."

"Go ahead," he told her, "I don't mind." He waved to the pack she had brought along. "Sorry about that. Catch you all next time."

The wheeze of relief came after he shut the door. She was right about it being too hot to sleep, though. He had been merely tossing on that bed. With the humidity it felt like he was trying to survive in a fishbowl. He went to the store for a cold beer and brought back his folder of bills to do his monthly accounts.

One hour later he went to pour himself a drink from the bottle of Seagram's he had chosen not to waste on that pack from Zacky's. It warranted a celebration. July represented a complete turnaround. The numbers had given a powerful boost to his trade. Over four weeks he was writing an average of four hundred and thirty bucks a week, his cut only one-thirty, minus the forty for McCann and Doheny—but that ninety was free and clear and, naturally, tax-exempt. The ninety was the nut. The magnet of the numbers had given a tremendous shot to his luncheonette and grocery trade, put them back in the black.

Auer lit another cigarette and did more calculations. In just one month, his first month, in one milk bottle per day Glenn and Vince had taken back to their bankers approximately $1,204, minus $420 in hits, or a $784 profit. Almost pure profit. Eight hundred dollars out of this one dumpy store in this one shitty, miserable neighborhood in one month. No wonder they could talk to people who could make a few phone calls to City Hall and call off Starker's dogs.

It took a bit of the edge off his triumph—the fact that powerful interests in South Philly were backing him—but his bottle tilted into the glass again, and he relaxed deeper into the sofa. He was in the black. It was not the money that gave him this deep sense of accomplishment. Money was not the measure of a man. Even though that was about all this society respected. If a man said he was a millionaire, he said it all. But his was a sense of personal accomplishment. He was going to beat them all and come out of this. None of them believed he could survive this, and he was triumphing over Bunny, Jerry, Uncle Joe with his lousy job offer, insurance companies that did not pay off, the scummy Johnsons, the berrypickers who did not pay their bills, the white trash who scorned him because he moved Peggy in, prissy Silverman the principal, and all of the other storekeepers who wanted him to move away, the indifferent police who refused to patrol his corner, and Starker, with all of his lackeys at City Hall. Sam the *shmuck* was going to defeat the whole yelping pack.

Auer rose and gave his reflection in the parlor mirror an obscene sign with an upward thrust of his stiff forearm. The old "focal point of tension" was in the black. Sam the *shmuck* had beat them all.

August should have been the greatest month in his life. He was waiting for September, when Jeanette Lewis would be back at the Thurston School, and this time, he promised himself, his voice would not crack or be stilted. He would not be such a sap. He would be able to make a substantial offer. But the first week in August, Glenn and Vince were sitting at his counter, enjoying their wine punch and sandwiches he had prepared, and Vince, with his mouth filled, said, "You make a good hoagie, Sam. You must have some wop in you somewhere."

"Well, I got all these Italian guys over the wood factory, and they bitched till I got it right."

Vince hunched his shoulders and examined the interior. "But how come you keep this place so cruddy? Those boards outside are depressing. That green color, too, Sam. I'd crack up if I had to spend the whole day in here with just that light coming through the door."

"You get used to it after a while," Auer said. "I told you about all those problems I had back in November with the bricks flying through my windows."

Glenn poured himself more wine punch and said, "That was a long time back, man. This place could probably do a lot better if it didn't have such a cruddy atmosphere."

"I've thought a lot about installing windows again," Auer said, "but I'm still leery about it. The family I had all the trouble with got thrown out of the neighborhood, but I still see their kids around here a lot, up at Morse's candy store. Their last word was they were going to get me."

"Yeah?" Vince said. "What's their names?"

"Lou Johnson. They moved up to around Nineteenth and Thompson. A big family. About fifteen of them."

"We've got people around Nineteenth and Thompson," Glenn said. "Spades," he added, and glanced toward the rear to see if Peggy was around.

"That's a shame," Vince said, "that a straight guy like you can't even operate his business without getting harassed."

"I tried to get the police. . . . ."

Glenn smirked up at the ceiling, and Vince said, "Nah, you don't want to bother those guys. They're busy. Let me look into this thing for you, Sam. We'll see what we can do. I like your hoagies, and I'd like the sun to be shining through the windows when I have my wine punch."

"I wouldn't want you to put yourselves out."

"It wouldn't be us," Glenn assured him. "We've got people around Nineteenth and Thompson who owe us a few favors."

After they left, Auer was sorry he had given the Johnsons' approximate whereabouts. It was all over with the Johnsons, and he did not even want to hear them mentioned again. Worse, he would owe Vince and Glenn another favor. They kept on hinting about this location being put to more lucrative uses, and he had the sense that he was being sucked into something way over his head. He was not sure what he would say if they put it to him.

Two days later the word spread from the Green Room to Shor's and Zacky's, and then throughout the entire neighborhood: Lou Johnson had been beaten up. A professional job. Three Negroes had jumped out of a car, dragged him back in an alley, and broken his left leg and his right arm, kicked out a few of his teeth. No money taken. They just worked him over real bad.

At the Green Room that evening, Auer believed that he would be glared at with hatred or resentment. Quite the opposite. There were effusive greetings from people he hardly knew, pats on the back, greetings for Peggy, and Sy Green was unusually amiable. They went to Zacky's and it was the same scene. He had become extremely popular. On their way back up Seventh Street, all the berrypickers greeted him with a "Hi, Mister Sam," and several wanted to put down quarters and dimes, but he told them he only did business out of the store.

In the morning Auer had a telephone installed, and the helpers from Manny's arrived that afternoon to tear down the boards and install windows. An eerie sensation. Like a film running backward, the pounding and scraping, nails coming out, a repetition of last November in reverse, the emptiness, and then he blinked at the glass, the sight of Leah's store across Sixth, Grace's through the door glass, and the school through the Cottonwood window. He blinked like a blind man recovering his sight after many years in shadows and darkness.

Vince congratulated him when they came in for the milk bottle at six. "That's really an improvement, isn't it, Sam? Your take keeps up, you'll really be able to shape this place up."

"From the reports I've got, that was some working over my old friend was given."

"He ain't dead," Vince said. "You told me you were going after him with a pistol and a switchblade all the time."

"I notice you didn't hesitate to put the windows back," Glenn added.

Those words stuck in his mind. They managed to dim the brilliant sunlight pouring through his windows that August. It should have been the greatest month of his life. For reasons he could not fathom, he had become attractive to and masterful with women. He could not understand his new luck. At first he attributed it to Peggy maybe having spread the word that he was a good lay, but he was scoring with women who could not even speak English. Three days after the windows were installed, he spotted Señora Gomez in the open window of Leah's second-floor front. With the steaming August afternoon she was wearing only a slip. He remembered the night of the ambush, his bleeding head, how gorgeous she had been in that purple brassiere and how they had stared at each other for a full ten seconds.

She made no move to close the curtains or draw the shade. He crooked his finger at her. She shook her head no. He crooked his finger again, and she pulled the shade down. Shrugging, he returned to his lunch dishes.

Ten minutes later he saw Señora Gomez coming across Sixth Street, in a red blouse, black skirt, and black high heels. She entered the store, and his heart pounded. Petite and busty as she was, she stood by the doorway with great dignity. Indicating the rear apartment with her chin, she said, *"No está Peggy?"*

She waited for him to lock the front door, and they went back to the parlor for a long kiss. Auer swept her up into his arms and carried her to the bedroom. She pushed him away to undress, and as her blouse came down over her shoulders he was pleased to see she was wearing her purple brassiere. He wondered whether she had put it on especially in his honor, to commemorate that night they had looked at each other, or whether she just happened to put it on this morning, or if a woman gave any consideration at all to such things, if they were all just crazy notions bouncing around in a man's skull.

When he went to mount her, she pushed him back with a light, firm hand, made him relax back, adjusted herself over his massiveness. He buried his face in her breasts and black, pomaded curls, and for a while in the sultry afternoon he enjoyed the exquisite pleasure of a woman thrusting at him and whispering mysterious words in a foreign language in his ear.

"Me llamo Elena," she said when they were through.

"What?"

"My . . . name is . . . Helen," she managed with difficulty.

He kissed at the soft flank she presented as she reached for her clothes.

"You're very pretty, Helen."

"Graciàs."

Auer recovered his trousers and removed his wallet. She quickly touched his arm and said, "No."

"You're on welfare. You've got a lot of kids. You can always use a few bucks."

"No, mi amor. No es necesario."

Now he had another phrase swirling in his skull: *"No es necesario."* All this time he had been suffering, and there was a woman like Elena right across the street, who could say *"No es necesario."* Had any of this been necessary? Probably. If he had not been through all this, he would have been incapable of crooking his finger at her that way. And she would never have crossed the street.

The very next afternoon Maggie May came in for a quart of milk and to put a quarter down on 417. As he wrote out her slip, he caught her eye in a weak moment. She averted her gaze, and when she glanced up again his eyes were fixed on her pink halter.

"I'm Peggy's best friend, Sam."

"Good enough. That keeps it all in the family."

"You want me?"

He walked from behind the counter to lock the front door. "Can you spare the time?"

She checked the Pepsi-Cola clock. "I've got to be home in fifteen minutes, Sam."

"We'll see whether we can work it out."

Maggie May wasted none of her fifteen minutes on silly preliminaries. She went directly to the bedroom, hitched up her skirts, pulled down her panties, and Auer pushed at her, wondering why he had always made such a big deal out of sex. He tried to draw out his pleasure, but Maggie thrashed and complained, "C'mon, Sam, I've only got fifteen minutes."

As she quickly dressed, Maggie said, "You can come around see me, and we'll have more time."

Auer zipped up his trousers. "I thought you were supposed to be Peggy's big friend."

"She ain't treating you right, Sam. There's some things I could tell you, but it ain't none of my business." She gave him a quick kiss and whispered, "Drop around. Honest, I'll really give you a better time next time."

Auer still found the change totally inexplicable and mysterious. This sudden success. Perhaps it was the money rolling in now, or possibly these women saw some aura of power because he could get a man like Lou Johnson almost beaten to death. He walked with a new swagger and yet could not shake off his gloom, a sense of something being eternally wrong, from the second that his eyes opened in the morning till the moment they closed in sleep. When he made love to Peggy, she received him with gin-sweet breath and without protest, while he dreamed of Jeanette Lewis and hoped that this feeling would leave him when Jeanette returned in September—September ninth, she would be back. . . .

Big Vye finally fell. He gave her the same hard eye he had cast on Maggie May, and Vye complained, "Shit, Sam, knock that off. I'm with George, and you wouldn't want me to be unfair to George, would you?"

"Screw George. Get your ass back there."

"It's too damn hot and sticky. I'm all dirty."

"Go take a shower first."

"You got a shower?" Vye asked with sudden enthusiasm.

"Sure I got a shower."

"All we got over that crumby building is a bathtub down the hall, and every time I relax in the tub some sonofabitch starts pounding on the door, wants to use the toilet."

"Go back and take a nice cool shower. I'll bring in a few beers."

"Peggy won't be back?"

"Hell, no. She went out to Lancaster Avenue, to visit her aunt."

Auer was stretched on the bed when Vye came out of the shower with a white turkish towel tucked high over her bosom. In the shadows of the drawn venetian blinds he chuckled to see a woman with such a strong, splendid body grin like a bashful girl as she opened the towel and let it drop to the floor. He rose to suck on her breasts as she stood over him, and as they both melted to the bed he went down and drew the black, powerful thighs around his head. Vye moaned as he worshiped her, used her passion to dream of all the other women in the neighborhood he had wanted to do this to. Sophie, Pauline, Jeanette.

He scrambled up to enter Vye, and she whispered, "You're good, Sam. You're goddamn good."

Vye took another cool shower before she left. He gave her three more cans of beer for George, and then he took his own cool shower. Brushing his teeth, he abruptly laughed at the split reflection of the bull in his cracked medicine cabinet mirror. All those rules and fears and taboos that a man had in his skull. Nothing had happened. He had just gone down on big black Vye and found her pretty tasty. A big, dark taboo shot to hell in his skull.

He tapped the tips of his teeth together. Apparently they were not going to fall out. No earthquakes. No portents in the sky. No lightning bolt flashing down to scorch him. Just a damn hot afternoon and a refreshing sensation as he brushed his teeth.

Within minutes after returning to the store, he was perspiring. Customers had been waiting out there, actually sitting on his step, waiting to put their quarter or fifty cents down on a magic number that would temporarily solve all their problems. They offered him hot tips and read astrology charts, would come rushing in to show how certain numbers were popping up all over the place, the last three digits of the attendance figures from Shibe Park coinciding with the first three digits of the *Bulletin* circulation figure, and they would give it a heavy play, put a dollar on it.

The last week of August was the hottest on record. Every night the TV announcers spoke of historic temperatures for that date. Auer could hardly keep his soda box filled, and Sidonia was in three times a day with kegs of ice. During that week he crept up Leah's backstairs after midnight to visit Elena Gomez, made love to her while her children listened behind a drawn curtain partition. He had Vye again in the heat of the afternoon, and the following evening he told Peggy he was going for a walk and dropped by Maggie's room. When he came out and walked up Seventh, the berrypickers greeted him amicably. A few people who had just arrived from down South asked how this man could wander around here so boldly, and they were told about Lou Johnson.

During the day there seemed to be a film over the brilliant sunlight streaming through his windows. An invisible filter casting a dark tinge that only he could see. It infuriated him that he was not happier. He had won. He was beating the whole whining pack of them. He had taken Peggy over to the diner, and Zig and Gall paid their bill quickly and cut out rather than face him down. He had defied just about every rule in the book and gotten away with it. Yet all the sex was not helping out much. It was great while it lasted, but sex was not the problem. He seemed to have some film or stain on him, as if he had been swimming in the Delaware River. Not even a bath afterward eliminated the feeling of being stained. The sensation was getting thicker. Vince and Glenn were calling in their notes. They wanted him to rent an apartment upstairs to Winston. Winston would pay one hundred a week for a ten-dollar room. Forty of that would go to McCann for extra cigar money, and all the landlord had to do for his extra fifty was mind his own business. He was sure there would be more to it.

September arrived, and there was no break in the heat wave. At night the temperature dropped to eighty. That first Sunday in September, Auer walked down to Glendolph to listen to the choir of the Negro congregation that had taken over the Baptist church at Fifth and Cottonwood. Their singing was quite an improvement over the frail, reedy voices of the hillbillies. As they came out after the sermon, he observed that they were much more smartly dressed, and not as constipated-looking. He rose from his milk crate to return to the apartment, and Marge Coleman opened the door of her curtained storefront. Marge was in her sloppy nightgown covered by a terrycloth bathrobe. The well-dressed Negroes filing past all looked the other way.

"Hi, Sam. You still mad at me?"

"Nah, why should I be mad at you? Just because you're a thief?"

"How do you like these people buying the church? I think it's a nerve."

"They've got a better choir. And more rhythm," he added jokingly.

"Well, you're practically one of them anyhow, so I guess you'd have to think that way."

Auer lit a cigarette. "Yep, I see all their singing has put you in a fine Christian spirit this morning."

"Did you hear that Starker's was moving?"

He winced at the news. "No, I hadn't heard that."

"Yep, moving over to South Jersey. I heard it from some of the men who come to my place for lunch. They told me the old man was fed up with this area and was moving the whole plant to South Jersey."

Auer shrugged amiably. "That should hurt you. A few of the old geezers were telling me you gave a special lunch service for five bucks."

"It ain't no different than being a cheap bookie."

"Probably not, Marge. Take it easy."

Walking back up Cottonwood, he was sorry she had opened the door and ruined the glow created by that choir. Marge Coleman was like finding a roach in your scrambled eggs. He was not sure whether he was disturbed or pleased by the news that Starker was moving out. On the one hand, it would mean a drop in his business, a drop he could survive; on the other, this was another tribute to his endurance and perseverance. He was gutting this whole thing out. Starker had tried to run him out, and now Starker was fleeing. Sam Auer stood fast, with a chance to make a whole lot more money if he had the guts.

Auer lit another cigarette and sat on his side step. It was the long Labor Day weekend, and in Philly that was a long, long weekend if one did not get out of town. There was hardly any traffic. Everybody had already fled, except for a few Negro boys playing basketball in the schoolyard and a few drunks rapping at

Grace's window. Not even noon yet, and the temperature was approaching ninety.

He went inside, and Peggy was still asleep, sodden with gin. He dialed his number in Oxford Circle, and after four rings it was Bunny who answered, with a "Hello" obviously intended for somebody else.

"Hello. It's me, Sam. I hope I'm not disturbing you."

"No. But you're visiting rights aren't till next week."

"I know that. I was just wondering; if the kids aren't doing anything, I could take a taxi up and maybe take them off your hands for a while. Maybe take them to a movie and dinner."

"We have other plans, Sam."

"If it's not important, maybe I could like take them off your hands. I'd really love to see them."

"I'm sorry," her voice rose. "We've made other plans. You just can't call like this and. . . ."

"Please, I don't want to fight. I'll see you all next week. I'm sorry if I disturbed you."

"Be sure and call if you have one of your sudden brainstorms and decide not to come at the last minute, Sam."

"No, I'll be there. Have a nice weekend. Give them a kiss for me."

Peggy was still snoring in the next room. Auer rose and went across to the schoolyard, where the five colored boys had uneven three-to-two sides for their pickup basketball game. He asked whether he could join in, and they eyed his paunch dubiously. Then he surprised them with his left hook shot and his lightness on his feet. The surprise lasted about twenty minutes. He was sweating like a pig, his wind gone, and he was being run all over the court by these teen-agers. They asked him whether he wanted to try something more his speed—twenty-one for twenty-five cents a game. Hustling him, but that was all right. Back at Southern he had always been a deadly set shot, had dreamed of playing for the Sphas one day. He still showed them he had some eye left.

It took them two hours to clean him out of the three dollars' change in his pocket. To show them he was a good sport, he took them to his side door, went to the store, and returned with six cans of beer. They sat in the shade of the school steps and talked basketball, whether Central could ever beat Overbrook High and how good Chaney was at Ben Franklin.

When Auer returned to the apartment, he found a note on the television. Peggy had gone out to visit her aunt on Lancaster Avenue again. He wondered whether her aunt wore a moustache and an army fatigue jacket. It was going to be a long, long weekend.

On Tuesday morning people were waiting at his door before seven o'clock. They wanted to get their bets down before they went to work. Howie Williams was one of the first players in. He ordered a bologna and cheese sandwich to travel and added one dollar to the forty cents for his lunch. "One buck on 417, Sam. Right on the nose."

"How come you've got a buck for 417 and you're still into me for one hundred and fourteen, Howie? Your bill hasn't come down all year. Last summer you owed me a hundred, and it's over a hundred a year later."

"That's all getting wiped out tomorrow. There ain't no way that 417 cannot come out today. You ought to put down a dollar yourself, Sam. Put it on 417. No way it cannot come out."

"If you say so, Howie. I'm just glad I didn't lay down money on all the hot tips I got this summer. I'd be bankrupt by now."

From the door Howie said, "You're a funny writer. Winston always tried to get me to double my bet."

Auer shrugged, "If you berrypicking bastards paid your bills, I wouldn't be playing this dumb game."

Before eight o'clock he had written thirteen numbers, and he was struck by the fact that the fours, the ones, and the sevens were getting an unusually heavy play. Too much of a play to be ignored. He shook his head at his own ingenuousness and wrote out a slip for 417, tossed his own dollar in the milk bottle. He was really getting loony. Whoever heard of a croupier taking the house odds after watching so many suckers go down the tube on these odds.

Between eight and nine he wrote eleven more numbers and, checking them out, nine of the eleven contained a four, a one, or a seven. Everything was going right for him lately. Of course, he felt lousy, but everything was going right for him lately. It might break his skein of luck to ignore these significant omens. Auer scribbled out another slip and dropped one more dollar in the milk bottle. Now he had to pray it would not hit. He might be pushing his luck too far. If he hit for eight hundred dollars, the syndicate might get pissed off at him.

Tuesday was the busiest day he ever had, both for the numbers and his regular food and grocery trade. For once Peggy stayed with him all day and helped out. Auer noticed how even Heinie Schmidt joked with her at lunchtime. Eventually everything was accepted. Everything became normal. He asked the workers from Starker's about the move to South Jersey, and they verified what Marge Coleman said. They added that Starker had a sign on the bulletin board that no man would lose his job, that all could transfer out to Jersey, but a lot would be quitting because they had no cars and there was no adequate transportation out to the rural site.

The temperature rose to over one hundred degrees, and Auer did not sit down all afternoon, with kids running in for sodas and packs of Kool-Aid, and adults for groceries and to put down their dimes and quarters and dollars. Hot as it was, Labor Day meant the end of summer, and the real year, the year of work, was beginning.

In the evening, to reward Peggy for her beautiful performance, he gave her fifteen dollars, ten for a dress on Marshall Street, and he told her to spend the other five for a bottle at the State Store. She surprised him by returning promptly at nine-thirty, with the dress and a bottle of Seagram's. They watched television on the sofa, munched at a bag of potato chips, and drank their Seagram's with lots of ice and 7-Up.

"Are you happy?" Peggy asked.

"I couldn't say."

"That's a strange way to look at things."

"I couldn't tell you, Peggy. I've never been happy in my entire life. I've read about it in books, but I'm not even sure what it means."

She rested her head against his shoulder, and he patted her arm.

"Are you going to take Winston up on his offer? Moving upstairs?"

"You know about that?"

"He was talking to me the other night in Shor's."

"I don't know, girl. It's a big decision."

"Winston said there could be an awful lot of money in it."

"Yeah," Auer agreed.

"You know what it's about, don't you?"

"Yeah, I know what it's about."

It was almost impossible to sleep that night. The temperature dropped to the eighties, but with the moistness and humidity the wallpaper curled off the plaster, the glass panes ran with sweat. Sixth and Cottonwood seemed to be curdling and growing moldy in the depths of a tropical rain forest. Toward dawn Peggy said, "You know if you don't, they'll find some other place."

"I know that."

"If people want things, they're going to get them."

"They usually do."

A shadow crossed his eyes, and he slept deeply, mindlessly. When he woke at dawn, his chest was soaked with perspiration. He took a cool shower and brought his bundle of papers inside, unwound the wire, checked for the number. He blinked twice at what had to be an optical illusion. The product of wishful thinking. He checked it again, and the last three digits were 417. That meant eight hundred dollars. Auer laughed. He should be overjoyed, but abruptly he felt as nervous as the morning they picked their way through the fog in the North Atlantic with all the troops on deck for a U-boat alert.

Howie Williams burst through the door, waving a newspaper. "Did you see it, Sam? Did you see it?"

Auer looked at him. The ex-berrypicker was so excited he seemed ready for an epileptic seizure.

"Yeah, I saw it."

"Did you put any down? I gave you that tip, Sam. I told you there was no way 417 couldn't come out. You put any down?"

"Two bucks. Thanks for the tip."

For a second the joy drained from Williams's face as he realized that Auer had won eight to his four. He shook off the sudden envy and spluttered, "You see. I gave you that one, Sam. Right on it. I gave you that one."

"Want your usual cheese and bologna sandwich?"

"Shit, I ain't going to work today man! Screw that! Excited as I am?"

"They don't come with the payoff till six."

"Make me some bacon and eggs, Sam. I ain't going into that damn rubber factory today."

Howie hung around for an hour, telling every customer that came in about his hit, his four hundred and Auer's eight hundred. Their reaction was to play. A lot of them picking 417, remembering three years ago when the same 642 hit two days in a row.

A fever ran through the neighborhood that Wednesday. Howie Williams was out on the streets, bragging to all who would listen about his stroke of luck, his four hundred dollars. The news spread from the icehouse, and people charged over to Sixth and Cottonwood to get their money down.

Peggy came in at nine-thirty. She saw the crowd at the counter, yawned, and asked, "What's going on, Sam?"

"Howie Williams hit for a buck. Right on 417."

"And Mister Sam hit for two," Bowes shouted over the hubbub.

Auer winced as Peggy leaped and threw her arms around him. She kissed him three times, hard ones, then danced around the store. "We going to have a party tonight? We going to celebrate, Sam."

"Yeah," he said patiently, "I guess we could."

She kissed him again and announced to the crowd, "We're gonna have a nice party. We're going to have the best party this neighborhood ever saw."

The fever running through Cottonwood Street rose with the sun. Before noon Auer had run out of carbon pads and was using looseleaf paper and a sheet of carbon. The milk bottle was filling up to the lip with coins, bills, and slips, and he found this hysteria terrifying. Everybody was laughing, but it would take so little for it to spill over into violence, a riot. The bars were open, and the customers pouring in told him that Howie Williams was already drunk, staggering from Shor's to Zacky's to the Green Room, with parasites sporting him to drinks in anticipation of the payoff he would collect at six.

By five-thirty the corner was crowded, throngs on the school steps, people in front of Grace's, another bunch on Leah's sidewalk. The hot sun beat down on them, and they were talking and laughing, but there was a sullen listlessness out there. They were out there to see that money arrive. Auer shuddered at the thought of what might happen if Glenn and Vince failed to show up today. That mob would burst in here and tear this place apart. A red car passed by, paused, and decided not to investigate this gathering. Word of the hit had already reached the station.

Peggy was still puttering around in back. While he had worked his ass off all day she had been preparing for her stupid party, hanging up gay crepe paper, blowing up balloons, using Barry as her messenger boy to bring in cases of liquor and beer, fancy lunch meats from Marshall Street.

Auer saw Howie Williams pushing through the crowd in front of Leah's. Howie was blind, staggering, mean drunk already, and two of the gang from the icehouse were holding him up. Auer looked up at his Pepsi-Cola clock. It was ten to six, and they would have one hell of a party around here if his boys did not show today.

A low murmur from the crowd on Cottonwood. Auer recognized it as the moan that came from the crowd in front of Zacky's when they spotted the berrypicker buses returning on Saturday night. All this furor for a stinking four hundred dollars. Howie cleared about seventy a week at the rubber factory, so to him it had to be a big deal, but all of this fever and hysteria for an entire neighborhood was absolutely insane.

He emitted a sigh of relief as he saw Glenn's Chrysler through the stacks of cans in the Cottonwood window. The crowd on his sidewalk parted to let Vince and Glenn through. There was no jostling or pushing. Not for men who could order what was done to Lou Johnson.

Vince and Glenn wore broad smiles as they entered. Howie Williams was staggering across Sixth, aided by his buddies, and Vince said, "Two big hits, eh, and everybody wants to see the payoff with their own eyes. Looks like a swarm of crows out there."

"You'd better give me the four, Vince, so I can get all these people off my back."

Glenn handed Auer two envelopes, one marked with a four, and the other with an eight. Auer stuffed his in his pocket and went outside. All of the drivers in the cars speeding down Sixth had to wonder what was happening, and most of them quickly accelerated at the sight of fifty Negroes milling there.

"Here it is, man," Auer said.

A cheer went up from the people on the four corners, and Williams snatched the envelope proffered him and clumsily tore it open. In his haste to count, he almost dropped several of the twenty-dollar bills and had to grab and crumple them before they fell to the pavement. There was another whoop and cheer from the crowd. Auer said, "It's all there, Howie?"

"Yeah. It's all here. Four hundred."

"You going to give me any against your bill before you celebrate?"

"Shit, man! I gave you that tip. You got eight hundred dollars, didn't you? I gave you that tip! That should go against it, shouldn't it? You got that tip from me."

"Yeah, Howie, I guess you're right. Enjoy yourself."

Another cheer as Howie held the bills in his hands high above his head as if he were an Olympic torch bearer, or showing off a winning sweepstakes ticket. The crowd immediately swarmed after him as he strutted across Sixth and then broke into a run heading down Cottonwood.

Auer shook his head in relief as they disappeared. He locked the store door and wheezed again. Vince and Glenn were sitting at the counter.

Glenn said, "Lots of excitement today, eh?"

"A bit too much. I didn't have time to make your wine punch. Settle for a beer?"

"A beer'd be great," Vince said. "Thanks."

Auer set up beers for all around and said, "I'm really glad you guys showed up on time. They'd have ripped this place to shreds if there'd been any foul-up today." He brought out the two milk bottles of coins and bills and slips and was pleased by the look they changed at the sight of a two-bottle day.

"Who was your other big winner" Glenn asked. "Who got the eight?"

"I hope you guys don't mind. It's me."

Vince laughed. "Hey, now? Catch that action. That's good going, Sam."

"You guys don't mind?"

"Shit, no. Much rather you get it than one of these spades."

Glenn nodded, satisfied by the two bottles. "Best advertising in the world. Like the track. One sucker hits for a grand, and there are three thousand extra suckers out there the next day."

"Winning made you nervous, didn't it?" Vince asked in a

concerned, brotherly tone. "I could tell. Winning made you nervous, Sam."

Auer shrugged. "Yeah, I don't know. It just didn't seem. . . ."

"Maybe this is a very good thing," Vince cut him off. "This might be just what you needed. Like look. I can see that a stinking eight hundred bucks makes you nervous. You actually thought we were going to be pissed at you. You've got to learn to think in entirely new sizes, Sam. You have to change your whole way of looking at things. I've been telling people downtown about you. About what kind of guts you have. And there could be some good things coming up for you. A chance to make real money. . . ."

Peggy opened the door between the store and the rear apartment. She usually never came out when Vince and Glenn were around, knew to fade into the background. The three men fell silent.

"We're having a party tonight, to celebrate. You guys are invited if you want to come?"

"I think I'll skip this one," Glenn said flatly.

Vince shrugged. "My old lady wants me to paint the basement tonight. Maybe some other time."

Auer waved her off with a fluttering motion of the hand, and Peggy shut the door. Glenn picked up the milk bottles, nodding in appreciation of their weight. Vince rose with him and said, "A gutsy guy like you can do a lot better, Sam. If you just learn to stop thinking like a loser. Just get this one idea clear in your mind. There is money to be made around here like you never imagined. And that's what you're in business for, isn't it?"

Vince gave one long last swig to his beer bottle. As Auer let them out the front door, Vince again patted him on the shoulder. "Think about it."

Auer went back to the parlor, and Peggy said, "How's it look, honey?"

She had decorated and festooned the three rooms with gay crepe and about fifty balloons stretching all the way back to the kitchen. Barry had helped her to set up a bar with boards over his bookcases, covered by Christmas wrapping paper. An empty washtub was waiting for the ice.

"Just like New Year's."

"I'm going over to Zacky's for a drink. And when I come back, I'll bring the people and get Sidonia to bring the ice, and I'll bring in the potato salad and the cold cuts from the store. Is that okay?"

"Sure. Go ahead."

"If you don't want me to go, I won't go."

"No. Go ahead. I'll get a nap for a while. I've had it."

Peggy gave him a quick kiss and hurried out. He went to the bedroom, and without troubling to undress or pull down the spread, he stretched out, groaned in pleasure. Just to survive on a hot and humid day like this was a feat, and he had been running since seven in the morning after a sleepless night. He closed his eyes and immediately sensed that he was too overextended to sleep. Shifting his butt, he removed the switchblade from his back pocket and placed it on the nightstand. He lit a cigarette and smiled in the shadow of the bedroom. Beat as he was, he remembered a day at the wholesale produce place on Second Street. He was a young bull, nineteen, tossing around hundred-pound sacks of potatoes, should have been playing fullback for Penn, and as the afternoon wore on, order after order to be filled, truck after truck to be loaded, he said to the boss, "If business gets any better, I'm quitting." Zuckerman, the boss, thought that was so hilarious he gave him a ten-cent-an-hour raise on the spot. And for weeks after that Zuckerman would point him out and laugh, say, "You hear what that kid over there said: 'If business gets any better, I'm quitting.' " Auer pressed out his cigarette and, rolling over, slipped into a sleep that was like entering a dark room with the door snapping shut behind him.

A roar from the streets woke him. Auer sprang up, confused and disoriented, the key already turning in the parlor door lock. Peggy was shouting, "We're all here, Sam," and the crowd of revelers was pouring into his parlor, laughing, nudging each other, pushing, before Auer could make any protest about the number.

Sidonia came in with a huge keg of ice wrapped in burlap on his shoulder, and the guests cheered as he dumped it into the washtub and immediately got out his icepick and began chipping away. Maggie May was coming in with her portable record player and a stack of forty-fives. The whole pack from Barry's was arriving. Among the crowd Auer saw Cleveland, Skinner, Willard, Jonesie, but half of the people pouring into his parlor were total strangers. Peggy kissed him and said, "You don't mind, do you, Sam? I only invited about fifteen of the people, but the rest just came tagging along."

Auer was about to tell her off, but somebody grabbed Peggy by the arm and said, "Excuse me, gotta talk to her for a second," and pulled her away. John Hunter appeared at the door with two of his pals from the Green Room. Auer observed that he was slowly getting civilized. Hunter was still in his combat boots and khaki trousers but had on a dark green sport shirt, tan summer jacket, and gray porkpie hat. Smiling, Hunter bowed slightly at the waist, as though asking permission to enter, and Auer invited him along with a shrug. The three entered, and nobody bothered to shake hands.

A half hour later the party was in full swing, with possibly forty people stuffed into the cramped apartment. The furniture had been pushed aside, and several couples were dancing to the rhythm and blues screeching full blast on Maggie May's portable. Every few minutes there was an explosion as somebody applied a cigarette to a balloon. Maggie May was shouting in the bedroom, "Put that stuff away, Willard! We don't need that shit around here."

Obviously, she failed to dissuade him, Auer noted. To the smell of alcohol, cigarettes, and forty human bodies on a sweltering evening, the heavy taint of marijuana was added. Vye was signaling to him from the sofa. She was shaking her head, saying something, he could not hear over the din of the rhythm and blues. He pushed his way through three couples dancing to "The Story of Love," crouched on one knee next to her.

"What were you saying, Vye? I saw your lips moving, but I couldn't catch it with all the uproar in here."

"I was saying you're a damn, pitiful fool, Sam."

"Don't you think I know that?"

"Well, then you'd better hear it again, baby. You're a damn fool. What the hell you want to invite this trash in here and let them mess up your place and crush their cigarettes on the rugs?"

He was about to answer when Peggy grabbed his wrist and dragged him away to dance. She rubbed her belly against him and did an extra wiggle when the crowd cheered her efforts. With the open door, people were leaving and more strangers were arriving, attracted by the racket.

Peggy abruptly broke away from him and grabbed a drink from Cleveland's hand. Auer went to the bar and mixed his own drink, more straight whiskey and ice. The last hope for the party ending early was fading. The bottled whiskey was running low, but Barry was coming through the door with five milk bottles of Grace's home brew. Barry suddenly getting generous with that stuff Grace said was too raw the other day. Tomorrow there were going to be a lot of sick and nauseous people on Cottonwood Street.

With his eyes smarting from all the cigarette smoke, Auer ground his knuckles into his forehead to massage his headache. The pain behind his eyes felt like silver eels writhing as an electric current lashed them. He motioned to one of Hunter's friends to stop jiggling the handle and get away from the door to the store.

A crap game was going on in the kitchen. He pushed his way through the bunch blocking the door to his bedroom, waved his arms at the sweet, musty fumes of the marijuana being sucked in by about six people on the bed, and watched the crap game in the kitchen for a while, sipping on his drink. His presence was barely acknowledged. He thought about getting into the game, doing anything, just to have an activity to hide this sensation of being superfluous in his own house. And he could not. There were dimes and quarters on the white kitchen table. It would look silly to barge in on this penny-ante game when they all knew he had eight hundred dollars in his pocket.

Another balloon popped as some idiot in the bedroom applied a cigarette. The crap shooters were using his old stone mug as an ashtray. They had dumped the salt and pepper into the garbage can and were crushing out their butts in the brownstone mug. Auer saw his father's hand dipping into that mug, sprinkling a little pile of salt on the tablecloth, dipping his bread directly into the salt. Tomorrow he was going to have to tell Vince it was no go on the other thing. And if they got nasty, they could screw it. And maybe they could screw it with the numbers, too. When business got this good, maybe it was time to quit.

Auer pushed his way back into the parlor and double-locked the door between the apartment and the store. He pulled Peggy away from a conversation she was having with Skinner and said, "I'm going out for a walk, a breath of fresh air."

Peggy blinked at him incredulously. "You gonna leave with all your guests here?"

"You're a good hostess. You entertain them."

"You want me to send Barry to Barber John's up in the Project to get some more real whiskey?"

"Do what you like."

Outside, the dusk was a sultry gray, with clouds melting like cream in a thick, heavy soup. Kids were trying to get in their last game on the basketball courts. He shook himself violently and blinked away a tear at the thought that for a second he had considered dealing, bringing shit into this neighborhood to help fuck up those kids doing that ballet in the dusk. He rubbed his palms over his damp face, the harsh bristles on his cheeks.

Leah, Maddy, and Herbert were in front of their store,

Leah knitting, and the boys playing chess in the light from the
phone booth. He turned up Sixth, not brave enough to pass
them the way he felt now. His skin was crawling, open,
scorched. Laughter, mirthless and raw, came out of him as he
surveyed Green Garden Avenue. He had seen it a million times
and was seeing it for the first time. The brown brick leather
factory. The gas stations. The garages. The broad stretch of
black asphalt dividing into three tunnels under the railroad
bridge at Ninth. Every summer, squirrels got lost and wandered
all the way up from Franklin Square, scurried back and forth in
crazy zigzag patterns across Sixth Street, till one onrushing car
finally splattered them over the asphalt. About the only animals
that survived around here successfully were the rats, and the
pigeons who shit on the whole affair.

The neon light was flashing over Doc's pharmacy. The
druggist was at his door, preparing to close for the evening, but
quickly opened up as he spotted Auer.

"Come on in, big winner. I thought you'd close and take a
few days off. If I hit for eight hundred bucks, you wouldn't catch
me in this heat. I'd be up in the Poconos right now."

They moved toward the drug counter in the rear. Auer said,
"You've heard about it, eh?"

"That's all I've been hearing about all day. You and Howie
Williams. My soda fountain girl has been cursing you all afternoon, saying. 'Them that has, gets.' "

"I can't hardly argue with that one."

"You going to give Bunny a break this week? Slip her an
extra hundred so she can buy something for the girls. School is
starting in a few days, so she'll probably be shopping for fall
outfits."

"Make it for eight hundred," Auer said.

"What?"

"Eight hundred." The words had come out of his mouth
spontaneously. He had not even been thinking of entering Doc's
when he came up Green Garden in a daze. He placed the

envelope on the counter and was glad to be rid of it. Money obtained so stupidly would only be frittered away stupidly unless it was disposed of at once.

"That's going overboard," Doc clucked.

"No big deal. Bunny gets nervous without money, and when she gets nervous, she takes it out on the kids."

With the transaction completed and the pharmacy lights turning off behind him, Auer headed down Seventh. He felt better with those eight hundred dollars gone. Like some boil on his ass had been lanced, and all the puss drained out.

Junior Johnson was bopping to the jukebox in Hank Morse's candy store. Auer touched his pocket and remembered that he had left his switchblade on the nightstand. It was probably stolen by now, and he was glad. What was he going to do—stalk in there and do chapter fifty of his vendetta with the Johnsons? He had beaten the Johnsons. They had tangled with Bad-ass Sam Auer, and he had won, survived. Lou Johnson was still in bed with a broken arm and a broken leg, most of his teeth gone. Justice triumphs. It would have been okay if he had done it to Johnson himself, personally, but this other, this other was too much. It had been his big victory to triumph over the pathetic, disgusting Johnsons. He had given a case of clap to people already infected with the syph.

Auer entered Zacky's, and big Zeke frowned so hard the wrinkles appeared on his bald black skull. Zeke sloshed off the spot in front of him as Auer pointed to the forty-nine-cent special.

"I thought you was throwing a party over your place, celebrating the hit?"

"Got too noisy for me, too rough."

"Glad you took all that riffraff out of my hair for a while. They were in here all afternoon, gave me a terrible headache from all that racket and carrying on. I kept on turning down the volume on the jukebox, they kept turning it back up. Finally Zacky tells me to leave it up, and he drives off. I musta' taken ten Alka-Seltzers today."

Auer signaled for a double shot. "Williams needed a party, too. Every man is entitled to one blast."

"Party? You know what that fucking fool went and did? He came in here with his four hundred like a proud-ass fool, bought rounds for all this trash, dropped all his winnings."

"Blew it all?"

"Just about, Sam. I wanted to kick his ass for him. His old lady came back from work at the hospital about seven-thirty, heard about his hit, rushed over here, and he was already down to about fifty bucks. When she saw what he'd done, she just turned around and walked out crying. I thought I was going to cry myself, she looked so pitiful. I told him to get his fucking ass out of here, and he was gonna argue, but Zacky had come back and told him to move on."

Zeke rang up the sale and returned one penny. He said, "That's when they took off for your place. The whole pack of them. They still there?"

"I couldn't say."

The bartender rolled his eyes toward the ceiling. "You are one carefree fellah, Sam. Letting that bunch take over your house for a party. I'd get out there with a machine gun before I ever let that pack within fifty yards of my home."

"You're a good man, Zeke. You're all right."

The bartender shrugged and shuffled down the counter to attend to Lenny and his girl. Auer sipped at his beer. They could have burned the place down by now, and he would not particularly care. He had gotten what he wanted out of it. He had survived and shown them all.

Zacky's was eerily somber when the jukebox was silent. Seven or eight customers draped dejectedly around the square bar. Zeke rang up another forty-nine-cent special on the cash register, and the bell-like tinkle came out irritatingly loud in the Wednesday night gloom. Auer picked up his penny and wondered why Zacky charged forty-nine and not fifty cents. Was there a purpose, or was it so because it was so? He turned the worn penny in his fingers and examined the faded impression of

Lincoln. Abraham Lincoln also had his marital difficulties. A penny. All of his troubles started with one penny. A penny pinwheel. Ages ago he slapped little Louis Johnson's hand for stealing a penny pinwheel. Was that wrong? He was not sure anymore. Should he have said and done nothing? This was where all civilization started. With this damn penny. Lou Johnson would never have punished the boy. Linda Johnson would have said, "Fuck that Jew." And there would go another kid stunted, twisted, ruined for the rest of his life. So who had won? He was sitting on one of Lou Johnson's old stools, and they would be going on to more dingy furnished rooms, more bills to beat, more storekeepers on the corner. They had won. In the clash they had left him behind like a casualty on the road, wounded, so filled with hatred he had almost been ready to say yes, push drugs to those kids playing basketball in the schoolyard. They had won, but he was right. Society began with the penny. Without that confidence, without an open counter, everything fell apart, would have to be locked up tight with chains, barbed wire, rifles, police on every corner. It ended up with guys like Vince and Glenn dispensing justice.

Auer waved good-bye to Zeke and walked out to the caress of the sultry night. Seventh Street was seething in the darkness. It was all in the open here, trash cans knocked over, radios blaring blues, kids racing down toward the lumberyard. They managed to survive in all this squalor, had the energy to go upstairs later and make love behind those yellow shades. He nodded to the people murmuring, "Howdy, Sam," and he was far from the slow, clean death in Oxford Circle.

Hymns were pouring out of the storefront church at Marshall Street. The regular Wednesday night prayer meeting with Bowes on the electronic guitar, the shadows through the curtains of people swaying on the benches and clapping their hands. The soaring contraltos and deep basses were sending a chill shooting up his spine, a warm tingling through his neck and shoulders. Outside, he sang along, flatly, "Through this world of tears and cares, if I stumble, Lord, who cares. . . ."

They were moving him, their voices were inside him, tearing him apart. People never sang like this in a huge, stone church. It was painful, agony, to hear such beauty coming from behind frayed, tattered curtains with the old Salada Tea sign still over the grocery door. They were stirring him unbearably, and he had to ask what else there was. Shumsky, the intellectual barber, claims that religion was the opium of the masses, but Shumsky should be here right now and tell him what else there was. This music was the only beauty in this whole fucking neighborhood, on this whole rotten street with the dogshit on the curb and the drunks staggering out of Shor's. He wanted to ask that fucking Communist scum where else these singers should be tonight, what else could put that expression on their face, make them soar like this.

Chilled, trembling, the tears filmed Auer's eyes, and he smiled. If life were a movie, he could walk in there, sit on one of those benches, clap and sway with them, sing joyously, pray to God knows what, tell them he could not stand being alone and here, was sorry, sorry that he was filled with so much hatred, was tired of it, wanted it to stop, would do anything to make the world better for them and for his daughters, that he could not stand being so far from people with that music curling up his spine.

With his shoulder he brushed the tears from his eyes, only to feel more dripping down his cheeks. Life was not a movie. In life one did not go in and join the congregation. One continued down the street with blind eyes. The rhythm and blues from his room was growing louder in his ears, and through a watery film he could see more uninvited guests climbing the side steps to his parlor. Grace waved to him from her window, and he smiled. Poor Grace, had to enjoy the party vicariously, trapped inside that room, probably would die in there.

Herbert and Maddy glanced up from their chess game, and Leah rose immediately. "Sam. What's the matter?"

"I'm throwing a party, Leah. Can't you hear the music?"

Auer draped his arm around the mailbox, used it for support, rested his cheek against the cold metal.

"Are you sick, Sam?" he heard her saying in the distance.

The question was strange. He remembered this mailbox. Twenty-five years ago the gang was playing follow-the-leader and vaulted over this mailbox. Zig, Gall, Moony, Solly, and then Leah's kid brother Dutch Radin, with his withered arm, tried it and caught himself in the crotch, toppled over, and banged his skull against the curb. It must have hurt Dutch like he was hurting now.

"You look sick, Sam. Let me call a red car and have them take you to the hospital."

Auer opened his eyes and saw Herbert and Maddy frowning at the interruption of their game, and plump little Leah looking so concerned.

"You know, you're the only one who didn't get on me, Leah? Toward the end a little, but you were the only one who didn't get on me."

"Let me call the red car," she repeated.

"How's the trial going, Maddy? Going to beat the rap, kid?"

"It's not till the end of the month, Sam."

"You'll be all right, Maddy. Everything will work out fine for you."

"Sam, I can call Bunny," Leah interrupted him. "Let me go inside and call her. You sit down and rest on the chair, and I'll go inside and call her."

He pushed himself away from the lamppost and straightened up. "She'd be delighted. It would make her evening."

"I can still phone her," Leah called after him as he crossed Sixth Street, the headlights of the oncoming traffic illuminating his crouching, unsteady gait.

Auer winced at the racket pouring from his old, cramped apartment. Tomorrow he was going to put this dump up for sale. There was nothing more to win. There was nothing more to prove. He pushed his way into the smoke and din of the parlor, and this dump was no longer his. People were looking at him strangely, as if he were the intruder. The bedroom door was closed. Big Vye was shaking her head, advising him to forget it.

Leah shrugged. "I don't know why people do that to themselves. Twist themselves into knots like that. There's simply no reason for it."

"You're a sweet woman, Mom," Maddy said. "You just don't know about it."

"And you're so wise all of a sudden, my son? Eighteen years old, and you're already well on your way to making a fine mess of your own life."

"Heck, I'm only an accessory. Give me time, and I'll really do something impressive."

"Auer is just a bum," Herbert announced categorically. "He'll end up in Franklin Square with all the other bums."

"My other expert is heard from," Leah said and resumed her knitting. "All those books you read, and you just get dumber. . . ."

"Oh, my God!" burst from her lips as they heard the screams across the street. There was a loud shriek, and the door banged open against its frame with a crunch of splintering wood, swung back, and was pushed open again with a pack of drunks from inside tumbling down the side steps in a tangle of arms and legs.

Maddy leaped up, but Leah blocked him with her small, plump body, saying, "Oh no, mister. You get right back here."

From the Auer apartment they heard yelling, shouts, furniture being knocked over, the crash of a body banging into a mirror, while simultaneously the soaring voices of the choir reached them from Marshall Street. Leah tugged both of her sons back into the store, suddenly endowed with a surprising strength and quickness. The three of them watched the Auer door pounding open and swinging closed as men and women vomited out, tripping over each other, falling down the steps, and then glanced around quickly to choose their escape routes. Another tangle of four or five bodies came toppling down the steps after having fought to squeeze through the door at the same time.

Herbert giggled at their difficulties in unscrambling themselves, and Leah hauled off and slapped him in the head, but Maddy was also laughing. There was something horribly funny about the scene. It looked like the arrival of the midget car in the circus with twenty-five passengers disgorging. All of those people had fitted into Auer's narrow apartment, and an endless supply was pouring out, some running down Sixth toward Grenoble, but most fleeing down Cottonwood toward Fifth, cutting into the schoolyard or the empty lot and disappearing into the darkness.

Maddy escaped from Leah's grip as he saw Auer come out on the side steps, outlined by the light from the open parlor door. The grocer was poised there for a second and then collapsed to the sidewalk.

Leah shouted, "You stay out of it," but Maddy raced across Sixth, beating out two oncoming cars that seemed determined to run him down.

Auer had fallen on his back, with one foot resting on the bottom step and his head tilted at an odd slant. Maddy was about to kneel down and touch him when he saw the black handle of the switchblade driven into his chest, blood oozing through the white shirt, more blood where the skull had hit the pavement.

Maddy stepped back. He had lived around here too long to touch a wounded or dead man, foul up things for the police. Auer's chest suddenly rose, expanded as though it were going to explode or expel the knife, and then it sank and moved no more.

Fat Grace was bellowing, "Barry! Barry! you get the hell in here, Barry! Get in here off the streets. Get in here, Barry!"

Cottonwood was deserted all the way down to Marshall, where a few singers had come out of the storefront church. Grace changed her mind, abruptly pulled down the yellow shade. Maddy guessed that Barry must have made it back through the rear door to the building. He lit a cigarette and saw his mother in the phone booth.

The only sound now came from the scratching record player inside, the music over, the needle digging and scratching monotonously into the grooves around the label. There was a distant siren, and he saw a red light approaching around Tenth Street. People were beginning to gather. Pauline Kozak. All of the Colemans were coming up Cottonwood. Another whooping siren joined its wail to the whine of the police car. The ambulance was arriving. Maddy flicked his ashes. This was the second body he had seen stretched on a sidewalk in less than three months.

Later that evening, after witnesses had been picked up as far away as Girard Avenue, an alarm went out for John Hunter, Negro male, five feet eleven inches tall, around one hundred and ninety pounds, trimmed moustache, last seen wearing combat boots, khaki trousers, green sport shirt, tan jacket, and gray porkpie hat. Also for Peggy Moore, Negro female, five feet four inches tall, visible scar on neck, last seen wearing red high-heeled shoes and blue dress with red flowers.

Several days after that, people from the neighborhood said they had seen Peggy Moore around Seventeenth and Columbia. Others claimed to have seen her around Eleventh and Bainbridge, but most agreed that was not Peggy Moore. No, that was not Peggy Moore at all.